CITY OF RUIN

CHARISSA WEAKS

CITY OWL
PRESS

CITY OF RUIN
Witch Walker, Book 2

CITY OWL PRESS
www.cityowlpress.com

Cover Design by MiblArt. All stock photos licensed appropriately.

Edited by Tee Tate.

For information on subsidiary rights, please contact the publisher at info@cityowlpress.com.

Hardback Edition ISBN: 978-1-64898-274-3
Paperback Edition ISBN: 978-1-64898-143-2
Digital Edition ISBN: 978-1-64898-144-9

Printed in the United States of America

For my family, for cheering me on and letting me vanish for days at a time
And for my Rebel Readers, for loving these characters as much as I do

AUTHOR'S NOTE

The Witch Collector centers around Raina Bloodgood, a character who cannot speak and therefore uses a form of signed language to communicate. Signed languages use a visual-manual approach to communication. There is no universal signed language. For instance, BSL (British Sign Language) is a different language from ASL (American Sign Language). Sign languages have their own grammar and use hand movements, sign order, and body and facial cues to create that grammar, as well as gaze direction, blinks, and rests. For ease of reading, the fictional sign language in this novel reads as if it were SEE (Signing Exact English). It should also be noted that the term mute is not used in this text so as not to lend to derogatory language that has impacted non-speaking and Deaf communities. For more information, please scan the QR code on the left. And for a list of content warnings, please scan the QR code on the right.

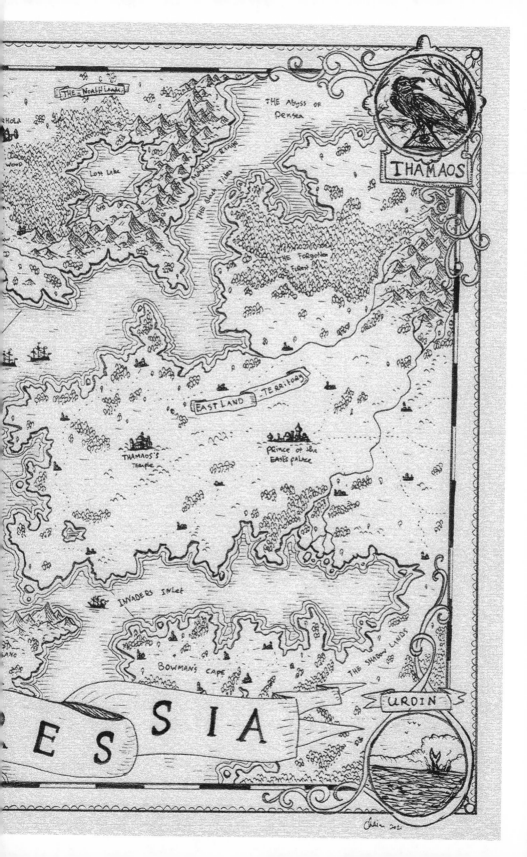

FURY

I've been dead to the world since the bitter winter after Urdin and Thamaos killed one another. I'm uncertain how long it's been since King Gherahn's authorities carried me north to torture me to death, chained me to the black, icy cliffs along the Abyss of Pensea—how many days, months, years, decades, centuries have stretched from then to now.

But I have an inkling.

Once upon a time, I beheld my future through the eyes of a weary traveler. Though much of my body has decayed since then, I still have my angry heart. More terrifying, I still have my godsdamn mind. Then again, creatures like me are hard to kill.

And we never—*ever*—forget.

When I wouldn't die, the king's Brotherhood locked me far beneath the earth, entombed in a prison of dirt, stone, and suffocating iron, and prayed to Loria that the kingdom's people would let me slip from recollection. What a gift if my immortal bones would turn to dust as forever came and went.

But here in this unforgiving crypt, with darkness and memories as my only friends, I still exist, my eternal torment paused like a held breath as the Ancient Ones' whispers reach my ears, the god spirits who've been waiting for my justice. My salvation.

My vengeance.

He's coming, they promise me, communicating the only way they can from the Shadow World's Empyreal Fields. *The man from the East. He's coming.*

I have been called Beauty. I have been called Love. But I am Fury, and some fool is going to bring me back to life.

❧ I ❧
MEMORIES

THE PRINCE WITH NO NAME

The Eastern Territories
City of Quezira
Min-Thuret Temple, Rite Hall

Thamaos's ancient ritual room is deathly quiet, save for the crackling of flames and the sizzle of my blood burning in the offering bowl.

"Hear me, my lord. I beg you."

My slit palm throbs as I squeeze crimson drops from my body for the third time today. This time, I let the blood flow. No gentle pricks. No careful measure. Instead, warm, scarlet rivers seep through my fisted fingers and pour into the fire.

I've knelt here long enough that the morning sunlight shining through the stained-glass windows upon my arrival has changed to the silvery glow of a coming winter's starlight. My back has grown stiff and my knees ache, having been pressed against the unforgiving stone floor for so many hours.

A servant enters the room to deliver fresh water. He sets the decanter near the altar along with cloths soaked in yarrow tincture for my ritual wounds. "Are you sure you're all right, my prince?" he asks for the second time within the hour. "You look so unwell."

"Because I haven't consumed a soul in over a week," I reply, my voice tight and hard.

When I sifted to this very room from the Shadow World, collapsing in the ritual circle with Colden Moeshka in my arms, I could barely move. Parts of my body were burned from Raina Bloodgood's fire, and my insides felt like they might crumble any second. Already, I starved.

But after feeling Garujo die, his Summerlander powers with him, and after so much death in the North, I couldn't stomach the thought of feeding. Since then, my skin has taken on a waxen sheen, and my veins stand out in relief. I need no looking glass to know my face is gaunt, my body thinner.

"Perhaps you should...*eat*," the servant says. He glances over the healing gash across my face before lifting his gaze toward the rafters.

The souls of three prisoners hover in waiting, silken and billowing. One smells like seawater, another like sweet earth, the final like the tall cedars in the East's Forgotten Forest. Tonight I will feed and begin the task of restoring myself. If I don't, I will die. And yet, miserable as I am, and much as I need to abandon these prayers and feast, I cannot make myself give up.

Not yet.

"*Go*." I force every bit of annoyance I possess into the word. "I want to be left alone, do you understand?"

He nods and hurries from the room, closing the wooden doors quietly.

It's been weeks since I've been inside the temple. Weeks since I last heard Thamaos's transcendental voice commanding that I go to the Northlands. I fear no matter how long I remain on my knees he might not hear me. Or perhaps he changed his mind about our plan and shunned me. I pray I'm wrong because I've brought him quite the gift.

From the moment I laid the God Knife on the sunlit altar, I swore my lord spoke to me from the Shadow World. A hushed murmur crept through the halls of this holy place, then all fell silent and still. I need his instruction. His direction. His assurance.

And so I bleed. And wait.

Once again, I dip my fingers into the blood and draw three runes on the altar. Connection. Faithfulness. Fealty. With a deep breath, I press my forehead to the marble dais, the very place where Thamaos and the Eastern Territories' kings and queens once rested, watching rituals performed in their names. An arm's length away stands the gilded throne that will soon be mine, an honor I must earn.

Eternal Emperor of Tiressia.

We no longer desire your world, Thamaos once said. *But the Nether Reaches are not our home, and our realm of Eridan is no more. The gods can rise and offer their immortal life forces to Tiressia's blessed lands. An offering to you, that you might know true power through us. Because you are the one who will unite this empire, my little prince. Perhaps even the world.*

A thought flutters through my mind. When I take the sovereign seat, will my lord grant the memory of my true name? The memory of who I was before I became his? A distant part of me longs to know, to be more than a nameless being hidden by shadows, surviving off souls. At times I remember that young man, like right now. Something in the act of worship and ritual is familiar in my marrow, beyond my years as Thamaos's chosen. Even beyond my years as a vagabond along the eastern coast.

I also remember magick. Potent, wild, and dark. Flowing hot in my veins.

My magick. Controlled by me and me alone.

A cold draft tickles the hair at the nape of my neck. I lift my head as the flames in every bronze brazier throughout the hall flickers but holds, as though a gentle breath has been blown over the fiery light.

"Little prince." Thamaos's voice drifts into this room of devotion, ritual, and sacrifice, and any rising memory is swept away. *"You failed,"* my lord whispers in a sibilant voice. *"You didn't kill them. Not all of them. Thanks to that Witch Walker from Silver Hollow."*

I shut my eyes, and a bead of sweat trickles down the side of my neck. It's cold in the ritual hall tonight, yet anger burns hot as a bonfire in my chest. Thamaos's last instruction had been to capture Colden Moeshka, the Frost King, and to destroy every Witch Walker living along the edge of Frostwater Wood. I did that. Save for that damned Raina Bloodgood and a handful of others.

And it wasn't easy.

"I hadn't the strength to last any longer, my lord. Garujo withered after the attack on Winterhold. My siphoning killed him."

I press a hand against the dark granite altar and inhale a ragged breath. I've turned many people to husks in my long life, but my misery over Garujo's death is suffocating. Though he offered his life for my survival, the loss weighs too heavy.

"The witch also had help," I continue. "Un Drallag freed Neri so he could protect the witch from Silver Hollow. Now I have a loose god spirit to locate."

One who supposedly wants to see me reign as emperor of these lands yet failed to offer his aid on Winter Road.

A flicker of reflected firelight snags my attention, and my gaze falls to the altar, to my grand gift. When I reach for the weapon, the entire piece —even the black-bone blade—is frigid. But at least it's here. Surely my lord will be proud.

"Two good things did come of this," I tell him, doing my damnedest to mask any hint of regret about the first matter. "I captured Colden Moeshka, and I learned that Raina Bloodgood had possession of your God Knife, my lord. After centuries of absence, *I* brought this treasure home." I extend the blade in supplication as a question rages, one I must ask, no matter how foolish. "Did you know where the God Knife was, my lord? That the king's collector was its Maker and Raina Bloodgood its Keeper? All this time?"

I've pondered this for days, if that was why he sent me to raze the valley. The only way I had known was because Garujo's soul recognized the Summerlander magick on the blade when the witch and I fought on the village green. Seconds after she ripped the God Knife across my face, Garujo's whisper of *Keeper* and all the understanding he could provide echoed through me.

A pregnant pause fills the air. For several terrible seconds, I'm certain I've overstepped, but nothing happens, save for an answer.

"Her father was the Keeper. The witch inherited his obligation the moment the blade returned to her family, and she grasped its hilt. When he died and his soul entered the Shadow World, I knew this time would come."

I cannot help but wonder how, but this time, I decide against inquiring further.

"In regard to all else," he says, *"you will be rewarded for capturing the Frost King and for sacrificing Garujo. As for Neri, for now he is no matter. I will deal with him in time. Your primary concern is to prevent that Keeper from setting foot in the City of Ruin. She and Un Drallag are no doubt on their way there now. If they are allowed to interfere in our plans, my resurrection and your future as the lord of Tiressia are but a dream."*

By all the sainted Ancient Ones. That insignificant witch is forever an obstacle. Though I'm beginning to question if she's ever been insignificant at all.

"I'll send word to my men in Malgros, my lord. My general is en route to the coast as well." I pause, carefully selecting my next words. "There's an issue though. I can offer no aid in locating the Keeper. Un Drallag bound himself to the witch. Claimed her. Carved his mark upon her skin. He will protect her. Even now he shields her mind from me."

Though I met him when he and Colden Moeshka visited my palace after King Regner died, I hadn't known his identity. In truth, I know little about Un Drallag, only what I've read in history books. If he's anything like Quezira's scribes depict in their tales, however, I'm not confident my assassins can stand against him. Much less him *and* Raina Bloodgood.

Anger roils beneath my skin. How could such a revered Eastlander share his sacred power?

So foolish. So traitorous.

So fucking problematic.

A resonating breath snakes through the room. *"Think, little prince. If Un Drallag is shielding her mind, his power is awakening. Take him as a source to siphon. You will require a fount of power to succeed with conquering the Summerlands. It won't be long until Un Drallag's magick grows strong enough to see you through any battle or war that lies ahead."*

I clench my offering hand so hard that blood flows from my sliced palm and drips to the stone floor. *Take Un Drallag.* The greatest sorcerer Tiressia has ever known. Feed from his power and soul.

If I can manage that, gods and men be damned.

A moment passes, and my lord continues as if he didn't just present the most impossible yet most desirable solution.

"For your second task," he says, *"you must unearth the Fury at Un Moritra.*

Soon. Her value is limitless. Use her, to whatever end, so I can return to the land of the living and ensure that Tiressia is yours."

Doubt and hesitance dominate my thoughts, as they have since this possibility was first mentioned many weeks ago. Though history holds that Fury died three centuries past, according to my lord, she's still very much alive. Like Un Drallag, she's a whirlwind legend I've only ever read about. A very *deadly* legend. Chained to the pits of the earth for attempting to over-throw King Gherahn's throne after Thamaos died.

Still uncertain, I soften my voice. "My lord. I don't possess the power to enter Un Moritra. I cannot break through your wall of runes. And Fury... After all these years in isolation, she must be mad. I need her whole, and that will be a struggle, as will convincing her to cooperate. I've a feeling she's going to be rather angry."

A low laugh rumbles from wall to wall and slithers around every massive column. I follow the sound, from the arched observation nooks along the sides of the room to the sloped rafters set into the high, mosaic ceiling. Though impossible, it feels as if Thamaos, long-dead God of the Eastern Territories, is *right here.*

"Un Moritra will know you," he says. *"And Fury will cooperate. Bind her with a clever deal before you free her. Offer her complete freedom in exchange for her aid. Restore her health. Then, if your men cannot rise to the task of capturing Un Drallag, Fury will. She will have no choice. Fury can see you and the Frost King safely to the Summerlands."*

The Frost King.

"My lord, you're certain Asha's curse doesn't extend to Mount Ulra?" Though I know better than to show doubt, I must know. "The king won't turn to dust if I take him there?"

"Why so worried?" Thamaos says. *"I need him. I would not ask if it could not be done. Mount Ulra is* not *the City of Ruin, and that was Asha's mistake. Do as I say, little prince. I have opened the way for you. All you must do is follow."*

The air moves once more, every firelight flares, then my lord's presence is gone.

After long moments, I stand on numb legs, and in the ritual circle of the moon and sun, study the runes etched beneath the Stone of Ghent, the transparent amber orb fitted into the God Knife's white granite hilt by none other than Un Drallag himself.

Take him, Thamaos said. Easier said than done. Then again, I've always enjoyed a challenge.

The thought of such domination makes me smile, much as it pains the knife wound Raina Bloodgood carved into me from temple to chin. I picture her then—the witch. See that pretty face contorted into her familiar scowl. Thanks to Un Drallag, I can no longer infiltrate her mind, and thanks to the Eastland Brotherhood's protections, she cannot see me with her gift of Sight.

But as I step into the full dark stretching over the vast and shining city of Quezira, I send her a message anyway, willing it across the many miles of land and sea between us.

"The rise begins, Lovely," I promise her. "And I'm going to make it hurt."

RAINA

The Northland Break
Frostwater Wood, Winter Road

The gift of Sight comes with deepest intuition.

A vibration in my blood. Chills across my skin. A tremble in the wind. I'm still learning the many facets of this ability, my exploration a shallow one. But each of those things are happening *right now*, as though the night itself contains a message I can't hear.

I *feel* the message though, tapping on the barrier Alexus erected around my mind to keep the prince at bay. The attempted intrusion is powerful enough to answer the question that has dominated our camp discussions since we left the castle.

"The prince is up to something," I sign to Alexus. *"I think he is on the move."*

Alexus sits across from me, a fire burning between us in a clearing on the side of Winter Road. The wood and all its creatures sleep, save for a white wolf howling mournfully in the distance, and a lone night bird singing a sorrowful song. Though the threat of a cold, hard rain hangs heavy in the air, Joran Dulevia, a water witch and Winterhold's bowyer, maintains a shield over us tonight. He's tired, so it won't last for long, but the respite is much needed.

The journey thus far has been trying for several reasons, mainly the downpours that have slowed our travels. Many from our group rest on a bed of pine needles, drying out near the blazing warmth. There were over two dozen of us when this journey began. Now there are nine. Some gave up early on. The rest turned back yesterday, too weary to continue. We need this rain to stop so we can reach the valley and let Finn and the others know we're alive.

Then we must head south. Malgros is a three-week ride from Hampstead Loch if we're swift and the weather favors us. Once there, a new battle awaits: securing passage across the Malorian Sea and, even more difficult, a way through the magickal wards surrounding Fia Drumera's City of Ruin.

Time is not on our side.

My sister looks up at me. She sits near Alexus, sharpening her dagger. To her left, leaned on one elbow, is Joran, hailing from the Icelander village of Reede. Callan Terzerak, a rune witch and diviner from the Mondulak Range sits beside me, drawing different runes in the earth. Hel and Rhonin are to my left, watching the flames dance as they share a pouch of pine nuts. Keth Rukano and Jaega Lor, warriors from the Iceland village of Tori, have already retired for the night.

"Did you see him?" Alexus signs. *"The prince?"*

I shake my head and toss the water from my wooden scrying dish, releasing the last crimson tendrils of a vision that wouldn't form. I've seen Finn and the other survivors roaming the burned villages, burying the dead, and salvaging anything they can find. I've also watched Vexx riding south on horseback, and I've seen Colden, cast away in a dungeon for the last nine days.

But the prince? He's as impossible to find as a mote of starlight in this lightless wood come midnight. All I see when I look for him is a red mist filled with dozens of floating runes linked by magickal threads, runes I've drawn for Callan, runes they say are for protection, invisibility, and blessing. Still, even though I can't see him, I'm certain his plans are sliding into place.

A piece of wood shifts in the fire, sending sparks flying. I flinch from the heat that washes across my face. Our nightly fire sometimes feels like a torment rather than a means of survival, just another portal into painful memories and nightmares.

I've struggled ever since we crossed the remains of the prince's campsite. One whiff of the death scent that lingered over the wood, and any memories I'd suppressed rose anew, sharp and violent. I relive it all too often. The fire, the death, the fear. Even the gates of the Shadow World antagonize me with their promise of an eternal cage.

I can still see all those souls waiting there, each one fixated on my presence when the prince dragged me under. I doubt I will *ever* stop hearing their hissing voices.

Keeper.

Seer.

Healer.

Resurrectionist.

Murderer.

Witch.

They were only wrong about one. I'm no resurrectionist.

Comfort caresses the bond, warming the rune above my left breast with awareness. When I glance up, Alexus's concern seeps into me, warm and assuring. He's so skilled with the bond, as though he's been through this before. Magickal scholar he may be, but if I'm the first he's claimed, how is this so simple for him?

For me, there's an insurmountable distance between us when it comes to the rune. When Alexus reaches out to me, I feel it so wholly. But when *I* try reaching *him*, I find myself standing on a precipice, looming over a beckoning void. Callan says the chasm is manifested fear or worry or some obstacle my mind has conjured. One I can't seem to conquer.

My thoughts are distracted because Joran is watching me. The gray of his eyes almost matches his gray-tinted skin, the argent ring around his irises gleaming.

He drags a wide-knuckled hand through his long, silver hair and gestures between me and Alexus, arm at rest on his bent knee. "Always so secretive, you two. Why not share? It's rude having open conversations most of us can't understand."

"Maybe you should try learning Raina's language like the rest of us,"

Callan says, wiping the gathering mist from their tan scalp. Half of Callan's head is shaved and marked with runes, the other half covered in black and silver hair, braided against their skull like Nephele's.

"It isn't easy, Joran," Rhonin adds, "but if *we* can learn, so can you."

A small smile forms on my face. I haven't known Rhonin or Callan long, but they've already won pieces of my heart.

Joran huffs, as if the very thought of learning to communicate with me is ridiculous.

"It's probably a wasted effort." Hel pops a pine nut into her mouth. "According to Nephele, Alexus became fluent in a matter of weeks. It would probably take you eons."

"Nice try," Joran replies. "I don't offend easily. Though I might find it embarrassing to be an immortal sorcerer with nothing better to do than learn a rarely used hand language so I can talk to a pretty girl."

Alexus trains his stony focus on me. The irritation in his stare shimmers, his impatience with the Icelander visibly rising. Alexus is our leader, a preeminent sorcerer with one weakness when it comes to learned power.

Water magick has forever eluded him.

With fierce archery skills and command over water, Joran knows his importance to our group. He hasn't been much aid with the unrelenting rain because of the physical demand while traveling for hours, but he may be critical in seeing us safely across the Malorian Sea and desert provinces of Ske-Trana, south of the Summerland's main port city of Itunnan. For those reasons, he holds little fear of being cast out.

A muscle feathers in Alexus's jaw. "All Raina said was that the prince is up to something."

His fingers worry with an old key that hangs around his neck like a pendant. *A memento from a long time ago,* he told me shortly after we left Winterhold. *A talisman.* For what, he can't remember.

"Up to something?" Joran mocks. "Genius deduction from our brilliant Seer."

A growl resonates from Alexus's throat. Joran sits dangerously within the Witch Collector's reach, my sister the only barrier. And not a good one. She drags a small whetstone down her dagger's edge and cuts a sharp glare at Joran before returning to her work. She and Joran are forever bickering, so I'm surprised when she holds her tongue, though thankful.

Another complication has been that some in our band—namely Joran —didn't take kindly to learning that Alexus turned the soul of a vengeful god loose on their homeland.

For me.

It's why I sit across from Alexus and not at his side. Why I sneak into his tent once everyone has gone to sleep. Why we keep our hands to ourselves until we're alone. The last thing we need on this journey is more friction, but the constant closeness is beginning to rub everyone raw.

Our only salvation is that Neri isn't in Winterhold. He and his wolves follow *us* instead, despite his bargain with Alexus being fulfilled. The wolves keep a healthy distance, and Neri has taken the form of a curious, cold wind at our backs. We don't know what he wants or if he'll make himself known. I figure there's a reason he follows so closely, though, and that his appearance *will* come. Like most dreadful things, it's only a matter of time.

At Alexus's right side, Helena holds her hand out to Rhonin. A long, red braid slips over his shoulder as he offers her the pouch of pine nuts. With a hard flick, Hel thumps a nut straight into Joran's chest. I've no doubt my friend had been aiming for the Icelander's face.

How I wish she'd hit her mark.

Joran swipes the front of his sweater. "Are you always such an atrocious child?"

Hel arches a challenging brow. "Are you always such an atrocious asshole?"

"Only when he's breathing," Nephele says.

Joran's smirk turns into a smug smile. "You once loved my breathing. Heavy and in your ear all fucking night."

Nephele whips her head around. Everyone's eyes go wide, including mine, as repulsion and disbelief tighten my sister's face. Gods. We've all felt the tension between her and Joran, taut and ready to snap. But until now, not even *I* knew why that tension existed. A reminder that there is much I still need to learn about my sister.

Alexus's voice is as deep as the low-rolling thunder to the west. "Stop talking, Joran. If you want to keep talking at all."

The Icelander just grins that insufferable grin, gets up, snatches a lantern, and turns to go.

Just when I think we're free of him, he swings back around. "You know. When I was a boy, there was a Seer in our village. A woman who lived near the edge of the Iceland Plains for a few years before leaving Tiressia altogether. Villagers claimed she descended from Loria's children, the first Witch Walkers. Those who were said to realm walk between Tiressia and Eridan. The first practitioners of vast magick. Born from Loria's will rather than her womb. Spawned from a god yet still mortal. A rare creature between a godling and a witch. People risked all to cross the Plains to see her."

Alexus turns a sharp look at the Icelander, as though something Joran said shook loose a recollection.

"My father swore the woman could break through any mental wards meant to keep her out, no matter the distance. That she saw far more than the present moment at hand. In fact, she learned to see into a person's past and could even glimpse their future." He narrows his eyes. "Did you hear that? *Their motherfucking future.*"

I feel like I know where he's going with this, and though a part of me wants to tell him to fuck off, another part is too intrigued not to pay attention.

Joran casts a glance across every face. "We all agree that the prince is striking now for a reason. We also agree that he's too godsdamn clever to place all faith in the hopes that Fia Drumera will surrender upon sight of her old lover held captive on the Jade River. Using Colden Moeshka as a ransom may indeed start a larger war, that's always been the fear. But the king is only a distraction. The Prince of the East has been at this game with the Summerlands for three decades. He needed a new tactic. The perfect weapons for his arsenal. He has *two.*"

Two. Because of me. Colden and the God Knife.

"But that isn't a trifecta for the resurrection he hopes to perform," Joran says. "He still needs that third element that will ensure his ability to break past the Fire Queen's wards and reach the Grove of the Gods." Joran shines his lantern in my direction. The warm light shadows the hard lines of his heavy brow. "Unfortunately for us, just like in the vale, *you* are the only one who can see what that weapon is, Bloodgood. If the prince is *'up to something,'* figure it out. You can't change the past, but you do hold the power to change the future. Don't fuck things up this time unless you want to live with even more death on your hands."

Joran's words should spark my temper. The *me* from a month ago would get in his face for those last remarks. But instead, my spirit sinks, even as my rune warms with bright heat.

Power rumbles through the camp, followed by an electric wind that rustles the branches above, filling the leafy canopy with blue, crackling energy that tingles over my skin.

Alexus's magick.

He's on his feet and facing the Icelander faster than I can blink, clenching two daggers of cobalt light in his fists.

Alexus's power revives more each day. Like the rest of us, he inherently sees certain threads and has learned to manipulate others. But he can also summon energy, absorb it, and concentrate it in various ways. He even taught *me*, with the sword of light I used to enter Frostwater Wood, the very magick that saved my life against an Eastlander on Winter Road. That was a smaller form of the same type of power Alexus harnessed to kill those men near the ravine. I can't imagine what he will be able to do once he's fully renewed.

In response to Alexus's daggers, Joran lifts his arms at his sides, and a dozen silvery arrows materialize around him, formed from the water saturating the forest, every tip aimed at Alexus.

The rest of us stand—except for my sister—ready to spring, though it's doubtful there's anything we can do if this sorcerer and witch finally clash.

Suddenly, hundreds of glistening vines slither from the wet wood, weaving together, quickly forming a wall between Alexus and Joran. I look at my sister, sensing her magick, vibrant in the air. She doesn't turn around to see her handiwork. She just smiles and continues sharpening her blade.

Joran huffs an arrogant laugh and flicks his hands at the wrists. His water arrows spear forward, stabbing into the living blockade before raining to the ground.

All he says as he wisely walks away is, "Interfering bitch. You'll regret that."

Nephele smirks. "I wouldn't bet on it."

In retaliation, Joran's shield vanishes, and an icy, spitting drizzle starts to fall. Nephele curses as her vines recoil, and everyone heads toward their shelters.

I go to Alexus. Still bristling, he watches the Icelander slip into his tent at the edge of our camp. When I touch his shoulder, he turns. His daggers fade into blue sparks, and then nothing.

We're alone, so he takes my hand and kisses me, the taste of rain and magick sweet on his lips.

"Ignore Joran," he says, as though he sees the yoke of responsibility I already feel around my neck. "He wanted to get under your skin. Don't let him succeed." He exhales a deep breath and wipes the rain from his face. "I let him succeed enough for the both of us."

But I can't ignore it. Because Joran was right. I failed my people before. I will not fail them again.

3

THE PRINCE WITH NO NAME

t isn't until the next morning that I'm able to return to Rite Hall and force myself to feed.

Sometimes I loathe this thing that I am, but I feel better now. Stronger. Complete healing will require even more feeding, but my wounds are already mending, the gash across my face tingling, my burns tightening.

After the deed is done, I leave and stroll the cloisters. The air is still and cold, the sun rising as I walk toward the western side of the quadrangle.

Rite Hall, formerly Thamaos's throne room, sits on the campus's eastern side, one of ten halls that surround the courtyard and meditative garden. The north side houses the Brotherhood's dormitories and living areas, while the south end contains their gathering, dining, and artisan rooms, still empty and quiet at this hour.

On the western side is the Triad—three buildings that mark the public areas. The worship hall and grand library, topped with gilded domes, and the central observatory—the temple's crowning glory—domed in panels of magick-tempered glass.

As I enter the wide expanse of the central observatory, the captain of my Royal Guard, Thresh, slips through the main entrance where two night sentries wait for the day guard to take their shift.

Thresh stalks toward me across the burnished floor. Clad in bronze leathers and tall boots, he stops outside the library's massive wooden doors where he falls into a severe stance. His feet are spread wide, his hands clasped firmly behind his back, his broad shoulders and strong chin held high.

Two torches mounted to columns that bookend the library's entrance, along with morning's first light filtering through the observation dome, illuminate the hall. The firelight reflects off the steel of Thresh's cuirass and the polished hilt of his sword. It even glimmers on the strands of his short blond hair, thick and tame and golden like his skin, save for that unruly darker lock that falls over his brown eyes when he glances my direction.

As I close the distance between us, my gaze slips past my captain to the library doors. Out of nowhere, a sharp pang strikes my chest and my throat burns, the way a throat burns to release a scream. A scream that howls in the recesses of my mind, drowning out the heavy raindrops pelting the night-dark glass above.

Taken aback, I pause. Look up. I've just come from outside. There's nothing in the sky other than a few puffy clouds and the promise of a cold, sunny day. Yet I'm filled with the inexplicable need to swipe at imaginary water dripping from my hair into my eyes. To rush into the library, a cry ringing from my lungs. The impulse is so strong that it takes all I have not to shove past my captain and haul those doors open.

In search of what, I do not know.

As fast as the feeling arrives, it passes. Bewildered, I swallow the tightness in my throat and keep walking, if a bit unsteadily. Thresh trains his gaze on mine for a long moment, spine rigid as a bowstring. I can see the question burning there.

Who did this to you?

I take the last steps separating us as he turns his eyes from me, staring straight ahead at the worship hall entrance instead. This is proper for the captain of my guard when standing before his prince and his men, but I sense a struggle as his throat moves on a swallow. His discomfort at looking upon me in this wounded, withered state.

"I didn't expect you back from the coast so soon."

Thresh keeps his voice down, low and tight. "I received word that you'd returned with Colden Moeshka and the God Knife. There must be much to do. With Vexx in the Northlands and Garujo...*gone*...I wanted to be here."

Gone. As if it were that simple. As if I didn't kill my oldest friend.

"I'm glad you came," I tell him, focusing on the business at hand. "I need you to retrieve one more criminal from the prison. Bring them to my chambers."

The thought gnaws at my conscience. Thresh will kill them for me, before he even brings them through my door. All I must do is inhale their souls.

A sick feeling arises anyway, and I mentally chide myself for such a reaction. *Eat or remain wounded and weak. Eat or die. The choice isn't difficult.*

Thresh turns his head, peering at me from beneath dark lashes. "*One* more? Given your condition, my prince?" He studies me for some flinch of correction.

He's right. Much as I don't want him to be.

"Make it three. We've a trip to Un Moritra in the coming days. I need to heal faster. Three should do the trick."

"Of course, Your Highness. Anything else?"

"Yes. Send Gavril and Crux to Malgros with a message. Alexi of Ghent and Raina Bloodgood are very likely headed to Malgros. I want them found, captured, and brought to me. Immediately. They share a runic bond, so they could possibly be a force to reckon with. But I want them in my possession. Soon."

Another nod. "I will go to the aviary now to see Crux, Your Highness. He should be ready to fly again."

"Make sure he informs Vexx that I want our enemies alive. Should the general feel the need to seek revenge, he may punish Raina Bloodgood before her arrival. Long as he leaves a little for me. But Alexi of Ghent isn't to be damaged. No more than necessary."

My captain inclines his head. "Yes, my prince. Consider it done."

Thresh awaits my dismissal. After a wave of my hand, he turns and stalks toward the main entrance and his sentries, obedient as ever.

When he's gone, my attention slides toward that damn library again. I can still hear a powerful rainsong dancing on the dome, rattling around like an angry ghost in the back of my mind, chased by whispers.

Hurry. We must hurry.

Annoyed by this incessant and vague recollection, I turn toward the doors that secure the Eastland Territories' history and lore. I'm not sure what's happening. Why the library that I've strolled past a thousand times calls to me now. But I'm compelled to look inside.

The archivists, librarians, and scribes who manage the library haven't gathered yet, so I tug the master key from beneath my tunic and unlock the door. The hinges creak as I drag open the heavy slab and step inside the threshold.

Only the first twenty rows of shelves on either side of the main aisle are given access to the public's perusal. All else lies behind a gilded, lattice wall and locked door, protecting historical treasures available to a select group: the archivists, librarians, scribes, scholars, the Brotherhood, and me.

To further protect the rare works housed inside the room, there's little light here save for the sun's first rays streaming through the tiny square windows on the upper floor, just beneath the golden dome. The hazy illumination lends a certain gloom to the winding staircase and dusty shelves of archived tomes and scrolls hidden within.

But that image shifts. The gilded wall vanishes, and the light changes to the silver of moonlight, as if what I'd seen before were a mirage. Lit candles and rush lights appear. Worktables filled with open books and scrolls. A main desk littered with texts and parchment and ink pots and quills.

Again, I feel the need to call out to someone who isn't there. This time, my gaze drifts to the top of the winding stairs, only to find nothing but darkness and the rumble of a threatening storm outside.

But I would swear on my soul that I smell and taste smoke and starlight.

"My prince, is something wrong?"

With a cold sweat breaking across my forehead, I grip the edge of the opposite door, panting, steadying myself as the scene corrects, swirling back to morning in the here and now. One of the archivists stands before me in his brown robe. His hands are pressed together, concern written across his lined brow. I swallow thickly, my blood warm with recognition and the most painful desperation, my mind haunted by the shadow of yet another lost memory.

"No," I tell him as I turn to go. "Just remembering."

4

RAINA

W e endure relentless downpours for two more days before the torrents cease.

But on that third day, the sun comes out, filtering through the trees, and that afternoon, the loveliest pink haze settles over the wood.

Come dusk, we pitch our tents as usual, on thick beds of pine needles covered in skins of leather to keep out the wet. The rain is still absent, allowing us time to clean up and wash in warmed rainwater, eat in the open air, and dry by the fire—without Joran's shield.

Only Alexus doesn't join us.

After I check the waters for the third time today, I head to his tent. When no one's looking, I duck inside. He sits on a bed of fur, leaning against his pack, dressed in nothing but his leather britches and that old key, writing by lantern light in a book at rest on his bent knee.

Sneaking from tent to tent in a chilly downpour isn't wise, so I've stayed with Nephele and Hel these last two nights. Alexus says it's just as well because he doesn't sleep well when it rains. But on the nights I *have* joined him, I've found him like this, transferring the contents of one text to another.

The book he copies from is an old journal. It lies open to the middle on a large piece of wool at his side. It's practically archaic, the pages brittle, the leather wrap worn to bits. I studied it one night, very carefully, trying to decipher the long-faded design on the cover.

The book in which he writes, however, is new. I recognized the moon and sun design and the Tiger's Eye stone affixed to the cover the moment he withdrew it from his bag the first night of our trip. It's the book I plucked from his desk at Winterhold. *Just proverbs and predictions*, he always says. The task keeps his mind busy. But from the care he gives those pages, I've a feeling the old journal contains more than that.

My eyes drift lower, over the broad muscles of his rune-covered chest, down the rippled plane of his abdomen, to where his britches are untied and partly open, revealing a dark trail of hair that's more alluring than it has any right to be.

"Care to go for a walk?" I sign.

In truth, after seeing him like this, a casual evening stroll is the last thing I want. But I have questions that can't wait any longer.

With an easy smile, he sets his book aside, grabs his tunic, and signs, *"I would love that."*

⚙❈⚙

WE HEAD SOUTH ON WINTER ROAD, HAND IN HAND ONCE THE CAMP IS out of sight. The graveled road is soft and riddled with puddles and a few ruts, but the day's sunlight has thankfully made it tolerable. We rarely have time alone save for at night. But this evening, there's no one to bother us, not even Neri's cold wind.

Alexus nudges his shoulder against mine. "Your glamouring is going well. I'm proud of you."

I glance at my hand, at my unmarked skin. Alexus and Nephele have taught Hel and I glamouring whenever possible. While we sat around the fire, when we could ride side by side, and for me, on many of the nights when I came to Alexus's tent. Glamouring will see us safely through Malgros and beyond, keeping suspicions at bay as we attempt passage and entry to Itunnan.

I rather like the nights when Alexus gives me lessons. We often end up naked, Alexus tracing every line of my witch's marks with his mouth and fingertips.

"I have a good teacher," I sign with a smile.

Before I break into interrogation, I decide to relax for a change. To feel something normal with Alexus. No surviving. No learning magick. No arguing with the others. Just us and this ordinary moment in the wood. I felt that way when we were near the ravine in the construct, the ache to be with this man outside of all that we've been through. All we're *still* going through. The notion of a peaceful life feels like an impossible dream when you live in chaos. But these glimpses remind me why peace is something worth fighting for.

We walk for several minutes in tender silence, enjoying each other's company and the rosy light trickling through the wood. Alexus's cheeks are tinged pink from the cold, his long hair loose, green eyes bright in this light. He looks content. Sometimes I can't imagine how he stays so calm, knowing that his life is tied to Colden's. He never seems worried to know that he could cease to exist any moment, while that knowledge eats at my nerves. If I couldn't see Colden in the waters and know that he's safe, I would be a disaster.

When we come across a bend in the road, Alexus pauses and glances around, getting his bearings. "My hunting shelter isn't far from here," he says, as though he'd been so absorbed in the peacefulness a moment before that he only now grasps where we are. "Maybe a day's ride. And, if we keep walking, there's a clearing just ahead. I bet we can see the stars soon."

"You know this wood so well," I sign, a woman who hadn't stepped foot within its shade until the last full moon.

"I do. Care to know why?"

When I nod—because *of course*, I'm nodding—he continues.

"As a boy, my father took me across the Northlands to the Iceland Plains to see an old water witch in hopes that my lack of skill could be corrected." He smiles at the memory and glances at me from the corner of his eyes. "It couldn't. But I liked the valley even then. Later, when I fled the East, I felt the Northlands was where I needed to be, especially near this wood. I've learned every inch of it, which would make my father proud. We spent a lot of time here on that trip. Some of the last days I had with him. It was good for us."

My fingers tense around a reply. I want to know more, but I hear the ache in his words, and I don't want to pry into painful parts of his life. So instead, I say, *"I miss my father too. Sometimes I imagine seeing him again. What conversations we would have. I was too self-absorbed to realize what a gift he was. I realize now, though."*

"Youth makes fools of us all," Alexus says as we veer around a puddle before coming back together. "I wish time was kinder. Even when you have eternity, there aren't enough second chances."

"Did your father teach you magick?" I sign. *"Is he why you are so good at* every-thing? *Including using the bond?"*

He tilts a look at me, eyes narrowed. "That's what's bothering you? I sensed something wrong."

I hate to spoil the easiness of our time together, but I answer honestly. *"The bond is such a simple thing for you and so impossible for me. How? If I am the only person you have marked?"*

Alexus pauses, and we face one another. "I've never claimed anyone but you. But someone once claimed me. My first love. First loves are powerful. And painful."

Don't I know. Each time I see Finn in the waters, I feel sick thinking about the moment we'll come face to face. I still don't know how I'll lie to the man I once believed I'd grow old with. How I'll convince him that I'm only staying with Alexus and his band out of some newly risen need for revenge on the Prince of the East. My only other choice is to tell Finn the truth, that the girl he used to love is now the woman who lies with the Witch Collector.

Every chance she can get.

Though I sense his reluctance, Alexus lifts his wrist and rolls back the cuff of his shirt. The runes that link him to the God Knife cover his strong forearm. But it isn't the runes he points to. It's a scar the size of a coin that lies over his pulse. A scar I've noticed but haven't asked about. When someone bears as many scars as Alexus, it feels wrong to make them remember their creation.

"We were sixteen," he says. "We kept it secret, for reasons. But her father found out."

Gods. I take his wrist and study the rough scar, its jagged edges. I let go and look up at him. *"Did you reverse the rune?"*

"No. Her father did, though. He wanted us to focus on developing our talents, not each other. He had us delivered to the temple where he cut the runes from our flesh and burned the skin in a holy fire. His sorcerer chanted the necessary song as we kneeled there, crying. Bleeding. Feeling every connection between us snap like ropes under too much weight. Until we both passed out on the floor."

I press his wrist to my mouth for a soft kiss, my heart breaking for a young man I didn't get to know. *"I am so sorry,"* I sign. *"That sounds unbearable."*

Alexus offered me the chance to reverse the rune at Winterhold. He's reminded me that it's an option twice since, when I tried to reach out for him and found myself facing a darkness that feels like it might swallow me whole. Losing this connection with him would be worse than facing my fear. I just need to learn to navigate the bond. To conquer the abyss that lies between us when I close my eyes.

He gestures for us to keep walking. "Unbearable is how it felt," he says. "Like my heart was being ripped from my chest. Her father was a master at cruelty. Even when it came to his daughter."

I can't imagine that kind of hurt. What fear the girl must've felt for a man who should've been a protector.

"Afterward," Alexus continues, "we became distant for a few years. We remembered our time together, and even the reversal ritual. But any emotion that connected us to those memories was gone. It was like a fever dream. Like none of that time had been real. Her father acted as though it hadn't. He kept us apart regardless, but sometimes we would see one another in passing—at the temple or at the school or even sometimes in training—and wonder."

"I'm sure that was uncomfortable," I sign. Two teenagers who'd been in love? Remembering things about one another? Probably quite *physical* things? Believing it was their imagination?

He shrugs. "It was. A simple locked gaze held so much curiosity, but we'd just keep moving. However..." He holds up a finger, a gentle smile on his face. "Curiosity eventually got the better of us, and we became best of friends. We pieced together our memories and realized what her father had done. What he'd stolen. But we were older. The fire of first love had faded. Loyalties had certainly changed. I'd become quite the dark soul, and she'd become quite the vengeful woman. Friends felt like a better route."

Unexpectedly, he takes my hand and stops us before turning me to face him. I revel in his nearness, suddenly enveloped in his heat. Because of his re-forged connection to energy, his magick warms every inch of his body, which makes cold nights a comfort.

He taps the tip of my nose. "Look up."

I do, and finally, after so many evenings sequestered in our tents or huddled beneath the forest's dense canopy, I stare up at a darkening twilight sky, still lit at the edges with the sun's glow, filled with the night's first stars. I study them all, watching as a few more twinkle into existence, remembering all the nights Nephele and I lay in the grass and traced constellations.

When I meet Alexus's stare again, my eyes wide, my lips curved into a smile, he takes my chin in his hand and steps closer. Where before the night was filled with shimmering stars and falling darkness, it's now filled with him.

"You like the stars?" He kisses me, his mouth warm and lush. "I can give you stars," he whispers.

The promise in that velvet voice flows over me, making me forget why I even came out here with him in the first place. *To ask about the bond and how to break through the barrier around the prince, Raina.* But the moment that thought enters my mind, it vanishes, because much to my surprise, hundreds of tiny golden orbs drift from the wood, floating like fallen starlight. I jump and gasp, pressing my hands to my cheeks, but it doesn't take long to recognize the familiar tingle in the air.

Alexus smiles and jerks his chin at the orbs. Like a swarm of fireflies, they zoom closer, each one mesmerizing as they hover and flicker, illuminating us and the road. The rich musk of Alexus's magick saturates the night like we're standing in a field of deer and wildflowers, its sweet flavor spilling over my tongue like honey. Captivated, I stare at the orbs with sheer wonder.

"They're just energy," he says. "They're also only the beginning of what I can do."

Holding my gaze, he slips the left side of my cloak over my shoulder and tugs one of the strings tying the collar of my wool tunic. The knot unravels, and the neck of my shirt falls open.

Alexus pulls the fabric aside, revealing my rune and the swell of my breast. My nipples harden as he dips his dark head and kisses the rune, trailing his tongue over the mark. I close my eyes and sigh. I don't understand why a kiss to the rune feels so good, but it sends a chill through me.

When Alexus lifts his head, he says, "You brought me out here to ask about the bond and breaking through the prince's barrier, didn't you?"

Completely caught off guard, I blink, trying to clear the haze of lust hanging over me and make the most innocent face I'm capable of making.

The side of his mouth quirks into a crooked smile, and that dimple returns. "Dismantling the wards around the prince will not only require the ability to read runes, but also the ability to rearrange those runes to unlock an opening. To do this through Sight, from thousands of miles away, will be the most complex magick you've ever worked. It will require immense concentration. Your attention cannot be easily diverted." I'm trying to listen. Trying so very hard. But he bends down again, trailing his mouth beneath the rune, and gently bites into my breast, making my knees give a little. "You must maintain two magicks at the same time," he continues, folding his arm around my waist, his voice warm against my skin as he drags his lips to my ear. "The balance would be quite difficult."

Quite difficult is right. I can't even *think* right now. Which, I quickly realize, was exactly his point.

Alexus pulls away, revealing my bared chest, which is now unglamoured, covered in luminescent witch's marks. Glimmering gold for life magick, bright scarlet for healing magick, icy silver for common magick, deep violet for Sight, and the occasional warm, ocher shadow for fire magick. I shiver when he trails his fingertip up and down a flourish that swirls from between my breasts. I swear he leaves a trail of magick on my skin.

"No matter how difficult, I've a feeling you're going to be persistent about learning," he says. "And I think it can be done. So I suppose I can teach you."

The nights when he taught me to glamour flash through my mind, and my reply bursts from my hands. *"Can we start now?"*

He laughs, the sound low and soft and sensual in the night. "You are an absolutely wicked little witch. I wish I didn't love that about you as much as I do."

I smile, brighter than I have in days, and before I know it, we're heading back toward camp hand in hand, jumping over puddles, laughing as his little starlights cluster around us, lighting the way.

Unfortunately, no birthbane tonic remained amid Winterhold's destroyed apothecary, and the dose I took the night before the harvest supper won't last much longer. But it's still safe to be with Alexus for a few days more, until the next full moon, and I plan to take advantage of that time with him.

Alexus slows our steps, lingering in the nightfall as a wolf howls in the distance. As we walk, taking our time, I ask one more question.

"Your first love. What was her name?"

I stare at him, waiting for a response, watching as her memory washes through him, the pain of recollection evident on his face.

"Fleurie," he says softly. "Her name was Fleurie."

THE PRINCE WITH NO NAME

The Eastland Territories
City of Yura, Un Moritra Ruins

The iron gates shimmer, wrapped in glistening, ancient magick that thrums through my bones, luring me to reach out and touch it.

When I do, silvery ribbons fold around my wrist and caress my arm beneath the silken sleeve of my jacket. A warm sensation floods my core, and I revel in the bliss, feeling so alive. So right. A blessing from Thamaos.

"Revius," I say, using one of the most basic Elikesh commands. It shouldn't work against the wards around these ruins, but as though I'd weaved some spell of unmaking, the iron gates open wide like a yawning maw.

Thresh and Bron—my right-hand, my closest advisor, my physician—wait behind me with lit torches in hand. Neither makes a sound of shock, but I know they lacked confidence in this mission. In *me*. And not because I'm still shedding the last layers of weakness.

No. Bron and Thresh doubted me because no one has opened this gate or stepped foot on this land in *centuries*. And yet here we are.

In all my years as Thamaos's chosen prince, I've never commanded magick without a source. Then again, I've never been sent *here*, where my lord's power still clings to the living world like fresh rain.

Power that knows me. Just as he said.

"You don't think we should've brought Gavril?" Bron asks. The warm light of her torch adds a golden glow to her pale skin and silvering copper hair.

A scoff leaves me before I can restrain myself. "If a sorcerer were all we needed to protect us from the creature beneath these grounds, she wouldn't be here. We just need *this*," I pat the God Knife strapped to my hip. "And you, of course, and Thresh to carry her out. As long as she's willing and doesn't try to kill us, this should go smoothly."

We leave my entourage behind and cross the grounds where gardens once flourished with renowned beauty, or so say the paintings in Min-Thuret's library. Now the land is covered with thorny bushes, weeds, gravel, and dirt. The dead version of what once was.

I visualize the old map Bron and I studied on the journey from Min-Thuret and move accordingly. Thresh lags a handful of steps.

"This was the famed monastery?" Bron asks, holding up her torch. Her life since she arrived in the Territories two decades ago, fleeing the North's complacency, is one of luxury at my palace, not the outskirts of a dirty city.

For the first time since I came to know her, I hesitate to answer. Given the events of the last few weeks, I'm wary. Unsure who I can trust. Even Bron.

Especially Bron.

Thanks to her son's treason in the Northlands, there's been plenty of reason to doubt her, much as I don't want to. She passed the Brotherhood's tests and questioning, but I'm no fool. If Rhonin Shawcross didn't act alone, and if betrayal is indeed in the air, I will sniff it out.

"Yes, this is the monastery," I reply. "Five hundred years old. Transitioned into the original scholarada where many of King Gherahn's young recruits trained. Only a select group advanced to the Order of Night at the school in Quezira."

"What happened to the rest of them?" she asks. "The ones who weren't chosen to advance."

"Conscripted to the guard. Unless they died in training first." I give her a sidelong glance. "At least my army isn't so brutal with its youth."

She says nothing, no doubt disagreeing after what happened with her son.

We pass the old dormitories' rubble. Though bandages hide beneath my trousers, protecting the healing burns along my calves and thighs, I join Bron and Thresh and crawl over the refectory's crumbling wall. Together, we walk through the infirmary and stumble over what's left of the bath house's cobbled tiles as a shortcut. While it requires a bit of care, particularly on my part, the trip across the decrepit acreage isn't half as dreadful as I imagined. At moments, it even feels nostalgic. Not a rush of memory like that night at the library, but as though I'm connecting to a part of my ancestors' past.

Until we reach the temple ruins.

"This feels dangerous, Your Highness," Bron says as we stare at the haunting remnants of the worship hall. The stone glows, bathed in the golden hues of a fading sunset.

I take the torch from Bron and aim it toward the darkness waiting before us. "Yes, well, best make friends with danger. It will be a constant companion in the days ahead."

Careful, I duck beneath a deteriorating stonework beam that bisects the opening where the main entry used to be. Bron keeps close as we step into gloomy shadows and walk inside a pool of torchlight, swatting our way through dense cobwebs, climbing over mounds of rocks, debris, and shattered mortar.

I imagine the hand-crafted stained-glass windows and granite altar that must've been here once upon a time, the wooden pews carved by men and women who revered their god and felt sure their work would have greater meaning in the future to come.

Gone now. Turning to dust. All of it.

What is the meaning of life if even time can steal our legacy?

Soon, we find the old hatch that leads underground. Thresh goes first. Once we're beneath the earth with the heat of our torches on our faces, my captain strains against the old iron door leading to the cells buried further below.

There's no magick down here that I can break through with a simple

Elikesh order, but there was never a need. Thamaos's outer protections surrounded this entire property, and beyond that, this place is a crypt, sealed by a door that, without an ability like Bron's, is an immovable slab.

Though we're cramped inside the small space, I sweep my arm between Bron and the door. "Your turn, my dear."

She takes a deep breath and steps forward as Thresh shuffles out of the way. Her concentration is single-minded, her stare eerily intense. For several minutes, she studies the curved line where the door meets stone, seeking threads within the metal's structure, threads that I've never been able to find, no matter how hard I look.

"Lana suun revius," she finally says. The Elikesh rolls off her tongue, smooth as unfurling silk. "Lana suun sal."

With a wave of her hand, the door drags open, painfully slowly. Mice scatter as the bottom edge scrapes the gravel, and the hinges screech their ages-old protest, reluctant to grant us more than a couple feet through which to enter.

But it's enough.

Truly admiring the way she's learned to dominate metals over these last years, I say, "See? Why would I want a dramatic sorcerer snipping at my heels when I have you?"

Those cerulean eyes glimmer in the torchlight, and brave as ever, she draws her dagger and leads the way forward.

Into the gloom, we creep down more crumbling stairs to the prison. Skulls of those who died here line the stairwell walls, framed behind thick, metal slats and the trapping power of more heavy iron, protections King Gherahn put in place ages ago at Thamaos's command. Though he was far before my time, I imagine the old king would spin in his grave if he knew what I was doing.

But he's not here. And like the thief that is time, I've come to take what he left behind.

On the last turn into the cells, dank air hits us from the arched tunnel ahead, like a foul wind rolling off a field of rotting corpses. We turn our heads, retching from the smell as water drips and pings against metal somewhere in the darkness.

"It may not even be alive." Bron forces the words, covering her nose.

"She's not an *it*." My voice is oddly harder than I mean for it to be.

"And she *is* alive. Centuries of starvation and isolation are not enough to kill this god spawn." Something at the end of the lightless corridor moves. Something that sounds like chains dragging along grit and stone. I glance at Bron, then to Thresh. "Though we may soon wish it were."

We enter the tunnel. Our torchlights reveal one empty cell after another, the massive iron bars rusted but still intact. Reinforcing iron plates have been forged into the stone walls between each chamber, along with iron piping that leads somewhere above ground for minimal ventilation.

A prison fit for trapping an immortal godling indeed.

Every step we take is met by that same sound—claw, then drag—until I hear the ragged intake of wet breathing as well.

I pause. Ahead, just within the outer rim of the torchlights' reach, a hand slips through the bars of a cell.

Long-nailed and bony fingers splay across the dirt floor, and a rust-covered iron cuff clangs against the bars. The creature known as Fury pushes her emaciated arm through the gap even further, her skeletal hand so stiff it trembles.

Thresh gags, the sound echoing through the tunnel as I take the final steps between me and the Eastland Territories' forgotten daughter.

In case the iron somehow fails, I unsheathe the God Knife and loom over her.

My shadows roil across the ground like a blood-drenched fog eddying into her cell. Surrounded, she lifts her head and stares at me with wide, rheumy eyes that dart wild as a lightning strike. She's confused, taking me in from head to foot. Understandable, given that she hasn't seen another face in centuries.

Though it turns my stomach, I absorb the sight of her, the body that has withered to nothing more than rotting patches of skin, glistening innards, and brittle bones. Little more than an animated carcass.

I almost feel sorry for her.

Almost.

I remind myself that she has a purpose. A tool of great use.

Crouching, I offer the wasted godling her real name, something no one has ever offered me, along with the warmest smile I possess.

"Well, hello there, Fleurie. Your father sent me to make you a deal."

6

ALEXUS

"You're up early."

From beneath his hooded gray cloak, Rhonin jerks his chin at me and takes a seat on a log near the fire, next to my scabbard and swords. It's cold, the air still dark and damp, the wood swathed in a fog too thick to ride against.

"Didn't sleep well?" He scrubs his hands down his dark britches, then reaches his pale hand for an empty mug and the flask of watered-down ale that sits near the heat.

"The opposite, actually. Slept like a rock."

And I did. When Raina and I slept. At least she didn't have any nightmares.

Rhonin sets the flask aside and lifts his filled mug to his lips. "Why are you awake, then?"

Visions of Raina lying before me flash across my mind. Her back arching. Her lovely nipples peaked and glistening from my kisses. Her mouth parted in ecstasy.

Her leaving my tent to avoid being seen...

That I had to let her go a short while ago makes me even more pissed at Joran. Raina doesn't want to feel responsible for further tension between

the members of this group, and I'll honor her wishes. But I don't give two
fucks about what the others think. I've been alone for a very long time. I
might've given my body away in the past, but my heart has been as caged as
Neri and my magick.

Until now.

"We're just so close to the valley," I say, poking at the fire with a stick.
"I'm more than ready to be riding toward Malgros. You?"

He leans his thick forearms on his knees. The tin mug clasped between
his massive hands looks like a child's toy.

I look at him then. *Really* look at him. His bloodshot eyes and their
purple shadows tell me all I need to know.

He scrubs his brow. "I'm not sure if I'll sleep well until this is over. I
can't stop thinking that an answer lies in the past. An answer you must
know in that enormous mind of yours."

That coaxes half a grin out of me. "*Many* answers lie in the past. I have
a friend in Malgros, Captain Osane, who always says, '*The past helps us understand the present, Alexus.*' But connecting lines across the ages isn't an easy
thing."

"I'm sure it's not. It might help if we talk it out, though?" His face
twists into a slight wince, as if he's presenting the question to a snake ready
to strike.

I sit my mug aside, toss the stick, and hold my hands toward the fire.
Fuck. I like this kid. I hate it that he had to leave his mother and siblings
in the East. I'm certain that's part of his torment, a reason for his sleep-
lessness.

But after my conversation with Raina last night, the last thing I want to
talk about is the past. While I remember certain parts so clearly, others are
riddled with black holes, muddling the history of my long life. Such is the
way when you face an endless existence, I suppose. Time isn't kind.

It devours.

And yet, I find myself glancing up at Rhonin and saying, "Sure. We can
talk it out."

His blue-green eyes light up, as though I said the words he's longed to
hear. Maybe I did.

"So Neri cursed Colden," he says, leaning closer, his voice laced with determination for answers. "And the ruling gods commanded that the truth about what Neri did to Fia and Colden be kept secret from the people. No record."

"Yes. Gods want to be revered and glorified. Not doubted. So they did their damnedest to make certain the Tiressian people believed what they wanted them to believe. And it worked. Three hundred years later, the Tiressian gods are all dead, and yet people still worship them."

I only learned the truth after I met Colden, as a spy, before I finally left the East. There were years when we tried to convince the Northlanders about Neri. Most only saw us as deceitful, as though we wanted them to worship *us* instead. We learned all too quickly that it is no small task to strip people of their gods. No matter how false they might be.

"And only those of you who were there know the *real* story," Rhonin replies. "And the chosen Witch Walkers. And now us, of course. Which is what I can't stop thinking about. How the tale made its way to the Prince of the East, after all this time. Where did it come from?"

My mind reels to that moment in Hampstead Loch, watching the prince's army riding like a squall of death into the valley.

"I've tossed that question around in my mind since this game started," I tell him. "I've wondered if there was a traitor in our midst at Winterhold, or if Fia confided in someone and the news made its way to the prince. Or perhaps it was a mouthy wraith determined to cause trouble. I'm not sure we'll ever have an answer." I meet his eyes. "You're certain you don't remember anything from your time at the palace that might point us in the right direction?"

I've asked this before, but the answer is always the same.

"Trust me when I tell you that I've scoured my brain. Other than many trips to Min-Thuret lately, all has been the same. Then again, I wasn't made privy to many details having to do with the prince's affairs, unless they came from my mother. Especially prior to being moved up the ranks."

Min-Thuret. If I could purposefully forget anything, it would be all the times that I kneeled for Thamaos and King Gherahn, and the crimes I committed in their names. I spent so many days in that temple, so many hours on my knees. Yet even those memories have splintered over the centuries. The last years of my life as a mortal in Quezira feel like a patchwork existence. If those years were a puzzle, a quarter of the pieces would be missing.

But there's one thing I didn't forget.

"Wait." I narrow my gaze at Rhonin and lean forward, clasping my hands between my widespread knees. "Where does the prince go when he visits the temple?"

The glistening Shara Palace is a week's ride from Min-Thuret. Two weeks' ride from the coast, where the prince's massive army remains stationed. Safety lies inland. What could he need at the old temple badly enough for frequent journeys?

Books? Codexes? Scrolls? There are ancient tomes and texts, well enough. Maps upon maps. Letters between past rulers and gods. Works on ritual and worship. On mathematics, medicine, law, astronomy.

I would know. The original collection housed and cataloged in Min-Thuret's library had to pass through my hands before ever arriving at the archivists' doors.

The last thing I expect him to say are the two words that leave his mouth.

"Rite Hall," he answers, keeping his voice low as some of the others stir from their tents. "Every time," he adds. "Alone, except for servants who tend him. They say he cuts himself when he prays. Does that mean anything?"

I close my eyes for a single breath and open them. Fuck all.

Staring at my clenched hands, I turn my right wrist toward the sky and study the nearly faded scar that lies across my palm in a diagonal. How many times did I pray to Thamaos in Rite Hall? Summon him from the realm of Eridan to the temple for King Gherahn?

Enough times to know that Thamaos was the only Tiressian god who required a blood sacrifice to deem someone worthy of his revered presence.

But he's gone now. Not even the Brotherhood bleeds for him when they pray. Rite Hall is a museum. A well-kept and hallowed hall, an honor to Thamaos's history. So why would the prince kneel in that room and spill his life's blood for a god bound to the Shadow World?

I think back to last night. To the journal entry I was translating when Raina came to me, from day number one hundred and seventy-four. There are a handful of entries mistakenly scribed in my journal by an archivist or perhaps an assistant, though if I ever knew who, I can't recall now. Still, I've rewritten those faded Elikesh words so many times that I know them by heart. They always draw my eye, the way the faded shadow of each letter is perfectly formed.

The gods may die, but they can still find you. They arrive as a whisper in the night. A chill in the wind. An ember from a flame. A wave on the shore. Listen for them always and watch your back. Because even when the worst of them is dead and buried, you will not be safe.

A whisper in the fucking night.

Thamaos certainly knew about Colden and Fia. He had a hand in Asha and Neri paying for their crimes with the Fire Queen and Frost King. He knew that the Northland king could be used as a pawn. A distraction.

Bait.

He just didn't have time to do anything about it before Urdin stopped him. *Before Urdin ended them both to see Thamaos condemned to the Shadow World.*

Is Thamaos manipulating the prince from beyond? Using the prince to his own devices?

Surely, I'm wrong. *Surely.*

Before I can spout the litany of curses rising inside me, Callan and Helena walk up. Callan, donned in their dark green cloak and layers upon layers of beaded necklaces, takes a seat beside me, a piece of salted meat in one hand, their pack in another. Hel sneaks up behind Rhonin. Her black hair is tied in a loose weave, her golden-brown face still puffy with sleep. Trying to startle him, she jerks his hood down, revealing his braided, red mane.

Rhonin tilts his head back to peer up at her. His cheeks instantly blush, and a lovesick smile spreads wide across his face.

Hel leans over him, smiling too. "What do you say we eat and then spar a little? Swordplay while the fog clears."

"I say I'm in. And that *I'm* keeping score this time. You cheat."

She splays her hand across her chest and bats those dark lashes at him. "Me? I would never cheat. Honor and all that."

Rhonin laughs and pushes to his feet as Helena strolls toward the tent she shares with the Bloodgood sisters, but when his gaze catches on my face, his smile falters.

After a moment of hesitation, he crosses the few steps between us and places his hand on my shoulder. "Are you all right? You look pale as me."

My pulse picks up pace. I know what I must do, much as I don't want to.

"I am not." Standing, I grab my scabbard and swords and shrug them over my shoulders. "I need you to keep everyone distracted while Callan and I go for a little walk."

From beside me, Callan says, "That sounds ominous. I try not to do ominous things this early in the morning. I haven't even eaten yet."

With my attention on Rhonin, I fasten the holster around my chest and waist.

Rhonin trains his voice low. "How exactly am I supposed to keep them distracted with you two missing? Have you met Hel and Nephele and Raina? They'll murder me for answers."

"Raina and Nephele are still sleeping. I only need an hour. We'll be at the rocky outcropping just west of here. About a five-minute trek if you stay true west. If we don't return by mid-morning, then I suggest you come looking for us."

"Mid-morning?" Concern fills his eyes. "It's what I said about the prince, isn't it? It means something really fucking bad."

Looking west at the misty forest, I arch a brow, praying to the Ancient Ones that I'm wrong when I say, "It means everything."

Callan rises and sighs, tugging their hood closer around their face. "All right, Old One. What are we doing?"

"Wait, can I come?" Rhonin asks.

"No," I answer.

"Why?"

"Because I need magick, and you have none." When he grumbles, I clasp his shoulder. "I trust you to keep things calm here," I say. "You are my right hand for the morning, all right?"

He nods, but the frown on his face tells me he isn't exactly happy about agreeing.

"Grab your pack, Callan," I say. "I need your help. And I think you'll enjoy witnessing the unthinkable."

"And what might *that* be?" Quickly, they fall into step beside me as I leave Rhonin and stalk deeper into the tangled, foggy wood.

I meet their hazel stare. "Believe it or not, I'm about to pray to Thamaos."

❧ II ❧
OLD FRIENDS

7

ALEXUS

Callan and I walk through the slumbering forest.

I tune my ear, listening for Neri's wolves, my neck bristling as I try to sense his nearness. This exercise could devolve into a disaster quickly if Neri scents what I'm up to. But I don't feel him, for now, and there's little sound this morning. Only that of a night bird's mournful cry as dawn breaks over the stony clearing.

"This should do perfectly," Callan says, their voice soft against the quiet wood. They shrug off their pack and withdraw a ritual knife, the wooden handle smooth from years of dedicated use. When they hand me the blade, I test the heft of its weight, the sharpness of its edge, promising in my hand.

"Ready?" Callan asks, their bronzy skin glistening in the misty air.

"As I'll ever be."

Inhaling the scent of rain and cedar, oak and pine, I climb onto one of the nine large rocks half embedded into the earth, each the width of a healthy stride. Carefully, I cross to the middle. The moss-slicked stones are worn flat by centuries of rain, their pattern reminding me of honeycomb.

It takes all that I am to do what I do next.

There, standing beneath the heavy canopies of mist-shrouded and ancient trees, I kneel.

Callan removes a pouch of blessed salt, a tinder box, and a small hammered-metal dish that sits atop a miniature brazier from their pack. They use these items to burn sage and sweetgrass, mugwort and juniper, for cleansing. Today they're being used for a summoning.

In minutes, a flame burns inside the brazier, heating the bowl that will soon hold my blood. Callan takes my hand and pours a small mound of salt into my palm. They watch as I drag the ritual knife in a circle around myself, carving a line through the damp moss on the single stone beneath me. I seal the threshold with a ring of salt. A protective barrier. The *first* one. Between me and the space where Thamaos's will have reign.

Callan acts as my ritual guardian, performing the same salt ritual on a larger scale. They walk around the nine stones, pouring salt, creating the second circle, one that will keep them and the rest of the world safe from Thamaos's reach. A god's consciousness is too powerful and manipulative for us to go about this summoning any other way.

"It isn't required that he answer your call," Callan says, closing the circle.

I rest my hands on my thighs and let out a breath. "I have a feeling he won't deny me. But I need to make certain that I'm heard. Instead of three runes, I'd like to mark nine. Nine runes that all but demand his presence."

Callan inclines their head. "So be it, Old One. You are the master."

With great care, Callan marks runes of protection around the outer circle with salt. When they finish, I do the same to mine, then remove the bowl from the heat and set it on the stone. It's been ages since I bled for Thamaos, but when I hold the ritual knife to my palm, my mind remembers exactly what to do. How to position my hand for the least damage. How deeply to drag the blade.

The pain is sharp but swift, yet it stabs with memory. After all this time, this rite is still ingrained in my bones.

I tilt my hand and squeeze my fist. The hiss and sizzle of my blood on hot metal stirs the darkest shadows tucked away in the deepest part of me. I repeat the action, squeezing over and over, until a crimson pool fills a third of the dish.

I dip my fingers into my blood.

"Connection," Callan says. "Always first."

Oh, how I remember. A rune to cross boundaries. Gods know that the separation between Thamaos and I, the space between the living and the dead, is vast. I draw the bloody rune on the north side of the stone on which I kneel.

"Faithfulness is next," Callan says. "Then fealty."

As my blood soaks into the moss, I glance up at my friend. "I remember this pattern, all too well. What I wouldn't give if there were others that could stand in their places. Anything that doesn't scream that I'm crawling back to him like some pious worshiper."

Callan arches a brow and holds their hands out. "These three are the basis of this rite, which was created for Thamaos alone. We cannot change that. You know this."

I do. But after three hundred years, a man can fucking wish.

Grudgingly, I finish the first three runes and look to Callan for wisdom to make certain I get the next part right. "It's been a very long time since I worked with layering runes, and I'm a bitter son of a bitch, so you should probably guide me."

"Strength is next," Callan says, their lips curling at one corner. "So that he knows you are not weak. Then Sacrifice, to show that you have offered your blood for a chance to communicate. Courage, to remind him that you do not fear him. Determination, to announce that you will persist until he answers. Then Need, to make certain he knows you have an unfulfilled desire only he can answer." They pause. "And last, the Shield of Loria. Because I'm about to pray for the goddess's favor to fall over you."

Callan's chants begin as I draw fresh blood from my palm to form the additional runes. If these don't work, if Thamaos doesn't heed my call, I'll have to try again.

When I finish, a web of light forms around Callan's ring, spreading from one rune to another, then it begins in my smaller circle, ringing me in protective magick.

Satisfied, I face east for Thamaos's direction. True disgust saturates my senses as I bow, pressing my forehead and hands to the damp rock as Callan chants Loria's grace around me.

"Come on, you bastard," I mutter. "Come and find me."

It isn't much of a prayer, and this isn't much of an altar, but it's the best this bitter sorcerer can do.

We wait. Minutes pass, until a thin, quick wind rakes its bony fingers through my untied hair, giving rise to goosebumps that chase along my spine and arms. At first, I think it's Neri, but...

"Alexus, look."

At the sound of Callan's command, I glance up. They step back, shielding their face with their cloak, distancing themselves from that same wind from before that's now growing into a whirling gust inside the second circle. With a whistle at its edges, the air swirls into a funnel cloud, picking up speed, swirling around the stones. It gathers pine needles and detritus and raw, gritty earth, spinning it fine as sand, until the remains fuse, forming into the shape of a naked man standing tall and strong, wearing the face of a long-dead god.

It's no man though. And it's certainly no god. Its skin is pale green like the leaves and moss, its hair dark and rich as soil. Its towering body appears smooth and hard, gray as the stones beneath me, wrapped in wooden twigs, its irises bright and clear as a stream in early morning light.

I know what I'm seeing. I know this is only a mirage. An illusion. That unlike Neri, this is Thamaos's mind, not his soul made manifest. His impossible reach through tactics such as this used to amaze me, and even now, I am shaken by his skill. To manipulate the living world from the depths of the Nether Reaches is a feat. To do it so dramatically an even greater accomplishment.

But most of all, it gives me some idea of what we're up against.

The forest-made thing smiles, making my blood ice. "Alexi of Ghent, old friend," Thamaos says in that too-familiar voice. "So we meet again."

⚜

"I DIDN'T EXPECT YOU SO SOON."

I sit back on my haunches, watching Callan from the corner of my eye. Carefully, they make their way around the stones to stand at my back. Thamaos's creature watches too, studying Callan with curiosity in its eyes. Even under such scrutiny, Callan continues chanting a prayerful song to the Ancient Ones. To Loria. Their voice is low, but I feel its immense power in the air.

"And I didn't expect *you* at all," Thamaos says. His mirage remains eerily still. "I thought you'd forgotten me."

There's a glimmer in the creature's stare. Some pointed glint of knowing.

"Believe me, I've tried to forget you," I reply. "But you just won't stay buried."

That first part is a lie, and when the creature's mouth curves into a mocking grin, I know Thamaos tastes my dishonesty.

I've tried harder than I care to admit to remember our final days together. The entire last year of his existence feels like a blur of time scattered with random memories. Him visiting the library at the scholarada where I was headmaster of the Order of Night and Dawn. The two of us standing together, face to face, tensions high, in the Great Hall of his palace, a place that doesn't even exist anymore. Him staring down at me as I knelt in my own blood in the ritual circle at Rite Hall.

I tried to be a dutiful servant. Tried to worship him. But those days are gone. Now, my loathing is as vast as the universe, for many reasons, even if I can't recall some of the more trivial ones. It's probably best that I can't remember. I just wish time would erase the damage I've done.

His creature glances around, taking in the scenery and the protective web of magick before leveling a stare on me. "What do you want, Un Drallag?"

Always to the point, even now.

I stand upon my stone, feet wide, and lift my chin boldly in his direction. Even still, his animated being is taller than me.

"You're using the Prince of the East, aren't you," I say. "Guiding him. Perhaps controlling him."

The earthen creature clasps its hands behind its back, an evil grin on its face. Leisurely, it begins walking around the stones, so close to the circle's salt edge. Callan moves too, safe beyond the circle's barrier. They keep pace with Thamaos, refusing to show alarm.

"What does it matter?" Thamaos says. "Either way, your true fear is that I will rise again. And I *will*. Soon. Much thanks to you and your new friends, the Frost King is in our hands, and the God Knife is finally home. Before long, we will be reunited, my throne reclaimed."

Thamaos's creature trails a glance over me as I turn, slowly following him with a narrowed gaze. "By whom? You or the prince? I'm fairly certain the prince believes it's him who will reign over Tiressia."

The creature huffs, blowing the dusty remains from the forest floor into the air. "I have always seated kings, Alexi. What makes you think I don't plan to offer the prince a place at my side?"

"You're assuming he can restore your life. Resurrection won't be so easy," I warn. "The God Knife doesn't give your puppet prince a key into the Grove of the Gods. Neither does having possession of Colden Moeshka. If you think Fia or I will allow you or your man anywhere near the City of Ruin, you are sorely mistaken."

He tosses his dark head back and laughs. "My, my. Such empty threats." He slices a steely look my way. "Your memory must, fail you, Un Drallag. You should know better than to think that I don't have a plan."

"I will stop you," I promise him as a chill wind that feels far too much like Neri breezes over me. "I will fight until my last breath before I ever see you walking and breathing in this world again."

Suddenly, the forest creature is looming over me, bending until it's staring me in the face, toeing the line of blessed salt around me. Its pale green skin roils like a storm trapped beneath glass, eyes aglow like embers of a stoked fire.

It glances at the key around my neck, then opens that earthen mouth to speak.

But before Thamaos's voice pours from the depths of this wind-borne creation, its eyes slither to my left, widen infinitesimally, and glow even brighter.

"*You*," he hisses, the word trembling the air with a visceral hatred I feel throughout my being.

I expect to hear Neri's voice, but there is no reply. And that rattles me even worse than if the God of the North had shouted across the clearing. Because for the first time since I carved it into my skin, my rune warms with vibrant, flaming heat as panic and a fierce furor rushes through the bond, nearly taking me to my knees.

The raging fire of a protective woman.

Raina.

8

RAINA

R un. Run, run, run.

The moment that *thing* locks its gaze with mine, my instinct screams that single word over and over. Or maybe it's Alexus, sending an order along the bond, a connection I now feel so entirely that I'm shaking from the power of it.

I don't get a chance to decide which one is sounding the alarm, my body or my lover, because as Alexus swings around, the creature standing with him explodes into a whirl of detritus.

Just as quickly, the thing reforms at the edge of the stones and slams against a tangled web of light, a *shield* between us. It roars like an unholy demon, the sound booming through the wood, stirring birds and creatures from their nests.

There are a few strides and a magickal wall keeping us apart, but I still flinch and lift my dagger, waiting for an attack.

What *is* this thing? A forest wraith?

I sniff the air, waiting for the scent of brimstone to strike me the way it did with Hel in the construct, but it never comes.

"Callan, break the circle!" Alexus tosses Callan a knife, the weapon flying end over end. By some miracle, Callan snatches it from the air like a master, by the hilt.

The creature jerks around to look at Alexus but turns back to me. "You will pay for all that you've done, Witch Walker. There will come a day when no magick, no sorcerer, not even time, distance, or realms, will keep you from my wrath. Know that. Don't *ever* forget it." It presses its massive hands against the shield, a malevolent smile curling the corner of its mouth. "I am Thamaos, God of the Eastern Territories, and I'm coming for you and all you hold dear, Raina Bloodgood."

I swallow hard. Thamaos.

Thamaos?

In the next instant, the web of light flickers out, and the creature disintegrates again, but this time, the million pieces of the forest that this thing seems to be made from fall to the ground in a lifeless heap.

Still shaking, I dart a glance at Callan, on their knees and panting, hood fallen around their shoulders, hands pressed to the earth. The salt ring around the stones now has a broken place, all magick within gone.

Alexus jumps down from the rocks and hurries to me. I sheathe my dagger, and he takes me in his arms, drawing me to his chest. I cling to him, trying to understand what in the Nether Reaches just happened, but also reveling in the bond, the connection thrumming and alive, open for both of us. I can feel his relief, his worry, his...

Blinking, I look up at him, stunned. Eyes wide, I search his gaze as heat flashes up my neck. He studies my face, and I know he sees the question there, the realization and recognition of all he holds inside his heart for me. But he makes no mention of it, and the feeling disappears from the bond, as though he's tucked it away in some dark corner for now.

Tenderly, he kisses the top of my head and says, "Are you all right?"

I nod. I'm just rattled and brimming with questions and feelings and...

I am not all right.

Alexus brushes my hair from my face, and I notice his bloodied hand.

I look at him, my brow furrowing.

"A ritual wound," he says, instinctively knowing my question. "I summoned Thamaos."

Summoned. Hearing that word right now, standing in this forest having just looked into the eyes of a creature, dredges up a memory.

"Do not summon me," Neri had said on Winter Road. If not for those words and what I just beheld, I would've never known such an option

existed, to summon a god. Not that I'd ever *want* to summon one of those bastards.

Careful not to hurt Alexus, I cradle his hand in mine and imagine the flesh healed, the strength that lies in his grasp returned, the care that lives in his touch restored.

Loria, Loria, una wil shonia, tu vannum vortra, tu nomweh ilia vo drenith wen grenah.

The old Elikesh words sing through my mind and the gash begins to close, stitching itself together, the sparkling red threads of his injury weaving into a tight line. When the healing is complete, Alexus cups my face with his other hand, stroking my cheekbone with his thumb.

"Thank you." His voice softens to that deep, rich sound that calms every frenzied nerve inside me. "For this," he says, lifting his healed hand. "And for crossing the abyss for me."

I did cross the abyss. *I did.*

Emotion swells, making me clench my fingers into a fist. I'd been terrified when I saw that creature towering over Alexus, terrified enough that the chasm between us seemed to vanish as I broke through the trees. I just needed to reach him. Physically. Mentally. Any way I possibly could. And so, inside my mind, I leapt.

And I would do it a thousand times more.

Gently, he presses his forehead to mine and brushes a kiss across my lips. "I suppose I have some explaining to do."

"Much," I sign between us as Callan approaches.

"Well, *that* went smoothly," they say before turning a look of concern on me. "Raina, are you sure you're all right?"

"Only shaken," I lie. Alexus translates to make sure they understand.

"I would suppose so." Callan's brows rise as they haul their pack over their shoulder. "It sounds like you've made quite the enemy, my friend."

A grim shadow falls over Alexus's face. "The question is why. The Prince of the East, who I fear might be the true pawn in this game, must've told Thamaos what happened with Raina on Winter Road. Perhaps she thwarted the prince's plans more than we realized."

"Or *Thamaos's* plans," Callan says. "And that painted a target on her back."

A cold wind blows as Alexus and Callan work at clearing their runes from the earth and stones, then we head back toward camp. As we walk, Alexus explains why they came here. I listen, but with every step, I must work to banish the echo of Thamaos's voice from my mind. His words feel far more foreboding than Joran's ever could, more like an omen, a promise, and something inside me warns that the god spoke no lies.

"At least now we know that Thamaos is involved," Callan says, clutching their cloak tight against the gusts. "The prince must be summoning him often, and there's no doubt who's controlling the situation." They dip beneath the branch of an oak tree, and we follow. "I'm going to pray to Loria that this is the last we see of the eastern god, though."

Prayer or no prayer, I know better. Odd as it seems, I can sense the verging of our paths taking place even now. Mine and his. A witch and a god. A collision looming on the horizon.

No. I have not seen the last of Thamaos, God of the East. Of that, I'm sure.

And he has not seen the last of me.

❧

EVERY EYE FIXES ON US WHEN WE RETURN TO CAMP, AND ALEXUS LAYS out the truth for all to hear. He believes that the Prince of the East has been summoning Thamaos, and that Thamaos plans to be resurrected so he can rule, not to be used as a siphon for the prince. Whether the prince is being manipulated into becoming a second-hand ruler at Thamaos's side, or if he's trying to fool Thamaos into a trap is the question.

Either way, the game feels more dangerous now.

There's a break in the rain, so we travel hard for the rest of the day. Alexus and I try experimenting with the bond, even as we ride. The connection can't remain open constantly; it's too overwhelming to sense another person's thoughts and feelings without ceasing. But we can call upon the connection when needed, like knocking on a door between us. Though each time I try, that looming abyss still awaits me.

Late that afternoon, when we break to set up camp, Nephele, Hel, and I unsaddle our horses to give them a rest. The dusky sky is choking back a downpour that we're all too tired to endure.

"I wish you'd told me you were going to check on Alexus this morning," Nephele says, unfastening the girth straps from her horse's saddle.

"Agreed," Hel adds, leading her animal from a rootbound patch of earth to more level ground. "We're a team. The next time the men try to pull one over on us, let's show them that they can't."

"I understand Alexus's need to keep things quiet," Nephele says, flashing her eyes at me. "But you are not alone. Before you go tearing into any battle by yourself, be sure we're at your side. We're stronger together than apart."

Pressing my lips into a thin, guilty line, I tilt my head and nod.

"Tuethas tah," Hel says and signs the words. Nephele and I smile and do the same.

Tuethas tah. It's not just *my sister* anymore. But my *sisters*.

We work in silence for a few minutes, until Nephele clears her throat. When I look at her, I notice her cheeks are warm with a flush.

"I need to explain what Joran said the other night." Nephele's voice is tight as she hefts her saddle from her horse and sits it on a bed of brown leaves and pine needles.

I take a deep breath and glance at a wide-eyed Hel. Nephele has avoided this conversation since Joran mentioned their past relationship. In her defense, I wouldn't want to talk about it either.

"I loathe him," she says, peering over her animal's back where Joran stands across the road, unloading his pack from his horse. "It was just once."

"Just once?" Hel asks, smiling. "It didn't sound like it was *just once.*"

"All right, three times, damn it. But just one night. Last year, after a wedding at Winterhold. I'd had far too much wine."

Smiling, Hel removes the saddle cloth from her horse's back and runs her hand along its flanks. "Obviously."

"He is quite handsome," I sign, trying to make Nephele feel better. Sex with Joran *has* to be a regret.

"And a part of me is drawn to that, unfortunately." She keeps her voice low. "Pale hair, a brazen attitude, and a big cock are my weakness with men, especially when they're not talking. But I'd need to gut him and start all over in order to tolerate him on a normal basis. He's a rotten-hearted prick."

Hel laughs but then groans. "Gods, now I'm going to think about what's between Joran's legs every time I look at him. Disgusting."

I smile, but I'm still surprised that Nephele slept with the Icelander at all, last year no less. I saw the way she and Colden looked at one another. The adoration.

"Why be with him, then?" I sign. *"What about Colden?"*

Finished with her horse, Nephele strolls over and strokes Tuck's white mane. "What about him? He wants me to find a special someone, though we both agree that Joran is *not* him."

My eyebrows rise of their own volition. *"I thought that special someone was Colden."*

"Me too," Hel says.

"No. Colden is special. We love one another dearly. But for me, he's safe and easy. For him, I'm comfortable. Someone he can trust. We have fun, but there have been others for us both."

"Well, I'll add that to the list of surprises when it comes to Colden Moeshka," Hel says, shaking her head.

Nephele furrows her brow. "What do you mean?"

Hel turns toward my sister, one arm slung over her horse's back. "He wasn't what I imagined when we came face to face on Winter Road. For my whole life, I pictured the Frost King as an old man. I'm still trying to wrap my head around the fact that he's not only young and beautiful but also a warrior, even though I saw it all in action with my own eyes. Now you're telling me he's fun too, when I pictured a serious, sour-faced king whose greatest skill was wielding a table knife."

"Ah," Nephele says. "Understandable. I remember feeling similarly the first time I saw him. I was stunned." She grins at the memory. "But Colden doesn't allow silence for long. He's quite the character, and yes, quite the soldier. Magickless or not, I expect him to outsmart the prince and find his way to freedom."

Gods, I pray to Loria that he does. But my mind clings to the rest of Nephele's words because I had no idea their relationship was like this. Though I suppose I should have. When Alexus first told me about Nephele and the Frost King, he called my sister Colden's *high servant* and *paramour*. His right hand and lover. Not a partner. It was *me* who defined what exists between them before understanding the truth. And I, of all people, should know that things don't always appear as they seem.

Still, I can't imagine sharing Alexus. The thought of someone else being with him now the way that I am—touching him, kissing him, fucking him —makes my chest tighten and my blood heat.

"I like our arrangement," Nephele says, and I hear the truth in her words. "Colden and I are... different. He would never admit it, but I believe he aches for something immortality has stolen from him. A chance to spend a normal lifetime with someone he loves without the promise that he will eventually face their loss day after day for however long he might live. As for me, I'm not made for tenderness. Not the kind you and Alexus share, anyway. I know the rune's bond is part of that, but I can see an intimacy between you two that I can't fathom feeling for another person. Though I admire it."

I think about all I felt from Alexus earlier this morning after facing Thamaos, and a sudden hollowness fills my chest. Immortality carries with it eternal loss and pain. The thought of loving someone, only to know that time would take them and leave behind grief for ages, would be... excruciating.

For the first time, I consider the boundaries of what we share, how much of a risk it is for Alexus to feel anything for me at all. Perhaps that's why he smothered his feelings as soon as I sensed them this morning. We're lovers, like Nephele and Colden. But with every passing day, whatever this is that lives between us grows. I might only now realize the truth of the situation, but Alexus has known all along what he stands to lose if this continues. Knows that he will remain constant long after I am no more than a fading star in the sky.

Yet he looks at me as though I contain infinities.

"By the way," Hel says, brushing the dried mud from her horse's golden coat. "How do you feel about the bond now? After what happened this morning?"

"Things have certainly changed," I sign as Tuck nuzzles her nose against my shoulder. *"I feel tied to Alexus in a different way. A good way. But different."*

Nephele's eyebrows pulls together as she gives me a tender stare. "Two lives can become so entwined, Raina. Not that that's a bad thing, but it's very personal and unique to every couple. There are levels of control to be mastered. I recommend a chat with Callan. They're bonded to many friends, a sort of guide. They might be able to offer an outside perspective and could help you know what to expect so that you aren't taken by surprise as things continue to change."

That night by the fire, Alexus begins teaching me the meaning of the protective runes I see when I look for the prince. I tell myself that I'm going to talk to Callan too. But the rain comes, and we all escape to our tents early, and the moment passes.

Tomorrow, I tell myself later while I drift to sleep. Tomorrow.

9

RAINA

I'm alone in a deep, narrow hole, face wet with tears and rain.

Blood runs from my fingertips as I claw the earthen walls. But no matter what I do, no matter how much magick I summon, I can't get out.

Voices drift to my ears as water rises around my ankles—sounds of laughter, life, freedom—and I imagine the comfort and shelter of the monastery, thirty feet above. Frantic, I fling away the mud lodged beneath my fingernails and the black mire coating my palms. In desperation, I cast another spell into the night and call forth any energy I can find, hoping to propel myself anywhere but here.

Nothing happens, save for the light of day and dark of night repeating their dance overhead. The rain keeps falling, and the water keeps rising, until it creeps up my waist, up my torso to my throat, my chin, until mud slides into the pool and the taste of soil floods my mouth. Every time I steal another suffocating inhale, the world grows blacker and blacker...

I jerk awake, gasping, and take in my surroundings.

It wasn't real. It's just a dream. I'm safe.

Restless, I shove away the furs and slip from beneath Alexus's arm. Thanks to the fear clutching my throat, it's hard to breathe, so I sit up and draw a breath of cold night air.

After a harsh exhale, Alexus pushes up behind me. "Are you all right?"

Suddenly, a handful of starlights penetrate the tent's canvas, tiny lights floating in the darkness.

Trembling, I face him and nod, making the sign for *nightmare*, though I'm still connecting the pieces.

He brushes my hair aside, kisses my shoulder, and skims rough fingertips over my collarbone, down to my rune. "I'm so sorry, Raina. I live under the weight of memory, it seems."

Regret and guilt lurk at the edge of his voice.

Regret for the rune. Guilt for the dream.

Because this time, the terror doesn't belong to me. It belongs to Alexus, coursing into me through our bond.

A nightmare of his childhood.

A nightmare of torture.

A nightmare he can't forget.

"Is this normal for bonded people?" I sign, wishing I'd spoken to Callan the night before last. Tomorrow, I'd told myself. And yet tomorrow came and went.

"It *can* be." He scrubs his hand through his hair. "It's obviously true for us. I'm sure the fact that we're communicating through the bond so often now has something to do with it. The rune forges many types of connection. It appears it's created a subliminal link between our dreams."

Gods, I would hate for him to experience the panic that comes with my nightmares. But I can't even think about those for all the images swirling in my mind.

Images that don't belong to me.

I touch his face, worried for him.

"I'm fine," he assures me, reading my face. "I'm more concerned about you."

"I will survive," I sign. *"But you lie. You are not fine."*

He isn't panting like me, and when I touch his forehead, there's no slick of cold sweat. There isn't even so much as a quiver in his ancient bones, and had I not awoken, he might've slept through it all. But I felt his torment.

Ruthless, raw, and real.

He lets out a long breath. "It isn't a lie, Raina. I swear I'm all right. Nightmares are so common for me. I have over *three hundred years* of memories. Sometimes they unearth themselves as they please. Facing Thamaos again must've triggered this one. He was there that day in the dream, the first time I ever met him. But that particular event in my life was just... an unhappy experience. A *test*." He slides his hand across my waist. "Now come. Lie with me. It's cold."

The thought is tempting, but I stop him from drawing me back to our pallet. I *know* what I saw in the dream was a test. I *know* how hard he cried when the proctors from the School of Night and Dawn came during the rainy season, pried him from his parents' arms, and carried him on horseback to the outskirts of a city called Yura. I remember his fear as though it were my own when he realized where they were taking him, the scalding-bright terror that flashed through his ten-year-old body as King Gherahn's men lowered him into one of the ancient wells at the Un Moritra monastery, better known as *The Death Pits*, and left him in the pouring rain to prove his skill. A little boy who couldn't work water magick.

Pass or fail. Escape or die.

I've never been to Yura or Quezira, yet thanks to this nightmare, I now remember what every nook in those cities looked, smelled, and sounded like over three hundred years ago. I can picture the dilapidated buildings cast in the shadows of new construction, and the ancient city that sits near the temple. I even recall how Alexi used to say that there were *two* cities of ruin in Tiressia, the one in the Summerlands and the one that time left behind in Quezira.

I also know that Alexi from the tribe of Ghent would've called the School of Night and Dawn a *scholarada*, a word I've never heard him use before, and that when he was sixteen, he advanced from the Order of Dawn to the Order of Night. I know they took him from Yura and sent him to the elite school newly erected in Quezira, and that he hated it so much he wanted to burn it to the ground, but that in time, he made friends and came to consider it home.

Then there's Min-Thuret. Thamaos's temple. The original kingdom seat. The awe Alexus held for that place is palpable. The structure now lives as a fresh memory in my mind, its glass and golden domes visible from the school, high upon a grassy knoll near the ruins, surrounded by rain-dampened air and marigolds trembling in the wind. I even remember the smooth cuts of timeworn carvings on the outer walls, protective archaic runes Alexus admired with a child's wonder. I recall his little heart thudding like an anvil tapping the bones of his chest as he crossed the threshold of those massive doors, strolled the cloisters, and later knelt in Rite Hall before that opulent throne.

So yes. For him, perhaps the nightmare was just an unhappy memory. For me, it's a slice of Alexus Thibault's long life that feels so real I could've lived its every second.

"What happened was torture," I sign. *"It haunts you."*

"Many things haunt me, Raina. This is the least of them." He takes my chin in his hand. "Which is why you need to hear me. I may be your hero now, but in another story, I was the villain. The worst kind. Men like me and the prince learn to live with our miseries and sins, even if that means being haunted by a legion of ghosts."

My chest tightens. Compared to the Prince of the East, Alexus is a saint, yet I understand the two men were cut from the same cloth. They've both hurt people for the eastern throne. They've both fought in wars, and on the wrong side at that. And they've both used their power to break the laws of nature and cross into the Shadow World, walking where only death dares trod. The line separating them may be thin, but they are not the same.

I can't believe they are.

Alexus grazes a touch across my cheekbone and pushes his fingers into my hair. "Listen to me. I've loved every night we've shared since Winter-hold. Every conversation. Every kiss. Every touch. But if we continue exploring this bond, continue allowing it to fuse our lives together, I fear you will learn firsthand how haunted I truly am." He pauses, swallows. "I can't say that the thought of you witnessing my old life doesn't scare me. Because whether you like it or not, facing the ghosts of my past *will* make you see me differently. Are you prepared for that?"

"I do not know," I reply honestly. I wasn't prepared for any of this, but... *"When I said that our darknesses could be friends,"* I sign, *"I meant it."*

My heart pounds as Alexus presses closer. "I fear you might not understand what you're saying."

"I am not scared of you," I tell him. *"Not even Alexi of Ghent or Un Drallag."*

He stares into my eyes for a long moment, then he kisses me, trailing his fingers down the slope of my breast, caressing my nipple, his rough fingertip circling the sensitive flesh. That strange vibration I'd felt the other night on our walk returns, lingering in the wake of his touch.

I press against his hand, wanting his palm on my breast. Alexus responds, gripping me hard as Mannus whinnies from across camp, alerting us that sunrise is a couple of hours away.

"Are you sure?" Alexus asks. "We don't have long before you must return to your tent. If we're to keep up our ruse, that is. I cannot say I care anymore."

The heat of his breath on my mouth sends a chill across my skin as he drags my lower lip between his teeth and kisses me, a kiss as tantalizing as it is teasing. Slow and deliberate, sensual and sweet.

I need him one more time before we reach the valley. I don't know what that confrontation holds, if Finn or his father will want to accompany us or not. If they do, I can't imagine many nights in Alexus's arms between here and Malgros.

"I am sure," I sign and take him by the wrist.

Holding his heated gaze, I slip his hand beneath the blankets puddled around my waist and place it where I need him, and where I know he wants to be. With soft lips, he seizes another kiss and glides his hand over my sex, his fingers playing along my center, until he slides one inside me, then eases another, matching every motion with his tongue.

I endure him for as long as I can, but I jerk away to catch my breath, each inhale coming shallower and shallower as he works me into a frenzy, plundering my body until I'm clinging to his shoulders and panting harder than when I woke from the dream.

Carnal longing guides me as I rock against his hand, needing more, needing *him*, already seeking sweet relief.

"Please," I sign against his chest.

"Mmm, *patience*." He lowers his head and sucks my nipple into his mouth, all while stroking his thumb over the little bud that makes stars explode behind my eyes.

Gods, I'm already so close.

Before I can reach that pinnacle, he releases my breast and takes his hand away. I almost grab his wrist and draw him back to me. But I become entranced by the shape of him in the dim light, the lines of his muscular form outlined by his starlights' amber glow as he slips his fingers into his mouth and slides them back out.

"You taste so fucking good," he says, and every inch of me burns.

Alexus kisses me, sharing my taste. With his tongue moving in soft, sweeping motions, he pushes his fingers back inside me and leans into me, over me, using the weight of his body to push me down to our bed of fur. He doesn't stop touching me until he fits himself between my legs.

He smiles and lifts his chin like he did the other night, and his power shimmers over my skin, a trickle of heat in my veins. The orbs drift closer, illuminating our nakedness.

With a beguiling glint in his stare, Alexus shifts his weight to one arm and skims his fingertips over my bared torso—from the hollow of my throat, between my breasts, down my abdomen, to the mound of my sex. I can't hold back the shudder that quakes in my bones as he grips me between my legs.

His voice is honey tongued as he runs his rough hand over my body once more. "I need to see you. Need the image of you naked and writhing beneath me seared into my memory." Using a deft touch, he traces the witch's marks blooming over my hip, winding around my navel, dancing up the curve of my waist, flaring across my ribs. "Gods, you're so beautiful, Raina."

My breasts grow heavy and tight as he teases my nipple between his fingertips. That same sensation from earlier returns, a vibration radiating from his touch.

I cover his hand with mine and give him a curious stare. All of this is so new.

"Energy," he says. "Almost as good as tangling our magick."

To prove his words, he licks a tantalizing path up the swell of my breast, swirling his tongue around my nipple, sending a restless ache straight to my clit.

We haven't tangled our magick since Winterhold. There's too little privacy for all that entails, especially now that his magick has returned. We could set the wood on fire for all we know. But that there is *more* than the combining of our magick, is difficult to grasp, even though I can feel this trace of his power. That he can gather energy from the ether and use it for destruction one minute and for pleasure the next is nothing short of baffling.

When he lifts his head, hunger glimmers in his green eyes. "Hard and fast or deep and slow?"

He asks this question each time.

"Both," I sign.

He groans from low in his chest. "I was hoping you'd say that."

Turning his attention between us, he fists his cock, long and rigid, and with cruel precision, rubs that wide tip against my clit. I'm not sure why I don't expect it, but that concentrated energy from before vibrates from his flesh, the sensation echoing through the most sensitive part of me, robbing me of breath.

On the edge of a ragged inhale, I push up on my elbows. Alexus smiles that knowing smile, and then, by the light of his magick, we both watch as he glides his swollen tip up and down my slit, his pulsating head growing slick with my desire.

"Just a taste of magick," he says, teasing me with a trickle of power, rendering me near mindless.

I drop my head back, fighting the urge to squirm against him, all while trying not to die from bliss as he plays. If this is just a taste, what in gods' stars am I in for? I already want him everywhere. In my hands. Between my legs. In my mouth.

Everywhere.

My desperation gets the better of me. I lift my head and let my hips fall into his rhythm, greedily stroking his length. He lets go of himself, eyes focused where our bodies touch, and a restrained groan rumbles inside his chest.

"You are the sweetest torture, Raina Bloodgood." A curse falls from his lips as he leans down and circles his tongue around each of my nipples, flicking the tender tips until another tingle shoots straight to where he grinds against me.

I fall back to the fur, and he follows, sucking my pebbled nipple deeply. After a drag of his teeth, he bites into the soft curve of my breast, sucking there as well. A sensation builds, reaching that delicate and addicting line where pleasure meets pain, a line I grow fonder of by the day.

Keen to have him inside me, I run my nails over his muscled back, down the sleek curve of his long spine, and urge him closer. Beneath my touch, chills rise across his skin.

"I mean to make certain that you remember this." He brushes a warm kiss over my rune, then over the skin between my breasts. "That you remember what it is to be *mine*."

As if I could forget. Alexus Thibault has marked me in more ways than one.

My rune comes alive, throbbing with passion, lust, need. Alexus doesn't hold back, letting me experience everything he feels in this moment. Admiration. Longing. Even that tender affection he'd hidden before. It's overwhelming, enough that tears well.

Wanting to give him the same, I close my eyes. I'm met with the ribbon of light that is the runic bond.

I let my mind roam toward Alexus, let myself drift on that silken ribbon. It still feels dangerous as I face the darkness between us, that seething void that awaits me every time I seek our connection. It feels as though I'm a moment away from falling off the edge of the world and entering a darkness from which I will never return.

But then I'm with him, and I know he feels me and my longing to give him a fraction of what he's given me. My adoration. My trust. My desire and yearning.

"Fuck yes, Raina," he whispers against my mouth. "I swear to the gods that nothing else exists when I'm inside you. Nothing but us. The Empyreal Fields are not as perfect as this."

I kiss his bearded cheek and press my face to his. I feel the same way. Good or bad. Villain or hero. Light or darkness. Right now I cannot care, because of this feeling. Of *him*. Inside me. *Bound* to me.

It's everything.

Moved by the emotion between us, he kisses me, our mouths open and hungry. When he finally pulls away, he buries his face in the crook of my shoulder, hooks my ankle over his hip, and in one swift and punishing stroke, plunges all that breathtaking hardness inside me.

Gasping, I bury my fingers in his hair and arch my spine, so wonderfully filled with him. He grips my ass and pushes in even deeper, until I can't think of anything other than the incandescent desire flooding my veins.

He rests his forehead against mine, closes his hand on my thigh, and begins to move, slowly at first, and with the same expertise that shocks me each time he takes me. It isn't long before he's thrusting, tip to root, each deep rub angled perfectly. Somehow, he knows exactly how to ride that tender place inside me that sends my mind reeling.

But that pulsating energy...

That concentrated power...

I can hardly stand it. Each withdrawal and advance muddles the remains of any coherent thought I've tried to hold on to.

An almost pained sound of deepest need leaves Alexus as I tighten my legs around his waist and curve my hips toward his. I'm fully aware of what it does to him, but I'm utterly stunned by what it does to me with this new sensation pulsing inside me.

My release still looms so close, and Alexus seems to sense it, perhaps through the bond, because after a powerful thrust that pushes my entire body up the fur beneath us, he pulls out.

All the air rushes from my lungs, my orgasm left teetering on the edge of a cliff as he pushes to his knees, hooks his arms under my legs, and drags me close. With those strong hands, he presses my legs apart.

"Do you like it when I taste you?" He drags his thumb along my slit and licks my wetness off the tip. "When my tongue is inside you?"

Any remaining composure crumbles to nothing. Wanton, I nod and lift my hips again, bearing myself completely. A desperate plea.

A wicked grin curves his mouth. "Always so eager," he says, tightening his grip on my thighs. "What must I do to teach you a little patience?"

I begin to reply, the words burning inside my hands absolutely lascivious. But the orbs of light flicker around Alexus like moths drawn to a candle's flame, and I become captivated by the sight of his rugged, scarred body kneeling in their golden aura. His knees are spread wide, his slick cock hard and jutting, the broad head swollen and ready.

With his green gaze on my body, hunger raging in his eyes like he could devour me, he buries his mouth between my legs and licks a long line up my center.

My eyes roll back, and I tangle my hands into his hair as he teases my clit with his tongue, his magick trickling over that sensitive bud. I could come from this alone, but Alexus is a master with my body, knowing exactly how much is too little and how much is enough. Right now, he withholds, keeping me teetering on a cliff's edge, plunging his tongue inside me like he can't get deep enough.

When he finally lifts his dark head, lips glistening, those bright, feral eyes almost silver in the orbs' light, a shiver crawls up my spine.

He is glorious.

He rises to his knees and angles his tip toward my entrance. "Much as I want to taste your release, and I swear I fucking will, soon, I need to feel you come. There's little sweeter than that tight little flutter on my cock."

Gods. I almost sign that if he doesn't stop talking like that, it's going to happen sooner rather than later. But he pushes inside me, deep and slow, just like I asked for, stealing my breath and staying my words, every delicious inch of him threatening to unravel me.

As he moves his hips, taking his time, he splays his hand across my abdomen and touches his thumb to my clit, rubbing circles with perfect pressure. It feels so good, so needed, my body clamps down on him in response.

He utters a guttural sound, and the pulse of magick in his cock intensifies, making me writhe and pant, my hands clutching the fur beneath me.

"Fuck all, Raina. If I could do this the way I want, the earth would quake from here to the godsdamn sea."

The promise in his words sends a surge of excitement through me—*and* through the bond—and with a ravenous ferocity of my own, I meet his long thrusts, forcing him deeper, aching as his building release swells, mingling with the awareness of my own threatening climax.

I reach for him, and as though compelled by my need, he crawls over me. With that beautiful face staring down, I draw him into a bruising kiss, keeping us close so I can swallow the too-loud sighs and moans that will inevitably leave him.

Because I can't hold on much longer.

As we kiss, the slow slide of his cock turns to a rhythmic pounding, hard and deep, until the tension inside me—coiled so painfully tight—unfurls into mind-shattering ecstasy.

Alexus rips away from my mouth as my body seizes his, clenching him, wave after divine wave. "El om ze pera," he utters between shredded breaths, eyes intent on mine. "Lohanran tu gra."

His words are Elikesh, words he's never spoken to me, but I sense their devotion along the bond, their significance as his restraint shatters.

With powerful thrusts, his orgasm spills inside me. I gasp with each burst of pleasure, the release only magnified by his magick. The pulsating surrender is a heart-stopping sensation I will crave for the rest of my days.

I hold him close through it all, kissing him as he groans into my mouth. I inhale every moan, reveling in the shudders rolling through this ancient, magnificent body.

A body that trembles just for me.

For several minutes, as his little starlights flare then soften and fade, Alexus lingers inside me, our heartbeats thrumming like the rhythm of a song. He presses tender kisses along my shoulders, across my face, over my eyes, and after a while, my racing heart slows and my quivering legs still.

"I think we should stay in this tent all day." He nuzzles my neck, trailing his tongue over my pulse, then moves lower, playfully biting my nipple. "I could show you more of my skills."

When he leans away, I shift my hips, moving on him, wet with our pleasure. *"I am more than a little curious after that demonstration,"* I sign.

He grins and nuzzles my neck again. "Don't tempt me. We have a king and a world to save."

There isn't much to smile about in that last statement, yet my mouth curves a little anyway, even with Joran's and Thamaos's words still lurking at the edges of my mind. Alexus said *we*. Because we're in this fight together.

Much to my displeasure, he withdraws from me and rolls to his back. I flinch at the emptiness, but he wraps his arms around me and tucks me into his side, and the empty feeling fades.

"Can I confess something?" he asks. "Without sounding mad? I've wanted to tell you since Winterhold."

I nod and trace the sculpted muscles of his abdomen, wending my finger up and down the trail of dark hair below his navel.

"After we arrived at the castle, I dreamed of you. Of what it might've been like if we'd met some other way, in some other life. That dream was so vivid that when you came to my chambers the next night, and I finally got to touch you and kiss you the way I'd desired, you felt—and tasted—familiar. Like my body had been made for yours. Not because of what happened between us in the wood either." He kisses my temple and pulls me closer. "It felt like I was exactly where I was supposed to be."

My face warms as I rest my chin on his shoulder, meeting his gaze in the dim light. Still smiling, I run my fingers through his beard.

I send my answer along the bond, growing braver each time I use it. I don't think he's mad at all. From the moment he first looked at me, it was like he could see into my soul. And that night in his chambers, he'd told me how right I felt in his hands.

While I can't say I understand it, I'm beginning to believe that maybe, just maybe, Fate has had her eye upon us for a while.

🐉

I REST IN ALEXUS'S ARMS UNTIL THE RISING MORNING LIGHT REMINDS me that I must face the day. From his place on the fur, still naked save for the blankets draped across his thighs, he watches me with an affectionate smile as I clean up, shrug into my traveling clothes, and braid my hair, an attempt at making myself somewhat presentable.

As I work, I trace my gaze over his body. It's impossible not to admire him, how his black hair pools beneath his head like a puddle of spilled ink, or the way the ancient scars on his sweat-dampened skin call to me in the faint light of early dawn.

If there must be a god in this land, it should be him.

Wind wheezes through the forest and whips the tent, fracturing the moment. It's as though Neri means to push us further south, out of Frost-water and into the valley. In a matter of hours, after too many days of rugged travel, he will succeed, whether I'm ready to face what awaits or not.

Alexus rises on an elbow and brushes his knuckles along my jaw, reading my mind as he so often does, even without the bond. "Stop your worries and go, or someone will catch you, and we'll have even more trouble to face today. It's already taking all my strength to endure Joran."

I roll my eyes and bob my head in agreement, though leaving him is becoming harder to do. Here in his tent, nothing and no one exists but us.

It feels so good, yet it's false contentment. Because out *there*, the enemy awaits, and the world is in chaos.

And we're walking straight toward both.

"Fine," I sign. *"But before I go, what does El om ze pera, lohanran tu gra mean?"* I messily spell the unknown words as best I can.

One corner of Alexus's mouth curls as he leans closer. "After we reach the coast, if you still like me as much as you do right now, I'll explain."

"Promises, promises," I sign, shoving at his warm chest. *"I will ask Nephele."*

He laughs and keeps his voice down. "Ever impatient. But I want to be the one who tells you. I'm not sure Nephele could anyway. It's a very old dialect."

"Old dialect," I sign. *"Like the kind you're translating in your book?"*

I glance at the corner of the tent, at the carefully wrapped books stacked beside Alexus's pack.

He gives them a thoughtful glance. "Yes. Exactly like that."

I'm curious, proving him right. Patience isn't a virtue I possess, but for now—*for him*—I'll wait.

Mannus whinnies again, more insistent, which is unusual. Alexus ignores his animal and takes my chin between his thumb and forefinger one last time. "Lohanran tu gra," he whispers before stealing another kiss.

Reluctantly, we pull apart. Alexus reaches for the old iron key, discarded with his clothes, and slips the leather over his head as I move to the tent flap and loosen the ties.

I peer out at the still sleeping campsite. The banked fires have long-since died, and a thin mist of silver fog creeps across the ground while daybreak lightens the wood. I'm reminded of my last morning in my mother's cottage. Like then, I dread the day, but for very different reasons.

With a final glance over my shoulder, I catch Alexus tugging his trousers over the loveliest backside I've ever been blessed to see. He grins and winks, and I can't help but smile as I throw up my hood and slip outside.

I make it a few strides before I step on a thick twig. The echo as it snaps in two cracks through the wood. Frozen in place, I glance at the other tents, waiting to be caught.

"Don't move," a low, tight voice commands from behind me. "Show me your hands."

My heart stutters to a halt, and Mannus whinnies once more. Damn. The second time wasn't a wake-up call.

It was a warning.

I inch my hands into the air to prove I'm unarmed.

"Now turn around," he says, his voice a demanding whisper. "Easy."

There's something about that voice. Even ground down to a hush. Something that makes me forego reaching for Alexus through the bond.

With my hands still lifted in surrender, I do as I'm told and eye the man behind me.

A man aiming an arrow at my heart.

10

RAINA

The man before me looks so different, even though I've seen him in the waters for two weeks now.

His sun-browned skin is windburned, his unkempt hair hanging over his eyes. He even wears a scruffy beard on his usually boyish chin, and he's lost weight, making him look like someone else entirely.

But I know the hand-carved curve of his father's yew bow.

As tears build on the rims of my eyelids, Finn approaches with unsure steps, bow still raised in his gloved hands. He pauses, breathing hard, blinking, as though he thinks he might be imagining me.

Though I'm thinner too, I'm sure I otherwise look much the same. Still, I'm certain he envisioned the worst end—that I met death weeks ago at the tip of an Eastlander's fiery arrow. And from his expression as I lower my hood, he's realizing just how wrong he's been.

Finn slackens and lowers his bow. "R-Raina? Am I... Am I dreaming?"

Though there's six strides between us, I catch the crack in his voice and the gleam in his eyes, dark irises shining like polished stones. Something pinches in my gut. I've always hated seeing Finn cry. It's a rare event, but it destroys me.

Loria, be with me now.

I shake my head and sign, *"No, Finn. You are not dreaming. The Eastlanders are gone, and we remain."*

With whip-quick movements, he slips his arrow into the quiver at his hip, slings his bow across his chest, and starts toward me, a man determined, just as he'd been the night of the harvest supper. He even wears the same clothes. The forest-green jacket Betha made him—rumpled and stained with more things than I care to imagine—and his crisp white tunic, now torn and dingy. But the sight of him takes me back in time, regardless.

An arresting, white smile breaks across his face. Faster than I can think of what to do, he lifts me off my feet and swings me around as he howls his joy through the forest.

"Thank the gods," he cries, no doubt waking everyone in the camp. "Do you hear me, oh Ancient Ones? You brought her back to me! And I thank you!"

An uncertain smile forces its way across my lips. I've missed Finn. Worried about him. Felt so much guilt. Now he's here, alive and whole. Yet no matter what I envision, I can't see any scenario in which this ends well.

When I look down, Finn kisses me like we're the only two people in the wood. It's a cold shock, Finn's taste mingling with the memory of another man's kiss.

Breathless, we break apart. I'm dazed, but not so rattled that I don't notice the optimism on Finn's face as he sets me on my feet. I can't remember a time when this kind of light radiated from him.

This kind of *hope*.

He cradles my face. "How?" He strokes his thumbs over the marks along my jawline and down the column of my throat. "How do you have these marks? And how in the gods' names are you here?" The amber flecks in his deep brown eyes glint in the morning sunlight, but there are thankfully no tears. He's too happy.

I can't decide which is worse.

"I don't even care," he laughs, still caressing my skin. "The marks only make you more beautiful. And who am I to question the gods about why they spared you? I'm only grateful they did. So grateful, Raina." He kisses me again, short and sweet, before continuing. "There are survivors. Twenty-three, including my father and the hunters. We've been camped near the loch for the last week. It's only a day's ride from here."

I smile and nod, unsure how I'm going to explain that I've watched them in the waters for a long while. I haven't been able to discern how many there were, and though I wish there were hundreds more, I'm glad not everyone was lost as I'd believed.

Taking a steadying breath, I grip Finn's wrists, anchoring myself. Words swirl inside my head, but like him, I allow myself a few moments to just be thankful he's here. There were a thousand and one ways I could be mourning him right now instead of feeling his pulse thrumming against my fingertips.

But that's not all I feel. My rune warms, throbbing with heat, and a surge of power beats the air, followed by the buzz of static on my skin.

Agitation travels along the bond, a steady, rhythmic vibration, like the well-timed plucking of an instrument's strings. As though sensing it too, Finn lifts his head, and his elated smile falls.

A mask of contempt slams down over his face, and with his nostrils flared, his entire body tenses, primed for action.

Primed for a *fight*.

He drops his hands from my face and touches the curve of his bow. "What in the fucking Nether Reaches are *you* doing here?"

It takes a heartbeat for me to turn and move in front of my friend, arms outstretched in a protective stance.

Joran stands in the middle of camp, crossbow raised, loaded, and aimed. Wisps of silver hair dance around his face in the morning wind, but that heavy-lidded stare is locked on us, sure as his bolt. The belt of knives that normally hangs from the waist of his dark gray britches is missing, as is his sweater and the leather vambrace that rarely leaves his forearm. This morning is the first time I've seen this much of him, and the soft azure marks that cover his water witch's skin.

Behind Joran looms Rhonin. His auburn hair whips around his head, and his shirt plasters his torso. He looks disoriented. Startled. But an arrow still sits nocked in his short bow, his shoulders tucked and rounded with tension.

A few other witches from Winterhold dot the campsite—Callan, Keth, Jaega. They're half asleep, but they each hold a weapon.

Finn's question wasn't directed at any of them, though.

It was directed at Alexus.

He stands a few steps away at the edge of his tent, panting plumes of cold air. A shaft of first light pierces the treetops and glints off the razor-sharp sword laid over his forearm. He rolls his shoulders, muscles bunching and flexing, but after a long and weighted moment, he relaxes from his fighting stance.

His britches are untied and hanging loose at his hips, and he's still shirtless, the scars of his many runes and the fresh, pink scratch marks from my fingernails on display in the rising light.

"Thibault!" Joran draws out the end of Alexus's chosen name, waiting for orders.

"Raina," Alexus says, but he keeps his gaze trained on Finn.

I hear a dozen unspoken questions in that single word.

"Tell them to stand down," I sign. *"This is Finn."*

I'm unsure why I announce that last part. It's clear he's already pieced together who our visitor is, or he never would've lowered his sword.

"It's all right." Alexus stabs the point of his blade into the ground. "It's Helena's brother."

The others lower their weapons. Joran too. I look straight at Rhonin, jerk my chin toward Nephele's tent, and sign Hel's name. He heads that way, understanding my desire that he wake my friend. Already, I can feel a strain in the air, one I need her to help erase.

Finn steps around me as though he didn't even hear his sister's name, glancing from the tent to Alexus and back to me, as if he can see the invisible bond between us. A familiar, sick feeling swirls in my stomach. My oldest friend looks confused, blinking fast, like he's attempting to put the pieces of a complex puzzle in their right places, yet none seem to fit. There's no doubt he saw me leave Alexus's tent before, and now I'm followed by a half-naked Witch Collector who not only looks like he's been well-had more than a few times, but who just understood my sign language and spoke my name with utmost familiarity.

I slide a worried glance at Alexus. He returns my glance with a wave of calm through the bond and a comforting, almost imperceptible nod.

But not imperceptible enough.

Every muscle in Finn's body grows rigid. He studies me with those bottomless eyes, reading truths I cannot hide.

"Earlier..." His throat moves on a hard swallow, as though his next

words are so disgusting that they choke him. "Were you with him...
willingly?"

Joran barks a haughty laugh. "Of course she was. She's willing nearly
every godsdamn night. Quite the champion, that one."

Alexus and I stare deathwishes into every inch of the Icelander. I
understand why Joran dislikes me, but this moment of arrogance is bold.

In those seconds, when Alexus and I have our eyes on the bowyer, I
glimpse Finn moving in the corner of my eye. I spin on my heel, but I can
only watch as he steps forward, rears back, and drives his fist into Alexus's
jaw.

The impact causes Alexus's head to jerk to the side, slinging a curtain
of dark hair over his face. But for all the power in Finn's blow, the Witch
Collector stands steady as a tree.

Alexus twists his head, cracking his neck, and with a swipe of his
thumb, smears the thin stream of bright blood running down his chin.

He holds up a finger. "You get one shot, blacksmith. *One.*"

"Or maybe I get two." Finn rips his bow free, and nocks an arrow,
aiming its broad tip at Alexus. "You'll be lucky if this is all I do. I
should've let that fiery arrow sink into your black heart back in Silver
Hollow."

"And perhaps I should've let that Eastlander slice you to bits," Alexus
says, a knife-sharp edge to his voice. "But I didn't. And here we are."

It takes a moment for me to grasp what they're saying. They saved one
another? The night of the attack?

"I'd put that bow down," Joran calls. "The Collector isn't my favorite
person either, but we need him. Besides, fast though you might be, I'm
faster."

The smile in the Icelander's voice is audible. Even without looking, I
know that wolfish grin is stretched wide, and that his crossbow is once
again raised, loaded, and aimed.

When Finn doesn't relent, I move to stand between him and Alexus.
"You do not understand," I sign. *"Put down the bow and listen. Please."*

He shifts his aim a few inches to the left, over my shoulder, never
taking his eye off Alexus who sweeps a brawny arm around my waist and
pushes me behind him.

He turns a quick glance at me, brows knitted so tightly that two deep lines form between them. "Never put yourself in harm's way for me. Do you hear?"

"There isn't much to understand, is there, Collector?" Finn says, disrupting the moment. "I can see what you've been doing. Preying on a young woman when she was alone and at her lowest. Is this what you do to the witches you take?" He draws back on his bow to recover the inch he's lost, his strength weakening. "I should pluck your eyes out, then leave you in this godsforsaken forest to be eaten by the wolves."

Regardless of Alexus's previous command, I move again. This time, I stand with my back against his chest.

"Raina." He grits the word through clenched teeth. But I hold fast.

"He did not force me to do anything, and he has never hurt me," I sign. *"We have endured so much these last weeks. He is not the man I thought."*

Finn's arms tremble, a dangerous position for an archer with someone they love standing at the end of their weapon. Though it's obvious that it kills him to do it, he lowers his arrow.

Alexus exhales a breath and threads our fingers together. His other hand settles heavy on my waist. It's meant to be a comfort, but I can feel the feral nature in the act, a territorial move.

That's all it takes to elicit an appalled scoff from Finn as understanding dawns.

Arrow dangling from one hand and a strung bow teetering on the fingertips of another, he steps back, chest rising and falling fast.

Panic beats a tattoo through my blood. This isn't how I wanted any of this to happen. I thought I'd have time to explain the past few weeks to Finn. Time to make him see that what Alexus and I went through changed everything. But I wasn't granted time, and much as I wish I could, I can't salvage things now.

I let go of Alexus and move slowly toward my best friend. *"Finn. Come talk with me."*

A growl tears from his throat, and he slings his bow into the wood. A snapping sound cracks the air, his beloved weapon exploding under the stress. Yet he's unfazed. He drops his arrow, shakes his head, and stares at me with the blankest expression, like I'm a stranger.

"What's there to talk about? You let him *touch* you, Raina. And yet... you *despised* him." The last hint of disbelief in his voice and on his face turns to abhorrence. "This man you loathed, this bastard you wanted to kill. You let him *inside* you, didn't you? Let him do things to you only *I* have ever done." He smacks his chest. "*Me.* The man who has loved you for your entire life. How? Why?" I reach for him, but he jerks away and levels me with a glare. Beneath his rage lies so much pain. "Did you *ever* love me, Raina?"

My mind races as I try to think of something to say, anything to convey how sorry I am. All I manage is an empty, *"Of course I loved you. I still do."*

Disgust radiates from his every pore as his features twist into a sneer. "But it's like you said on the green, isn't it? On our last day together? Our kind of love isn't enough." I lift my hands to reply, but in a manner I'm far too used to, Finn grabs my wrists. Hard. Holding my hands apart. Silencing me. "It's been *weeks*!" He all but spits the words in my face. "And you've already let him fuck you like some common wh–"

"Enough!" A second wave of power ripples the air, rustling the leaves in the treetops as Alexus pushes between us. He shoves Finn so hard my old friend not only staggers but falls. The muscles along Alexus's shoulders and neck tighten, and his scarred back flares as he stalks toward Finn and straddles him. He leans down, grabs a fistful of Finn's tunic, and jerks him up. "If I *ever* see you touch her like that again, I'll carry your head around on a motherfucking pike."

Under the haze of humiliation, a snarl curls Finn's lips, and he reaches for the dagger sheathed at his thigh. I gasp and start toward them, but I freeze when Alexus seizes the dagger first and presses its deadly edge to Finn's throat.

"Brave or stupid," he says. "That's always the question with you, isn't it? I fear the answer is stupid." He stabs the dagger back into the sheath, and with the strength of a single fist, hauls Finn to his feet, bringing them nose to nose. "I am not a mountain you want to cross, boy. I will *bury* you. But for now, I'll give you one more chance to use the brain Loria gave you. If you speak to Raina with respect and keep your hands off her, I'll let you continue breathing. But if you lay a single, angry fingertip on her or so much as *think* a slur about what she and I do in the dark, I promise you, I will dig the hole for you myself." Alexus lets go of Finn's shirt with a shove, then wipes his bleeding lip with the back of his hand.

The expression on Finn's face as Alexus returns to my side is one of rage, his eyes violent. He opens his mouth, but before he can utter a response, Hel calls his name. A keening wail leaves her, a sound so filled with relief it pierces my heart like a needle.

She stands near Nephele's tent with Rhonin and my sister, dressed in the clothes she slept in—a white linen tunic, untied and hanging off one golden brown shoulder, and gray leather britches barely shoved into her boots. Her long hair is a tangled mass of black waves, surrounding a face still soft with sleep.

Rattled by the familiar yet unexpected voice, Finn turns his frenzied gaze upon her as more shock piles onto the heap already weighing his back. "Hel?"

She runs straight for him and collides as only Hel can, throwing her arms around his neck and her long legs around his waist. Finn stumbles a step and lifts his hands, and after a few moments, looks at me. I can read the questions in his eyes.

Is this real? Is any of this real?

I nod, and as Hel's little death dances in my heart, the tears I've been fighting since I first saw her brother fall down my face. Finn lets the moment between us live one last second, then he wraps Hel in his arms, crumbles to his knees, and weeps.

11

RAINA

"One of us should check on them." Rhonin squats near the campfire and adds a handful of forest duff to the weak flames. "I know there's much for Hel to explain and that this is difficult for her brother, but it's already late morning. There's only so much daylight."

Joran strolls to a downed log and sits next to my sister. She recoils at his nearness. But at least he's clothed now.

"Or perhaps we should leave their miserable asses here," he says. "It isn't like they can't find their way to the valley."

Alexus stands with his back against a tall oak. He's an impressive sight, clad in black from boots to fitted leather pants to a jacket buckled over a midnight tunic. His arms are crossed over his broad chest, and though he stares distantly into the low-burning fire, Joran's words are enough to make him stiffen.

"I'm not leaving *anyone* behind," he says, his voice sharp-edged.

"We could divide into two groups," Rhonin offers. "Nephele can lead some of the others to the loch and after the next hour passes, if Hel and Finn still haven't finished, I volunteer to break up their reunion. I'm sure they'll understand. Then we can all be on our way."

Alexus lifts a brow. "You think more highly of that boy's temperament than I do." He touches his thumb to his wounded lip. "I expect we'll come to blows again before we reach the valley. Possibly before we leave this wood."

That can't happen. Finn *does* get stupidly brave when he's angry. It isn't either/or. It's both.

"I will take care of it," I sign to Alexus. Then I pick up what's left of Finn's shattered bow and head for the last tent standing.

"Does she know they killed her mother?" I hear Finn say as I approach, and the fissure that formed in my heart when my mother died cracks a little wider.

"She does," Hel says. "She saw it happen."

A heavy sigh. "I buried her, you know. Ophelia. In the cemetery. Next to Rowan."

A breath of sadness flutters through my veins. The memory of my mother cloaked in magick and trying to save me—to save us all—is never far from my mind.

"I'm certain Raina will be thankful," Hel says. "She should hear this from you, though."

"I can't. I wanted to share a life with her, Hel. When she got her head out of the clouds. Now I don't even know who she is."

"She's *Raina Bloodgood*. Your best friend long before she was your lover."

"*That* woman isn't my Raina." A tempest rolls in his voice. "*That* woman is someone else entirely."

The tent flap slaps back, and Finn ducks into the open. I stumble back as Hel follows her brother. She rubs her hand across his back, and after giving me a somber look, walks across the campsite's small clearing to stand with the others. Finn watches her go, then lowers his gaze to the fragments of his bow.

A cold sweat dampens my palms as I extend the wooden remains. He accepts, careful not to touch my fingertips.

"Please talk to me." I clasp my hands together for a moment before my next words. *"Let me say my piece."*

"Why? Nothing will make this better." He turns and starts south, back the way he came. It might be pointless, but I hurry after him, grabbing his arm.

He swings around and shrugs me off. "I'm *leaving*, Raina. Hel says you're coming to the loch. I won't be there. Have a nice trip with your boyfriend."

"Finn, do not do this," I sign. *"War is coming."*

He laughs. "And exactly what are *you*, a powerless village witch, going to do about it? Are you going to kill the Prince of the East like you planned to kill the Frost King and his collector? Better warn Thibault since you tend to fuck the men you decide to murder."

The bond between me and Alexus shudders with rage. When I look at him, he's gripping the hilt of his sword, the fire in his eyes promising that he could take Finn's head for that comment alone.

I pour my disapproval through the connection between us and force my intent into my glare. In answer, Alexus rolls his shoulders and releases his weapon.

I face Finn and make one last effort. *"I have been through far more than you can imagine,"* I sign. *"And I may not be skilled yet, but I am more capable than you give me credit for."* I gesture to my marks. *"I have these for a reason, Finn. Stay and let me show you. Let me explain. Tiressia needs us."*

Moments pass, a few brief seconds of contemplation on his part. "Tiressia doesn't need *us*, Raina," he finally says. "How can you not see that? It needs *Neri*. And now it has him. He will find his way back to his true form and end the feud between the Eastland Territories and the Summerlands once and for all. When that happens, this perilous game you're playing with your life and my heart will have been for *nothing*."

At the mention of Neri's name, a cold gust whips around us, and a tinkling sound floats in the air. Alexus must hear it too, because my rune throbs, and concern crawls along the bond. I hunch away from the wind as it deposits a thin frost on the ground, coating our boots. Finn grimaces and turns his face, but he doesn't know to notice the presence lurking near, the phantom sliding a touch along my spine.

A malevolent *hello.*

The hair on the back of my neck prickles, but I refuse to give Neri the satisfaction of a reaction. He's here, though. As he has been since we left Winterhold. Watching. Listening.

"Neri is not some gentle god determined to guard his people," I sign, wondering if Hel explained Neri's true history to her brother and he simply refused to

believe her. *"He is a self-serving bastard. He had the chance to help Colden Moeshka, but he stole his power instead."*

An irritated groan resonates from Finn's throat. "He also fought a war for *many* years against Thamaos and his rulers, to keep the Northlands and the Summerlands free. That's more than I can say for a murderous Eastland traitor who spins tales that make him look like the hero." He glares over my shoulder at Alexus, daring him to take offense, then turns his eyes back on me. "Neri—a *god*, Raina—could be our leader, instead of a pathetic Frost King and his Witch Collector. Thamaos and the Prince of the East will roll right over them. Hide and watch. At least Neri could give them a fight."

The disgust I felt every time I walked into Finn's father's forge and saw Neri's pennon hanging there is nothing compared to what I feel right now. I can only stare at Finn as my stomach clenches to the point of sickness. Such piety for a god whose rule he's never experienced. A god whose amber eyes have never held him captive.

He feigns being taken aback. "What? You really thought I'd fight someone else's war? That I'd happily watch from the fringes of your life as you go on some pointless quest with *him?*" He stabs a finger at Alexus and then leans in, brown eyes glistening. "I love you, Raina Bloodgood. I've always loved you. I'm sorry if it wasn't the kind of love you wanted. That it wasn't perfect or exciting or dangerous or whatever the fuck that bastard makes you feel. But know that I died in that valley because of you. I thought of your suffering and imagined your misery, and I wanted to *cut out my heart* to stop the pain. I couldn't sleep. Couldn't eat. I wanted to take back every single time I refused to leave this godsdamn valley with you. I *hated* myself. Maybe I still do. And maybe, when I kissed you earlier, I thought about how I'd do anything you want. *Anything.* Just to make certain I never lose you again." A rogue tear slides down his cheek. He scrubs it away like it offends him and begins walking backward, face filled with disappointment. "Except for *this*. I won't do *this*."

My heart lurches inside my chest, reaching for him. With every step he puts between us, another tie that binds our friendship snaps in two. But unlike my heart, my feet root where I stand. My choice is made. And it isn't with him.

I press my hands to my face, tears spilling from my eyes as he turns his back on me, and I let him go.

He only pauses once, spearing me with a glance over his shoulder. "Good luck having a life without me, Raina. I've a feeling you're going to need it."

12

RAINA

The Northland Break
Hampstead Loch

We reach the loch the next afternoon.

The blue expanse shimmers under the sunlight as a cool breeze ripples the tents lining the beach. The scent of burned wood still lingers on the wind, though the village down the way was turned to ash weeks ago now. Such a loss will live with me forever, but despite the fiery memories, my heart swells at the sight of life in the valley.

Unfortunately, I'm distracted by the lack of safety here. Willow trees line the lakeshore along with Brigot's Rock, the lake's defining feature, and several rocky outcroppings good for shielding coastal winds sloping off the western range. But there's no further protection and nowhere to hide. The villagers didn't know the Eastlanders' fates on Winter Road, or that they haven't been vulnerable to another raid. And yet they remained steadfast, gifting our people proper burials anyway.

"I'm not telling Father about Finn," Hel says as we ride. "Not yet." With Northland and Tiressian flags heralding our approach, she and I lead our band. If the flags don't ease the survivors when they notice a band of warriors riding their way, perhaps two recognizable faces will. "I'll tell him later," she continues. "After all the news has been delivered. If Finn didn't beat us here."

To keep my mind off what Finn did or didn't do, I concentrate on erecting a glamour over my witch's marks to avoid unwanted discussion when Warek sees us, in case Finn *didn't* come this way. It isn't an easy task with my emotions still running high, but I remind myself that this is a means of protection I need to be able to maintain, no matter what I'm facing. I must master the skill. And soon.

The moment one of the survivors glimpses our horses, the villagers form a wall, though no weapons are drawn. I tell myself it's because of the flags, but after Warek, Saira, and Tuck greet Hel with a tearful homecoming, her father turns to look at me. I can see the knowledge in his eyes, the uncertainty in his every move as he lets go of Hel and starts toward me and Nephele.

My sister and I dismount, and Warek pauses an arm's length away. Stiffly, my father's oldest friend kisses my forehead, then Nephele's. "I'm so proud to see both of you. So proud you endured, and the Ancient Ones saw you home."

Home. Home was the cottage and Silver Hollow. It was hot summer afternoons playing in the stream with Nephele before she was chosen, my parents watching from the grassy bank, folded in one another's arms. Home was my sister's laugh, my father's knee, my mother's soft hands. It was Finn's hungry mouth on my body behind the forge, Hel catching us under the stars with wide eyes and a giggle. It was the excitement of harvest celebrations and trading days in nearby villages.

It was the dread of Collecting Day.

It was also years of blissful innocence and ignorance about the real world beyond the valley. Days I can never get back.

Glancing eastward, I realize this valley isn't home anymore. Not for me. For the first time in my life, I am completely unmoored to this stretch of land.

Warek takes a shuddering breath, snapping me out of my thoughts. He tightens his hand on my shoulder, but there are no more words spoken between us.

If he didn't know the truth about me and Alexus, he would tell me Finn is okay. He would tell me Finn is only out hunting, that he will shout to the gods when he beholds my face. That's what Warek Owyn would say if he didn't know I'd broken his son's heart in two and will probably shatter it to unrecognizable pieces before all is said and done.

Instead, he lets go of me as unease creeps across his expression like a rain cloud, and his shadowed stare slides past me. Nephele and I turn. Alexus, Rhonin, and Joran approach. Still draped in black, Alexus carries twin double-edged swords crossed over his broad back, and long daggers are strapped to his thighs. Rhonin left his bow with his horse, but his sheer size is enough to garner wary glances.

As for Joran, he might not have the other men's stature, but with his belt of knives, that silver hair blowing behind him, and that sleek, dark crossbow hanging from his belt hook, he's still intimidating. The three of them, a stalking force against the wind, would raise anyone's hackles.

Alexus pauses at my side, keeping a comfortable distance from the villagers but a close stance next to me. Though he brushes his finger along the back of my hand, I can sense his tension, the way his body stiffens as he endures their stares, each face unsure about the Collector's presence.

Including Warek.

"My lord." Warek's voice is quiet, yet stern and cold. "My son has been here and gone. Forgive me if I'm at a loss right now. I've yet to tell everyone the details. In truth, I'm still struggling to parse everything that's happened." Warek glances at me. "I don't know what to think right now."

Alexus lowers his voice as well. "There are far more important matters at hand than your son's love life, Mr. Owyn. Or what Raina and I have been through. I'm happy to go somewhere private and talk with you if needed. I can explain what happened with the prince and Thamaos and Neri, and what it means for the days ahead. Then you can decide how to inform your people. We ride south to Malgros come morning regardless. Then on to the Summerlands."

"We?" Warek strokes his graying beard and peers at Hel from the corner of his eye. "As in?"

"As in anyone who wishes to travel with us," Alexus answers.

Warek hesitates, the wheels of his mind visibly churning with concern for his daughter, the beginnings of a father/daughter battle in the making.

But instead of getting into the matter now, he drops his hand and says, "Of course, my lord. This way." He gestures at the villagers still waiting behind him. "Help our guests with their horses and tents. Then prepare an evening meal in their honor."

As everyone scatters in our direction, the camp is revealed. It's no village, but a makeshift green with rough-hewn tables and benches encloses an area of cut switchgrass, and at the green's center stands the pyre for the bonfire, encircled by a ring of perfectly placed rocks from the lakeshore. The familiar stone circle is Mena's doing, of that I'm certain. Knowing that she's here lifts my spirits.

Before he follows Warek, Alexus takes my hand and squeezes, sending a flood of comfort through the bond, easing my tense muscles. When I squeeze back, he kisses my temple and winks a dark-lashed eye, clearly no longer worried about anyone knowing just how intimate we've become.

"Glad I'm not a part of this," Joran says as Alexus trails behind Warek. "I'd rather peel my own hide with a splintered twig as endure that fucking story again. I'll be back come nightfall." Snagging a leather flask from his pack, he takes off toward the lake's north end without another word, not even to Keth, his apprentice, who sighs and drags a hand through his chestnut, spiky hair as Joran stalks away.

"He's not a people person," Keth says with a shrug, to no one in particular.

Jaega rolls her eyes as she and Callan hand their horses off to a villager. "As if we don't know."

"Hey." Rhonin bumps into my shoulder and jerks his strong chin toward the willow trees where an old woman pushes through the swaying green curtain, a basket of harvested herbs in her grip. Her hair, a shock of copper and silver, blows wildly behind her.

The sight steals my breath.

"That is her," Rhonin signs, spelling the words, and quite well for such a new learner.

Tears prick my eyes. *"Indeed."*

"She moves like my mother," he adds, his voice cracking on that last word.

As though sensing us, Mena lifts her head. She freezes, and a moment of disbelief passes, snatched by a cool breeze. She drops her basket, and with her skirts gathered in her fists, begins hobbling across camp.

I hurry toward her. In those impossibly long seconds, my hold on the glamour slips, but it doesn't matter with Mena. She saw my marks the last time we were together, inside her burning cottage. And somehow, I think my marks are something she would love to see.

We pause two strides apart, taking one another in. Mena cups her hands over her mouth, laughing through her joy, and I smile so big it hurts.

When we close the distance, our meeting is a gentle thing. I clutch her fingers, then she presses her chilled palms to my face. The scent of soil and herbs accompanies her, so welcoming that I inhale a lungful of her earthy aroma. It's a scent that awakens memories of days long past in Silver Hollow, of the cottage and summer moons and midnight fires.

"Raina, my girl. You are such a beautiful sight!" The wrinkled corners of her mouth quiver. "You cannot know how happy I am to see this face!"

"Happy as I am to see yours!" I sign.

She embraces me. "I could hardly believe Finn's news. But here you are. *Here you are.* Whole and divine as any witch I've ever seen!"

Though her words are filled with love, my stomach still sinks. She must know that I hurt Finn too.

We hold one another for a time, swaying in the breeze, until Mena pulls back and brushes the tears from my cheeks. She directs a feeble smile behind me, and I turn to find Helena, Saira, and Rhonin, all wearing soft smiles.

With a shaky hand, Rhonin runs his palm down the laces of his leather vest. For all the days I've known Mena, I've only heard her daughter's name mentioned on a few occasions, as though the word brought too much pain. Rhonin, on the other hand, has talked about his mother many times on the trip from Winterhold, sharing tales of their life in the East. He loves his family. Prays every night that his mother and siblings are safe after his obvious deception. He believes his mother is clever enough to lie her way out of her son's betrayal. At least that's always been the plan if one of them were found out.

Mena is part of that family, the mother and grandmother Bronwyn left behind for the sake of Tiressia. Now Rhonin gets to know her, after all this time.

A moment of wonder crosses Mena's face as I take her marked hand with its many shimmering whorls and flourishes and place it inside Rhonin's bare, calloused palm. From that simple touch, Mena's eyes shine with distant knowing, the kind of truth that creeps up slowly before landing a stunning blow to the heart.

"*Mena Shawcross,*" I sign. "*Meet Rhonin. Your grandson.*"

⚜

WHILE MENA AND RHONIN GET TO KNOW ONE ANOTHER, AND HEL plays with her sister, I reconstruct my glamour and spend a little time studying the wards between me and the prince. Now that I know what the runes mean, I must learn to track the quickly moving web of lines that connect the floating sigils, a required skill if I ever plan to open a doorway through the Brotherhood's blockade.

It's never been clearer that I have no idea what I'm doing. I might as well be facing a journey over the craggy mountains of the Mondulak Range with my hands tied behind my back.

When I can't stand staring at that red, nebulous cloud and the labyrinth of glowing lines any longer, I abandon the waters and join the others, helping raise shelters and tend horses. After an hour or so we finish, every tent prepared for the night.

Alexus is still with Warek, and a couple of elders have joined, so I grab my bowl and the hairpin from Winterhold that I've been using to prick my fingertips and meet Hel and Saira by the lakeshore.

As the girls play with Tuck the dog, I sit on a smooth boulder, legs crossed, and search for Finn. According to Hel, he didn't tell their father where he was going, only that he couldn't be here when we arrived. But I can see him. He isn't far. He's lying on a blanket somewhere along this very lake, arm bent behind his head, eyes closed against the cold day and bright sun.

Next, I try to see Neri, a fool's errand. An icy, white cloud appears over the water and dissipates, leaving a slick of frost on my hands. Though I can't decide if it's real or just my imagination, I swear I hear him laughing in the distance.

I scrub my frosted hand on my tunic and curse the northern god in my mind.

After rinsing and refilling my bowl, I search for Colden. He's still in the dungeon, though he's finally resting, lying on the dirt floor of his cell, head propped on the crumpled ball of his blue velvet coat. This time, a tin dish and mug sit near him. At least the prince isn't letting him starve.

Before I can stab another finger and begin the work of looking for the prince yet again, Nephele appears from behind and slides onto the rock next to me, a bundle of clothes and bath linens in her arms.

"Any change?" she asks, a dull sparkle in her eyes.

I shake my head. *"Colden is resting though,"* I sign. *"And he has eaten."*

Relieved, she takes a deep breath and sets the bundle aside. "Some of the villagers offered to launder our clothing before we leave." She retrieves four lumps of soap from her pocket and holds them to her nose. "They gave me these too. They smell divine. Herbs and wildflowers. There's a good bathing area down the way. What do you say?"

Thanks to the rain, Joran's water magick, and Hel's growing ability with fire magick, we managed a moderate cleanliness while traveling. But now there's an entire lake at our disposal, and I'm filthy from handling dirty tent stakes and horses. Still, I hesitate. Every time I look at the bowl, the duty I feel to see the prince overwhelms.

Nephele arches a sharp eyebrow and faces me, glancing at my reddened fingertips. "Raina, I love that you check on Colden as often as you do, and I appreciate how much you want to break through the barricade between you and the prince. But the Brotherhood—an entire *council* of sorcerers—is protecting him. Alexus nor I possess any ability to see them or reach them with our magick. If we are no match for them, imagine how incredibly difficult it would be for *you* to dismantle their wards, even if Alexus had months to instruct you."

"I understand," I sign. *"I know I am no match for them. But the Seer Joran mentioned could have done it. So I must try. If I could just—"*

"Just what?" She tilts her head and shoves the soaps in her trouser pocket. "What can you possibly do? Listen. The woman Joran spoke of was Petra Anrova, one of Loria's descended. Even with the power of the goddess of creation in her veins, she spent years learning to see more than what the gift of Sight alone allowed. You and I come from two common Northlanders. A father who was a reaper and a mother who—"

She stops abruptly. I hold her gaze while her mind works behind her eyes and mentally finish her sentence for her. *A mother who was more than we ever knew. A mother who went to the grave with a host of secrets.*

"Perhaps that is why I should try," I sign. *"Mother and Father hid so much. The truth about the God Knife. Father being a Keeper of the blade. Mother's power. What else do we not know? What might we find if we dig a little deeper?"*

"Or perhaps they hid things for a reason," she says. "Because maybe the truth was more dangerous than lies."

"I do not fear danger," I sign. *"I fear being someone who does nothing while those she loves stand in the enemy's path. I have been that person. I do not wish to be her again."*

"Raina." Nephele clasps my hand, sadness in her eyes. "You didn't know to watch the waters. You didn't know the enemy was near."

Alexus said nearly the same words not long after we entered Frostwater Wood the first time. It's still hard to feel blameless when all that remains of the valley is less than two dozen villagers trying to find life again around this lake.

My sister and I stare at one another for several long seconds before Nephele sighs, obviously spying the resoluteness on my face.

"Fine," she says. "Let's pilfer some wine and bathe. Afterward, we can discuss seeing past the prince's barriers. Like Alexus, I'll help you any way I can. Even if I must summon Neri myself and *make* him grant the ability you desire."

Her words sink inside me like a stone dropping to the bottom of a lake. No. Not a stone. An idea. A seed. In verdant ground.

And it quickly takes root.

Do not summon me. Those words breeze through my mind yet again. If not for this simple command from Neri on Winter Road and what I beheld between Alexus and Thamaos, I would've never known such an option existed.

I still don't. Not really. Not for me, anyway.

But as I walk with Hel, Nephele, and Saira toward the rocky outcroppings in the distance to bathe, I make a decision.

Tonight, when no one is watching, I'm going to find out.

13

RAINA

Dusk falls when we return to camp, and a storm looms over the
mountains to the west.

As some of the women set our clothes up to dry near a small
fire, which I hope isn't pointless given the threat of rain, I realize that
Warek has already retold Alexus's tale to the villagers, leaving a somber tint
to the air. Most eyes that meet mine look confused, like they're trying to
decide whether to believe anything we say. I'm certain that hearing the
truth about Neri shook many foundations of belief. Such is the way when
faith is tested.

There's still no sign of Finn, and Alexus and Rhonin have gone to the
lake's north end to clean up and look for Joran before the evening meal.
That those two are together makes me smile. They've grown closer than I
would've expected these last two weeks. It seems perhaps they both need
the friendship.

While Nephele and Hel begin helping the men and women in the food
tent, I stroll through the camp and find Mena. We sit together for a while,
watching two villagers stack wood for the pyre. Eventually, we talk about
all that's happened over these last weeks, listening to another night bird
sing its melancholy song.

"I am worried for the days that lie ahead," I tell her. *"What Fate has in store. It feels as though the real journey is just beginning."*

She takes my hand and presses a kiss to my knuckles. "Sadly, I'm certain you're right. This is only the start of a much larger story. But Fate isn't what you think it is, my girl. Fate doesn't carve our life's road, nor does it decide our destiny. *We* do. Fate only places people, events, and choices in our path. It's up to us to navigate the labyrinth of love, loss, happiness, and pain that is borne from those experiences. Granted, sometimes Fate fights for two souls to come together, and that is not a thing to take lightly." She smiles and touches my face. "Trust that you are making the right decisions, Raina. Trust your instinct. You are here because your blood sang a song of trust and you listened. Believe that your intuition is a gift that will never fail you."

With those words of wisdom in mind, I walk Mena to her tent so she can clean up before dinner, then I head down the torchlit path that leads to Brigot's Rock, scrying dish and hairpin in hand, dagger strapped to my thigh. My hair is still damp, and the rain-scented wind off the lake is cool, but my borrowed wool tunic has a hood. I toss it up and march to the lapping waves where I fill my vessel to the rim, then tuck myself in the crescent-shaped shelter of Brigot's Rock.

I don't know if Fate had a hand in what I'm doing, or if I'm just too persistent for my own good, but I'm hoping that Mena was right, and that I'm making the right choice tonight.

Callan explained the summoning process after the incident with Thamaos. I listened, though I felt certain it was magick I would never perform. I remember the runes they mentioned, though. There were nine, because Alexus requested them. But only three are required for a summoning, along with the runes of protection. Three of the many runes Alexus taught me the other night by the fire.

At least Neri never required a blood offering, something I'm quite thankful for as I drag my dagger through the pebbly sand, carving the outer runes before closing myself inside the first circle. I sit cross-legged in the middle and repeat the motions on a smaller scale. Finally, I draw the runes for Communication, Faithfulness, and Fealty.

Confessing such sentiments for Neri makes my stomach turn. But if Alexus endured Thamaos for answers, surely I can endure Neri. *He's just a soul,* I tell myself. Unfortunately, he's a soul that can send a moving wagon flying off the road. A soul who can strip power from a person like a beast ripping out an organ. He has no reason to hurt me though. If he'd wanted to, he could've already ended me.

Though prayer isn't my best talent, I close my eyes and think a few lines anyway. After three attempts, however, nothing has happened. Certain that I've done something wrong, I grab my filled dish and prick my finger. Using Sight to see Neri has failed every time before, but tonight I also pray to Loria that my gift might forge the first link between me and the being I'm searching for.

"Nahmthalahsh. Show me Neri."

The water swirls, a captured tempest. But then it stills, and vapor rises, moments before ice forms over the surface and drapes along the bowl's rim. On the wind, a whisper of laughter.

That bastard is mocking me.

Irritated, I smack the bowl against the ground to dislodge the ice and return to the water's edge to refill the vessel, careful not to break either of the circles.

When I return to the rock's shelter, I stop and stare at my work, rolling my eyes at my severe lack of knowledge. I might not have disrupted the circles, but did I disrupt the magick by leaving it?

There's only one way to know, so I sit down and try again.

"Nahmthalahsh. Show me the God of the North, the White Wolf."

The water froths into white foam, and after a blink of my eyes, morphs into a bowl of useless snow. I toss the fluff and slam the scrying dish onto the sand and rocks.

"Such a curious woman," a deep voice says, caressing my ear. *"Quite the little voyeur, aren't you?"*

I go still as the ancient stone behind me, my hands tightening on my vessel's rim.

I know that voice. Neri.

Discreetly, I rub my still-bleeding fingertip against the wood to center my mind so that I don't somehow inadvertently signal Alexus through the rune. Like he worried about Neri rupturing the summoning of Thamaos, I worry about what might happen if the Witch Collector senses my trouble and storms to the shore. Though I should probably welcome that idea, Neri is right. I'm as curious as ever.

I don't know if it's possible to communicate with a god who doesn't know my hand language, but before I can sign, he says, *"Thank you for sparing me Un Drallag's presence. Have you any idea what being trapped inside that lover of yours was like for me? I owe him much misery."*

My heart races, and my breaths come fast.

He can hear my thoughts.

The air tightens, compressing against my skin, and his voice deepens to a growl, grows colder. *"I only hear your mind because you called me here. So that's your fault, Seer."*

Even as a cold night descends, beads of sweat pearl on my forehead. I form a thought in my mind. *"I didn't think it would actually work."*

And I didn't. I'd only hoped.

"And yet here you are, asking your gift to find me. In Loria's name. That, to cure your ignorance, is a true summons. Not this ludicrous rune circle." Suddenly, the sand around me scatters like a wind just rushed across the shore. *"That magick is for Thamaos's ego, and you did it incorrectly anyway. Only those who've been involved in a deal with me in some manner can seek me out. But I distinctly recall telling you not to do so. Now, what am I supposed to do about such disobedience?"*

Uncertainty tremors in my bones. Do I reach for Alexus through the bond or just run? Somehow, I sense that both scenarios would be thwarted, so I sit my dish aside instead and look around the empty lakeshore, simultaneously slipping my hand down the outside of my thigh to my dagger's hilt.

Neri laughs again, a menacing sound that rumbles through the pit of my stomach, matching the distant roll of thunder. But around that laugh, the air tinkles and chimes like tiny bells of ice have been strung through the willows.

A frigid fog rolls off the water, and the lakeshore turns hoary with frost. One moment I'm alone, shivering with low-thrumming panic, and the next Neri is there, a crystalizing, hulking form squatting beside me.

On the edge of my vision, his wolfish face comes into focus a short distance from mine. With an unnaturally quick tilt of his head, he bores his gaze into my skull, reminding me of those agonizing seconds when his wolf cornered me on Winter Road. Slowly, trembling under his scrutiny, I gather the courage to meet his amber eyes.

It's strange looking upon him. His skin is the same as I remember, white as snow and glittering like moonlight on the lake. He's terrifying yet beautiful, the way the prowling white wolf is beautiful, stalking through a wintry wood—a thing to admire from a distance but to avoid at all costs.

He skims a glance over my face, and the corner of his mouth curls, revealing a long and deadly fang. "Terrifying *and* beautiful? Thank you for the compliment. Two kindnesses in a matter of minutes. Whatever did I do to deserve that?"

Leaning closer, he lifts a massive paw-like hand and trails a claw-tipped finger along my jaw. I sit unmoving as a thin dusting of frost forms in the wake of his touch.

My fingers tighten around my weapon's hilt, my grip shaky and clammy. The blade is as useless as the dagger I clutched when Neri attacked Colden. What earthly weapon can be wielded against the soul of a god? Not my steel dagger, forged for close combat with the living. Not even the God Knife. But if Neri means to kill me, gods be damned if I'll go down without a fight.

He *tsks*. "I'm not going to kill you, Seer. And no, your little knife is no threat. I show mercy because of your puerile nature, and because I suspect that, even with such inexperience, I'm going to need you in the future." He angles his head again, his white, silky hair revealing a pointed ear and a thickly muscled shoulder. "Now tell me what you want from me," he whispers.

A moment of uncertainty passes. Tell him or don't? The decision is easier than I expect.

Again, I think the words.

"The Eastland Brotherhood has hidden the Prince of the East from me. I cannot see our enemy or what he has planned. You can help me. Help your people. Restore their faith in you."

He laughs, the sound so powerful it ripples the lake. "You would have to make me a deal," he replies. "And I doubt you'll be willing to grant what I desire, no matter how badly you want help."

My eyes narrow into a glare. His words are meant to be elusive. They feel like a puzzle, something I'm meant to sort out, yet he hasn't given me enough clues.

"I don't play games," he says. "I want to be resurrected so I can stop Thamaos's return. Why do you think I've followed you this far? I listen. I hear. I see. I know." He pauses. Curls his lips over his fangs. "I saw your lover summon Thamaos in the wood. I will not watch that monster live again while I'm hunted and sent back to the Shadow World, because that is what he will try to do. Anyone who thinks otherwise is a fool or severely manipulated. If you help to bring *me* back before that dark prince succeeds in digging up his wretched lord, I'll help you with whatever you ask of me. If you don't, we each fend for ourselves." He leans back, broad chest lustrous as a moonstone. "Now, do you want to deal or not?"

So cut and dry. As if resurrecting him is a simple thing.

"I have no remnant of you," I tell him. *"The prince has the God Knife, made from Thamaos's bone. I couldn't resurrect you if I wanted to."*

"Do you really think any god would be so witless as to not prepare for such things? Knowing that the laws of their kind provide a method for true eternal life? I had liegemen devoted to protecting my remnant. They were charged with my resurrection because of my unjust death. They failed, thanks to Fia Drumera's protections around her land. But now I'm granted another chance, it seems. With you." He tilts his head closer. "I know where my remnant is. I can lead you to it. And so I offer you a deal."

His aid is what I wanted. This just isn't how I thought that aid would be granted.

Fuck. If Fate oversees what choices lie before us, then that son of a bitch has one cruel sense of humor.

"I need to see what the prince is up to now, *not later,"* I tell Neri, digging as deeply as I can into my sense of self-preservation and perhaps my own powers of manipulation. *"If you're correct, then Thamaos wants you sent back to the Shadow World. If he's truly guiding the prince, and the prince gets to the grove first, what makes you believe Thamaos will let the prince leave your grave intact? It* must *remain intact if you want to live again. As it stands, we could already be too late."*

Sighing with annoyance, Neri growls and spreads his massive hands. "Then I cannot help you. Because until I am whole, I have no power over the magick of men. Only my own and any I doled out three centuries ago."

I suppose that explains why he was able to remove Colden's curse.

"The council's barrier is as impenetrable for me as it is for you," he adds. "But I've a sneaking suspicion that the prince is nowhere near ready to attack the Summerlands. In fact, if my old deal bonds are singing correctly, then he's going to need a little time. Which gives you a window of opportunity. Find my remnant and reach the Grove of the fucking Gods first." He raises his white brows. "So. Last time. Deal or not?"

Oddly, I want to trust the god crouched before me. But I need time to think this through.

He huffs a laugh. "I thought you had more fire, Seer. If you decide you want to play, you know how to find me. Until then, I'll be on the lookout for other means to make my resurrection happen." He stands, and like an apparition, begins to fade at the edge of Brigot's Rock. Before he vanishes completely, though, his voice reaches my mind. *"Perhaps you should keep an eye on your king,* he says. *One of the answers you seek now lies with him. The knowledge will not save you or Tiressia, and it will not stop the prince, but it will allow you to prepare."*

A second later, Neri is gone. His words linger though, repeating in my head, and for reasons I can't yet understand, I believe everything he said.

Listening to Mena's advice, I decide to trust my instinct. With a slight shiver, I get up and walk to the shore to fill my scrying dish. Using the hairpin, I prick my finger and bleed into the water one last time tonight.

"Nahmthalahsh," I sign, releasing a shaky breath as a great clap of thunder cleaves the air. *"Show me Colden Moeshka."*

14

COLDEN

The Eastern Territories
City of Quezira
Min-Thuret Temple, Dungeon

There's a dead woman in the cell next to mine.

A tall, blond guard carried her into the dungeon moments ago. Now he looms over her, covering her corpse with a blanket, like he's tucking her in for a long night's sleep.

At the guard's side stands a woman dressed in black trousers and a bronze tunic, holding a basket of medicinals in hand. A physician. Which seems quite pointless given that the body is a rotted mess of remains and bones. She sits the basket aside and withdraws a thin, iron collar that she places around the exposed sinew of the dead woman's stringy neck.

The maid's face is familiar, that pale, pearlescent skin. And her hair... The color of straw under summer's late dusk. Not blonde and not red, but something softer in between. Silver threads streak her braided locks now, and her body is leaner, harder than I recall, her face more lined. It's been nearly twenty years, after all. She's one of mine, though.

Bronwyn Shawcross.

"I take it that digging people from their graves is the only way you can force anyone to spend time with you," I say.

The guard and Bronwyn glance up, and though I catch a glint in Bronwyn's eyes, she's the epitome of calm, her facade never once wavering. If I were a betting man, I'd wager that her pulse didn't even quicken.

But I wasn't speaking to Bronwyn or the guard.

The Prince of the East, whom I haven't seen in many days, stands two steps behind them, hands stuffed inside his trouser pockets, blood-colored shadows roiling like a miniature storm around his feet.

My words were meant for him.

He pierces me with a cold look, and from my place on the ground, I take him in. The fitted lines of his leather jacket. The deep cut of his raven-black tunic. The copper embroidery in the silk. He looks nearly whole again. Farther from death's door than he appeared when he brought me here. How many souls were lost to achieve that sort of healing?

Hands twisting in his pockets, he jerks his head at the guard and Bronwyn, dismissing them. Without a second look at me, they head to the stairwell, though I know this is not the last I've seen of Bron.

Once they're gone, the prince strolls to the bars between us and leans his shoulder against the iron. "I have no problem persuading people to *spend time* with me," he says. "You of all people should know that."

Only four torches illuminate the dungeon. The warm light softens the harshness of the small prison, casting the prince's scarred face half in shadow. A face I once admired while drunk on the Eastland Territories' renowned black wine and my fair share of feverish kisses in the late hours of a summer night.

The distant memory of that visit, of being with him—and remembering how much I liked it—makes me nauseated.

"That was thirty years ago," I tell him. "When you weren't such a despicable, soul-sucking louse. Just a handsome prince. Which I rather liked."

He smirks. "Speaking of liking things. Do you like your temporary home?"

Home? My cell is barren. They've given me no chair, no bed, no blanket. Just a few of the luxuries granted to the dead woman before she arrived. Servants flocked into the dungeon and filled the neighboring cell with a narrow brass bed, fresh linens, a regal, high-backed purple velvet chair, a colorful handwoven rug, and even a dainty mirror, basin, and ewer.

A cell fit for a princess. Not a decayed carcass.

Who she might've been and why she's here, I can't gather. But given that the prince has ties to the Shadow World and his prisoner is bound in iron, I can't imagine it's good.

I lean right and appraise the covered body. "Let's just say that, for a corpse who smells like she's rotted for centuries, your newest guest has the better accommodations." I set aside my bloodstained blue velvet coat, wadded into a makeshift pillow. "Given our past and who I am, I find your poor hospitality insulting."

He laughs, and I grimace. How easily I recall enjoying that sound.

"Insulting? My prison isn't fit for a king? What would you prefer? An entire temple wing? A pretty maid to prepare your meals? A copper tub with a handsome wash boy, perhaps?"

I flash a bright smile. "That sounds outstanding. I'll take all of it."

"You'll take the ground," he says, his voice hard. "Be thankful I'm not offering less."

After a deep breath of dank air, I narrow my eyes and study him. "What in the Nether Reaches happened to you? The last time I was here, you were no war-mongering murderer. You were so pleasant for a man shrouded in secrecy, and might I say *more* than determined to see that I enjoyed my stay."

"You were here a long time ago. Thirty years, according to you. I'd forgotten. It clearly wasn't memorable. And people change. Best to remember that. As you said, I'm not so pleasant now."

"Not in the least." I wink. "Though still willing, I bet."

Another smirk, then he grips the bars and faces me. There's no humor on his face anymore, and his eyes—eyes that were hazel if memory serves —are now darker than mine.

Voids. Hollow orbs.

Like they were on Winter Road.

"Don't think that one night decades ago means I give two fucks about you now, Colden Moeshka. Because I don't. You're lucky you're not bleeding from every orifice and begging for mercy in Yura's pits."

To stoke his ire, I stand and—though weak—cross the cell. Teasing, I slide my palms down the tattered remains of the tunic I've worn since Neri stole my power. I tug it open to reveal my bare torso. A starburst scar now streaks my skin, from the hollow of my throat to my navel, but the glimpse of nakedness still catches the prince's attention.

He tracks my every move as I slip my fingers down my abdomen, until he drags that bottomless stare up to meet mine. The tiniest shimmer of recollection flickers there. Something he cannot hide, even within the shadows suffocating his soul.

Holding his gaze, I wrap my fingers around the bars above his fists, making sure our hands touch. "If I remember correctly—" I lean in and lower my voice, noting the sweet smell of sweat in his hair and dirt on his skin "—it's *you* who does the begging."

His gaze slides to my mouth. An eternal moment stretches between us before he jerks away from the bars, takes a step back, and rakes his fingers through his dark hair. "Still so godsdamn arrogant. I only found you beguiling back then because I saw that arrogance as... *confidence*. Now I see a man who pretends to be something he is not, to whatever end he desires."

I lift my hands and clap. "And that, ladies, gentlemen, and all fair people, from a prince who doesn't remember his own name." The bars feel colder when I grasp them a second time. "Your very existence is pretend. You play the role of a mighty, conquering prince when you have no notion where you came from." I lower my voice to a hush. "I told no one about our night together, but I remember everything. I can still hear you saying *Colden* across my lips, and I can still see your panic when I asked what *I* could call *you*. The horror in your eyes when I wanted to whisper your name, and you couldn't even utter a single syllable. Don't you ever wonder why you can't recall your life?"

Though his exterior is composed, the distress behind his eyes is clear as glass. It's a mirror to the past, that look so similar it's like we've slipped back in time.

"My life is none of your concern." The words grit between his teeth. "And know this: you meant nothing to me then, and you mean nothing to me now. A scenario that might be your norm. Should Fia Drumera surrender once she learns your life hinges on her decision to cooperate with my forces, I'll keep you beyond her citadel's gates. Alive. But if she doesn't, if you are as insignificant to her as you are to me, then I will end you. If not for the sheer pleasure of proving how unimpressive that night with you was, then to bask in the moment when your friends watch you turn to dust." He looks over his shoulder at the dead woman. "If all goes to plan, Alexi will join us soon. Once his power has returned in full, I will siphon from him, and there won't be a damn thing anyone can do to stop me."

He lets that thought linger, as though he's had the last word, and exits the dead woman's cell, closing and locking the door. I'll give him a point. His declaration pierces me, even though I know that capturing Alexus Thibault once he has complete control of his magick won't be a simple errand.

As the prince turns to leave, a slow smile unfurls on my lips. I'm too much of a bastard to let this chance pass.

"Ahhh," I moan theatrically. "The *bliss* of knowing something your enemy does not."

The prince pauses, right hand opening and closing into a fist. In his left hand dangles the keys to these cells.

"Don't toy with me, Colden." He swings around, a half-snarl on his lips. "I know your tells. The way you taunt to detract from the truth."

I walk to the cell door, slip my arms through the bars, and rest my elbows on the crosspiece. "Or maybe you don't know me at all. Like you said, it was only one night. Only a few meaningless, breathless kisses."

His face hardens. "You were in my home for days. Don't think I didn't watch you even more closely when wine wasn't clouding my better judgment. And after these last minutes, I doubt anything has changed about you."

I make sure there's a mocking tilt to my smile as I give him my surest stare. "I thought you said you'd forgotten our time together. Me and my unimpressive mouth."

Words I know are lies. On Winter Road, he'd repeated a part of our conversation from that warm summer night together. Words that only held meaning for him and me. Thirty years ago, I made a jest about living forever without any sort of power, and once he sensed that my power had been torn from me, he'd thrown my words in my face. *What's the point in living forever if you're boring?*

He stares at me, his expression one of held-back rage. He wants to throttle me, which is perfect, because I want him to come a little closer so I can snatch those godsdamn keys.

As though my words command him, he stalks forward. Close, but not close enough.

"Stop baiting me," he demands, "and speak your mind. Or I will carve that tongue you think so highly of from your throat with one of these." He flashes the keys.

The image of his threat jars me, I'll give him that.

But I hold all the cards.

"Well, you see, here's the thing. A long time ago, possibly before you were even an urge in your mystery father's blue balls, Alexus did a stupid thing. He bound himself to me with Summerlander magick that has held for three hundred years. His immortality depends on mine. If you kill me or let any fatal harm come my way, you lose him too."

I can't resist an enormous grin.

The prince's eye twitches. His chest rises and falls faster as he processes my words. "You're bluffing."

"Oh, but I am not. Why do you think we've stayed together all this time? It isn't because Alexus can't resist me, because I assure you, he can and has. Now he's like a brother to me, one who cared enough to help keep me alive. To give me a reason to live another day." I tilt my head. "Again, do you never ponder these things? How did you imagine he'd survived the last three hundred years?"

His brain is working. I can see it.

"You want me to believe that Alexi of Ghent gave you his... *eternity*?"

I've never heard it described like that, but now that the words have left the prince's mouth, I'm not sure I'll ever stop hearing them.

"Yes, because he *did*. It ate at my conscience for years, but what was I to do? At one point, I wanted to die. An unending existence as a Frost King, even with Alexus at my side, seemed a horrendous fate. But how could I end his life too? It seemed he wanted to live, that he was searching for something I couldn't understand. Besides, after enough time, one adjusts, and living forever begins to feel like it was meant to be." I pause at the honesty I'm revealing and search for my cavalier veneer. I find it quickly and wear it like a second skin. "You wouldn't know anything about such a plight, seeing how you must eat souls to live." I *tsk* to annoy him, and a disgusting revelation strikes. Was he already devouring souls when I met him? I think of the woman in the cell. "That's what happened to her, isn't it?" I jerk my head toward my rotting roommate. "You devoured her essence, then had second thoughts. Is she going to reanimate? Wake up a flesh-eating monster? Is that why she has a collar? Where's the leash? I should know since I'm being forced to sleep next to her."

Wearing a sadistic grin, the prince tucks the keys in his pocket and heads for the stairs. His shadows follow like the rising tide of the Eastland Territories' Black Sea. When he reaches the third step, the last one within view, he pauses and looks my way.

In a voice laced with wicked delight, he says, "I suppose you must wait and see what she is. Just as I must wait and see if you're the liar I believe you are."

He disappears up the stairwell, and I return to my place on the cold, hard ground, thinking about the prince's plan for Alexus. As thoughts race through my mind, I focus on the matted tuft of dark red hair flowing from one desolate patch of scalp at the back of the dead woman's head. The sight puts me on edge, and I find my thoughts shifting, waiting for her to crawl from that bed in her skeletal remains.

Nonsense. Pure nonsense.

I tuck my wadded jacket beneath my head and lie down. I don't know if it's night or day, only that I'm fucking tired.

"Sweet dreams, princess," I mumble before closing my eyes. "Try not to let the maggots bite."

It isn't until minutes later when I've started to drift that I swear a draft of power winds through the subterranean dungeon, carrying a whisper-voice into my cell on the end of a raspy, wet breath.

My eyes dart open, but there's nothing to see save for the flickering torches and the unmoving body, still hidden beneath that blanket.

I must be going mad down here because what I felt and heard is impossible.

"*I'm no princess,*" the voice had said. "*My name is Fury, and I'm a fucking god.*"

15

ALEXUS

"*Her name is Fury.*"

Panting from her sprint from the lakeshore to camp, Raina carves her hands through her long, dark hair, dragging it back from her face. She stands at the end of the table where I've been sitting with Rhonin for the last few minutes discussing Joran's whereabouts. I haven't even had time to look for her. I'd assumed she was still with Nephele and Helena.

Though I'm startled by her abrupt arrival and declaration, I school my features into a mask of calm and temper my emotions. With a steady grip, I lower my mug of ale and rest my hand on Raina's waist, an effort to ease her. Her witch's marks are revealed, bold in the dark of night, and her end of the bond is closed. She's so rattled that her distress is shutting down everything.

Luckily, I can read her emotions regardless. They're so often written on her face and in the way she signs.

"*Whose* name is Fury?" I ask with a confused shake of my head.

My heart skips a beat at the feel of that name on my tongue. A name I haven't heard in a very long time. A name I wouldn't call a name.

It was a rebellion.

"*The weapon,*" she signs with hasty movements. "*Joran was right. The prince needed a third weapon. I do not know what she is capable of, but she is the weapon. I have no doubt."*

As a chilled sweat breaks across the back of my neck, everyone begins to gather for dinner, their eyes on the storm clouds shadowing the sky in the distance. A few stares have started watching us, though, given Raina's obvious agitation.

"We're going to talk in private," I tell Rhonin as I stand. "If Joran isn't back soon, send Keth, Callan, and Jaega out to look for him. If the storm breaks, though, they need to get back here. I don't want anyone to lose a night's sleep because Joran is an idiot."

"Will do," he replies, turning up a healthy swig of ale.

I lead Raina toward the willows where we take shelter beneath the swaying fronds. Despite the increasing wind, the bonfire is high tonight, a dancing symbol of defiance as the survivors face the very element that devoured their families. Its light reaches us even here, though it isn't enough. I need to see Raina's eyes. Her expressions. She says so much with that beautiful face when she signs, and right now, I don't want to miss *any* detail.

Quickly, I call forth the energy of the night—the heat of the fire, the power from the moon, the strength in the wind. I'd rather not draw the villagers' attention, and I feel stronger today, so when the force of each entity arrives, I draw it all through my veins and channel it into pearls of light at the ends of my fingertips, releasing them into the darkness around us.

Raina's eyes widen, but there will be time to explain my ever-changing magick later.

"Take a deep breath and start from the beginning," I say as she leans back against the tree. The sight of her like this—underneath this willow, her dark blue eyes staring up at me... It stirs something deep inside that I try to recognize but can't.

I let her sign. Let her tell me everything. From Nephele's mention of Neri to that bastard finding Raina on the lakeshore to her seeing Colden in Thamaos's old dungeon.

Once she pauses, I say, "But you refused to make a deal with Neri, yes?" Thank the fucking Ancient Ones, she nods. "And you couldn't see the prince at all," I clarify.

"I could see nothing but Colden and red shadows at first. I could not hear them either. I never do. I only knew that Colden was still locked in a dirt cell, speaking with someone," she signs, *"and that it had to be the prince. So I waited. Longer than usual because of what Neri had said. Eventually, the shadows faded, and I saw the woman through Colden's eyes. Somehow, I heard her too and felt Colden's unease."*

From the stricken look on Raina's face and the way she shivers at the thought, it's evident that she'd love nothing more than to scrub the image from her mind. A decomposed body. A woman with a single streak of dark red hair. Flesh rotted, and yet she was somehow alive and worthy of being caged and secured by an iron collar and bars.

A woman who called herself not a princess, but a god.

A Fury.

"She could be anyone." My voice comes out weaker than I mean for it to, my throat constricting painfully as I speak. I swallow. "A former siphon, perhaps. A sorceress."

I want to believe my own words, even as I absentmindedly touch the centuries-old scar on my wrist. The moment I feel the rough skin, I yank my hand away, because the suggestion my mind is trying to conjure needs to be shut down. Now. It's only the anxiety of this entire ordeal getting to me.

Because Fleurie died. The Brotherhood killed her after the battle between Thamaos and Urdin, at King Gherahn's command. Once they reduced her to no more than a lifeless form chained to the rocks at the Abyss of Pensea, they let her wash away in the brutal, icy waves.

Her death is one part of those last years with Thamaos that time hasn't leeched. I watched it happen. Chained as well and on my knees in the frigid cold, forced to witness my friend's torture for days, screaming until I couldn't speak, until her bloody body slid down the black cliffside and vanished into the sea.

All because she wanted to take her father's empty throne.

Fleurie cannot be alive. I would've known. She would've found me.

Unless she couldn't. Unless she's been trapped or imprisoned all this time.

"She is not just anyone," Raina says. *"My intuition tells me that she is a force."*

Her intuition. Growing and changing with every passing day, every call upon her gift of Sight.

I blow out a breath as thunder rumbles over the land. Again, my fingers itch to touch the scar on my wrist, and a chilled sweat breaks across my skin. Suddenly, it's harder to breathe.

How I wish I could see Raina's vision. I trust her, but this is something so hard to believe that I long to know for sure.

She stares up at me with that weary gaze. *"I do not know who she is,"* she signs. *"Only that Colden radiated concern. That concern was not only for himself. It was also for you."* With tenderness, she presses her palm to my face before signing, *"I see you, Alexus. What are you not telling me?"*

As she stares into my eyes, I'm reminded of our time at the refuge when she showed me the God Knife. How stunned I'd been to see a lost part of my past, returned by her hands. This moment feels very much the same.

Impossible.

This time, I don't wait to tell her the story. Instead, I snuff out the orbs and take her hand, walking with her toward the green so the others can hear as well. Because there is only one reason the prince could want to see my old friend roaming the world again. The one reason that made her father long to control her, though he never could.

Fleurie can take the prince straight to the Grove of the Gods. Before we even get a chance to leave this godsdamn valley.

16

ALEXUS

"A portalist." Disbelief edges Nephele's words. "Thamaos's godling daughter is a *portalist*? And she's alive?"

Nephele, Helena, Rhonin, Callan, and Mena sit with Raina and I on tree stumps placed around a nest of lanterns inside Warek's meeting tent as wind beats the thick canvas. Warek stands by the entrance, arms folded over his barrel chest.

"Yes. She was—*is*—a portalist."

"What does that actually mean?" Rhonin asks.

A long sigh leaves me. Not from annoyance. But because I can't believe I'm having this conversation.

"A portalist can create an opening between two places and carry things across that divide," I tell him. "They use the gift of farsight to visualize the location to which they want to travel. But it's only a temporary visit. They're bound to whatever point they originated from. So even when Fleurie fled her father through a portal, the moment that opening closed, she'd find herself back where she started. She was but a courier and a visitor."

"I've heard stories about Thamaos's lovers," Mena says, "and that he spawned a child with a sorceress, but one never knows what tales are true. So many lies have been spun to erase our true history."

I nod, too aware of how right she is. "This tale is certainly true. Fleurie's mother was called Isidore, an Eastland sorceress. When Fleurie was nine years old, Isidore confessed to Thamaos that they'd conceived a child, and that the child had a powerful ability she feared. He didn't view the unexpected daughter as anything more than..." I pause, shaking my head as the only appropriate word comes to mind. "A *weapon*. And he meant to wield her as such in the Land Wars."

"But is she alive?" Callan asks, running their fingers up and down one of the many long strands of beads hanging from their neck.

I scrub my fingers through my beard and look at Raina. I fear this is especially difficult for her given that Fleurie is the only other person to whom I've ever been bonded.

"I don't mean to negate what Raina is experiencing with Sight and intuition," I say to Callan. "But I can't imagine how she can be here after all this time. Unless she truly was immortal."

"Some godlings recorded in the East's history books in the grand library *were* listed as immortals," Rhonin says, leaning his elbows on his widespread knees. "Like the ones still living in hiding across the world. You thought otherwise with Fleurie?"

He doesn't understand how well I know those history books.

"I did," I answer. "Even *she* believed that she was mortal. Inherited immortality wasn't the norm in the age of gods. It was the exception. The very reason that relations between gods and mortals became forbidden. Immortality couldn't be tested without a long passage of time or a risk of life. And besides..." I swallow the swelling sickness swirling inside my chest. "I *watched* her die. At least I thought I did."

I close my eyes, trying to suppress the images rising in my mind's eye and failing. As a strong wind howls, I picture Fleurie trapped by some glacier or rock at the bottom of the sea, pinned beneath an icy ocean of inky darkness, in pain and drowning, wishing for a seam in reality through which to escape, longing for death and never finding it, for three hundred years.

I pray to the Ancient Ones that the woman from Raina's vision isn't her. That this is all a grand mistake. Because the alternative couldn't have gone well for Fleurie.

"Can the prince force her to open a portal between him and the Grove of the

Gods?" Raina signs, staring into the flames flickering inside the lanterns a moment longer before lifting her head and leveling that sapphire stare on me.

"Not by force alone. It took a hundred sorcerers to prevent the two of us from escaping the East. A hundred more to chain us against those rocks. The prince is but one man. I can't imagine him or his modern-day Brotherhood being that capable, even if he held the most powerful siphon in existence captive."

"You realize that *you* might very well be the most powerful siphon in existence," Callan says. "And the prince might want to use Fleurie to find you."

Raina looks at me, a glimmer of worry in her eyes.

"That's very possible," I reply. "And Raina has seen Vexx riding south. I could be walking into a waiting trap. But if I want to reach the Summerlands, I have no other choice than to go through Malgros. As for Fleurie tracking me down... Thamaos gave Fleurie the moniker of *Fury*. He denied her true name, using Fury in moments when she showed weakness or rebellion, as a mockery. A slur. A goad. But even *he* saw what she truly was. She would annihilate the prince. Especially if she knows he means to harm me."

"But she might not know," Hel says. "It's been three hundred years, and it sounds like she's been tortured for all that time. Her mind might not be the same anymore, or the prince could've lied. But also, remember that, like their parents, godlings are vulnerable to iron. And if this woman *is* Fleurie, then the prince has the upper hand. For now, anyway. With her collared and jailed like an animal, he can prevent her from causing any damage to him or his efforts."

Nephele arches a blonde brow. "Yes, but to use her ability, he must let her go at some point. The question is, what does he have up his sleeve that will insure that she *doesn't* annihilate him? That she does what he wants instead?"

The answer strikes me as sure as lightning.

"A deal. Her help in exchange for him rescuing her." Like the deal Neri tried to make with Raina. Like the one I made with him in the ravine.

"That's the only way to truly bind a god or godling's word," Callan adds.

I think of Raina's gruesome description of my old friend. "She might've been so far gone that she didn't know what she was agreeing to," I say.

Nephele stands and begins pacing a short path behind Mena. "Fuck. This is bad."

Warek, a silent sentinel, clears his throat, the sound loud over another wind that whips the side of the tent. "There are still obstacles," he says. "If the prince intends to use Fleurie, and if Fleurie is in the deteriorated state Raina says, then she must heal, which buys a little time. She may be part god, but surely three hundred years of slow decomposition cannot be undone in a single day."

"Probably not without a talented Healer," I interject.

"And he doesn't have one of those," Rhonin replies. "He has my mother. Knowledgeable as she is, she only holds the power of herbs."

"Secondly," Warek continues, "Fleurie must be capable of breaching Fia Drumera's protections. Protections that have withstood attacks for ages. Can Fleurie's ability bypass such magick?"

"Unfortunately yes," I answer. "To a living god or godling, the magick of men is more an annoyance than an unbreakable wall. It's why the East-landers came so close to entering the City of Ruin during the Land Wars. They would have succeeded if not for Colden and his men. There was god magick versus god magick. Two very equal forces. But Thamaos and his army were up against Asha whose lands were fortified by a league of mages as well as Neri, a scattering of Witch Walkers, and his soldiers. Once Fleurie became skilled enough, Thamaos tried using her to take his armies through the City of Ruin's gates. But Fleurie wasn't capable."

Callan looks at Warek. "Portals require immense control and strength to open and hold open. It's difficult enough to ferry another person through. Let alone hundreds or thousands."

"Still," Nephele says. "Warek is right. Fleurie needs to heal, so we have time."

"But we cannot know how much time," Raina signs. *"This three-week journey must happen as quickly as possible."*

Mena exhales a long breath. "Is it even her, though? That remains the biggest question."

Something inside me caves. For the first time since Raina said the name *Fury* to me, I know that it is indeed my friend. In the wood, Thamaos told me that I should know better than to think he doesn't have a plan. I just couldn't fathom the impossible at the time. That his daughter lived, and that he'd finally found a way to trap her into doing what he desires.

"Until we have more proof through Raina's visions, we must assume that it is," I reply. "And move on from here accordingly."

"Meaning we should probably leave tonight," Nephele says. "Before this storm arrives and slows us even further." Thunder immediately rolls in the distance, and she crosses her arms over her middle as though the ominous sound rattled her.

Gods' death. We haven't slept. We've barely eaten. But I know she's right.

I scrub my hand over my face. "Agreed. We need to get ahead of the rain. As far as possible this time."

"Sounds like you have a plan, then," Mena says.

Rhonin nods in my direction. "I'm at your side, Alexus. Whatever you need."

"And me," Raina signs. *"You have me. We bear this burden together. To the very end."*

"To the very end," I sign back, my heart full.

Nephele stops her pacing and gives me a soft wink. "Me too."

Hel lifts her eyes, that dark gaze rimmed in soot-black lashes, and defiantly stares at her father. "Me three."

Warek's chest swells, and his face reddens. Earlier, he'd told me that he would insist Helena stay back. But he doesn't get a chance to argue the point, because Finn and Joran duck inside the tent, rumpled and wind-blown, surprising us all.

"Me four." A muscle quivers in Finn's jaw as he grits his teeth, as though speaking to me in a civil manner is the most colossal of efforts. He swallows so hard the knob in his throat visibly moves. "I offer my sword, my bow, my hunting and tracking skills too." He glances between Hel and Raina. "I can't let either of you go through this without me. I hope you can tolerate me."

Raina stares at him for a moment, expression filled with concern, hurt, and uncertainty. She turns her gaze on me and sends a feeling along the bond, like a question, tugging my mind for an answer. When I nod that it's all right with me for Finn to join us, she inclines her head toward her friend, an acceptance of his offer, as though his traveling with us is a decision she and I had to make. Not just one or the other.

I only hope I don't regret agreeing to it.

"I've tolerated you for almost nineteen years," Helena says. "I think I can handle *this*." She smiles and crosses the tent, embracing her brother. Warek eases, the pressure inside him visibly releasing, though worry still creases his forehead. Two of his three remaining children are headed into harm's way. Without him, it seems.

Helena lets go of Finn and cocks her hip, glaring at Joran. "What about *you*, asshole? You're awfully quiet for a change. You in?"

Muscled arms crossed beneath his thick chest and silvery brows curled inward, Joran tilts his head like a dog listening for a high-pitched whistle. "Yes, *I am in*." He cuts a look at me. "A pack of white wolves couldn't keep me from this adventure."

Mena stands, her back crooked, and gestures for me to join her. When I do, she takes my hand in hers and opens my palm toward the sky. With a curious touch, she runs a finger over the lines crossing my hand. After long moments, she lifts her head and looks up at me, her aged eyes wider and glassy as she studies my face. That look makes my spine tingle.

"Unfailing," she whispers, so low that I'm sure only I can hear. "Forever unfailing." Before I can ask what she means, she touches my face, then motions for everyone else to draw closer. "Come, come," she orders. "All of you. Form a circle. A prayer before you leave."

No one says a word. They do as she says.

"Now stretch out a single hand. Everyone."

We obey, though some of us more reluctantly as we realize what Mena intends. Slowly, we place our hands one atop another, our arms like the spokes of a wagon wheel, an act I would never have imagined happening with these six people a month ago.

Mena begins chanting to the Ancient Ones. Her words take on melody, flowing into a lovely song. In minutes, as the wind blows stronger and stronger, her magick washes over us.

Not just a prayer. A blessing. A protection.

When she finishes, we leave the meeting tent to gather our belongings and horses, braced for the long night ahead. As a crash of thunder rumbles over the mountains, the sound like ten legions of horses racing through the sky, it isn't lost on me that, although we go our separate ways, we stepped into the brewing storm together.

III

BEGINNINGS

17

FLEURIE

The Eastern Territories
City of Quezira
Min-Thuret Temple, Dungeon

E ven the most raging misery can be bliss.

I sit inside my newest prison, on the edge of a soft bed, staring at my rot-ravaged legs. Bronwyn, the healer, kneels before me, my bandages in her grasp as she inspects the progress.

The burning pain of healing lives in a constant swath of red misery over my still-distorted vision. But even without Bronwyn's reports, I can see well enough in the torchlight to know that my legs are improved today. Slivers of white bone are still visible in places, as is the glistening pink and red of reforming sinew, but there's more skin now. Its edges are crusted and blackened around the remaining open wounds. But *I have skin.* Everywhere. Intact and smooth as cream.

I can't stay upright for long, so Bronwyn reapplies her stinging oint-ments and replaces my bandages before helping me lie back down on my side. It takes some effort to find a position that doesn't make me wish I could scream.

"You'll be walking in a matter of days, Fleurie," Bronwyn says, her voice as gentle as her touch. "And the prince has agreed to let me take you outside a little at a time once your skin has renewed completely. Sunlight and fresh air will be good for you."

Sunlight. Fresh air.

I caught a glimpse of blue sky when the prince's guard carried me from the wagon to the entrance leading under the temple. Though I knew more darkness and captivity awaited, that moment had been a holy experience, seeing the light of day after such an age. I can't fathom basking in the light, but how I long for that simple freedom.

"I'll return in a few hours with more bone broth," Bronwyn says. Carefully, she tilts my chin. "Your throat is closing nicely. Receiving nourishment should be a much different adventure now."

I see genuine happiness on her face. I've also heard it in her voice over the past few weeks as my healing has improved. *Not an enemy.* I find myself thankful that I can infer such things at all anymore. That my raging hatred is compartmentalized inside my heart and mind, saved like a bottled hurricane to be unleashed on the one being who deserves my wrath: Thamaos.

Even if I must see him raised from the dead to do it.

Bronwyn stands and takes up her torch. When she turns to go, I notice that she pauses at the cell next to mine. Whispers scrape the air, and this isn't the first time. I can't make much of it, other than the prince's healer shouldn't be secretly fraternizing with a prisoner. Yet she is. Which is curious.

After a few more moments, Bronwyn leaves, and the dungeon door clangs closed.

"I must say, you're looking much better than when I first saw you. It won't be long until you're ready to take over the world. Literally."

I glance at my roommate. What I can see of him. Colden Moeshka.

During my first few days in this prison, I second-guessed how many years I believed had passed, though I'd felt so certain before, as the Ancient Ones whispered their promises on the wind. Colden Moeshka lived in *my* time, a bane to the gods, one of Neri's cursed soldiers from the

Northlands. It felt as though I'd fallen back three hundred years in time rather than three hundred years having passed.

But then I remembered the truth of it all. Here was the Frost King, telling me his name. Telling me that he knows Alexi. That he's heard Alexi speak of me.

That Alexi lives. As I had once been informed he would.

Alexi told me about Colden too. I recall clearly when my friend was sent to spy on the North, how he met the new northern king and even went with him to the Summerlands. Alexi did no harm there, much to Thamaos and King Gherahn's dismay. Upon his return, he confessed that he didn't dare reveal himself amid a city of Summerland mages.

The truth was that his journey changed him. He came back a different man. A *conflicted* man. A man who was about to face the most trying year of his life and didn't even know it.

Colden leans against the bars that divide our spaces. He's kind to me, but he talks a lot, his accent strange to my ear, his humor even more so. I long to tell him that I don't want to take over the world. That I never wanted that. And I ache to the dark pit of my core to ask him about Alexi, or perhaps to rip open the air and find my friend myself. But that isn't how things will unfold. This I know. And besides, I haven't been so lucky as to regain my voice or my magick.

And even when I do, *if* I do, it won't matter.

The prince keeps me collared, though the collar I wear now is thinner than the last. Less iron allows for faster healing. But it still serves its purpose, like the bracelets my father had his blacksmith weld around my wrists ages ago: to keep me pinned like a butterfly that would otherwise fly away.

But I wear another collar too. An invisible torque of magick. It stayed my tongue and even my hand three hundred years ago, when I had so many truths to share with the world, truths that might have saved my dearest friends.

After all this time, I still feel the torque's dominion over me.

The door creaks open, and then clangs shut again. I know it isn't Bronwyn by the sound of our visitor's feet. That soft, lazy slip of his boots on the stone steps as he makes his way into the dungeon. He's always dressed in dark-colored clothing, a smear of red around his feet.

His Highness, everyone calls him.

Except for Colden.

"Well, if it isn't the prince with no name. Back again."

"Fuck you, Moeshka," the prince says as he lets himself into my cell, though his words seem to hold less and less bite with each time he comes here.

"Oh, don't you wish," Colden jabs.

The prince's voice is the shadow of a voice I once knew. Given our current circumstances, the sound shouldn't make me feel comfort in the least, and yet it does. I long to see his face more clearly, but he never enters my cell with a torch in hand, like he doesn't trust me near open flame.

The prince squats at my bedside, hands clasped between his legs. "Bronwyn was right. You're healing so very well."

"What's her purpose here?" Colden asks. "I think *I* know. If the stories our very dear friend, Alexus, told me are true. But I also think *you* should tell her the gruesome details. That way her wrath is properly placed."

I can hear the mocking laughter in his voice. He thinks I don't know what I've done, why I'm here. They both do.

I made a deal. It had occurred to me when the prince stood over me in the pits, offering freedom for my aid, that I could say no. But I already knew I wouldn't. I know our future. I have seen it. This story began such a long time ago. I know the names and faces of the main players in our tale, one of whom is kneeling before me, lost to himself as he has ever been.

It's a thoughtless thing to do, but I reach out and touch the prince's face, tracing my finger over the soft curve of his strong cheekbone, remembering. Everyone's little prince.

Colden had called him the *prince with no name*.

But he has a name. And I know it.

How many hundreds of times has his name fallen from my lips?

He turns from my touch and pulls my hand away, placing it on the bed. The air between us pulls taut with a strangeness. Something more than general discomfort. Something like inquietude.

"When you're fully healed," he says, clearing his throat, "we need to have a chat about the specifics of our deal. It won't be much longer. Then, when it's over, you're free to roam this wide world as you wish."

I just nod. There's no argument to be had when you already know the outcome of a decision made. I'm going to open the world like a knife through time.

And change an old friend's life forever.

18

ALEXUS

Northland Break
Gravenna Mountains, North Side

F or the next week, we travel down the Northland Break toward the Gravenna Mountains, outrunning storms and stopping only for short rests.

Fleurie and Colden are still imprisoned, Fleurie's agonizing healing indeed causing an obvious delay in the prince's plans. Each day, Raina checks the waters three times, and each night, I thank my old friend for the reprieve she's given us, my heart sick to know she still suffers.

I also dream. Mostly of my time as a student and later headmaster of the School of Night and Dawn. But sometimes I dream of dying alongside Colden, and other times I dream of Fleurie—our secret rendezvous when we were young, fighting on the training fields once we were older, our days and nights chained to those horrific cliffs.

Sometimes I even see her coming for me, holding out her familiar hand. If the prince means to use her to find me, if he tricked her into a deal, then she must deliver or forfeit whatever she bargained. Likely her freedom. Which means she and I could end up in a very difficult position.

Raina dreams as well. Of the prince. Of her parents. Of Finn. Of me. She sleeps with Nephele now, to prevent more hot blood between me and Finn. But through the bond, we share every dream. Sometimes the effect is miniscule. Sometimes it's emotional and difficult. Other times I wake hard as a hilt, aching to be inside her. Then there are times that wound as deeply as any knife.

I'd be a liar if I said I didn't envy Finn the time he's had with Raina. Time he wasted. Time that I might never get.

But we travel on. And I keep breathing.

By the time we reach the Gravenna foothills a handful of days later, our food stores have dwindled. The scattered homesteads between the loch and the mountains offered meager supplies given that the valley's four main trading villages and their harvests are now gone. We've only a week and a half of travel left, through the mountain pass and on toward Malgros. But we won't make it unless we find more food.

After we build our nightly fire, it's decided that we must hunt, even though the area's main food source comes from the mighty Great Horn, the very beasts Warek and Silver Hollow's hunters had been pursuing when their village was attacked. It's a task Finn, Joran, and I quietly volunteer to take on while Raina, Nephele, and Helena clean up before we dine on mushed meal.

Come dawn, the three of us meet by the banked fire with our horses. Rhonin is there too, his hair unbraided and pulled back in a tail, bow and quiver in hand.

"I know a few women who won't be happy when they find out I let the three of you go off into the mountains together. With weapons, no less. I'm already on their shit list."

Finn buckles a thigh sheath around his leg, replete with two hunting knives, and straps on his quiver. "We're the best hunters in the bunch." His dusky face remains impassive. "It only makes sense."

"And I've no fear of a fiery wench," Joran says as he attaches two wound ropes to his saddle so we can drag the beasts from the wood. "Nephele Bloodgood holds no sway over me."

Nephele might not have held sway over Joran before we left Hampstead Loch, but now, something has shifted in the way he looks at her. They bicker every godsdamn second, but the moment her stomach grumbled last night, he decided he was in on the hunt.

"Fiery *wench*?" Rhonin says. "I *dare* you to say that to her face." With a snort-laugh, he hands me his quiver. "I'm more fearful of *them* than any of you bastards. Hel will have my balls strung from her belt."

Without breaking a smile, Finn says, "I don't think that's where my sister wants your balls, Rho. Lucky for you, I guess."

Rhonin's face flames as he rests his brawny hands on his hips. "Just try not to kill each other. For my sake."

"Whatever do you mean?" Purposefully, I unfurl a sly grin. "The three of us are becoming fast friends. Can't you tell?"

I peer at Joran who's already glaring at me, then I look at Finn. He grabs his bow, bracing it against his foot as he strings it. Every movement is so familiar and practiced that his eyes remain on me the entire time, narrowed and hardened with bitterness he pretends he doesn't feel.

"Pretty sure you'd all rather starve than be alone together," Rhonin says. "I can go in someone's place if you want. I'm no hunter, but these hands can kill just about anything if I can get close enough."

"A Great Horn might be a challenge even for you, my friend," I tell him. Quickly, I check the knives at my hips and the quiver across my back, and I drape the rope that ties four water flasks together across Mannus's back. "Besides, there are more people to consider than ourselves. The three of us will survive." I glance at my companions as Rhonin gives me his bow. "Won't we?"

Joran's only response is a huff of breath as he mounts his horse, cocks a silvery brow, and rides into the mist toward the tree line, leaving me and Finn to follow.

◉⟡◉

HALF AN HOUR LATER, GUIDED BY THE FRAIL LIGHT OF DAWN, WE CREEP through the Gravenna Forest. Quietly, we fill the group's flasks with fresh water from a spring, tie the horses, then Finn and I follow Joran as he takes the lead.

He weaves through the tall pine trees, soundless as a shadow. The mist looms, but it's thin enough to see the forest floor. With a sharp eye, Joran studies the ground for tracks, droppings, and beds, eyeing the massive pines and cedars for rubs and nearby ground scrapes. He's doing everything right, but I'm still not convinced this arrangement is best. To my knowledge, he's never been this far south, and though he might be a talented bowyer, Gravenna territory is a stranger, its beasts foreign. Great Horns are different animals from the deer of the North, something I explained earlier only for him to turn his ear. They're carnivorous and fast, a herd of predators that will take down anything that moves. Their heads are armed with a crown of antlers made to gore, their mouths loaded with two rows of razor-sharp teeth for ripping apart meat. This is their home. In this forest, *we* are the prey.

And yet Joran stalks onward with no fear, as though he designed this wood and its every inhabitant himself.

Finally, we hear water and move toward the sound, slipping across the wide stream, from rock to rock. Once we reach the other side, Joran points to what we all knew we'd find if we located a water source: a trail, worn and covered in hoof prints, a path traveled often. Not because the Great Horn doesn't know that using the same trail is a giveaway to where they nest, but because they don't care. They do not fear the humans that enter this wood.

The Icelander starts forward again, walking parallel to the path. And again, Finn and I follow with me bringing up the rear. We move on for a long while as the gray morning light turns the shade of a bruise. There are ten to fifteen paces between each of us, our steps careful and quiet as we duck under low-hanging boughs and lunge over fallen limbs. If we catch the beasts sleeping, we'll have a slight advantage. Great Horns know how to protect themselves, and if they sense us in the least, we could already be walking into a trap.

Joran takes a left turn behind a giant boulder, still following the curve of the herd's path. When I round the rock, I find Finn and the Icelander standing stock still, except Joran stands about thirty strides ahead, face to face with an enormous Great Horn.

And nine more beasts waiting behind it.

Finn reaches for an arrow, but I grab his wrist. These ten animals could be a distraction. I can feel more, can see their shapes taking form in the

surrounding mist lurking between the trees. Watching. Closing in.
Salivating.

Finn jerks from my grasp. "Don't fucking touch me, you bastard."

My blood rises. "If they attack us because of you, I'm letting you die
this time, you little shit."

So much for working past our differences.

A rough wind rushes through the wood, twisting around trees,
whistling over the forest floor, rustling leaves. That wind is cold. *Stinging*
cold. Like a *northern* wind. One we shouldn't feel this far south. I glance
down, only to spot a dusting of frost around me.

Neri. That bastard is *still* following us.

I scan the wood once more, searching for any sign of the northern god's
spirit, but there is none. Not even the usual tingle of awareness that drips
down my spine when he's near.

I summon energy from the wood, earth, and rising sun, as some of the
Great Horns bristle and snort, bearing their teeth and pawing the ground
as though they sense something wrong in the air too, other than our
presence.

Power tingles in my hands. If these beasts *do* attack, I'm not certain
that I can stop them all without harming Joran and Finn too.

Another wind blows, hard enough that Finn leans with the force of it,
but after a few moments, the strangest thing happens. The beast standing
before Joran turns sideways, standing still and perpendicular to us, vital
organs vulnerable.

A second Great Horn moves from the back of the herd and joins the
first beast, positioning itself the same way, almost as though volunteering
to be an offering.

Joran takes three strides backwards and gives a slight, reverent bow.
Before I can do anything to stop him, he whips an arrow free from his
quiver, notches it, and lets it fly, the fletching whistling straight toward the
first beast's heart.

The arrow sinks into the leader's massive body, a perfect, clean shot,
and the Great Horn falls. I watch the other animals closely, power crackling in my hands like clenched lightning, waiting for nine Great Horns to
rush us with those murderous horns. But instead, when Joran sinks the
second arrow into the second beast, the rest of the herd lets out low,

vibrating growls that morph into sorrowful groans, as though mourning the loss. The last thing I expect is for the animals to turn and leave, but that's what they do, vanishing into the trees.

Finn blows out a long breath. "Neri. Raina told me what it was like when he's near. I felt him, and I prayed to him. And he provided."

Letting my gathered power dim back into the atmosphere, I look at Finn as though he's dim. "Neri would never help feed us."

Though it *would* explain why two Great Horns offered themselves as a sacrifice rather than burying their antlers in our guts.

"Maybe not *you*," Finn says. "I don't want to put food in your belly either, but I don't really have a fucking choice since we're all in this together."

"Or perhaps you're *both* wrong." Joran unstrings his bow and rests it against a tree. Glaring at us from beneath his heavy brow, he unsheathes his hunting knife and stalks to the felled animals where he kneels, says a quiet prayer, and begins the unmaking of the animal. "Gods rarely do anything that isn't self-serving, right? This could just be part of his plan."

"Feeding us?" I join him, roll my sleeves, and begin dressing the second animal.

He opens his beast's belly. "Keeping you alive so he can strike a deal for help once he gets to the City of Ruin."

"I've made one deal with that bastard," I reply, cutting through the tough hide. "That was enough. Never again."

"Not even for his aid? Not even to stop Thamaos and the prince?"

I pause my work and meet the Icelander's gray stare. "There are enough evils in this world. I've already freed Neri's spirit. The last thing I'll do is give him life again, and that's what he wants."

Joran sits back on his heels, scrubbing the wrist of his bloody hand across his forehead. "Evil? Perhaps you should reconsider your definition of that word, and then what *evils* you're willing to endure, Collector. Malgros is nigh, then you face the Malorian Sea and the Summerlands. The battles ahead are many. Perhaps this band could use a mighty weapon of its own."

"It *has* a weapon," I say. "Me."

With that, we drop the conversation. After a half-hour of work, I wash my hands as best I can with water from one of the flasks, then Finn and I leave Joran to finish the carcasses while we trudge toward the stream for the horses. Finn stalks alongside me, quiet, but I can feel his eyes on me from time to time.

"Just say it," I tell him. "Whatever it is you're fucking thinking."

"I'm thinking that you're a godsdamn coward and fool for not helping Neri, and for telling Raina to not help him too. If you plan to fight a battle, or worse, a war, you need him on your side."

My temper flares, but again, I refuse to have this discussion. It isn't easy, but I say nothing as we near the stream.

Finn isn't so silent now.

"She's going to see you for what you are, you know. Eventually."

I step over a downed tree and pause, irritation drawing my muscles rigid. "And what exactly is that?"

Finn stops too. "A fraud. A cold-hearted murderer lies beneath that skin. A traitor. An enemy of the north. She will see. Hopefully before we leave Malgros's shores. Regardless, I will be there when she does."

I step closer to him. He tries to hold my gaze, but he looks me over. I washed, but I'm still a sight. My hands still have speckled blood on them, up to my elbows. Blood stains my tunic too. I even feel a little splattered on my face.

"Want to know what *I'm* thinking?" I ask.

He swallows. Hard. "Not really."

I lean in. Get in his face. "Too bad. Because I'm thinking that most of what you said is true. I *was* that man a long time ago, but I'm not anymore. Except maybe the cold-hearted part, which places you in a heap of fucking trouble. Because of all people, it will probably be you who learns just how cold-hearted I can be."

I start walking again, leaving Finn standing in my wake.

"I don't follow," he calls.

And I don't reply. I just know that I meant what I said earlier.

Next time, I'll let him die.

19

RAINA

The Northland Coast
Malgros

Malgros shines in the distance, radiating a golden arc across the starlit sky.

Alexus and Mannus guide our band with me and Tuck close behind. We're bone-weary and sore, hungry and dirty, but the promise of relief is finally near.

There are lookouts and gates at each of the seven rocky hills surrounding Malgros, with a looming city wall connecting each one to the next. Starworth Tor is one of those lookouts, the very first to the west. The property overlooks the shoreline and consists of Captain Osane's home and Malgros's old lighthouse.

That's where we're headed. Starworth Tor is the only gate Alexus believes might provide safe entry to the city because it's rarely used, located so close to the cliffs. He knows the captain well, but their friendship is a secret, a way for Alexus and Colden to have privacy when they come here.

I tighten my hands around the reins and try not to think about getting caught as we ride through the night, nearer to the wall. It's at least four stories high, hiding the city that lies beyond. Even from this distance, I can see the wards shielding the gates and the many braziers and torchlights glowing atop the dark stone ramparts. I imagine the sentries from the Northland Watch patrolling the battlements.

Tears prick my eyes, stinging in the wind. My parents shared tales of their time serving in the Watch, but I never pictured a city so vast and filled with enough life that it lights up such a large stretch of land.

Alexus takes a sharp right turn, leading us parallel to the city wall and Palgard Gate. According to Rhonin, this is the gate through which the prince and his army passed under the cover of darkness—without difficulty. I've yet to break through the barrier that shields the prince, but there's no doubt that he has people inside this city who will be watching for our arrival. Including General Vexx, who I *have* seen.

To our benefit, the night is as dark as the abyss that lives in my mind. Earlier, we traveled with Alexus's starlights, but now we lean on the gift of our horses' night vision. Alexus rides confidently, though, and soon we're safely out of sight of Palgard Gate.

We ride until the distant crash of the sea against the rocky coast meets my ears, and a comfortable, briny wind tangles my hair. There are cliffs near, so Alexus deploys his starlights again, scattered about the night like fireflies.

As we near the end of the wall on the western side, we slow our horses to a trot. Here, the wall has tapered to a lower height. Two stories, perhaps. Only two guards stand between torches on the battlements, but Starworth Gate is otherwise secured by wards. They don't appear as strong as the wards that surround the prince, but their tangled web glimmers a threat in the darkness, nonetheless.

"Let me handle this," Alexus says over his shoulder. "But glamours up."

Everyone bristles, even me, and a gentle wash of power fills the air as those of us who need to erect shields over our witch's marks quickly construct our glamours. Nephele glamours our weapons.

"Be convincing, be clever, or have a windfall of luck," I hear Rhonin say, repeating Alexus's words from our meeting in the library at Winterhold.

"I think we're trying for all three tonight," Hel replies.

My heart begins a steady, hard thumping as I move my hand to rest on the dagger sheathed at my thigh.

"Easy, Raina," Finn says, bringing his horse adjacent to mine. "I'm here."

As though I need his protection.

I try to ignore him, but it's becoming ever more difficult. Time for anything except riding, checking the waters, and learning to dismantle runes has been limited on this journey. But Finn has seen me practice the sword with Helena and Rhonin a few times. Thanks to a year of training with Hel, I can wield a blade as good—if not better—than her brother, even when I'm hungry and exhausted. Finn knows I'm not a defenseless, helpless creature. And yet he still treats me as one.

My irritation is distracted by a gravelly, woodsmoked voice that drifts from the ramparts. "Who goes there?"

One of the men takes up a torch and holds it over the wall's edge.

"Harmon?" Alexus calls. "Is that you?"

"'Tis me. Who's you?"

Familiarity. This is good. *Very* good.

Alexus laughs and summons his starlights closer to reveal his face, though he doesn't say a word.

The man leans forward. There's a pause, and then, "Oh, my lord! My lord! Just a moment!" He disappears, but I can still hear him. "Dru! Open the gate! It's Master Thibault!"

Our group exhales a collective sigh. I unclench my fingers from my weapon and take a deep breath. Sometimes I wonder if I will ever know what it is to live peacefully, without panic rearing its head.

"Thank the gods that was easy," Nephele says from beside me, arching the long line of her spine into a stretch. "I can't get off this horse fast enough."

"You've certainly had your practice at riding these last weeks," Joran says from behind her, where he stays. "You just need a little instruction on how to better sit in the saddle." His voice deepens. "I'd be glad to teach you."

Groans resonate from the riders behind me. Hel and Rhonin mainly.

My sister tosses a disgusted glare over her shoulder. "Why do I hear sexual innuendo in those stupid words?"

Joran enjoys poking my sister like the bear she is, so I'm not surprised when one side of his mouth pulls up and he says, "Why indeed?"

Fuming, she opens her mouth to land a retort, but thankfully, their bickering is cut short. The portcullis rises with a screeching groan, and the wooden gate beyond is thrown open. Harmon bursts from the darkness carrying his torch. Smiling, Alexus holds out a hand, and Harmon grabs it.

"My lord, it's been ages!" The older man lifts the torch and waves it around to better see the rest of us. "We weren't expecting you."

"I know, and for that I apologize. Though I hope we're welcome," Alexus replies.

Harmon waves him off. "My lord, you're welcome here anytime. Your rooms remain well kept for your arrival. Always." Harmon looks at the rest of us again. "Does this have something to do with the Watch's heavier presence at the gates?"

Alexus frowns and shakes his head. "What do you mean?"

"The gates, my lord. As of late, anyone who enters is taken to the Watch. There were rumors that a large band of foreigners snuck into the city from the docks and through Palgard Gate one night many weeks back, but little was said about it. Now the gates are being watched so closely. No one knows why, for sure."

"I think I have a good idea," Alexus says, peering up at the ramparts. "No heavier surveillance here though?"

Unease flashes across Harmon's face. "Even here, my lord. I sent the guards from the Watch home for the night a couple of hours ago, to give them a rest. The cap'n doesn't like 'em around. Luckily, they don't want to be here either."

"Luck," Rhonin murmurs behind me.

"I see," Alexus says. "That could be a problem during our stay, but I'll speak with the captain. For now, please keep word of our arrival silent."

Harmon bows. "Of course, my lord. As always, no one will know you're here. You and yours are safe with us."

Two tall young men with blond hair and golden, sun-kissed skin walk through the gate carrying torches. They appear to be twins. Alexus swings down from Mannus's back and nods at them in greeting.

"Dru. Drae. If some of my friends help, can you two join your father in seeing our horses to the stables while I take everyone else to the main house?"

The young men hurry forward. One of them takes Mannus by the bridle. "Absolutely, my lord," he says. "I'll help. Drae should notify the cap'n that you're here."

"Very well," Alexus says, motioning for Drae to come closer. He says something privately to the boy, eliciting a small smile. When Drae turns and bolts through the gate, Alexus removes his pack from Mannus's back and slings the strapping across his chest, facing us. "Good ride, all. Let's go get some food and rest."

With groans and sighs, we dismount our stiff bodies and follow Alexus and Harmon, guiding our horses into the shallow tunnel that leads to the main property. As Callan and I pass the gate, they take me by my elbow and pause.

"See this?" They tap a finger on the wood and drag it along a glimmering line, from rune to rune, and back up a second line. "This portion of the ward's construct allows the gate to be opened from the *inside*," they say. "Just not from the outside. It's all in the design. Do you see how?"

I look closer. The runes for protected passage are there. Twice. The mirrored versions are reversed.

Callan taps their temple. "Something to remember, should you ever need to seal yourself away."

Any magick can be undone. I can't help but remember those words from my father. But magickal knowledge is magickal knowledge, so I lock that tidbit in the back of my mind for safekeeping.

When we step from the tunnel into the open night, Alexus's starlights rush forth and multiply, swelling like light-filled bubbles, illuminating the rear of the sprawling white stone estate and lighthouse. The structures sit perched on a rocky cliffside dotted with tufts of seagrass, a ledge at what feels like the end of the world.

We all pause, staring wide-eyed at the sight, taking in this home and Alexus's magick moons, the salty wind soft around us, laced with a floral scent. Jasmine, I think. The beauty in the moment takes my breath.

"That's new," Harmon says, motioning toward Alexus's magick. "But I like it!"

Dru, Finn, Callan, Keth, and Jaega, gather the reins of our horses and lead the animals down a worn path toward the stables. Before Harmon follows, he smiles and claps Alexus on the shoulder. "It's so good to have you back on the tor, my lord. I wish you a peaceful and uneventful stay."

Alexus smiles too and returns the gesture, resting his hand on Harmon's stooped shoulder. Though I can tell he's happy to be here, I also feel his worry seeping through the rune.

Uneventful is unlikely.

"It's good to be back, my friend," he says.

Then he turns and leads us to meet the captain.

🐍

ALL I CAN THINK AS WE CLIMB THE WIDE STEPS TOWARD THE MAIN house is that Starworth Tor is unlike anything my mind could've conjured. Even with Alexus's magick extinguished, the white stone facade glows beneath the soft moonlight. Candlelight warms the massive windows that cover the front and side of the house, and ornate wooden shutters— chained to the stone—flank each glazed opening that overlooks the sea, sentinels awaiting an incoming storm.

The world seems so quiet and peaceful as we reach the vestibule near the main entrance. There are six torchlit stone pillars flanking the pathway between us and the main door, an arched, wooden affair with intricate carvings. When the door opens, we pause between the vestibule's first two columns.

Except for Alexus. Pack slung across his broad chest, he keeps walking toward the tall, umber-skinned woman stepping across the threshold. She waits at the doorway, inside a triangle of candlelight radiating from an outdoor chandelier. Wearing sand-colored trousers and a black linen tunic, she shoves at one of her rolled sleeves, pushing it to her elbow.

Despite the woman's loose-fitting clothes, it's obvious that her long form is lean and strong. Her black hair is close-cropped and beginning to gray, and her shoulders are squared and her chin set. She's a little intimidating with such stature and those piercing, dark eyes.

The captain.

With a book dangling from one hand, she moves further outside and meets Alexus nearly eye-to-eye beneath the chandelier. The stare she directs over his shoulder makes me want to recoil, uncertain if we're as welcome here as Harmon said. Nervously, I shift my pack from one shoulder to the other as she devotes her attention to Alexus.

"Zahira Osane," he says. "It's been too long, old friend."

Alexus has told me about his friends here, how he met them while in Malgros for meetings with the Watch years ago. But I still find myself unsure what to think as the pair stand face to face *or* when the woman rips off her spectacles and gives Alexus a thorough and measured once-over.

"Yes, it has," she replies. "Three years." She draws a deep breath, tucks her book beneath her arm, and slips her spectacles into her trouser pocket. She looks so severe. But then a bright smile spreads across her face. "Which is far too long, you beautiful, magickal bastard. Don't just stand there. Kiss me, for gods' sakes."

Light-hearted joy floods the rune as Alexus cups Zahira's face and kisses both apples of her cheeks. He presses his forehead to hers, and she fists a handful of his hair, holding him to her. They remain frozen in that intimate stance for several long moments, happiness radiating from them both. That feeling fills my heart with warmth.

"You have explaining to do," I hear her say.

"You have no idea," he replies.

Another woman, wearing a cream-colored tunic and leggings, appears in the doorway behind them. Her hair is pinned in a crown of loose curls, the dark mane interspersed with silver strands that compliment her golden-brown skin.

"Alexus Thibault? Is that really you?"

Zahira steps aside, still smiling, while the other woman bounds toward Alexus and throws herself into his waiting arms. The impact knocks a laugh out of him, but he barely stumbles, holding her against him, her feet off the ground.

"You act as though you've missed me, Yaz." He lowers her until her bare feet touch the stone entryway once more and kisses her forehead. "And I know that can't be true."

"*Never.*" Yaz presses one hand to his face and clutches the buckles of his jacket in the other. She lets a gentle smile unfurl and winks. "All right. Maybe a little."

Breaking the tender moment, Zahira raises a brow. "We're thrilled to see you." She gestures our way. "But is there a reason you've brought a small army to our door? Without Colden?"

"Unfortunately, yes." Alexus glances over his shoulder, then faces the women again as his voice momentarily dims.

As he talks, the women's expressions turn grave, and the color drains from their cheeks. Zahira wraps a comforting arm around Yaz's shoulders. Shaking her head, Yaz presses her hand to her stomach, then to her mouth, as though what Alexus is telling them is making her sick. I'm sure it is.

Alexus's voice finally becomes audible again. "I'll explain in more detail later. For now, these Northlanders need rooms for a few nights, if you're comfortable with having us in your home."

Zahira reaches for Alexus's hand and gives it a squeeze. "Of course we are." She steps to the threshold and rings a small bell that hangs near the door. "If some of you can double up, there should be plenty of beds."

The house is expansive, but can it be so easy to care for so many on a whim?

Yaz motions for us to join them. Nephele, Hel, and I lead the way, and Alexus rushes through an introduction of each member as we approach.

The moment I reach his side, he says, "And this is Raina."

Gently, *lovingly*, he brushes his fingers across the back of my hand. After so little contact these last weeks, this simple caress is enough to make my heart skip a beat. Unashamed and with no fear, I take his hand in mine. He stares down at me with surprise that softens into a smile. Gods, I've missed him.

I inhale a shaky breath and face our guests. Zahira and Yaz lift their curious stares from our hands and study our faces instead, as though they see something more than what stands before them.

My cheeks heat.

"Nice to meet you, Raina," Yaz says. "Nice to meet you *all*. I'm Yazmin, Zahira's partner. You can call me Yaz."

Her gaze travels back to mine, and though I return the smile she offers, I make no move to sign. I'm too exhausted to get into that discussion tonight, and there will be questions later regardless. I can already see them dancing in Yaz's stormy eyes.

Having been summoned, a young woman, older than Hel but younger than me, hurries outside in a white nightrail and robe. She draws up short at the sight of our haggard mob of warriors, standing like statues in the middle of the vestibule.

A sea wind writhes through the columns, lifting her chestnut-colored hair, revealing blue and copper witch's marks on the pale column of her neck, marks she quickly glamours as she assesses the unexpected situation. Fire *and* water magick. A combination that explains the ability to quickly prepare baths for a horde.

The woman's attention is distracted by Joran who breaks away from our clan and strolls toward the rocky knoll that overlooks the dark sea beyond, as though he's bored by the formal introduction. As Joran passes the young woman, she gathers the front of her robe in her fists and shrinks like a wilting flower, a wary gleam in her eyes.

Good instinct.

Joran holds up a hand. "No fear, darling. Bit young for my taste."

He glances at Nephele, so brief I almost miss it. I slip a look at my sister, easily reading the irked expression on her face. She would throttle him if we didn't need him.

"Guard dog?" Zahira asks Alexus.

"Not at all." He watches the Icelander with a sharp eye. "Water witch. Bowyer. Jackass."

"Ah," Zahira says, as though that's the only explanation needed. And I suppose it is.

Yaz motions for the young woman to join her. "This is our friend Mari. She helps tend the house. Mari, this is—" She pauses, as though reconsidering her words.

"It's all right," Alexus says. "If you trust her, so do I."

Yaz lets out a breath. "This is our friend Alexus Thibault, and his friends. They'll be staying with us for a few nights."

Mari bows. "Nice to meet you, my lord."

Alexus dips his head in greeting. "Nice to meet you, as well." He turns to Zahira and Yaz. "There are ten of us. A few are helping Harmon and his sons with the horses. He looks at me and holds my gaze for a long moment. "I can take the lighthouse as usual, of course."

I feel a question vibrating along the bond. It isn't spoken, not something audible I can hear. But a knowing. He's asking if I want to stay with him now that we're here. In the lighthouse. Separate from the main house. *Private*.

A tender chill courses over my skin, and I respond, squeezing his hand. *Yes. Yes, yes, yes.*

Alexus's mouth quirks up, and his dimple appears, as if I just made his day a thousand times better. And that makes me happy. I must think about us right now. What we need in this sliver of time we've been given. I can't worry about Finn's feelings forever. He chose to come along on this journey, knowing my situation. He won't like the arrangement, but he will have to accept it.

"Of course," Zahira says, glancing between us with a subdued grin. "The lighthouse it is."

"Mari, can you prepare the rooms and baths?" Yaz asks.

Mari stares at Alexus for a moment longer, then turns a second look over her shoulder at Joran who stands near a ledge, leaning his weight on the stone, the wind playing in his silver hair. I sense hesitance in the woman, especially when Joran turns his head and meets her gaze.

She breaks the stare-down between them and nods to Yazmin. "Certainly. I'll be quick, my lady."

When Mari vanishes inside the house, Zahira heads toward the main door. At the threshold, she smiles at our weary crew and sweeps an arm inside. "Welcome to the city by the sea, everyone. And welcome to Starworth Tor."

20

RAINA

The inside of Starworth Tor's main house is just as impressive as the exterior.

Decorative bronze sconces and candle chandeliers illuminate the home with warm and inviting light, showcasing the high ceilings, elaborate staircase, and exposed wooden crossbeams above. I don't mean to gawk, but the entry and sitting parlor are larger than the cottage I shared with my family. There are more candles in this single part of the house than I've probably burned in my entire life. They aren't tallow either. The smell of beeswax permeates the air. Honeyed. Sweet. A little musky.

It reminds me of Alexus's magick.

Zahira guides the rest of us deeper inside the house. She doesn't so much walk as she glides, her footsteps soundless on the slate-tiled floor. As we enter, I cling to Alexus's hand while, on his other side, Yaz links her arm with his.

Hesitation fills me and lines every face around me when we reach the great room. It isn't the size of the space that gives us pause, though. It's massive enough to seat us all, even if a few must take the floor.

But the fine furniture and rugs... They're more exquisite than anything I've ever seen, even at Winterhold. Each piece is unique and exotic, made from pale, smooth woods covered in lush fabrics and pillows.

Far too lovely for a bunch of filthy travelers.

We crane our necks to take it all in. Artwork and tapestries hang along the white-plastered side walls, while packed bookshelves line the back of the room. Each cracked, gilded, and pristine spine beckons.

Windows make up much of the wall that houses the stone hearth, a stately affair that—like the bookshelves—reaches the ceiling. A low fire burns to ward off the slight chill from the sea wind, but the air here is far warmer than what I'm accustomed to this time of the year. A refreshing change.

"It's all right," Zahira says. "Come in. Get off your feet. Let those glamours go. Yaz and I will bring food and wine while you wait for your rooms."

How did she know?

Again, I squeeze Alexus's hand. When he looks at me, I form the question on my face.

"She can see through glamours," he says softly. "Quite handy to have around."

As everyone cautiously drops their glamours and packs and finds a place to rest, Yaz and Zahira head toward the corridor that must lead to the kitchen. At the same time, Joran swaggers into the room, nearly colliding with Zahira.

"Beautiful home," he says to both women. "Fit for the gods."

Zahira clasps her hands together and inclines her head. "Thank you, but somehow I doubt Starworth is any comparison to Eridan's luxurious palaces of marble and gold."

Joran skims an appreciative look over the room. "I think we'd be surprised to learn what some of the gods considered luxury. Especially Neri. Though I'm beginning to think we could always just ask him."

Alexus, paused with me by the bookshelves, turns a dark look on the Icelander, but before he can say or do anything, Nephele interrupts.

"Uhm, about that food and wine." She steps forward, forcing a smile. Her body is tight as a drum, as though she's as worried as the rest of us that if Joran is allowed to talk for too long, he might insult our hosts. "I can help in the kitchen," she says. "Three pairs of hands are better than two."

Joran eyes my sister, obviously aware of what she's doing. His irises all but glow with the fire of a welcomed challenge, the way they always do lately when Nephele is abrasive towards him, as though he likes the rub. "I can help too," he says. "Four pairs of hands are better than three. Even if I must dodge Nephele's icy eye daggers."

My sister fists her hands, the muscle in her jaw ticking. "Or real ones," she hisses.

Yaz sputters a laugh. "I can see that you two are a ball of fun. I'm surprised you made it here in one piece, Joran."

"No more surprised than me," Nephele says.

Zahira looks at Alexus, her eyes widening a fraction before she turns back to Nephele and Joran and gestures to the corridor. "Come. I'm sure Yaz and I can use you both. Just keep your hands off the knives."

The moment passes as Yaz and Zahira lead my sister and Joran from the room. With the tension gone, everyone relaxes, some settling into their seats, some taking in the home's beauty.

Alexus sits on the edge of an elegant desk, strips off his pack and mine, and pulls me onto his knee. It's such a comfortable action, a closeness I desperately need, yet it takes a moment to relax against him. It's been nearly two months since the night of the attack, but we haven't had the chance to be open with our affections, or to share them with each other these last weeks at all.

Hel looks us over and bites back a smile, then walks to the windows near the hearth that I now realize are doors. Beyond, as far as the outdoor torchlight reaches, I can make out a veranda and pots of vibrantly colored flowers.

"Damn the gods, Alexus," Hel says. "You chose a cold castle over *this*?"

"I did," he answers, squeezing my hip. "The valley and the wood always felt more like home, though I do love it here."

Rhonin crosses the room to stand with Hel, hands stuffed in his trouser pockets. He brushes a shoulder against hers. "Feel like a stroll along the beach? I'd love to show you the water."

Hel's dark eyes light up. "I would love that." She turns to Alexus. "Is it all right, you think? Safe?"

Alexus nods toward the veranda. "Yes, it's private. Go out the doors, take the stairs to the left. There's a gate that leads to a secluded cove. Yaz usually has a few chairs down there." He smiles. "Have fun, you two. Careful of the tides."

Bouncing on her toes, Hel drags Rhonin outside. The smile on that boy's face is so bright it could give the moon a challenge. It warms my heart to see how much he cares for Hel, even if she hasn't succumbed to his charm quite yet.

Several minutes later, Mari strolls into the room, fidgeting with the sash of her robe. Her eyes are downcast. "The chambers are ready, my lord. Baths too. I can show everyone their accommodations, even those who are still at the stables."

I'm amazed how quickly she made that happen.

"Your efforts are much appreciated," Alexus says. "Especially at this hour."

"Yes, thank you, Mari," Zahira says as she and Joran enter the room. They carry silver platters of food while Nephele and Yaz follow, cradling several bottles of wine in each of their arms. The platters are placed on two marble tables positioned before the settees where members of our group have perched their tired bums. Fruits, cheeses, and salted fish fill two platters, portions arranged on individual white linens made for carrying, while an array of breads fill a third tray.

"Dig in," Yaz says. "And we'll show you to your rooms."

Any hesitation preceding the moment vanishes. Everyone swoops in, Alexus and I included, our stomachs far too empty for etiquette. Joran is the only one who holds back.

Alexus reaches into the crowd gathered over the tables and procures a bottle of wine in one hand, while the other hand plucks a bundled linen of food. He hands me both before grabbing our heavy packs and slinging them onto his body.

"I'll talk to you two in a while if that's all right," he says to Zahira and Yaz. "For now, I'd like to get Raina settled in the lighthouse and get cleaned up."

Zahira holds up her hands. "Go. Get that woman off her feet."

He looks at me, a twinkle in his eye, and jerks his head toward the veranda. "Ladies first."

21

RAINA

Now I understand why the night air is tinted with such a lovely aroma.

We reach the end of the veranda and climb two flights of stone steps that lead to an iron gate, the source of the scent is clear. Drae is there, standing on the other side, and behind him stands a long arbor lit by hanging torches. They illuminate a gravel path that bisects a grand garden.

The flagstone walkway is lined with winter jasmine, the arbor smothered by woody, twining wisteria vines. There's even a large bird bath in the center of it all.

But my gaze rests on the towering lighthouse at the garden's end. Mullioned windows surround the top of the structure beneath the cupola, but they're dark tonight. It's the few windows below that are aglow.

Harmon's son opens the gate. "Welcome home, sir. Father is taking your friends to the main house now. I lit the candles and lamps in the lighthouse for you and the lady and started a fire in the hearth. The loft's catwalk needs repairs, so I wouldn't use it until the rusted steel has been replaced. Also, Father, my brother, and I live in the garden house now. Should you need anything, just ring the bell."

"Good to know. We should be fine, Drae," Alexus assures him. "Thank you for your help tonight."

Minutes later, I'm standing in a rather large, round room that couldn't be more like Alexus Thibault. Where the home decor of the main house was bright and white, soft and neat, this space is filled with an eclectic array of rich wood furniture, the upholstered pieces covered in gray, black, and blue jacquard. Books are everywhere, stacked neatly around the candlelit room, and a display of ancient weapons hangs above the hearth.

There's no tub on the main floor though, which disappoints me a little. Okay, a lot. I don't mean to be ungrateful, and I absolutely want to stay with Alexus tonight, but I'm certain I must reek like horse. A thin coating of old sweat, dust, and grime clings to my skin.

"Here, let me." He takes the food and wine from my hands.

"Do you stay here often?" I sign. Drae called it *home* after all.

"Not as much as I used to." Alexus looks around as if to make certain all his things are in their proper places. "When the lighthouse went out of use, and the new one was built further east, Zahira decided this could be an excellent guest house. I came here one summer to help with the renovations and repairs, added the chimney and hearth and garden house, and I took a liking to this place. Zahira dubbed it my second home, and that's what it's been for nearly ten years now." He nods at a stack of mugs on a small table near the hearth. "Grab two of those and let's go upstairs. I have a surprise."

I curl a finger through the handles of two mugs and trail behind him up the winding staircase until we reach the loft. Surprised, I pause near a dressing table and floor-length mirror to fully take in the cozy quarters. There's a wardrobe, two cushioned chairs, and a simple table with an oil lamp in the center. There's also a small writing desk with everything a writer might need, and a narrow sitting bench made from driftwood. The anchoring piece is a finely carved four-post bed with dark blue linens and white gossamer draped from canopy to floor.

The bed is appealing, especially given the fact that I haven't slept in one since Winterhold, but it's the glass door covered by a sheer curtain to my left that draws my eye.

"Catwalk," Alexus warns as he sets the wine bottle and food on the table and strips off our packs, dumping them on the floor with a *thud*. "Lovely view out there, but if the walkway is unstable, we'll be avoiding it during our stay."

More disappointment strikes. I make a sullen face, envisioning strolling outside to watch the sun rise and wondering what the stars must look like from up here. I realize that might be how this place received its name.

Alexus unbuckles his black jacket, revealing the midnight tunic beneath. He tosses the jacket on a chair, then leans against the bedpost, one hand resting on his hip. Humor dances in his eyes, chased by a naughty glint.

"That pout of yours is adorable. It does things to me you can't possibly imagine. But it's unnecessary. The lantern room is above us, and it has a catwalk too. Besides, would you believe that I can do far better than either of those views?"

Stealing a glance at the continuing staircase, I decide that I will most certainly enjoy that view come morning. But for now, I'm more curious about this lure Alexus is so easily baiting me with. I set our mugs beside our dinner and move toward the Witch Collector. He looks so inviting standing there, somehow even more devastatingly handsome when he's filthy.

"*I would believe you capable of nearly anything,*" I sign before slipping my arms around his waist.

His grin curls a little at the edges, and he touches my face, the way he always touches it, like it's made of delicate glass. "That's what I was hoping you'd say," he whispers, leaning down to kiss me.

He kisses me slowly, sensually, and I savor every moment pressed against him, folded in his arms. When he pulls away, we breathe each other in like air, like we've been holding our breath for the last three weeks.

"Now," he says, shaking his head as if to clear it. "Back to the surprise I mentioned before you completely distracted me with your mouth." I smile as he jerks his thumb over his shoulder toward an inconspicuous door I haven't noticed until this very moment. It's arched and painted white to match the plastered walls. "Want to see?" he asks.

I nod emphatically.

Smiling, Alexus crosses to the wardrobe and retrieves a stack of clothes and a black silken robe from the cabinet. He lays them out on the bed and says, "For later."

I find myself reaching for the robe, rubbing the silk between my fingers. It's his, as are the tunics and all else, and I long to crawl inside each piece.

Alexus pours our wine. After hooking the mugs with his finger, he offers me a piece of bread smeared with goat cheese and gathers our bundled food.

He lifts his occupied hands and glances at the door. "Do you mind?"

Munching on an enormous bite of rye, I hurry across the room and drag the heavy slab open for him, unprepared for the sight that awaits. In fact, I swallow my lump of food and blink, certain I must be hallucinating or dreaming.

There's a landing. And another set of stairs. They lead to a mass of rocks below the lighthouse, at the edge of the tor, lit up by three blazing torchlights and a flaming brazier. And there, nestled inside those rocks, under a sea of stars, is a small, steaming pool of bright blue water.

I turn back to Alexus, flabbergasted.

"Go on." He winks and flashes a playful smile. "I promised you wine and a bath days ago, and I always deliver."

My excitement is uncontainable. I stuff the rest of the bread in my mouth and hurry down the stairs. Alexus follows—I can feel his smile through the rune—and his starlights suddenly appear, safeguarding my rushed steps.

On my left there's the lighthouse, which is beautiful enough. But on my right lies the mouth of a small cave, yawning around the bright blue pool. The lightly steaming water somehow glows with its own light. Above, the black sky is full of silvery stars, not a cloud in sight. And out there in all that darkness lies the Malorian Sea. The moonlight shimmers on its surface, its waves pounding the rocky shore.

Awestruck, I pass the brazier and a lone lounging bed with plush cushions, and bend down at the pool's edge to slip my hand into the balmy water. I glance at Alexus as he carries our wine and food toward a flat rock that extends a few hand widths over the pool. Two bathing linens, a small tray of seashell-shaped soaps, and a clear glass cruet filled with purplish liquid have been neatly arranged there, waiting.

Alexus planned this. He had Drae do all of this for us. *For me.*

"It's a thermal pool," he says, joining me. His leathers creak as he squats at my side. "Part of the geography here. Thermal pools are hidden in caves along the coast. This one drains to the sea and refills from a crack in the earth somewhere beneath these cliffs."

My parents talked about the caves and thermal pools, similar to the hot springs south of Hampstead Loch where my father found his brimstone. But I don't recall mention of this stunning light.

"How is it so blue?" I sign. *"So incandescent?"*

"The heat seeping from the earth reacts with something in the algae that creates the azure color and makes the water glow. The algae offers healing properties, and the warmth... Well, there's nothing like a hot soak."

He reaches over his head and tugs off his shirt, then stands and toes off his boots. Like the seductive sorcerer he is, he holds my gaze as he unlaces his trousers and drops them, along with his braies, before kicking the garments aside. There's nothing remaining save for the iron key around his neck, which he sheds as well.

My mouth waters. It hasn't been that long since I last saw him naked, but it feels like an eternity. I memorize it all. Those broad, round shoulders and that powerful chest, the corded muscles of his arms, the hard, rippled plane of his abdomen, the V-shaped dip of sinew aiming toward that absolutely perfect cock, hanging long and heavy between his legs.

"You are cruel," I sign, my face warming, my core tightening.

His laugh drifts between us as he holds up his hands in mock defense. "I swear, I'm not trying to be. It isn't like I'm denying you anything you want."

He wades into the water, down the wide stone steps. The muscles of his tapered back and rounded ass flex with every movement, and I have to admire the view. When he reaches the deepest end, he disappears beneath the surface. I watch him swim for a few moments, then I glance at the gibbous moon.

Alexus might not deny me what I most desire, but nature and time already have. At least until I find some birthbane.

When Alexus reappears, he wipes the water from his face and beard and heads toward our food and wine. I allow him a moment to arrange our dinner and settle on a slab that acts as a seat in the water, his light, golden skin wet and glistening under the firelight.

After a long drink, he pops a couple of pieces of fruit and bread in his mouth and stares across the pool at me, a wicked look on his face. "Are you coming in? Or are you just going to sit there and watch me?"

"What is the harm in watching?" I sign. I often think about our first night together. The watching in the window. How exciting it felt.

How much he liked it.

He shakes his head. "Not a damn thing, you little vixen. But if you blushed before, I promise you, you'd be absolutely scandalized if you could see me now."

I'm so impossibly tired, and yet I cannot fight the smile that stretches across my face, or the need to make certain he's telling the truth. Hungry for more than just Alexus, however, I procure a few bites of fruit and cheese and a long sip of wine to dull the ache in my stomach.

Then I stand and unfasten the toggles of my jacket.

Alexus watches me closely from beneath a hooded stare, holding his mug of wine. With a sly smirk on my face, I lay my jacket aside and strip off my tunic. My boots and socks are next. I kick them out of the way and peel off my trousers and underpants, until I'm standing in nothing but my stays.

Alexus's heated gaze skims down my body, but he returns his attention to my hands once I begin untying the strings holding my stays together. "I'm fairly certain you're the one who's cruel," he says. "A part of me could watch you undress all day. But a more eager part wants you to hurry up."

I laugh and step into the warm water, still unlacing the ties.

One step. Two steps. A pause.

Gods, the water and heat feel so wonderful.

Alexus sets his wine aside and pushes through the water to get to me. He takes my hand and helps me deeper into the pool. With one arm wrapped around my waist, he takes over my work, unthreading the laces quite a bit faster.

"I like taking your clothes off anyway," he whispers.

Those green eyes sparkle under the torchlight, watching me as I rest my hands on his shoulders. The moment he tosses the stays aside, I inhale a deep breath and sigh, reveling in the freedom of being naked and the bliss of the healing heat.

He drifts his hands over my breasts, then lowers them to my hips. "Much better, I imagine."

"You have no idea," I sign.

I kiss him then, pressing against him, my soft to his hard. I sense his magick stirring, the night coming alive around us, the thrill of his power rising with his desire, that honey and sandalwood scent mingling with fire smoke and winter jasmine.

Starlights flicker to life around us as he lifts me up so that my legs wrap around his waist. He wasn't lying before. He's stiff as stone between my legs, and yet I can't have him.

Releasing a groan, he draws away from the kiss and rests his forehead against mine. "All right. Let's talk, okay?"

I nod.

"I don't yet know how long we're going to be here, but I swear on all that is holy in this world, unless we manage to secure passage to Itunnan tomorrow, I will oblige your every desire while here. But for now, I think we both understand that we must be careful. I'll speak with Yaz tonight. She's a former apothecary and still provides services for people who need her. That's why the gardens here are so extensive. If anyone has birthbane or something similar, or might know how to get it, it will be her."

I exhale a long breath and nod again. That would be splendid.

"Secondly." He brushes yet another kiss across my mouth. "There are other ways to find relief, and I can't wait to share each one with you. But first..."

He sets me on my feet and swims to the ledge. While his back is turned, I duck under the water, soaking myself thoroughly, basking in the heat that loosens every muscle. When I break the surface, Alexus sits on the stone slab with the cruet of purple liquid in hand, water sluicing down his muscled body.

He curls a finger, and in a voice I cannot resist says, "Come here."

His starlights follow as I swim to him. With an arm around my waist, he lifts me onto the slab, nestling me between his legs.

"Tilt your head back."

When I do, something cool pours onto my crown, and the scent of lavender fills the air. Alexus sets the cruet aside and slides his strong fingers into my hair. With firm motions, he massages the liquid into my scalp, creating a light lather.

My body goes limp, and my eyes roll back. With every soft scrape of his fingertips, I relax more and more. This is bliss. It's also arousing. My breasts grow heavier, my breathing comes faster, and my nipples peak in the night air.

I grip Alexus's thighs as he scrubs. This might not be as good as an orgasm, but it's pretty fucking close.

He chuckles in my ear. "Are you all right?"

Shivering, I shake my head and sign where he can see. *"So good."*

The hair on his chest tickles my back as he leans down and kisses my shoulder. "I can do even better." He drifts his soapy hands over my breasts. "Rinse and let me show you."

First, I face him and return the favor, washing his midnight-dark hair. I even work the lather through his slightly longer beard.

He closes his eyes and sighs, beads of water pearling on his feathery lashes, a devilish smile at play on his lips. "This is making my dick hard again."

A laugh shakes through me. I love how comfortable we've become, even though we've shared no intimacy for weeks now, and how wonderful a simple bath can be when shared with the right person.

Hands still buried in his hair, I kiss him, gently dragging my teeth over his bottom lip, then I fall back into the water. Sinking down, I drag my fingers through my hair over and over and scrub my face too. Alexus joins me, and we swim together for a little while, exploring the deeper waters inside the cave, the algae-covered rocks on the cave floor. It's magickal. Our bodies wind around each other like remnants of silk cast to the sea, every movement smooth and languid.

We break the surface for air and swim toward the shallower entry until the water is chest deep. Alexus feeds me more fruit, a kind I've never tasted, white and pink and delicious. When he pushes the fruit past my lips, I suck on his fingertip. His eyes darken, gaze fixated as I clasp his hand and take his finger deeper before slowly dragging my mouth from his skin.

"Gods' death, don't tease me like that," he says, his voice suddenly ragged. "I dream about doing many, many things to that mouth."

"I know," I sign. *"I have seen."*

His dreams were difficult at times. Especially those when he was young at the scholarada. But other times, they buoyed me, assuring that his deepest desires lie with me.

A warm blush touches his cheeks, which would be adorable if not for the ravenous expression that takes over his face.

He traces his finger over my lips. "You liked what you saw."

Not a question.

"Very much," I sign, trying to breathe at a steady pace.

Those eyes narrow on my lips again. Gently, he tips my chin up and slants his warm mouth over mine, sharing the sweetness left by the fruit. His every lick, taste, and bite is hungry and promising, while every suck of my lips and swirl of my tongue is a reminder of what I long to do to him.

Reluctantly, he pulls away. "I'm trying to remember what the fuck I was doing five minutes ago. I had a plan. I think."

I laugh again. *"I believe you were going to wash me,"* I sign.

He holds up a finger. "Yes. Soap."

He retrieves one of the formed seashells that smell of jasmine and lavender. Hands lathered, he begins a slow glide of his palms over my shoulders and arms, rubbing deep circles into the muscles with his strong fingers. Again, I soften against him, and he drags his hands to my neck, rubbing long lines up and down my tired tendons and muscles before he rinses me.

Soon, I'm slicking my own palms and washing him too. His stare burns as I work, those eyes so intense as I trace my hands and the warm water over his lovely body.

With his eyes holding mine, I slide my hands over the thick curve of his chest, drag my fingers over his hard nipples and down his abdomen. When I skim a touch along his rigid length, he sucks in a quick breath and kisses me, his lips wet, his tongue consuming.

I stroke him, loving the feel of him in my hand, the silkiness of his skin, the perfect, punishing hardness beneath. His chest begins to heave as I play, and his hand tightens in my hair as I learn what makes him flinch, what makes him sigh, what makes goosebumps rise along his skin. He likes it when I squeeze harder, so I do that, moving my hand faster, dragging my thumb over his sensitive tip.

"Sweet fucking gods," he murmurs against my mouth, and after two more strokes, he hauls me against him. "Arms around my neck, legs around my waist," he orders, and I obey.

Gripping my ass, he climbs out of the water with me clinging to him. As we pass the brazier, the fire burning low, he offers a single glance at the dimming flames, and they flare high again at his silent command. Beneath the starry night, he lays me down on the lounging bed. It's just big enough for us to lie side by side, face to face. I can feel the heat from the brazier on my skin, cooled by the sea wind drifting through the rocks.

Alexus slides one hand beneath my head, then trails the back of the other along my jaw. "I really like being with you."

I swallow the knot that forms in my throat. *"I really like being with you too,"* I sign.

He grazes his fingertips down my arm and over my hip. I part my legs for him, and gasp when he touches me. He leans up on his elbow and pushes my legs apart even more, opening me. His little starlights draw near and hover.

"So beautiful," he whispers, teasing a finger up my center before leaning in to drag his teeth across my throat. With a low growl, he pushes two fingers deep inside me, and everything in me turns molten. "You're so tight and warm," he says. "I want to bury my cock inside you and never leave."

A vibration of desire moves through the rune and air, skittering over my skin, tightening my body in all the right places. Alexus moans and finds that place inside me, that tender spot he manipulates so well, and in seconds I'm panting with need.

Wanting to please him as well, I grip his thick cock and squeeze, slipping my thumb over his already slick head.

He hisses through an inhale and rocks his hips, throbbing against my palm as I stroke him from base to tip. "Just like that," he whispers, a raw ache in his voice. "Fucking *exactly* like that. Can you feel what you're doing to me?"

I nod. I know what pulses beneath his skin. The orgasm *and* the magick.

Aching, I grind against his fingers. There's a plea in my mind, one I send over that roiling abyss and let travel through the bond, one I let burn in the rune.

Don't stop. I need more.

As if I'd signed the words, he thrusts another long finger inside me, filling me to the point that it almost feels like him. He teases my clit with his thumb and lets his magick flow, that torturous pulsing vibration that makes my toes curl.

"That's my girl," he whispers. "Tell me what you want. What you need."

His cock twitches in my hand, and he thrusts harder into my grip, murmuring my name into the night. He kisses me, every stroke of his tongue demanding that my body relent to him, every graze of teeth across my lips destroying me.

He pulls away from the kiss, and the hand that rests beneath my head curls into a tight grip at the roots of my wet hair. Not so gently, he tugs my head back, making me look at him while we touch each other.

"I'm going to come so hard in your beautiful little hand. Is that what you want?"

I'm barely able to nod, because with those words, pleasure ricochets through me like lightning.

Alexus's magick intensifies, and he works his fingers harder. "Look at me when you come for me," he demands.

I meet his stare, my body spasming around his fingers as I writhe. Lust shines in his green irises, sweet longing, the deepest ache. I feel those things too, pounding through the rune as I ride out my pleasure on his hand. But there's something more. Something that scares me a little. Something that makes my heart lurch as though he's beckoning it to him. Even the little death I stole for him in Frostwater Wood flutters in a dark corner inside my chest. And the abyss in my mind? It rages awake, as though it hears his siren call.

It's what I saw in the wood after Thamaos's summoning, though it shines brighter now. Like a beacon. It's more than affection. More than adoration. More than fondness.

Before I can think the word, Alexus gasps around his rising orgasm. His face pinches with pleasure as I stroke him harder, but he never looks away.

"Fuck," he cries out. "Don't stop."

In ecstasy, a quiver tremors through his body as he breathes my name —*Raina, Raina, Raina*—and his release shudders out of him, surging again and again, spilling warm over my hand.

Finally, he breaks our stare, tipping his head back, gasping, his mouth parted, as the last soft pulses of his orgasm pour from his body.

When he meets my eyes again, I trail my mouth up the column of his throat and nibble his ear. Smiling, he captures my lips, kissing me hard and hungry at first, but the kiss changes, becoming soft and sweet, his lips plush and pliant, his tongue gentle and thoughtful in its caress.

Once we regain our composure, Alexus cleans us, then we lie together the way we did that night at Winterhold, staring at one another for a long time, spent and sleepy.

"I've missed you," he says, and I feel the honesty in the rune. "How do you miss someone you've only so recently met?"

I shrug, though I know why. What I saw in his eyes is the reason.

"I have missed you too," I sign, unsure what that means for me, if I've already turned down the path of no return and just haven't realized it until now.

He will remain constant long after I am no more than a fading star in the sky.

Where that terrified me before and made me feel selfish, now I feel greedy, as though one lifetime won't possibly be enough. My eyes drift closed, and something inside me twists painfully knowing that I might not get another month, another week, another day. Maybe not even another hour, minute, or second.

"Come on," he whispers. "Let's get you in bed." He kisses my forehead, then stands and gathers me in his arms.

Yes, we're in the middle of chaos, and nothing that lies outside Starworth Tor holds any good for us. Not even time. But as Alexus carries me upstairs to the lighthouse loft, I fold my hands around his neck and rest my head on his shoulder, certain of only one thing. If all we have is now, I will fight like an unholy terror to keep him safe. To protect this special magick we've found, this portal to peace and contentment we travel into whenever we're together. However temporary.

And I dare anyone to try and take him from me.

22

ALEXUS

I leave Raina in the loft and head to the main house to speak with Zahira and Yaz.

I don't make it halfway down the corridor to Zahira's office before I turn around, tuning my ear to voices in the foyer.

"But sir, perhaps you should speak to the captain before you leave."

The rough scrape of boots on stone echoes down the hall.

"It's all right, Mari. I won't even be missed."

Finn.

I eat up the hallway in eight long strides. When I turn the corner, Finn is standing at the bottom of the stairs with the house girl, his pack hanging from his shoulder.

"Where do you think you're going?"

He looks me over with bloodshot eyes, from my damp hair to my clean clothes to my polished boots. His face goes red.

"To an inn. I can't stay here, and somehow, I don't think you really give a godsdamn."

I rest my hands on my hips. "Mari, please go rest. You've done far more than enough tonight. I'll take care of this."

The young woman nods and vanishes up the stairs. Once she's gone, I level my gaze on Finn.

"Half of Malgros could be looking for us. You can't go roaming about wherever you please, especially not before I have a chance to speak with the captain. You don't even know how to get into the main part of the city from here."

He takes a step closer, stretching his spine, an attempt to meet my eyes. "First of all, I'm not ignorant. Harmon said he would take me. He has friends who own a tavern and inn. They'll give me a room for the few days we're here, no questions asked, and Harmon will relay any important news. Secondly, no one is looking for *me*. If they have a mark on anyone, it's *you*."

I narrow my eyes. "You're doing all of this because Raina doesn't want to sleep with you?"

The moment I speak the words, I feel like a hypocrite. Much as I want to pretend that I could live with her decision if she chose to be with Finn, deep down I know I couldn't. I'd be an utter asshole to this boy for taking what feels like mine.

"No," he spits. "It's because I can't deal with knowing she's sleeping with *you*. I'm trying to protect myself from doing something stupid where you're concerned. But also, don't think you can make me stay here, because you can't. You have no power over me."

I raise a brow. "I assure you that I *can* make you stay here, and I have more power over you than you can imagine. But if you want to leave, then get the fuck out. Know this though. If you bring harm to this house or anyone in it, I will not hesitate to make you pay."

"And if *you* bring harm to Raina, I will not hesitate to make certain that the Witch Collector finally dies." He walks around me and heads to the door. "Keep her safe, you son of a bitch."

"No fucking worries."

For the briefest second, I consider stopping him. It's what Raina would want. But when I turn around, and he glares at me, I can't make myself ask him to stay.

Instead, I watch him slip out the door.

"Gods, this is worse than I thought."

"Yes," I reply, crossing my arms over my chest as I sit on the edge of

Zahira's desk, having divulged every detail of the last nearly two months, along with the truth about me—my past as Un Drallag and my caging of Neri. Things I never shared.

Zahira gets up from her seat near the fire and begins pacing across her fine rug. Other than the new green velvet chairs where she and Yaz have been perched for the last hour, the room looks much the same as the last time I was here. The space is filled with eclectic furniture and hand-carved bookshelves lined with perfectly ordered magickal instruction texts, an entire row of old captain's logs, and a collection of Yaz's botany tomes. Intermingled with the books is a veritable jungle of vining plants, and above the hearth is the old helm from Zahira's sailing days. I've rarely felt at home anywhere, but I feel it here.

"Obviously, the prince has the Watch looking for you," Zahira says. "Or the traitors *within* the Watch, anyway."

"And more sentries will arrive at our gates for patrol duty tomorrow morning," Yaz adds. "I'm not sure how we can hide the fact that nearly a dozen people with no approved passage papers are staying here."

"Nephele can build a small shielding construct around the property," I say. "I'll help her so that it isn't too tiring to maintain. She's skilled in vast magick and has built far more complex constructions."

"That won't be noticeable to a witch's eye?" Zahira asks. "Like wards?"

"No, not unless they know what to look for, and few understand vast magick. The house will appear normal under any protections we use here. With the construct, we could be standing in the vestibule shouting to the tops of our lungs, and they'd never see or hear us. We'll just need to use the beach to get into town to avoid the sentries seeing us come and go."

"Very doable," Zahira says, pausing her pacing. "Wonder how Nephele is so skilled in vast magick?"

"I taught her. For eight years."

Zahira gestures to her wall of books. "Most any magick can be learned, yes, but it took you seventeen years if I recall? From age ten to age twenty-seven? Eight years seems... fast."

I scrub a finger over my chin. "As I said, their mother had more power than we realized. I didn't get time to study it, but that power clearly lives inside Raina and Nephele."

"Well, good thing," Zahira replies. "Because you need all the magick you can surround yourself with right now. In fact, if you haven't had time to help Raina master harnessing your shared power through the rune, you should do that while you're here. Imagine if there were secretly two of you. *Two* cataclysmic weapons instead of one. As long as the prince doesn't find out."

"He can't see her," I explain. "I have her mind thoroughly protected, so exploring the sharing of our power isn't a bad idea. Though I'm not sure what kind of training that will entail."

"Start small," she offers. "No blasting sea stacks and cliffs to oblivion. Start with harnessing light like you mentioned, and any other small tricks you carry up your sleeve."

I smile at that statement of the obvious, but my smile falters. "I just hope I'm granted time. I try not to think about it, but it's becoming harder each day. That I could just stop breathing. That I could leave Rai—" I pause to correct myself "—leave *everyone* to deal with the prince alone."

Her eyes soften. "I don't think you need to fear death via Colden's demise as much as you need to fear being used by the prince. There's no way Colden hasn't informed him how you two are connected. If he loses one, he loses both. And you are a great asset to a prince who needs other people's magick to thrive."

I take a deep breath and blow it out. "Indeed. That's all I've thought about these last few weeks."

"You cannot get caught," she says. "Not by the Watch. Not by this General Vexx person. And not by the prince and your friend Fleurie."

Instinctively, I touch the key around my neck and grip the edge of the desk. "I'd like to see them try. I'm not the man I was the last time you saw me." I glance at the open door to her office and focus on the energy outside the room. With a simple thought, the door slams.

Yaz startles, and Zahira spins around, looking at the door. With a mental command, I re-open it and let it close this time with a quiet *snick*.

"Gods above," Yaz murmurs.

Zahira faces me, eyes narrowed. "Impressive."

"That, my friend, is nothing. I couldn't have done that an hour ago. I get stronger by the minute."

"I have no doubt. Your awakened power was evident the moment I saw you in the vestibule." She points a long finger at me. "But strong as your magick might be, Alexus, your selflessness for those you love is stronger. All I'm saying is don't let those feelings make you act out of desperation. That can only lead to trouble."

I nod. "Understood."

"Now." She rubs her palms together. "About getting you to the Summerlands and to Fia Drumera's gates. I can tell you that Dedrick Terrowin's last trade ship went out a few days ago. It should arrive in Itunnan soon, but you could be facing a five-day wait for it to return. He's still the only smuggler this side of the Malorian."

"Fuck. Five days? That's a damn lifetime given our situation."

"I'm sorry. I'll send word first thing tomorrow for him to come see me at his earliest convenience. He's very likely being watched if your foes are worried about you heading south. It isn't unusual for Dedrick to come here with questions for the old cap, though, and it isn't unusual for me to send communication through Harmon or the boys if I'm expecting a shipment. But I live in my books or on the beach now. I rarely go to the docks anymore, so it's best not to draw suspicion with my presence."

I scrub my hand over my face. "Not what I wanted to hear."

Zahira shrugs. "I know. But Dedrick will respond soon. He always does. Then we can work out a plan. In the meantime, at least Raina can watch the waters, and Yaz and I will pray to Loria daily that the prince remains immobile. There's unfortunately little else you can do right now."

"Oh, I can think of plenty of things he can do," Yaz says as she stands and moves to a brass tea cart parked beside the fire. She's already gifted me two vials of birthbane, the small glass bottles hidden away in my pocket. With a generous hand, she adds a mixture of fresh tea leaves from a jar that says *CHAMOMILE* to a fine porcelain cup, then uses a doubled cloth to snatch the kettle hanging in the hearth. She adds a splash of cream and drop of honey and hands me the final, steaming concoction. "Your people need rest and time to recover. I see weariness but also much needed healing. You've all endured great loss and have had little to no time to process that loss. Healing will be found in one another, and in Starworth Tor, if you allow it."

"Always so wise, Yaz." I take a careful sip of her piping hot tea.

"Wise enough to know that you won't listen to all we say." She lifts her soft chin, and her perceptive hazel eyes shimmer. "Now, who do you mean to kill?"

I take another sip of tea before answering. "There are likely several people here who need to pay for what they did. Once I know Dedrick's schedule, I'll figure out how I mean to go about making that happen. It will be quick and clean. I'll be gone before the bodies are even found."

"I'm holding you to that," Zahira says.

"You have no worries."

She arches a thin, sharp brow. "None? You're a good friend who has just arrived in what should be friendly territory, Alexus, yet it has become a place that harbors the enemy. I have worries."

"Colden and I have eyes and ears here too," I assure her. "I'll check with those I know I can trust tomorrow. I'll take Rhonin with me."

"Eyes and ears watching and listening for who?" she asks.

"Admiral Rooke, mainly. He's been a question ever since his appointment. I worried he couldn't lead the Watch with a level hand, but I never thought he would betray the people he was charged with protecting. But Rhonin was in the army that came through Malgros. He couldn't determine who from the Watch oversaw their entry, but he surmised that the betrayal stemmed from a high-ranking officer."

Zahira crosses her arms over her chest, brows drawn down in thought. "Rooke doesn't strike me as a crooked man, though corruption often weaves a deeply invisible thread. If you question him, my only suggestion is that you be wise in your strategy. He is guarded well. And if you find you must kill him, do so in the hours just before you leave, else you could place us all in jeopardy."

"I would never endanger you, Zahira. I was trained for this. It's been a while, but I've a feeling that I'll remember what to do."

"Just be careful," she says. "You might've been a killer three centuries ago, but that doesn't make you one now."

Doesn't it? Some things are embedded in our marrow.

Yaz clears her throat. "Well, I for one would very much like to find a way to show your friends around Malgros tomorrow, *before* you go murdering people and possibly painting a target on your back. Raina and Nephele need time here, probably more than you can imagine. Their parents met here, lived here, loved here. The connections they might find in Malgros could truly help them."

"I have friends expected in two weeks from the Drifts," Zahira says. "I've already received their passage papers. I can simply alert the Watch that they arrived early last night at our gate for a longer stay. Everyone will need to take turns using the papers, but I have five passage forms. Three women and two men. The Watch never questions me or Yaz."

"Of course not," I say with a smile. "The beloved Captain Osane and her dear Yazmin? They can do no wrong."

Grins spread across Zahira's and Yaz's faces. "Does this mean I get to take your lady friends shopping tomorrow?" Yaz says.

I almost spit out my tea. "Shopping? How is shopping healing?"

"They need clothing. You all do." She feigns innocence, laced with a little mischief. "And I promise, I'll make certain there's something in it for you too."

"You are one devious little woman," I say with mirth as I push off the desk and head toward the door. I stop and take a book from a stack—*Curses of the Lorian Age*—something to read while trapped here, and glance back at Yaz, lifting my teacup. "Just remember. I like red. And very little of it."

Yaz laughs as Zahira cocks her head and gives me her infamous once-over, the surprised ghost of a smile on her face. "Alexus Thibault. You really care for this woman."

Using my mind, I open the door and step into the hall. With one last glance at my friends, I give in to a little openness and say, "Yes. I do. I really do."

23

RAINA

I wake to the smell of seawater and winter jasmine.

A breeze drifts over me, and I squint at the open window where sunlight filters into the room. The soft crash of the ocean's waves reminds me where I am. A smile tugs at my mouth as images of last night flit through my mind. I stretch and turn over, only to find that Alexus's side of the bed is empty.

The surge of panic that thrums through me is accompanied by a wave of breathlessness. Thinking the worst, I toss the blanket aside to get out of bed, but I spot a folded piece of parchment on the bedside table, my name elegantly scrolled across the front in midnight-black ink. Standing next to the note is an ornate vial made from dark purple glass and a lone white flower from the garden that I can't name.

Rubbing my eyes, I prop up on my pillow and gather the note and flower.

Good morning...

You looked beautiful enough to ravish, yet too peaceful to wake. Nephele and I need to build a shielding construct around the house before dawn as there

*are sentries from the Watch arriving come sunrise. You and all within will be
guarded from view, so please don't worry.*

*Passage to Itunnan likely can't happen for several days. Rhonin and I still
have business in the city, so I won't see you until dinner. Yaz has a formal
meal planned. She says that she and Zahira are taking you, Nephele, and Hel
shopping today anyway, and I know better than to argue. Have fun but be
careful, keep your eyes open, and glamour yourself. Yaz and Zahira are excellent protection, and no one knows that we're here. Though should you need
me, remember that I am but a thought away.*

*Also, the vial is birthbane tonic, courtesy of Yaz—if you want it. I took a
vial myself, so either way, in two nights' time, you are mine.*

Always,
Alexus

We're going to be here, beneath the Watch's nose, for a while. I'm
thankful we're not traveling for a change, but I dread the constant worry
ahead. I just want this to be over.

And shopping? I've only ever shopped at the valley markets, mostly for
food. Are new clothes worth the risk of watchful eyes? One glance at my
threadbare, filthy attire piled on the floor and my worn-out mud-covered
boots, I realize the answer is probably *yes*.

I read the last part of Alexus's letter again. Two nights to let the birthbane take effect. *Two long nights.* I'm excited, but I've never been more
impatient.

Like the desperate lover that I am, I drop my hands to my sides and
exhale a frustrated breath, staring at the wood-planked ceiling. My body
tingles with relentless desire, my skin so sensitive that even the slightest shift
of the blanket reminds me of Alexus's calloused hands caressing me last night.

The temptation to satisfy that burning need is almost irresistible, but I
clutch the note and vial to stay my hands. I can suffer for two more days.
Like he said, we can still be together in other ways. *Like last night.* Resisting
relief now will make it that much sweeter later.

I pop the cork from the vial. A sniff identifies the familiar remedy. It's always awful, but I gulp down the bitter contents and pray there's more for the rest of our journey.

The wind off the ocean calls to me. I grab Alexus's robe from the bench at the foot of the bed, slip it on, and stroll to the catwalk door. Surely a look won't hurt. Cautiously, I open the door and pause with my toes just over the threshold, taking in my first unencumbered view of the Malorian Sea. The sky is filled with fluffy, white clouds and flapping seagulls, and a gentle, cool wind rolls in from the west. It's later than I thought. The sun sits high, sparkling along the sea's white crests.

The ocean stretches and glitters for what seems like forever. I've never imagined anything so expansive. It's a little terrifying to think that, soon, we'll be out there floating on that endlessness for days.

Several fishing boats dot the shallower waters while ships belonging to the Northland Watch's fleet guard the blue waves further south. The green and indigo flags of the broken empire are visible even from here, the North's sign of a desire to return to peace and a united land.

A laugh bubbles up inside me when I glance down and see yet another note with my name on the front tucked securely into a pot of flowers near the door. Smiling so wide it hurts, I pluck the letter from the greenery, brushing my fingertips over the ink before opening.

You little rebel...

I knew you'd come out here, no matter what I said. I envisioned you standing here naked, those pretty, pink nipples peeking through the long dark hair cascading over your shoulders—though I figure you're wearing my robe instead. I saw you touching it last night. I asked Yaz to buy you your own today. Pick out something silky with a sash.
I have the most lascivious plans... Now go back inside.

With a heartfelt thank you,
Your Jailer

My smile turns to a laugh, but when I read the note a second time, heat centers between my legs in a heavy ache. I press the note to my lips and try to decipher what Alexus's words mean. My mind conjures all manner of lewd scenarios—prisoner and jailer—only making me hunger for him worse. Even the wind off the sea is torture, plastering the cool silk of my lover's robe against my skin.

Temptation returns in a flood. I slip my hand inside the robe and brush my fingertips over my damp heat, certain that Alexus Thibault is trying to kill me. Though it's difficult, I ball my fingers into a fist, turn on my heel, and head back inside.

Hands on my hips, I look over the room, my body still thrumming. Alexus unpacked our belongings. Our clothes, weapons, blankets, everything. I walk to his desk and run my hand over his journals and touch his quill, imagining him sitting here this morning writing my letters as I slept.

I don't know why I'm surprised to find a change of clothes and shoes and a pitcher and basin of fresh rosewater waiting near the dressing vanity. There's also a comb with birds carved into ivory, and a sleek wooden brush made of softened boar bristles. Both must've been imported because I've never seen such beautiful grooming items in the valley.

My hair is a mass of messy waves from falling asleep with it damp. Using the brush, I smooth out the strands and weave them into a long braid, tying the ends with a leather band. As for the clothes...

They're strange. In the valley we wore stays or linen undergarments made with boning that kept our breasts snug against our bodies and our posture good. Most of us worked much of the day, so support was a necessity. Our bloomers were nothing special, made to wick away moisture and that was about it.

Here, the underclothes are much smaller affairs. The top piece extends only a few finger lengths beneath the breasts, and the bottoms... While quite elegant, there's no way the laboring women in these parts cover their bits with such delicate items.

I put the pieces on anyway and revel in the comfort as I lace the front of the top piece and the sides of the bottoms. Next, I dress in the waiting clothes that probably belong to Yazmin: a pair of ecru linen trousers, a white blouse, and a dainty pair of leather shoes. As I turn toward the mirror and face the woman before me, I feel like someone else entirely.

Before I leave, I check the waters for the first time since yesterday at noon. Through Colden's eyes I see Fleurie, a woman I've come to know in ways I never imagined. I don't begrudge her the time she had with Alexus. I just wish I didn't have to relive it through his dreams. Worse still, I wish she didn't feel like a threat. Not because they were lovers. But because— much like death—she could snatch him away in the night. For the first time, that feels like a true possibility, because she's healing. Enough that I can now make out her face, one that resembles the pretty bright-eyed girl in my mind's eye. But Colden is sleepy, so Fleurie quickly fades from sight.

The prince is still barricaded. As always, I try to dismantle the wards around him, but whatever I'm doing is wrong. It feels as though there isn't enough focus in the world to break past that barrier.

When I look for Vexx, he's staring at the same view as me, from a different angle. Knowing he's here, hungry to cross paths with me and Alexus, makes me hope that maybe I *am* seen today. Maybe I'll look up and stare into his soulless eyes. Maybe I'll get to drive my dagger into his throat and rip out his spine, that bastard.

As for Neri, I don't dare ask the waters to see him anymore. If I want to summon a wolf-man-god, I know how. But I don't want to. Not now. Not ever.

I grab my dagger and thigh belt and head for the stairs, hoping that I'm never in a position where I have no other choice.

⚜

THE HOUSE IS EVEN MORE BREATHTAKING AWASH IN SUNLIGHT. EVERY piece of wood furniture has been polished to a shine, and there's not a speck of dust or sand on the slate-tiled floors.

No one's in the great hall, so I stroll down the corridor that leads to the kitchen and stop at a massive floor-to-ceiling window that looks over the sea. Below, Zahira and Hel sit at a table draped in white linens and filled with colorful dishes of food and an overflowing vase of fresh flowers. Zahira spots me and smiles, then motions for me to join them.

I don't know my way around the estate yet, but the short path to the lower courtyard is simple to navigate. As I step into the sunshine, I inhale the salty morning air and feel every trouble that's worried me for weeks evaporate. I can't believe how warm it is here in comparison to the valley. It feels more like early fall than nearly winter.

"Morning, Raina." Zahira raises her teacup. "Come. Have breakfast."

It isn't just her and Hel. Yazmin and Nephele are here too. Everyone is smiling, my friend and sister both dressed in foreign but beautiful clothes, their faces shining in the sun, their hair clean and neat. Nephele looks a little tired, probably from building the construct around Starworth Tor, but I can't imagine it was anywhere near as complex as the enchantment in the wood.

On the table, there are plates of pastries and bread, cheeses I could never identify, salted meats, more strange fruits, and a jar of fresh honey. It's like we've entered another world, another time. If trouble wasn't brewing across this stunning sea, I bet we could live here forever and be so happy.

I take a seat between Hel and Nephele and make the sign for *Good Morning*, hoping Yaz and Zahira will begin to learn some of my more common communications. Nephele translates.

After I set my dagger and thigh belt aside, I sign to my sister. *"Where is everyone?"*

"Sleeping, I suppose," she answers. "I haven't heard a peep out of anyone this morning, not even Joran. Which is highly unusual."

"Unusual seems to have become his norm lately," Hel says. After a pause, she nudges me and changes the subject. "You look rested. I wasn't sure if Alexus would let you sleep at all." She winks. "That man looked ready to fuck you until you couldn't walk."

Nephele sputters into her tea and reaches for her napkin. "Helena!"

My smile freezes into a tight line as my cheeks warm with mortification. Under the table, I kick my best friend's ankle.

"Ow!" she cries. "What? It isn't like they weren't there. It was obvious."

"We were exhausted and had no birthbane," I sign with quick movements, unsure what else to say in front of Alexus's friends, even though they can't understand me.

Yazmin pours me a cup of tea. When I meet her eyes, she's biting her upper lip, holding back a smile that threatens to take over her face.

Zahira is the first to respond, though. She lifts her teacup in Hel's direction. "A woman after my own heart. My tongue has no leash either." She looks at me, grin widening. "It's okay, Raina. Trust me. Yaz and I are thrilled to see Alexus acting like a giddy young man, especially given his current circumstance. We haven't seen him this way in..." She glances at Yaz who finishes the thought with... "Ever."

I snatch my teacup and take a long sip. My face grows even hotter, but underneath my embarrassment, a thought rises to mind. I'm falling in love with the fact that I make Alexus Thibault happy. That I make him smile. That even under the weight of impending death, he has found joy with me. It's the last thing I ever expected.

"Enough talk about Alexus," Yaz says, setting my tea aside. "Now that you're all here, I'll admit something. Shopping was just an excuse. We can certainly grab clothes for the three of you, but there's more to the day's plan than what I shared with our beloved Witch Collector." She leans her elbows on the table. "I have a proposal. One that might provide much needed answers if you'd like to hear about it."

Nephele, Hel, and I share a glance. "Of course," Nephele says as she makes me a plate of food the way Mother used to. "Do tell."

Yaz gives Zahira a look, and only after Zahira nods does Yaz continue. "There's an oracle in the city. The Memory Catcher, we call her. She's different from Seers like you, Raina. She reads people's blood and sees the memories that live there. I would've tried convincing Alexus to see her today, but he's never cared for her insight. She's never failed us, though."

The one name that comes to mind is the one Nephele shared with me at Hampstead Loch. Petra Anrova. The woman Joran spoke about who lived in the Iceland Plains for a time. This can't be her, but seeing memories is like seeing the past.

Nephele sets the dish of food in front of me. Before I can think to school my expression, I give her a wary look. Zahira reads the question that must be clearly painted on my face.

"The past helps us understand the present," the captain says. "And Ingrid, that's the oracle's name, is especially skilled at revealing past truths we need to make sense of our present conflicts. History holds answers if we're only brave enough to seek them out. According to Alexus, your mother and father hid many things from you and Nephele. Perhaps we can uncover something that will help you both make sense of why they did what they did and how it connects to this time in your life."

The three of us look at one another again. My curiosity gets the better of me.

"Why does Alexus dislike Ingrid?" I sign before I begin eating. This time, Hel translates.

"Because she sees the past, I suppose," Zahira says. "He's never been one for revisiting memories. Of course, now we realize why and what he didn't want revealed. He might still scold us with more than a few choice words when he finds out we've taken you to see her, but I trust her tellings." She lets out a breath. "I'm not certain there's any man in all of Tiressia who has more regrets and pain than Alexus Thibault. I didn't realize how deep that pain and regret ran until he explained last night. I think a part of him wants to know all the things he's forgotten, but another part wants to keep those lost memories buried. They don't sting that way."

I understand all too well the misery of wanting to forget pains of the past, and yet longing to uncover other truths that might wound just as deeply.

Hel squeezes my knee with a gentle grip. "It's worth a chance. We should try. You might remember something about Rowan or the God Knife."

I turn to my sister. Her eyes are focused, deep in thought. She blinks out of her daze and meets my stare. "I agree with Hel. Speaking with the oracle might be helpful."

All eyes rest on me, waiting.

"We will see the Memory Catcher then," I sign as Hel translates. *"The past is the past. It cannot hurt us now, right?"*

Zahira's eyes grow dark. "Let's hope not."

24

ALEXUS

The bell above the barber surgeon's door jangles when Rhonin and I enter the small, empty shop.

It's dark and gloomy here on the back side of the Merchant Quarter. Most of the shops are set far from the coast, lining narrow streets, nestled below cramped living quarters. There's a window, but the grime coating the panes muddles what little light finds its way here. Still, the bloodstains on the wood floors remain, some in big, saturated splatters beneath the surgeon's table. Others in rings from buckets around the barber's chair.

Rhonin makes a disgusted sound beneath his breath and taps his finger against a wide-toothed saw, one of the many rusted surgical instruments hanging on the wall. It screeches on its hook.

"You have interesting friends," he says. "Who apparently like to murder people. Gruesomely."

I eye the backroom door, covered by a dirty, dark green curtain. "You haven't even met him yet."

"Little scared," Rhonin replies, raising his red brows. "Not gonna lie."

Just then, Emory pushes through the curtain. He's a short, round man with a red face and bulbous nose who always smells like meat. He's wearing a blood-stained apron over his normal clothes.

"Master Thibault!" Eyes bright, he hurries across the room and embraces me, patting my back so hard it jars my teeth. When he pulls away, he gives Rhonin a once-over, then says, "What brings you to Malgros?"

I withdraw a small bag of coins from my pocket, enough to feed his family for two weeks, and hand it to him. Then I flip the lock on his door to ensure no patrons interrupt. Mornings are busy in the city, the citizen's focused on their work and comings and goings. Rhonin and I made it here unnoticed thanks to a bath, a change of clothing, and a quick glamour over our weapons. But we need privacy to talk.

Emory's face falls as he rolls the bag of money between his fingers. "Oh dear. You're here for information."

"That I am. This is a friend of mine." I gesture to Rhonin. "You can speak freely in front of him."

Emory nods at Rhonin. "All right. I suppose this is about the Prince of the East bringing a small army through here."

I clasp my hands behind my back and widen my stance. "It is. I know they arrived by ship, and I know they were allowed to port. I also know they were given horses by the Watch and slipped through the city and out Palgard Gate in the dead of night. What I don't know is who in the Northland Watch is in league with the East. I was hoping you could tell me."

"Come sit," Emory says as he slips the coin in his pocket. He crosses the small space and perches on a tall stool.

I take the barber's chair as Rhonin glances at the surgeon's table, the only other seat in the shop. He purses his lips and folds his arms across his wide chest. "I think I'll stand."

Emory shrugs and looks at me. "Word in my chair is that there are at least half a dozen officers working for the prince. No one knows how he infiltrated our shores originally, but even the admiral is under his influence."

"What about Dedrick Terrowin? Is he a conspirator? The army transferred from an Eastland ship to a Northland Watch ship, mid-sea. Did he have anything to do with that?"

Emory makes a face. "Dedrick? No, my lord. Dedrick isn't the straightest arrow, but he's loyal to this land. The only things he brings back on his ships are common goods and the occasional Northlander he smuggled across the sea in the first place. It's one thing to want to leave Tiressia. It's an entirely different game to Dedrick if someone wants to come in."

"Good to hear." I lean back in the chair. "Back to Admiral Rooke. I've been told it's difficult to find him alone."

Emory's stare widens a bit. "Yes. Especially now. I imagine they're expecting *you*, my lord. Perhaps even the king."

I don't tell him the situation. He's trustworthy and has been for years, but word of an empty throne could be a trigger for more problems.

"Precautions against *something* have been obvious," he continues. "Though the admiral must believe that his extra protections at the gates are an excellent shield."

"Why do you say that?" I ask.

"He has a dinner planned in a few nights. Not a large affair, but large enough. I have a patron whose wife works at Brear Hall in the kitchens. Preparations for twenty people have been made for a week now. I don't know much else, other than a man from the East is certainly attending, and a few of the other names I heard are those believed to be traitors."

A man from the East. General Vexx.

I dart a look at Rhonin who reads me well. "Sounds like we're going to a party," he says with a crooked smile.

"And that the ladies aren't the only ones doing some shopping today," I reply.

Emory moves to the table behind me and turns my chair around to face the mirror. The very *dirty* mirror. He grabs a small bucket with the day's fresh water and dips a cloth into it, then washes and dries the mirror.

Staring at me through the glass, he says, "You'd be a lot less conspicuous if all this hair was gone. Both of you. It isn't the way here. You look like Icelanders. Or worse, part of the Eastland army."

I stare at Rhonin through the mirror.

"You fucking first," he says with a mocking laugh, as though he thinks I won't do it.

I don't want to look like the man I used to be. Don't want to look in any mirror and see that person again. But Emory is right. Blending in while here is a wise decision. The fewer eyes on us the better.

Still. This will hurt. That much I know. It's easier to face the day when I feel like someone else.

"To the shoulders," I tell Emory anyway. "No shorter. And shave the beard."

He nods, and with a smile, takes up his shears.

RAINA

Nephele, Hel, and I walk up a busy cobblestoned road with Yaz and Zahira hand in hand at our sides, fraudulent passage papers in our pockets.

I've long dreamed about Malgros. Envisioned my parents roaming around a sunny city by the sea. Those images formed by a young girl's imagination are nothing compared to the real thing.

The street is elevated above sea level at the top of the cliffs, arching along what's known as Village Hill and Malgros's sea wall. On one side there's a seemingly endless row of tall buildings made from various types of stone—shops and homes, offices and businesses, taverns and inns. The buildings with signs creaking in the breeze are often crowded, people moving in and out of doors, while others still lie quiet for the day. There are food carts and stalls, children playing in public fountains, and fishermen climbing up the hill from the eastern beach access, their morning's catch in tow.

My chance of being noticed at all dwindles with every step. I've never seen so many people in one place.

On my other side lies the sea. I struggle to stop staring at its shimmering surface over the top of a shoulder-height crenelated wall. All that glittering blue, and the coast's long stretch of golden sand is so inviting, even with the Watch's fleet floating on the water, sails billowing in the wind.

I pause to take it all in, resting my hands against the wall's sun-warmed stone. It's a cool day, but still pleasant. To my right, a mourning dove perches on the next merlon, hooting like an owl, watching me like it has something to say.

The little death I stole for the dove that struck our door on Collecting Day flutters, then coils its shadow inside my chest, like a child curling up to sleep.

Are you following me? I ask with my mind, but the dove flies away.

"Makes you wonder why Mother and Father ever left, doesn't it?" Nephele says, stopping at my side. "Their stories were so real it feels like I've been here before."

For the first time since I was old enough to wonder such things, I think I truly understand why Rowan and Ophelia moved north. It's hard for Nephele and me to imagine turning our backs on this place now that we're here, but I'm reminded that fear feasts on those with something to lose. There's been war on the other side of that sea for ages. If I had a partner and children, I'm not sure I'd feel safe raising them here either, beautiful though a home by the Malorian Sea might be.

"They did it for us," I sign.

Nephele squints at the water. "They did. I still doubt that it was easy to say goodbye."

"That's where Finn's staying," Hel interrupts.

Nephele and I turn around. Hel holds the piece of parchment where she jotted the name of the tavern after speaking to Harmon before we left. She hadn't wanted to mention Finn's departure at breakfast. Didn't want me to worry. But when I almost went upstairs to see him, she knew she had no other choice but to divulge what happened last night, the way he'd decided to leave no matter what she said.

She points across the street, a few buildings down from where we're standing. The large wooden sign swinging above the door is the shape of an ale cask and reads: *The Bitter Barrel.*

"I'm going to check on him," she says. "Just buy whatever you think I might need. Nothing fancy."

For a moment, I consider accompanying her. Everything with Finn is so broken. But if he was ready to accept my relationship with Alexus and to put the pieces of our shattered friendship back together, he wouldn't have left Starworth Tor last night. I need to give him the space he wants, even if it worries me.

"I can go with you while Yaz takes Nephele and Raina to shop for clothes," Zahira offers. "It'll be safer." She turns to Yaz. "We'll meet you at Ingrid's in a couple of hours?"

They kiss, and we part ways, and soon, Nephele and I are standing in a shop filled with women's clothing that's like nothing we've ever worn. Nephele's eyes are wide as she takes in the gowns and day dresses hanging around the room. There's a table covered in hand-sewn lacy underthings too—far more provocative than my usual attire.

My attention snags on a red dress, silken and beautiful. The last time I wore red was at Winterhold, a darker shade, and I didn't care for it. But *this?* This red reminds me of passion.

"These clothes are all too... *elegant?*" my sister says, clasping her hands in front of her chest. "We need traveling attire." There are only two shop-keepers in the room, busy at the window, but Nephele lowers her voice anyway so that only Yaz and I can hear. "We need *fighting* wear," she says. "Leather. Linen. Boots. Belts. Leather halters. Also things made for the desert. Not lace and silk, unfortunately."

Yaz is petite, yet formidable. She stands up straight, pushing out her chest, planting her tiny feet, as though rooting where she stands. "Those items are in the back, and we'll purchase all that you and your crew need. But I'm not leaving unless you two and Helena have a couple of lovely items each to wear to dinner while here." She winks at us. "And maybe something that Joran, Rhonin, and Alexus will fancy."

Nephele huffs and gawks, her mouth agape in disgusted horror. "If Joran Dulevia ever sees that much of me again, it'll be because I died that way and he found me. I would never purchase clothing for that man's benefit."

"Then for your *own* benefit," Yaz says, gesturing to the room. "Take your pick. Something *you* like."

I blush and look to my sister for any salvation from this moment. I can see in her tight expression that she *still* wants to argue with Yaz, but Yaz's sternness reminds me of our mother, meaning we've met our match.

Nephele reads my mind. Reluctantly, she snatches a sleek, vivid blue dress from a rack—the bold color suits her well—along with crisp, white undergarments. I reach for an emerald dress for Hel, and something just as bold for myself. The red dress. With its fluttering sleeves and low neckline, its crossover skirt and sash, it feels *right*.

Lastly, I turn to the undergarment table and gather tops and bottoms for Hel and I. Hers, a lighter shade of green. Mine, dyed the same color as my dress, the bright red of a blooming rose.

A big, white smile spreads across Yaz's face as she strolls deeper into the shop, trailing her hand over more pretty dresses. "Red is a good choice, Raina. Exactly what I was going to suggest."

❧

THE MEMORY CATCHER'S SHOP IS NOT A SHOP AT ALL.

It's a tall, narrow, crooked house squeezed between more tall, narrow, crooked houses about a five-minute walk from Village Hill. The front door is black, the paint peeling and cracked from the sun and briny air.

Zahira clangs the knocker mounted to the door, cast in bronze to look like an eye. Suitable for a Seer of any type.

A boy answers. Recognition brightens his eyes when he sees Zahira.

"Hi, Laren," she says. "I've brought some friends to see your mother. Is she home?"

He nods but doesn't speak, then motions for us to come inside.

We enter a dark, cramped entryway. The walls are painted to match the exterior door, the curtains drawn over the windows. The furniture is ornate and old, lots of velvet and other rich fabrics, and so many mirrors. Candles light the visible spaces, the only illumination reflecting in the glass, even though there's a perfectly good sun outside.

The boy vanishes into a nearby room. Minutes later, footsteps sound on the tile floors, and a woman dressed in black appears in the doorway.

Ingrid, the Memory Catcher.

She's so slim and spindly that it's almost unnatural. Her skin is paler than Nephele's, white as a full moon, her hair coiled atop her head like a serpent, every strand the color of a cold winter's night. Her eyes are big and green, rimmed in kohl and dark lashes, her mouth full and red as the dress I bought today. The combination lends her an unearthly sort of beauty.

She smiles stiffly, as though the action requires effort, and walks forward, taking Zahira's hand. "Captain Osane," she says, bowing her head before looking back up. "You are here for a vision?"

"Yes," Zahira answers. "For my friends." She gestures to me and Nephele and introduces us.

"I'm Ingrid," the woman says. "You have payment?"

Before I can panic over my lack of preparedness, Zahira retrieves a handful of coins from her pocket and hands them over.

Ingrid jingles the money, slips the coins into the pocket of her black day dress, and says, "Good, good. Follow me."

Nephele eyes me warily, but we trail behind Ingrid through the house to a windowless, candlelit room filled with books and oddities. Yaz, Zahira, and Hel wait near the door, the space too claustrophobic for us all.

There are strands upon strands of tiny bones strung together with thread along the sides of an apothecary cabinet, and a dozen old, clear canisters containing dark liquids I'm glad aren't labeled. There are various animals too, preserved and mounted in every corner. The only ordinary items are the small table with a white cloth draped over the top which sits in the middle of the room, and the high back chairs that stand on either side of the desk.

"Sit," she says as she rounds the table and takes her seat. "Tell me a little bit about yourselves."

Nephele squeezes my hand, then we slide onto the cushioned seats of our high backs. I don't want to worry Alexus, so I close my end of the runic bond while Nephele gives a brief overview of our lives. That our parents were enlisted in the Watch, then moved to the valley when Mother became pregnant with Nephele. She tells Ingrid how we lived in the valley together until Collecting Day eight years ago. How Father died in the fields. That Mother is gone too. The only thing she doesn't disclose is that Mother died in the prince's attack, though if Ingrid is all Zahira claims, she will see that truth anyway.

Ingrid seems to absorb the information. Eyes narrowed in thought, she opens a drawer and retrieves a second cloth, this one black, embroidered with moons and stars. She lays the piece on the table, then lights a lone candle stub and sits it near the table's edge.

Lastly, she withdraws a needle, holds out her hand, and looks me in the eyes. "You first."

I truly want to trust Zahira and Yaz, but nothing about this feels good. I'm nervous, a little uneasy, and more than uncertain about continuing.

"It's all right." Ingrid holds the needle's sharp end over the candle flame. "All I'm going to do is prick your finger."

I give a little huff, more of an inward reprimand for feeling so awkward. I've done worse than a needle prick for weeks now, so I shake off my discomfort and offer Ingrid my hand.

The jab is quick and neat, resulting in a tiny bead of bright red blood. I don't expect what comes next, though I should. Yaz mentioned that Ingrid reads memories through blood.

Ingrid removes a small spoon from her skirt pocket and squeezes a few drops of my blood into it. Then she puts the spoon in her mouth.

Beneath the table, Nephele grabs my knee. In the seconds after, I feel nothing save for a slight sting, but Ingrid seems to feel everything. She rests her hands on the table, then closes her eyes, rolling her tongue inside her mouth as though savoring the taste.

Her breaths move through her lungs faster, her chest rising and falling in great swells with each drag and push of air. Suddenly, she stops and opens her eyes.

"Do you remember living here?" she asks me. "Your sister said you were born in the valley. But I see memories in Malgros."

Startled by her question, I shake my head, confused. *"I have never lived here."*

Nephele translates. "I never lived here either," she provides.

Ingrid looks between us with a curious glint in her eyes. Again, she burns the needle in the candle flame and holds out her hand for Nephele. My sister isn't as hesitant as me. She places her hand in Ingrid's hold, and in seconds, Ingrid opens her eyes, once again relishing the blood on her tongue.

"You lived here as well. You were eight years old." She turns to me. "You were only two."

Nephele blinks, tilting her head. "We did no such thing. I would remember. Raina might not, but I would."

Ingrid shrugs her shoulders. "I can only tell you what I see. You look like your mother—" she points at me. "And you," she points at Nephele, "look like your father."

"True enough," Nephele says, "but we never lived here."

"You *did*," Ingrid says. "Stay here long enough, and the memories will arise. I can see you both on the beach with your parents, playing in the sand and water." She clasps her hands atop the table. "There's more though."

Nephele looks at me, hesitation written all over her face. I let out a deep breath. *"Let her speak,"* I sign. *"We can decide what we feel about it later."*

"Go on," Nephele says to Ingrid.

"Your father used to go missing a lot."

Nephele presses her fist to her mouth, then lowers her hand. "Not *missing*. He just went to other villages to trade."

I don't recall that at all, but the moment she speaks those words, the abyss in my mind roils like a boiling, oily pit. I close my eyes and tighten my fingers around the edge of my seat, feeling dizzy, feeling compelled, like the wisest thing I can do is dip my trust in that utter absence of everything.

But I peel my eyelids open instead, fighting that call, that lure.

Ingrid glances between us. "You both have memories of his absences. Days, weeks. Once he was gone for an entire month. When I see memories, my gift singles out where I need to look. These particular memories that I'm sharing with you are suppressed to varying degrees. The time you had here in Malgros is a significant suppression for you both. The issue with your father's absence is more severe for Raina than you, Nephele. But there are hints to your here and now in those memories. Possibly even your futures."

"Our parents would've told us if we lived here," my sister says. "They wouldn't have lied. Mother was pregnant with me here, but they left. She told me of my birth in the valley."

My sister's denial is strong. I don't feel such disbelief that my Mother, at least, would've been dishonest.

"And yet your earliest memory is here in Malgros," Ingrid replies. "Toddling on the sand with your father, you just haven't recovered it yet. But surely you feel some familiarity here?"

She does. She said as much as we stared over the water earlier.

Someone touches my shoulder, and I jump, having completely forgotten that we weren't alone in this room. Zahira stands behind Nephele and me like a protective mother, as though she knows we've already had our fill of this little outing.

"I think these two are tired, Ingrid," she says. "Do you have any further suggestions for what Raina and Nephele might do to unearth these memories more fully?"

The woman leans forward, forearms on the table. "If you're going to be here for any length of time, I suggest taking a stroll by the barracks where you and your parents would've lived and spend some hours on the beach. Other than that, perhaps you should have Captain Osane check the years of your parents' time here. That information can be found in the Watch's enlistment logs in the archives."

We say our thanks and leave the room, quickly heading toward the home's peeling front door. I don't even hear Ingrid's last words as we depart, and when we stroll by the barracks and the Northland Watch's command post, I find I can't look at the buildings for too long without the abyss coming alive, causing a tightness to clamp my chest like a vise.

I just want to go back to the lighthouse. I want to sink into the warm water between the rocks and forget that a stranger just told me my parents were even bigger liars than I imagined.

When I'm finally alone at the lighthouse, I strip down to my skin and dive deep into that steaming blue pool. Less than half an hour later, I stand in front of the mirror in the loft, staring at myself, a woman whose life has been built on lies. A woman who might not even know who she is at all. A woman containing a threatening, silent darkness she must eventually face.

I close my eyes and edge my consciousness close to that inky emptiness, vast and void as the space between stars.

I'm listening, I tell it, clinging to courage. *Tell me what the fuck you want with me.*

I'm met with silence as the darkness roils on.

26

ALEXUS

I lean against the wooden post by the stairs in the lighthouse loft, staring at Raina.

She sits in the chair by the desk, her back to me, one flourished knee drawn to her chest as she reads the book on curses I borrowed from Zahira's office. She's wearing nothing but a red silky robe—new—and her hair is damp, falling down her back in loose waves. She's apparently so lost in thought that she never heard me come in.

"Hi." I brace for the moment she turns around.

When she does, she blinks and grabs the front of her robe to close it over her breasts, startled by the strange man standing in her room. It takes a few seconds, but she smiles, and everything about her softens. Her pretty blue eyes. Her gorgeous face. Her lovely hands.

She unfolds from the chair and comes to me on those long, bare legs, moving with all the grace of a sylph. Her robe is open, the exquisite, naked column from her throat to her ankles on full display.

Seeing the soft tuft of brown curls between her legs makes my blood rush, thinking of her silken pink center. The curves of her breasts are another temptation, heavy and sweeping. Beckoning. I want to touch every inch of her smooth, tawny flesh, trace every line of her witch's marks.

I swallow hard as she nears and drags her finger along my jaw, marking the lines where Emory shaved my beard down to a shadow. Raina's eyes widen and sparkle with what I think might be delight.

"Do you like it?" I sign, turning my head just enough to kiss her wrist.

"I love it," she replies. *"You are so stunning."*

She grazes her fingertips over my lips, fluttering them for a moment before she rises on her tiptoes and presses that lush mouth to mine. I open for her, relishing her taste, the sweetness and the warmth, like sugar and cinnamon. Her skin and hair smell like jasmine and lavender, two scents that are permanently sealed inside my senses and will forever remind me of her pleasure.

As I slip my hands beneath her robe to hold her bare waist, I can't help but think about how good she feels when she's riding me, when I'm holding her just like this, watching her take what she wants from me, watching her take everything I need to give.

The thought is too much, sending an ache straight to my balls, stiffening my cock. I make myself pull away, because as much as I want to lay her down and devour her, there are other concerns at hand.

With a tender touch, I tip her chin up and look into her eyes. "I heard about what happened today. I saw Yaz."

I wanted to reprimand my old friend for taking Raina to see the Memory Catcher. But in truth, my discomfort at Ingrid's mention only exists because I have long wished to ask her to read my blood. I want to retrieve memories but having someone look into my past never felt safe with as much as I had to hide.

A cloud of unease passes over Raina's eyes. *"More secrets thanks to my parents,"* she signs. *"More lies."*

I draw her close, my hands at the small of her back. "I'll help you figure this out. If you were born in Malgros, we'll know before we leave. Zahira plans to visit the archives first thing in the morning to see what information she can find. As for your father and his absences, I can't comment on what he might've been doing during those times away. But I can promise you that I'll be here when and if those memories resurface. If there's anything else I can do, you only need ask. I understand what it feels like to not be able to remember."

"I would rather not talk about it," she signs, and my rune warms with her desire. *"Zahira postponed dinner. We have the evening to ourselves. My only request*

is that you make me forget for a little while." She slips one hand over my shoulder and threads her fingers into my hair. Her other hand settles between my legs, rubbing at the growing erection I can't seem to tame, until it strains against my trousers.

A part of me thinks to deny her, to encourage her to talk instead. But she isn't ready, that much is clear. And besides. Raina Bloodgood is as persistent as a river rolling over rocks. She would wear me down easily.

I lean in and press my mouth to her ear, already struggling to maintain a steady breath. "I swear to the gods, you are my greatest weakness."

Truth, but not something I ever thought I would admit to another person.

She opens her robe and presses her naked breasts against me, still rubbing her perfect fingers up and down the length of my cock, as though memorizing the feel and the shape.

"I think a little magick practice is in order," I whisper. "Time for my lascivious plans."

She looks up at me with curiosity in her eyes and a question on her face.

I reach for the sash hanging untied at her waist, ripping it free. With a wink I say, "I suppose I'll have to show you."

27

RAINA

Prisoner and Jailer. I understand now.

"Are you certain you're all right with this?" Alexus asks.

The silken sashes he took from our robes are held firm in his fists. One red. One black. I stand before him beside the bed in the loft, naked, witch's mark exposed, body willing. The trust I have for this man astonishes me sometimes, but the thought of him binding my hands holds not a single spark of hesitation.

Only longing.

There's hesitation in *him*, though. He doesn't want to be like Finn. He hasn't said as much, but I remember the rage that burst from him at the sight of my hands being pinned in someone's grasp, my voice silenced. To prove I have no qualms about what he's proposed, I hold my hands between us, palms up and wrist to wrist.

His eyes go dark as sin as he jerks his chin over my shoulder and says, "On your knees on the bed. Facing away from the head frame."

A tingle drips down my spine, and desire pools low in my belly. I don't know what this has to do with learning to harness his magick through the bond, but I'm thankful Zahira mentioned the task and more than glad for the mental distraction this afternoon. I'm learning that this is how I keep from spiraling through these days of worry and waiting.

By losing myself in Alexus Thibault.

I crawl onto the bed, aware of his intense stare as I position myself. When I cast my eyes on him, I swear I see lust flaring in his gaze, feel it alive in this room.

He possesses no modesty as I watch him strip, the wait almost unbearable. With every item of clothing shed, I grow wetter and wetter, and when his hard length is revealed, my core aches to be filled with him.

Sashes in hand, naked save for the key around his neck, Alexus moves onto the bed, kneeling behind me. As the down mattress sinks beneath his weight, my heart picks up pace, my pulse fluttering like a butterfly trapped in my throat.

"Come a little closer to me and spread your knees."

I do as he commands, scooting backwards until he stops me. When I'm comfortably spread, Alexus slips his hand down my abdomen, down between my legs, and drags a finger through the slickness gathered there, from my entrance to my clit, flicking that little bundle of nerves, making my abdominal muscles tighten.

"So wet," he purrs, a moment before bringing that same finger to my mouth and dipping it inside, swirling it around my tongue. A silent whimper shudders inside my chest as he slides his finger from between my lips. "See how good you taste?"

Trying to maintain some semblance of composure, I nod as I grit my teeth and fist my hands at my sides, goosebumps racing along my skin. I feel certain I won't make it through this, whatever *this* is, and I wish more than anything that birthbane didn't take days to work.

Alexus takes my right hand in his and kisses my knuckles, then he winds one end of the black sash around my wrist, securing it with a knot I don't recognize. Next, he ties the other end around the slender bedpost, once again using a knot that looks complex enough I won't be able to go anywhere.

Once he repeats tying my left side with the red sash, he says, "Any discomfort?" and I shake my head. My arms are stretched, my breasts pushed forward, and this is quite possibly the most vulnerable position my body has ever been in. But I'm not uncomfortable.

Alexus ducks under my trussed arms, and then knees his way onto the bed in front of me. He grazes his hand along the curves of my side, admiring his handiwork. "This might be the best idea I've ever had," he says with a sexy smirk.

Seductively, he leans down and kisses my rune, tracing his tongue across the mark. I can't fight the shiver it causes.

Before I grasp what's happening, Alexus lies down on his back and uses the leverage of his feet planted on the mattress to push himself toward the head frame, resting his head between my legs, his broad shoulders butting against my thighs.

Heat licks up my throat and spreads across my face as I look down at his muscled body, his cock raging hard against the carved plane of his abdomen. He touches it. Stroking it. Thumbing the already glistening crown.

A ragged breath tremors out of me. This is torture.

"I'm going to feast on you." He presses a kiss to my inner thigh. "No release though. Not until you fill this room with *starlights*, as you call them. And I want your glamour up. Let's see if you can hold two magicks at once."

I send a bolt of bewilderment through the rune, chased by a question. I have no idea how to harness his magick, much less while I'm holding the construct of a glamour in place. We could be at this all night.

Not that I mind. But I do.

Sort of.

Gods above and below.

Alexus laughs and skims his rough hands up my thighs and over my hips, cupping my ass. "My power is accessible through the bond. All you must do is command it. Will it to behave as you wish. Focus."

I make a mental note to call him the worst magickal instructor ever born when this is over. But my mind gets sidetracked quite quickly because he's kissing the inside of my thigh again, and not a gentle press of the lips either. A wet kiss, his tongue making sinuous circles on my skin.

When he stops, he smacks my ass, just hard enough to arouse the slightest, most wonderful sting. "Glamour. Up."

A quiver rocks through my thighs, and my muscles clench, but I hold myself steady and try to think straight enough to erect a glamour. It's difficult, because I can feel his breath, warm on my damp flesh, making me ache even more. But the glamour rises. The magick of it chases across my skin, and my witch's marks vanish.

"Mmm, good girl." He spreads me apart with his fingers, opening me. "Now sit."

Every bit of my self-awareness tightens into a knot in my chest. When I don't move—because I'm so incredibly aroused yet somehow also simultaneously mortified—his arms tighten, and he draws me down to his mouth. I'm angled in such a way that my back is arched, my softness pressed to his mouth just right, just where I need him. But gods' stars. As he pushes his tongue into me, I feel like I'm suffocating him.

I inch up off his face, and a deep chuckle resonates from his chest. "Don't be embarrassed." He lifts his head and drags a long lick up my center, making me tense. "You are perfect and utterly delicious. This is bliss for me." Again, he folds his hand around his cock. As he pumps his fist, his other hand grips my hip. "I can make you climax like this."

No doubt.

He kisses my thigh. "Just call forth my magick," he continues. "And I'll fuck you with my tongue until you can't stand it anymore." He takes my hips in both hands again. "Now, come here."

There's no fight in me this time. No resistance. No bashfulness. I let him feast, let my pleasure build with the tempo he sets, leading me toward the crescendo of a song whose ending I know well.

If I give him what he wants.

I work very hard to compartmentalize everything within my mind: the bond, the glamour, the distraction of Alexus's talented tongue devouring me. Even though he avoids my clit, only licking over it a few times, there's a pressure building inside me, making me writhe against his mouth.

Focus, Raina, I think as I close my eyes.

There, in the darkness, with the world shut away, I see magick across the landscape of my mind. If I look to one side, I see Alexus's life threads, still wound with mine and Colden's. If I look to another corner, I see the pulsing magick of my glamour. In another floats the threads of Alexus's desire, his *passion*, threads I could tangle with my own if the time were right.

Alexus's end of the bond and the glowing threads of his power linger just beyond my abyss, pulsing like a flaring light. A *beacon*. Like a lighthouse across the dark shore of the chasm before me. On a leap of trust, I let my mind cross that pit of nothingness.

There's something there. A presence. A *force*. It's almost like the vestige of another bond, a soft shadow hovering behind Alexus's power. Limned in white light, the shadow is frayed at one end, like a shredded piece of gossamer caught in the wind. I don't know what it is, but it calls to me, as though it needs me to reach out and touch it.

Magick means connection. It always has. Tonight, this magick is about mine and Alexus's connection to each other, so I submit.

When I let my mind graze that shadow, Alexus groans into my flesh, and suddenly, his hands are everywhere. Squeezing my ass. Gripping my breasts. Reaching up to fold those long fingers gently around my throat. His touch is a heady thing, and I rock against his mouth, feeling more desperate for this release than any other before it.

In the next breath, I hear his voice, speaking to me the way he did when we were in the wood, harvesting fire threads. *Fulmanesh, iyuma tu lima, opressa volz nomio, retam tu shahl.*

Fire of my heart, come that I may see you, warm my weary bones, be my place of rest.

I can't explain why, but something compels me to think those words. I repeat them until bold, fiery threads emerge from Alexus's power within my mind's eye.

Bend them to your will. Force them to become light.

Is Alexus speaking to me? Is he communicating through the bond? His voice is so clear, as if he's whispering in my ear.

He presses his tongue harder to my clit, flicking that tender bud, sucking it, reminding me of the reward that lies ahead. With an image of my will in mind—those glowing orbs of light filling this room—I repeat the Elikesh lyrics in my thoughts, until those blazing threads cool into soft, white light.

The sweetest caress of power cascades over my body, my skin heating with desire and need. Alexus keeps feasting, and his hands keep roaming, rougher and harder, as though learning me anew.

Suddenly, Alexus smacks my ass again, making me gasp and arch my back.

More, I plead through the bond.

In answer, he sends a trickle of magick between his tongue and my clit, the pulsing current growing ever more powerful before fading away.

Needy, I close my hands around the silken sashes binding me to the bed and grind against Alexus's mouth. If I'd possessed a demure quality before, it is gone from me now.

The throb between my legs pounds harder and harder, but so does Alexus's magick, trapped within me, beating under my skin, wanting out. My rune heats, and my skin goes taut, drawn upon by a force so strong it's as though my very soul is being pulled from my core.

Alexus's magick pours from me, and the room brightens even from behind my closed eyes. When I open them, I'm met with a loft filled with tiny orbs of light. Hundreds—no, *thousands*—like sparkling stardust.

My excitement floods the bond, and I swear I feel Alexus smile.

He doesn't make me wait for my prize. He lets his magick thunder into me, vibrating through his tongue into my body, and in seconds, I'm in a state of utter rapture, swept up in the wave of a relentless orgasm that spasms through me over and over and *over*.

When I come to my senses, Alexus is soothing my swollen flesh with long, languid caresses of his tongue. But he's also stroking his cock. Hard and fast. I cannot stop watching, especially as a pearl of cum slips free.

I'm still floating in the haze of pleasure, still hungry. My hands need to feel him. I need to taste him. Need to drink him down.

I think of the sashes around my wrists—*the knots*. And with Alexus's magick still hot in my veins, I envision those knots untangling. At my command, the sashes untie and fall away, and I collapse forward, catching myself on the bed in sheer surprise.

Alexus catches me too, by the hips, before a laugh escapes him. "Fuck, Raina. You did it. My talented, wicked little witch."

He has no idea.

Without a second of indecision, I grip his cock, and for the first time, take him into my mouth.

"*Shit.*" His voice is rough and ragged around his gasp, his entire body jolting from the contact.

My legs are trembling, but I manage to turn myself around, until I'm on my knees between his legs, my breasts pressed to his spread thighs.

He tortured me. Now I mean to repay the favor.

All while I hold two magicks in play.

Alexus rises on his elbows, staring at me with a glistening mouth, his expression shadowed with longing. The light in the room shimmers in his eyes as I swirl my tongue around his broad, swollen head, sending the tiniest trickle of his own magick into his flesh, eliciting a groan.

"This." His deep voice shudders as he slides his hand into my hair. "This is going to fucking break me, isn't it?"

I smile and nod.

And then I begin.

COLDEN

The Eastern Territories
City of Quezira
Min-Thuret Temple

"Why do I feel like you're leading me to my death?"

I watch the prince closely as we walk across the wide courtyard beneath a soft, evening rain. The sky is gray, the air cool. Twilight here smells like incense and soggy earth and coal fire and cooking. I'm certain there's more to take in, but my attention drifts between the prince's strong yet slender form to the tide of red shadows swirling like a misty ocean in the wake of his feet.

When he turns a sharp glance over his shoulder, his damp hair—fittingly the blue-black of a raven's wings—falls into his eyes. The style is less severe than usual. It draws my attention to the raindrops clinging to his feathery eyelashes, black as kohl, the water sparkling beneath the brazier lights. I shouldn't notice. But I do.

"Thresh?" the prince says to his captain who follows behind me. "Did you prepare my whips and chains? The stocks?"

Thresh doesn't even snicker. "I did, my prince."

As we turn a corner and slip into the cloisters, I offer the prince a cocky, tilted smirk. "Oh, the things I would do to you if my hands and feet weren't bound."

I don't expect his next words in the least, even though he's become a little softer toward me these last weeks. It's usually me with the gibes. But he grabs the long, iron handle of a massive door, opens it, and when I pause before him says, "Don't tempt me, Moeshka. I might finally hold you to task."

Thresh punches the hilt of his dagger into my spine, urging me to keep walking. Tearing my eyes from the prince's gaze, I enter a cavernous space, a gathering hall, one Thresh guides me through until we're in a long, narrow corridor marked by several doors. Dormitories, I think.

I have to wonder where Rite Hall is. I hate that I missed it. Bron said eastward when she explained its current use, though I also hold knowledge passed down from Alexus. The old ritual room Alexus once frequented with eastern royalty is now where the prince communicates with Thamaos's spirit, that virulent bastard.

"Stop," Thresh says in that sonorous voice of his once we reach the end of the hall.

I roll my eyes. "Surely not."

He opens the door and shoves me inside. I take several steps across the stone floor, until my feet meet woven rugs and rush mats. The chains linking my ankles are just long enough that the effort of walking isn't miserable, but not so long that I could get away if I decided to try.

It's an apartment. What appears to be two rooms. Smaller than my chambers at Winterhold, but not cramped, though there are no windows save for one tiny rectangle pane through which I can see raindrops and gray sky.

The main room, with a small wood stove instead of a hearth, holds a sitting area and wine cart, along with a small library, empty writing desk, and copper bathing tub. One glance into the next room reveals a bed. Nothing extravagant, but after so many weeks sleeping on the ground and then a thin cot, I would give my pinky finger for a night's sleep beneath that canopy.

The door snicks shut, and I turn to find that I'm alone with the prince.

"Well, this is unexpected and awkward," I say.

With the smallest laugh ever laughed, he drags his fingers through his wet hair, strips off his dampened black jacket, and tosses it on the back of a chair.

"I suppose it's only going to get more awkward, so ready yourself." Cool and unaffected, he strolls to the wine cart and opens a bottle, pouring red liquid into two glasses.

An odd feeling flashes across the back of my neck, and I glance around, not necessarily nervous, but uneasy. The only thing I notice is that the bathing tub is filled and still steaming.

"You're going to boil me alive. Or drown me."

Another insignificant laugh. "Or *bathe* you."

My brain pauses, and I glance from side to side in utter confusion as he turns around. "*Bathe* me," I say, my words flat, prompting him for an explanation.

Casually, he walks toward me and slips a key from his pocket. An abrupt and unanticipated chill races up my spine when he moves closer and takes my hand in his.

I haven't felt his touch in thirty years, and yet somehow, it hasn't changed. The same formidable strength lives in those hands, those elegant fingers, yet he knows how to use them with a tenderness that once softened my cold heart and stirred my blood.

When he unlocks the shackles at my wrists, tosses them on a fine, velvet settee, and slowly drags his hand from mine, I am certain he must be unwell.

More than a bit taken aback, I narrow my eyes. "Have you any notion how good that felt? More importantly," I add, "have you any notion how many necks I've snapped with my bare hands?"

A nearly imperceptible curl forms at one corner of his mouth, one that doesn't reach his eyes with any sort of lightheartedness. "I didn't intend for it to feel good," he says. "Know that. And have *you* any notion how many necks *I've* snapped with *my* bare hands? Why do you think I need no weapon?"

"You're a liar. And you have a guard."

"Not a liar. And that I do. Right outside that door. A barbarian.

Though I don't think I'll need him. Something tells me I'm safe from your deadly hands."

The prince drops to a knee. I close my eyes for the briefest moment, swallowing hard as he unlocks the chains at my feet. When I glance down, finding him in a pool of red shadows, he looks up, not a drop of fear in him, though I could swear I see something far more damning moving in his eyes.

"I think I've dreamt this lovely scenario a time or two." My cock twitches, that traitor.

"And you'll have to keep dreaming." He stands and points to the tub. "In the bath, perhaps."

I rub my wrists where the chains had been and study the warm water. The tray of soaps. The sponge scavenged from the sea. "I'm not sure how to accept such a kindness from my enemy. Is there something in the water that's going to eat my skin off? I'm going to look like Fleurie did when she first came here after this, aren't I?"

Another tiny curl at the corner of his lips.

His violent edges have smoothed so much over these last weeks. Bron says he hasn't been communicating with Thamaos as often, that the lack of contact with the god spirit is why he feels less like a knife at the throat.

For me, he's more like a waiting kiss, which is even more dangerous territory if I'm honest. I know I'm lying to myself when my mind tries to convince me that enemies can be lovers. That there's no rule that says passion must extend to deeper sympathies. And yet those words are all I can hear right now.

The prince reaches for the wine and sets one of the glasses on a drink table near the tub. "Unfortunately for me, I need you. As you have continuously reminded me, I can't kill you, not until I find out for certain if you're bound to Alexi, much as death might be the most desirable end to your annoying mouth. But you *do* stink. Actually, you smell like something crawled into your clothes and died. So if you would please—" he gestures to the tub and moves to sit on its edge "—I would like to enter my dungeon without wanting to vomit. I'm sure Fleurie will appreciate the effort as well."

I scoff, pretending to be offended. "I have never been asked to get naked in such an insulting manner. But if you insist." I reach over my head and tug off my tattered and filthy tunic. "Your little buckets of cold water and floor cleaner haven't really been wonderful for grooming and, you know, *not eating my skin off*. Which I'm clearly concerned about."

When I look at him, his eyes are locked on mine. His wine glass is held inches from his lips, the muscles in his clenched jaw rippling, as if it's taking everything in him to keep his gaze on my face.

Fuck it. I toss my shirt aside and face him fully, slipping my hand to the ties of my trousers. "Are you going to help?" I ask, undoing the laces one at a time. "Is that the plan?"

His eyes drift down, and my blood warms.

Which is stupid. I should want him dead. A thousand times over. Brutally. But somewhere inside him is a good man that Thamaos has poisoned. I'm sure of it.

His eyes are dark and delightful when he lifts his gaze. I recognize the want there. The need. The ache.

"That is *not* the plan." He stands from the tub's edge.

"You sound like that's a disappointment when it doesn't have to be."

He takes a deep breath and moves toward the door. "It *does* have to be, Colden. And it would be best if we both remember that. We are not on the same side, and I fear we never will be. This little fire between us is nothing anymore. Time to snuff it out."

The problem is that his words don't match anything else about him. Not the look on his face. The tone of his voice. The glint in his eyes. *Nothing*. The man I knew is still in there, peering through the haze. *At me*. Someone on the *right* side. And someone who might be able to save him.

Also stupid. Because you can't save someone who doesn't want to be saved. Yet I find myself wanting to try.

"Consider the fire snuffed." A bold lie as I hold his gaze and drop my britches where I stand.

Naked, I move to the tub and slowly ease into the hot bath, groaning at how good it feels.

Aware of the prince's roving stare, I drag water over my shoulders and reach for a piece of soap and one last effort. "You know, Thamaos is using you," I tell him, sliding the soap up my arm. "He's likely why you don't remember who you are."

The prince leans against the door, arms crossed over his chest. "You know nothing about me. Or Thamaos. Don't pretend you do."

I rub my hands together, forming a lather. "I know that you were someone before he fucked with your memory. You probably had family and friends and a life. He took that from you, and you don't even care. That's how deeply he's infected you."

"I'm here because I want to be. Because Tiressia deserves to be united under one rule. No more war. No more division. No more existing as three separate continents and an archipelago when we were once *one* land. It can be that way again. Open seas. No fear. No fighting."

I rest my arms on the sides of the tub and study him. "You really think you're doing the right thing. That murdering an entire valley full of people was necessary."

He works his jaw. "War has casualties. Until it ends. Which it will if I have anything to say about it."

"And yet, *you* are the cause of war. The cause of division. The cause of protected seas and fear and fighting. All because, why? Thamaos whispers his desires to you when you pray to him? Is that how it happens? He slips that poison right into your brain, telling you what he needs you to hear so that he can once again live? Is he why you must survive off souls? What the fuck sort of deal did he force you to make?"

"I made no deal. My purpose is to unite Tiressia, and with Thamaos's help, that's what I intend to do."

Something in those words catches my attention like a shirt snagging on a nail, but I can't reason out why.

"If you think that he will have use for you after you resurrect him," I say, "you clearly did not live in an age of gods and don't have any notion what you're up against." I grab the sponge and begin washing again. "He'll probably kill you when he's done with you. And all of this will have been for naught."

I have no idea if anything I said will get through to him, but the seed has been planted. I'll have to work on making it grow, if Thamaos's poison doesn't kill it before I get the chance.

With a playful wink, I wring my sponge out and extend it toward him. "You're sure you don't want to help? It could be fun."

No reply, but the way he gazes into my eyes is intense enough that I eventually slip under the water to break the stare, holding my breath and counting to ten. If he's still standing there when I come up for air, perhaps I'll finally persuade him to stay. To join me.

To remember.

Luckily for us both, when I break the surface, he's gone.

29

ALEXUS

Raina and I sleep until we hear the clang of swords echoing from the beach the next morning.

I get up and go to the catwalk door, peeking through the sheers, only to find Rhonin and Hel sparring in the sand, the white-crested waves lapping at their feet.

They move like two lovers dancing, so aware of one another. So comfortable. This synergy has happened over the course of weeks now, their friendship and alliance. But sometimes I wonder when it will become something more.

Regardless, as a man who once taught the sword, I'm impressed by their skill. Watching Rhonin with all his Eastland army knowledge is one thing. But Helena is a warrior to her marrow, something I've known since I saw her bravery in the ravine. She's Rhonin's match in every way, pivoting, thrusting, and blocking as though she's wielded a sword her entire life.

More surprisingly, though, is the sight of Nephele and Joran—also sparring. And not as gracefully.

They're both skilled—I taught Nephele the blade myself. But where Rhonin and Helena move like lovers, Nephele and Joran move like enemies. Their faces are red in the early morning sun, their bodies stiff and sweaty and on edge. The only time either of them relaxes is when Joran bests Nephele and laughs in her face. When she attacks, he manages a block, but not before she sweeps his legs and straddles him with the length of her sword pressed to his throat.

"Your sister is going to kill Joran," I say lazily as Raina crawls out of bed and moves toward me.

She slips her hands around my middle and up to my chest. Rising on her toes, she rests her chin on my shoulder and presses her naked body against my back lovingly.

"Let her," she signs.

I laugh and turn in her arms, taking her face in my hands. "I need to go to the docks today."

She makes her pouty face, that full bottom lip curling, and gods' death, it makes my blood heat. It's ridiculous that such an innocent, playful expression gets to me like it does, but it makes me want to bend her over and fuck her right here. I have no explanation for why it affects me so brutally.

"Trust me," I tell her, lowering my hands to her hips. "I want to stay in this lighthouse with you for the rest of the day."

Repeating last night, until her hungry mouth reduces me to a sweating, panting, begging mess.

I can still see her lips around my cock. Still feel my own magick vibrating from her tongue, the way she continued stroking and sucking as my restraint shattered. I can see the ecstasy in her eyes as I took her throat as deep and punishing as I would've taken her body. And I can still taste her kiss, the taste of *us*.

"But this sanctuary is only temporary," I say, a reminder to myself amid a flood of distracting thoughts. "Or it's supposed to be. We've yet to hear anything from Dedrick Terrowin, so I'm going to see him. I'll take Rhonin with me."

"I could go with you," she signs.

I tighten my hands on her hips. "You should stay here and see what Zahira turns up at the archives. Go to the beach. Lounge in the pool. Visit Zahira's library or Yaz's gardens. Dress for dinner tonight. The docks can be rough. I somehow think taking a beautiful woman for a stroll around lonely seamen might not be my wisest decision. I'm trying to *avoid* attention."

She rolls her eyes but smiles and signs the word *Charmer.*

I lean in for a kiss. "Charm has never been my strong suit. Just know that this evening, the birthbane will have had plenty of time to take effect. Then, you're mine, and I won't be gentle."

Her eyes sparkle. There's a tug on my heart and a sweet hum through the rune. Though the day's deeds are pressing, I sweep Raina up and take her back to bed anyway. She snatches the silken sashes hanging from the bedpost on the way and slips them around my neck.

Placing one knee on the mattress, I lay her on the cooled sheets and crawl on top of her with a smile on my face. "Practice makes perfect, I suppose."

She grins and signs one word as I kiss my way down her body. *"Indeed."*

❦

"I'M HERE TO SEE DEDRICK TERROWIN."

Rhonin and I stand inside a small, dirty office located in a run-down warehouse near Malgros's shipyard, our weapons glamoured. It's already noon, later than I'd hoped to be here, but leaving my bed with a naked Raina Bloodgood lying in it wasn't easy. That man, Alexus Thibault, is gone now, though. I've shed him and taken on the old, yet still familiar skin of Alexi of Ghent.

The skinny young man behind the desk gives me a once-over that says he doesn't trust me in the least. As he shouldn't.

"I'm a friend of Captain Osane's," I tell him. "She sent word yesterday that she needed to speak with Mister Terrowin. I'm here to facilitate that meeting."

The young man scrubs his hand through his oily mop of hair and gives me yet another once-over. Warily, he spares a long look at Rhonin who stands a foot behind me like a guard. "Mister Terrowin isn't in," he says. "Hasn't been for days. I received the message, however, and when he returns to the office, I will surely give it to him."

I lean down and splay my hands on the messy desk. I can smell his lie. Even better, I can see it. Terrowin's signature dated from yesterday is *right there*, on a shipment inventory list, the lettering different from all the other refuse littering this desk—tins of fishy smelling food, scattered contracts, and random slips of scribbled-upon parchment.

"Then tell me where he lives," I say, lowering my voice, my face tight. "I'll find him my godsdamn self. The matter is urgent."

The young man sits back in his chair, his eyes round. "He isn't home either, sir. Last I saw him, he was leaving the Bitter Barrel, with... *a woman.*"

Fuck. "When?"

He hesitates. Which is foolish.

I rip my dagger free from its sheath and let it pass through the glamour. With a firm hand, I slam the tip into the desk. "I asked you nicely. *When.*"

He holds up his hands. "L-last n-night, dear sir. He'd had a lot of ale."

Rolling my eyes, I jerk my dagger from the wood and re-sheathe it behind the glamour. The young man's eyes track the movement. His gaze then follows my hand as I reach into my jacket pocket and retrieve a hefty handful of silver coins. When I drop them onto the desk, the man gapes.

"Find Terrowin," I tell him. "Drag him off that woman's pussy and get his ass to Starworth Tor before nightfall tomorrow. If you do that," I gesture at the money, "there's more where this came from."

As Rhonin and I turn for the door, the young man clears his throat and squeaks out a broken, "B-but wh-what if I c-can't?"

Pausing, I level a look over my shoulder. "Then I'll be back for my money, *dear sir*. And to commandeer Terrowin's motherfucking ship."

⊙⥊⊙

RHONIN AND I HEAD TO THE MERCHANT QUARTER. THE PORT WAS A long walk from Starworth Tor, but I'm still glad we chose against having Harmon cart us around like dignitaries. We take in the view of the cranes and the ships at dock, and the busy street that crests Village Hill.

"You sounded completely different back there," Rhonin says as we walk.

I shrug. "Sometimes it's necessary that I play Alexi of Ghent. That was a kindness, though. I was far more agreeable than he ever was in situations like these. Believe me."

Rhonin huffs a breath. "Glad I never met him."

I stare out over the sea, remembering. "Me too."

It isn't until we turn toward the back streets that I feel someone behind us. Rhonin notices too, slipping a glance over his shoulder.

"Two Northland Watch guards," he says. "Not as big as us, but close. They look curious."

"It doesn't matter if they're giants," I tell him under my breath. "This will end badly for them if they play the moment wrong. Just keep walking. We're simply two men among many strolling the Merchant Quarter."

We stop by Emory's shop, trying to appear as normal as possible. Unfortunately, he has a patron, so he slips me a folded note with the information I requested about Admiral Rooke's dinner party scrolled inside and glances toward the door. It's clear he doesn't want trouble or attention, so we leave as he so silently requested.

The bell above the door clangs as we step outside. I lock eyes with one of the guards, a Witch Walker. The tan skin at his throat is decorated with witch's marks of indeterminate colors. Many of those enlisted in the Watch are Witch Walkers, so it's nothing unusual. But I can't tell if he recognizes me or not. Is that look on his face because he knows he's spied the Witch Collector? Or because he only knows that I'm a foreign face?

I shove Emory's note in my pocket with Zahira's offered passage papers and guide Rhonin deeper into the Merchant's Quarter, circling back toward the shipyard. If things go badly, and they very well could, it's easier to kill two men in the shadows of abandoned warehouses than in the middle of Village Hill. It's also easier to lose them here, which is what I try to do as we pick up our pace.

Rhonin and I turn down the cobbled path into a narrow alley, heading toward the wharf, but it's a wrong fucking turn. We don't make it ten steps before we look up and pause. We're standing between two massive living quarters, not warehouses, the buildings replete with external stairs and balconies, the alley opening to a people-filled street in the near distance.

"Shit, turn around," I say, but when we do, the two guards are there, and a sudden, foreign power folds around me like an invisible hand.

At my side, Rhonin tries to lift his arm to reach for the sword crossed over his back to no avail. I could break through this magick easily, but I allow it for now, willing to play this game of cat and mouse with an unworthy opponent.

"Witch Collector," one of the men says. The one with the witch's marks, the one binding me. His hands are behind his back, and he wears a smug look, as though this is a trick of grandest magick. "I couldn't resist a trap," he adds with a smug expression.

"Bad decision," I tell him, my skin bristling as the air around us sparks. "Very bad."

Rhonin looks at me with wide eyes, shaking his head with infinitesimal movements. His face says *Don't do it* in about ten different ways.

As for the guard, he shows no fear. Instead, he laughs. "Is it, though? Do you know how many of our guard are at the wall waiting for your arrival? And yet here you are, already walking our city streets." He cocks his head. "At first, I wasn't sure it was you, what with the new look and all. But those eyes are unforgettable, and on top of that, I could sense something odd about you. A glamour, perhaps? How'd you manage that?"

The Admiral likely hasn't informed his men that my power has returned. Less fear among the masses that way. Foolish. That's like sending unwitting children to fish for a shark.

"Just tell me what the fuck you want," I grit out. "Make it fast. You're wasting my time."

The guard narrows his eyes. "The Admiral is looking for you. And we're going to take you to him."

The air sizzles with my power, and Rhonin groans. "Shit, that was either the worst thing you could've possibly said or the absolute best."

The answer is the *worst* if we're talking about what this means for the existence of these two men. If I let them take us, then yes, we'll be carried straight into the admiral's hive where I can destroy from within. But if Vexx isn't there, then I could hurt many people and still lose him, and that cannot happen. Once he hears of his fallen brethren, he'll likely leave these shores, and I might not be able to stop him. I need to happen upon Rooke and Vexx on my own terms, the party tomorrow night, but unfortunately, that means these two men cannot walk out of here alive with a story to tell.

It happens fast. Faster than when I destroyed those Eastlanders in Frostwater Wood. I summon forth all the energy that I can, sending power rushing through me, more controlled now, ready to be concentrated where I direct it.

I can feel my body changing, the surge of blood to my skin, the quick swelling of my veins, the electric haze that floods my vision. With my mind, I punch all that power straight into the pounding hearts of the two men standing before me.

The magick holding me and Rhonin vanishes as a cracking, squelching sound fills the alley. The men don't even get a chance to scream before their chests explode.

I manage to shield my face with my arm in time, but Rhonin is not so lucky.

"What the fucking fuck, Alexus!" he cries out as he looks down at himself, then at the fallen guards a few feet away, their chest cavities blown open. "Fuck, fuck, holy fucking fuck!"

He stands with his hands spread wide, his face masked with shock, his body frozen. I clamp my hand over his mouth and scan the alley. The balconies. The street ahead. No one has noticed us. Yet.

Quickly, I do my best to clean the bits of viscera from his tunic, to wipe the splattered blood from his face with my sleeve, but he's a bloody fucking mess. So am I, just not quite as bad. It will require two tightly woven glamours to get our asses back to the tor.

Rhonin picks away a sliver of bone stuck to his face. One look at it, and he vomits. While he's throwing up his guts, I stalk to a set of stairs leading to the top floor of one of the living quarters and take the treads two at a time. We need to get out of here and buy all the time we can.

At the landing, I grab one of the laundry wires that string across the alley and give it a hard jerk. It snaps and falls, and the freshly laundered bed linens billow to the cobbled street below.

As I hurry back down to ground level, Rhonin gathers himself, wiping at his face, and collects some of the still-damp sheets and throws them over the bodies. Blood soaks through the material on contact. He stares at the growing stains, glances at the balconies, then darts his gaze toward the mouth of the alley where someone could spy us standing over dead men any moment.

"What do we do now?" he asks. "The docks are too damn far away to dump them, and we can't just leave them here."

"The fuck we can't. Come on." I turn for the back streets as I begin constructing better glamours.

Rhonin grabs my arm. "And be seen leaving the scene of a crime? With a guy who looks like wraiths are about to crawl out of his eyes?"

I touch my face, having forgotten what I look like when I channel such immense power. I also sway a little, a twinge of nausea pinching my gut, like an aftersickness. It's been too long

"I'd rather not end up in a Malgros prison for murder," Rhonin continues. "Or any prison, for that matter. For any reason."

Shaking off my dizziness, I gesture around us. "Unless you can open portals or you're fooling us all and are skilled enough in vast magick to transport us out of here, you don't really have another choice, now do you?"

"Sorry. Just a magickless human here, remember?"

"You won't end up in prison," I assure him, placing a firm hand on his shoulder, in part to steady myself. "Not as long as I'm breathing."

Rhonin lifts his hands and in the same breath drops them at his sides. "Look, you're quickly becoming my hero and all, but somehow that '*long as I'm breathing*' bit doesn't provide much comfort given your current situation."

Even though there are two dead men in our wake, and even though I feel like shit on the bottom of a boot and am now certain I'm being hunted, I can't help but find a shred of humor in the moment.

"If you'd rather stay with the bodies," I tell him, "you're welcome to do so. But I'm leaving, wearing an excellent glamour. If I were you, I'd follow your motherfucking hero."

Though he groans his uncertainty, this time when I turn to go, Rhonin Shawcross is steady at my side.

30

RAINA

With Alexus and Rhonin gone to see Dedrick Terrowin, and Zahira and Yaz visiting the archives, I spend the morning with Nephele, Hel, and Callan at the beach. Ingrid had said to spend some time here, and so we do, though no memory reveals itself. I only know that I love the water, and that one day, if we survive this, I think I might like to live here.

Shortly after noon, when we tire of playing in the wind and sun and waves, we head back up the tor to peruse Zahira's library.

"I could live in this room forever and never grow tired," Nephele says, thumbing through an old tome. Her blonde curls are wild, her pale skin tinged pink from sun and wind burn.

We sit on stools placed around a tall table covered in the selected books of our choice. Every wall here is filled with them, from floor to ceiling.

Yaz provided each of us with pads of bound parchment and sticks of linen-wrapped charcoal for easier note taking, though none of us know exactly what we're supposed to be looking for. Nephele chose books about the recent history of Malgros, no doubt searching for any information about our parents, while I selected another book about curses and one about Loria's descended, doing the very opposite of my sister.

The book Alexus had brought to the lighthouse mentioned Soul Eaters, creatures who were once men, changed into devourers by an ancient curse cast by a faraway god on the rulers of his own lands. Though the text only skimmed the topic, it sounded so similar to the Prince of the East, I thought I'd dig deeper.

Hel glances up from *The History of Tiressian War,* the book she's been reading for the last half hour, and says, "Fia Drumera once destroyed an *entire* Eastland fleet of over five hundred ships with a single wave of fire. That is unfathomable."

"Summerlander magick is powerful," Nephele says, still skimming her gaze over the open pages before her. "Especially when wielded by an ancient queen cursed with even more power over fire."

"You know," Callan says, their hazel eyes sparkling with thought. "I've sometimes wondered if Neri wasn't a sly bastard, and we just disregarded him since he was a god." They close their book on rune magick and exchange it for another. "If you think about it, Neri gave Fia Drumera additional means to protect her land from Thamaos. The same goes for Colden. Granted, their powers were so similar in strength that they repelled one another, so Neri *did* keep them apart as he agreed in his deal with Asha. However, he also made Colden's lover immortal, giving his former Northland soldier eons to figure out how to be with her, if he wanted. And in doing so, he created two immortal weapons: one for the North and one for the Summerlands, a way to forever protect those lands from Thamaos's rule."

Nephele finally looks up. "Neri hated Colden because Asha wanted him, a human, more than she wanted Neri, a god. What he did to Fia and Colden was a punishment, not a blessing. For anyone."

"If he cared about having Colden as a weapon for the North," I sign as Nephele translates for Callan, *"why did he threaten to kill Colden in the wood? Why take his power? That was done in rage, to teach Colden a morbid lesson."*

"Or perhaps Neri was in love," a voice says from behind me. "And that made him foolish. Just a thought."

We all turn to look at the door. Joran leans against the frame, arms crossed over his chest.

"On an entirely different note," he says, "I thought you ladies might like to know that the Collector and the Spy are currently trudging up the beach soaking wet, like they took a swim with their clothes on." He smiles a wolfish smile. "Looks like they met with a bit of trouble."

"And that brings you joy?" Nephele all but spits the words as she slams her book shut.

"Immense," he says, grinning even wider than before.

We slip off our stools and hurry to the window that overlooks the sea to scan the shore toward the city. Nothing. Not even footsteps in the sand.

Just as I prepare to call Joran's words horse shit, Rhonin and Alexus come into view, entering the cove around an outcropping of rocks. Walking side by side, their boots are in hand, their shirts stripped and hanging from the belts, their pants rolled to their calves, their trimmed hair blowing in the breeze.

How did Joran see them before?

When I turn around to ask, the Icelander is gone.

❦

"So you are still not going to tell me what happened," I sign as Alexus slips a new black tunic over his head.

I stand beside the mirror in my robe, watching him scrutinize the neatness of his dinner outfit before reaching for a black jacket that looks as though it was tailored for him. The collar and cuffs are embroidered in glistening, golden thread that also decorates the long lapels.

"Trust me," he replies. "You don't want details." He keeps his attention on the man in the mirror as he slips the key around his neck and shrugs into the garment. "It was bloody and awful, but we made it out just fine."

I cross my arms over my middle and lean against the mirror while he pulls half his hair into a leather tie. Just fine? When I met him on the beach earlier, he was already weary from using his magick against those guards. But after helping Callan build protective wards behind Nephele's construct for reinforcement, and after chatting with Zahira and Yaz about their unlucky day at the archives, he only had enough energy to climb up the lighthouse stairs, dive into the pool for a bath, and eventually collapse on the bed in a naked heap. He slept for well over an hour before he felt himself again.

Running his hands down the front of his jacket, he slips on his shiny shoes and turns his attention on me. "I would rather not talk about that side of me, all right? Today made me feel too much like Alexi of Ghent, and he was a villain." Though he masks it well, I hear a twinge of self-loathing in his voice, or perhaps regret. Maybe both. "It's a bit of a mood killer," he adds, still covering his feelings. I can't even sense them through the rune.

I would never tell him this, but with his hair shorter and his beard gone and the dark, rich clothes, he looks like his old self. At least the image in my mind from our shared dreams. But appearance does not make the man.

"You are no villain," I sign. *"Ever the hero."*

He arches a dark brow. "We all play the villain in someone's tale, Raina." He falls quiet, but then he reaches for my hand and draws me close. "Listen. Tonight isn't about my past. It's about *us*. I want to go to the main house, eat the lovely meal Mari and Yaz are preparing, and then you and I are going to come back here, I'm going to tangle our magick, and we're going to rattle this entire city. Can we focus on that?"

Before I can answer, Hel and Nephele arrive downstairs to get dressed with me, laughing as they start up the lighthouse steps.

"Don't be naked!" Hel shouts. "Also, we brought wine and cheese!"

Alexus chuckles and kisses me. "I left you a gift on the desk. I saw it and thought of you."

I smile and squeeze his hand before he heads down to the main house. Since tonight is our night, it's an early dinner, at his request. A man who knows how to get what he wants.

But I can be persuasive as well.

Later, as Nephele tames her pale curls, and Hel works to make her ebony locks even glossier than before, I reach for my gift, wrapped inside a small golden box, and take my red dress and secret lacy undergarments from the wardrobe with one thought on my mind. At some point, Alexus Thibault is going to have to show me this other side of himself he so wants to hide. Maybe not tonight, but I've a feeling that it's inevitable.

I just hope I can handle it when he does.

31

RAINA

"Why did no one tell me this was a formal thing?" Rhonin says as I enter the dining hall. Everyone's here except for Finn which stings my heart.

Mari sets a dish on the table, leaning beside Rhonin, quite close. "I think you look handsome, sir," she says with an admiring expression. "I like the shorter hair and the smooth face."

"He *does* look handsome," Hel counters from my side, her voice stiff and slightly territorial. "Always."

Every head turns toward me and my sisters.

"Perhaps we overdid it a little," Nephele mutters under her breath, because every eye in the room is wide.

Alexus heads straight for me. His eyes grow dark as he skims a gaze over my loose hair and down to my neck where his gift resides. He bought me a simple gold necklace with a single pearl in the center, like my own little moon. It's perfect.

When he reaches me, his eyes fall to my exposed cleavage, then further down to the witch's marks trailing up my leg, visible through the slit in my dress.

He leans close to my ear, sending a rogue chill across my skin. "You look good enough to eat." My face warms as he leads me to my chair and pulls it out for me before taking his place at my side. Discreetly, he slips his hand over mine and whispers, "You make that necklace even more beautiful."

I shove away any worry about having eyes on us and kiss his cheek, feeling the slight stubble already growing along his jaw.

His mouth turns up. "Why, thank you."

Grinning like a fool, I turn back to the table.

Poor Rhonin, in his plain white day tunic and brown trousers, stands frozen with indecision. When Hel saunters toward him, she passes Mari on the way and gives her a look from the corner of her eye. But Rhonin's attention is solely on Hel.

With her curves on display beneath her clinging emerald gown, he blinks with astonishment, taking her in.

"Why are you gawking?" she asks. "Are you so used to seeing me covered in filth and wielding weapons that you've forgotten that I'm also a lady?"

"Not at all." He shakes his head insistently and moves her chair back from the table. "Okay, maybe a little. But if I forgot, I've certainly been reminded now."

She looks up at him and smiles.

In her silky blue dress that shows off her slender yet strong frame, Nephele stalks toward the last open setting at the table. The one beside Joran.

She grabs the back of her chair before he gets a chance. "I can seat myself. I don't need your help for anything."

He drenches her in a wicked once-over. "Anything? Are you so sure?"

With a look that says she's seconds from gouging his eyes out with a dinner fork, Nephele jerks her chair back. "Positive."

Once we're all set and no one is killing anyone, Mari and Yaz finish bringing the dinner in. The food here has been plentiful, but I haven't felt like devouring a full meal until now. There's a rich, red wine being passed around—not that I need more—and roasted chicken and baked fish swimming in some sort of fragrant yellow sauce and roasted vegetables and breads and even spiced pies for dessert. My mouth waters and my stomach grumbles at the sight.

Zahira and Yaz stand at the head of the table, arm in arm, wine glasses in hand. "A toast," Zahira says. "To everyone in this room. May the Ancient Ones show each of you intrepid warriors the truths you need to see and may Loria light your paths with clarity."

We clang our glasses together, and though Zahira's words resonate in each person's expressions, it seems our stomachs resound even louder. We dig in.

It's obvious that everyone tries their best to be reserved and polite, but I'm apparently not the only one whose appetite is returning tonight. Plates are filled, and most of the chatter goes quiet because our mouths are stuffed with food. As I eat, I can't help but wonder about Finn. If he's all right. If he's eating a hearty meal. Hel said he is well cared for at the Bitter Barrel thanks to Harmon and Zahira's generosity, but I can't help but worry.

Across the table, Rhonin hands Hel a piece of warm raisin loaf which he smothers in butter and honey. "Try it. I bet you'll love it."

The sound that leaves my best friend when she bites into the bready goodness is a deep, unexpected moan that makes Rhonin's mouth fall open. She eats the whole thing as he watches her lips, then she licks the honey from her fingertips.

"Gods, Rhonin. That almost earned you a sticky, wet kiss."

Rhonin closes his mouth and swallows. His face turns three shades of red. "Maybe next time?" he offers, and I nearly choke on my wine.

Callan laughs under their breath, Keth and Jaega snicker, and Alexus stares at his plate, a wide smile on his lips. Sweet Rhonin. I find myself wondering how many chances he was granted to find love before now, being in the Eastland army and all.

Dinner and too many glasses of wine pass far more quickly than I expected, given that our little band of fighters attacked the spread like they do everything else. As everyone chats, Alexus strokes my leg under the table, causing my overly full stomach to flip. Perhaps eating a large meal and downing nearly an entire bottle of wine before having possibly the best sex of my life wasn't the best decision.

With a grip of my knee, he stands and folds his hands around the back of my chair. "Raina and I are going to graciously dismiss ourselves so we can turn in early. It's been a long day."

"Exhausted," I sign, out of a nervous need to over-explain, and Hel translates with a smile.

Everyone knows we're lying. It's evident on their grinning faces. Except for Joran who, I realize, stopped caring about me and Alexus spending time together weeks ago.

I dismiss the thought and stand as Alexus pulls out my chair and motions for me to lead the way toward the veranda. "I'm right behind you," he says with a wink.

"I bet you are," Zahira says, and the room breaks into laughter.

Alexus just smiles and presses his hand to the small of my back. "Come on. Let's go have some fun."

๑ฟอ

THE MOMENT HE CLOSES THE CREAKY GARDEN GATE, ALEXUS SWEEPS ME into his arms and carries me down the flagstone path toward the lighthouse. Only he veers left, taking us through a labyrinth of tall hedges into a nook at the garden's edge where the last of the sun's dying rays barely linger. The space is filled with the beginning shadows of nightfall, the briny scent of sea and sand, and the aroma of winter jasmine that grows in a thick, white blanket over the stone wall.

There, beneath the setting sun and rising moon, with waves crashing against the rocks below, Alexus sets me on my feet, tosses my shoes aside on the grass, and presses me against the fragrant blooms. I cling to his strong arms as he kisses me deeply, licking into my mouth, hungrily exploring. His hands are firm and warm on my waist, his grasp sure as he draws me flush against him. He's already so hard that the pressure of his desire makes my heart skip a beat.

"I hope you aren't as tired as you claimed." He traces the shell of my ear with his tongue. "Because it's going to be a very long and eventful night if I have anything to say about it." He holds my chin between his thumb and forefinger and peers into my eyes. "I'm going to make you come on my cock in every position imaginable, Raina Bloodgood. Starting now."

There's no other warning for the delicious warmth of his power as it skims a teasing touch along our bond. I simply feel that familiar sensation, the air sparking alive with electricity, tickling my skin. My body is buzzing from the wine, so I reach for Alexus's threads with my mind, ready to draw his power into me like our night at Winterhold.

"Stop that, you little rebel." A quiet, deep laugh falls from his lips as he smacks my ass, making me gasp and arch into him. "I told you. Tonight, it's my turn." He grips me tight, kneading my flesh as he presses his erection against me again. "Close your eyes," he whispers, "and let me have my way with you."

An insuppressible smile spreads across my mouth, and as though he holds some spell over me, my eyes flutter shut. Before, at Winterhold, I hadn't known what I was doing when it came to tangling our magick, and Alexus's power had been so weak that he'd had no other choice but to let me lead us. And yet, every moment had been divine regardless.

This time, there's no searching for threads at all. No clinging to them with my mind. No novice at the helm, unsure what to look for, unsure what to do. This time, behind my eyelids, the threads of Alexus Thibault's magick shine, limned with golden light, already vining along our bond at a ravenous pace.

My heart beats faster with anticipation, every twist and weave heating my already burning blood. I cannot imagine what it will be like with him in complete control, his power so much stronger now than it was before. How can we bond any closer than what this night holds for us? Bonded not only in body but also through the rune, through the tangling of our magickal threads, and through the sharing of power.

We will be *one*.

No sooner does that thought travel across my mind, Alexus's power branches through me. A wave of stunning energy rolls over my skin, setting every nerve ending in my body on fire. That power intertwines with my own magick, sending a brutal trickle of pleasure straight to my core.

"Breathe," he commands, smiling against my mouth.

Obediently, I suck in a deep drink of night air saturated with the honeyed taste of his ancient magick.

"Now lift your dress" he says, his voice rough with desire. "And spread those beautiful legs for me."

At his words, my heart thunders with longing, but I hesitate. *"Harmon? The boys?"* I sign. They live in the garden house.

"Busy at the stables because I asked them to be," Alexus replies. "I want to lick you and fuck you under the stars if you'll let me. I want you to think of me every single time you walk through a garden or hear the ocean or smell jasmine or feel a godsdamn night breeze on your bare skin. I want tonight to be something you can't possibly ever forget."

That sends a flash of lust through my body that is so desperate I gather my dress around my hips in a hurry and spread my legs.

As I stand there, waiting, I realize that he hasn't asked me how I want him yet. Hard and rough or deep and slow. I don't think it's up for debate tonight. He means to give me everything.

With that hungry look in his eyes, he lowers to one knee and slides his hands up the curves of my thighs. Even that simple touch sends another bolt of pleasure zinging through me.

For a moment, he angles his head in a curious tilt, then brushes his fingertips back and forth between my legs. It's hard to focus on anything but the white-hot need raging inside me, but when a deep and seductive sound rumbles in the back of Alexus's throat—something torn between a moan and a growl—I blink away the haze of lust and look down at him.

He's seen the lace.

With a lick of his lips, he meets my stare. His green eyes are bright as sea glass held to the light of a high-summer sun—and filled with hunger. He strokes the delicate material again, and I flinch at the tempting contact.

"I want you in nothing but this and the necklace," he says, something dark and wild hovering at the edge of his voice.

It takes a matter of seconds before my sash is untied and my gown is gone, reduced to a puddle at my feet.

As I stand before him, naked save for the scraps of red lace Yazmin calls undergarments, ready to make love against this stone wall if I must, another sound leaves Alexus. It's a sound borne of appreciation and desire, escaping his lips as he admires my bare skin.

He reaches up and brushes his thumb across my nipple. The dark pink flesh is hard and peeking through the lace. The sensation of that touch is tenfold what it would be without our power joined along the bond, making me quiver. I can hardly bear it, yet at the same time, I must have more.

The leather tie holding his hair falls away as I slide my hands into his dark locks and clutch him to my breast. In response, he flicks his tongue over the tip, teasing and biting to the brink of pain, the way he knows I like. I still can't wrap my mind around how well he knows me. How well he's known me since that first night at Winterhold. I never have to instruct or guide him. He just *knows* how to touch me, how to *take* me, how to please me.

I hold him tighter, fisting my hands at the roots of his hair until I'm panting. The action seems to drive him because he grips my waist and everything changes. His mouth becomes hungrier, his touch rougher, and I find myself questioning what the tangling of our power does to *him*. Is he close to exploding like me?

Unexpectedly, he yanks at the lace garment covering my chest, ripping the flimsy top from its silken straps, and throws it aside.

I suppose that answers my question.

Alexus slides his palms across my exposed breasts, my waist, and over my ass, where he gathers the lace of my panties in his fist and tugs, putting gentle pressure where I throb for him.

I gasp, and a wicked tilt crooks his lips when he grins up at me. He keeps tugging, using rhythmic movements to torture me, knowing exactly what he's doing, all while moving from breast to breast, sucking me into his mouth, rolling his tongue and teeth around my nipples.

Gods, I could climax from this alone, and I half-think I might. But Alexus lets go of the lace and draws back, leaving me pulsing with need.

This night is far from over, so I take my hands from his hair and rest against the soft, crushed flowers at my back, trying my best for patience. With that same rougher touch, Alexus trails his strong hands and warm mouth down my abdomen, skims his broad palms over my hips, and slips his tongue along the edge of the lace.

"Red," he whispers, gripping the back of my thigh. "I love you in red."

In the next heartbeat, he lifts my knee over his shoulder, opening me to him. I can barely remain standing when he leans forward and drags his teeth over me, through the fabric, again and again, until I'm grinding shamelessly in time with his mouth, yearning to feel his tongue buried inside me.

Reading my mind, he hooks a finger in the lace and pulls the material aside. The night wind off the sea is tinged with the slightest cool edge, enough that a chill races over my skin at the exposure. I drop my head back against the wall and listen as my pulse pounds harder and harder in my ears. I've never been so starved for anything or anyone in my life. Never needed someone so much it hurts.

Again, I thread my fingers into Alexus's hair. His mouth is so close that when I curve my hips I can feel the damp warmth of his panting breaths. All I can think about is yesterday, straddling his face, his cock in my mouth, the bliss I felt when he came.

With that thought, the loud creak of the metal gate opening and closing screeches through the garden. My blood turns to ice, and Alexus shoots to his feet, bringing my gown with him, sliding it up, helping me slip my arms into the short, ruffled sleeves. Just like that, his magick uncoils from mine like a fraying rope under loads of strain.

He cuts his eyes in the direction of the path leading to the lighthouse, then drags me deeper into the shadows and nestles me in an alcove beneath a bower of foliage. Reeling from being startled, I close the folds of my dress to cover my nakedness and tune my ear to our visitor.

Just as quickly, I let out a steady breath of relief. I've been at Starworth Tor for such a short time, and I already recognize the *click-clack* of Yaz's shoes. This time, however, she's stalking across the flagstone, her steps hastened.

She bangs the knocker on Alexus's door, and the corner of his mouth curves with a mischievous grin. "Whatever it is can wait," he whispers in my ear, and by all the gods, I'm thankful.

But Yazmin doesn't give up so easily, which shouldn't surprise. She seems like the kind of woman whose most well-known traits are persistence and determination.

She bangs the knocker again, and a third time, with feeling—it almost sounds aggressive. Huffing and groaning, she moves toward us, her heels carrying her past our nook, *click-clacking* quickly toward the gate.

But she stops. Takes more steps. Backtracking. Until her shadow moves at the mouth of the short labyrinth, and finally, she appears.

Wearing a knowing smirk, Yaz walks closer and glances down, spying my discarded lace top and the sash to my dress. My face heats to what I know must be a shade as bold as the undergarment at her feet.

"For gods' sakes, Alexus," she *tsks*. "The least you could do is carry the poor woman into the lighthouse." She brings her hands to rest on her round hips and lifts a brow. "But first, if you would be so kind, we have business to tend. It's important."

I push back against the alcove wall, as embarrassed as I've ever been, hoping the settling darkness will swallow me.

"Business?" he asks.

"Dedrick Terrowin," Yaz replies. "He's waiting with Zahira in the office now."

Alexus frowns. "How'd he get through the wards?"

"Callan thankfully happened to be walking the grounds with Keth and Jaega and saw a horse-drawn cart approaching the main gate. They alerted me, and when I saw it was Dedrick, I hurried down to retrieve him. Harmon thankfully sent the sentries home again tonight, so Callan worked a little magick and let Dedrick through."

"All right." Alexus lets out an annoyed sigh and nods once. "I'll be right there."

Yaz offers me a genuine, apologetic smile, then turns and leaves, but I don't take a full breath until the gate creaks closed.

"Gods, I'm so sorry, Raina." Alexus groans and scrubs his hand over his face. "And believe me," he adds, "I loathe asking you to do this, more than you can possibly imagine, but would you care to wait for me in the loft?"

"I want to go with you." I sign the words with one hand, struggling to keep my dress closed, though I'm unsure why it matters right now.

"I know you do," he signs and cups my face. "But I can't take that risk. You might be part of our group on his ship, but I don't want a smuggling sailor knowing how important you are to me. Not until I know for certain that he's an ally."

My stupid little soft heart all but melts into my ribs.

Alexus kisses me. It's a tender thing, this kiss. Softly pressed with supple, swollen lips. Warm and wet and wonderful. I grip his wrists, wanting more, to finish this before he goes. I don't care if it's hurried or brutal. I just need *him*.

But he pulls away.

"Go to the loft." He strokes my face with his thumbs. "The candles should already be burning. There's more wine waiting too. Crawl in bed. Snuggle beneath the covers." He leans close. "Touch that perfect little pussy for relief. But remember that I'll be there soon."

Gods, that mouth of his. His tongue loosens with every encounter, and I think I love it. It makes my thighs quiver, especially as he takes a step back, leaving me standing there, aching for him.

He shoves his hands into his trouser pockets and walks to the mouth of the labyrinth. "Oh, and Raina." He turns a glance over his shoulder and spears me with an intoxicating smile. "Leave the lace on."

ALEXUS

"**D**edrick Terrowin."

The smuggler stands with Zahira, leaning on a dark green marble cane as they look over her collection of maps. At the sound of his name, he turns around. He's dressed in fine clothing not dissimilar to my own, as though heading somewhere important.

"The one and only Alexus Thibault." He holds out his light brown, tattooed hand as he walks toward me. I don't miss the emerald and pewter ring on his middle finger, designed to match the silver lion's head on the top end of his cane. "I heard I was summoned."

I accept the greeting with a firm handshake and determine that, as Zahira said, he possesses no magick. Then we get down to business.

"I trust that I have your silence on the matters discussed here tonight."

He pushes the bronze spiral curls hanging over his forehead out of his eyes, his warm, amber gaze reflecting the room's fire and candlelight. "Of course. My customers know I'm a man of my word." He glances at Zahira who inclines her head and nods.

"I need safe and comfortable passage for nine people on your next trip to Itunnan," I tell him.

"You know you'll be properly compensated," Zahira says.

Dedrick runs his finger over his thick eyebrow. "Safe, I can guarantee.

Comfortable?" He moves his head from side to side. "That could be an issue. Nine people require a fair amount of space. My next cargo load on the Lady Belladonna is small though, so perhaps, if the money is right, I can offer extra room and conveniences. It'll be tight quarters though, and a little more complex to get you off the boat once we arrive. But I'm not new to this game."

I incline my head. "That's what I was hoping to hear. When does your ship set out again?"

"Three mornings from now, if she arrives on time tomorrow. Is that soon enough?"

"It'll have to be," I reply, hoping that the dead men in the alley have no tales to tell.

He gestures toward the chairs by Zahira's fire. "I have about an hour before I must leave. Can we review the details now? I have a very busy schedule over the next two days. Much of it includes the Watch. I doubt you want too much movement with them around."

Not at all. Especially now.

I glance toward the door, thinking of Raina. I have a very beautiful woman waiting on me.

"Fine," I tell him. "But let's make it quick."

We sit at Zahira's desk for half an hour, working out an embarkment method, along with how the Summerland Guard secures and scours cargo and trade ships as they arrive in port. With the size of our party, the margin for error is greatly increased. Still, it's fairly straightforward.

"You're free to roam the ship until we reach Summerland waters," Dedrick says. "At that point, I'll send you and yours below deck. When we reach the port, you'll burrow into a false hull, from which you will *swim* to a specific dock under the cover of night. From there, my contact will take over. She'll get you through Itunnan and the Ske-Trana provinces unseen."

Somehow, I can't imagine it being that easy, but I'm not sure what else I can do but trust this man.

I walk him to the front door. Callan waits in the vestibule, ready to open a pathway for Dedrick to unwittingly walk through.

"Good night, Master Thibault," he says. "I look forward to our journey."

I force a smile, still too uncertain of this newest character in my story.

As he walks down the vestibule, leaning heavily on his cane, I call to him, and he turns around. "Where exactly are you headed?" I ask.

He smiles and reaches into the breast pocket of his slim-fitting black jacket. He reveals only a peek at a pretty, pearlescent envelope with his name scrolled across the front. "To a dinner party held by Admiral Rooke. It's the place to be tonight."

My blood stills. "I thought that was tomorrow night."

He shakes his head and raises his brows. "No. Tonight. And if I don't hurry, I will certainly be late." He turns and heads toward his waiting cart and driver, waving a hand over his shoulder. "I'll see you in a few days, my lord!"

Fuck all. More like within the hour.

I SLIP INTO THE KITCHEN WHERE RHONIN'S HELPING MARI CLEAN UP the dinner dishes and drag him into the hall, hoping to bypass Zahira and anyone else.

"Get upstairs, change into the formal wear we bought the other day, and meet me at the Emory's as soon as possible. Say nothing to anyone."

It's better if no one knows where we're going. I just haven't figured out how I'm going to get past Raina yet.

Rhonin is such a good soldier. He's curious, but he hurries upstairs without a word.

When I enter the lighthouse, Raina's dress and torn lace undergarment hang from the newel post by the stairs. I glance the winding staircase and notice that her shoes lie on two different treads, as though she stripped on the way up.

I follow her trail until I reach the loft, where I find her resting on the bed, on her stomach, two books cast aside, dressed in nothing but those tiny red bottoms I need to thank Yaz for and that little gold necklace. She slides a long leg up at an angle, granting me a lovely view.

"Fucking beautiful," I mutter, drinking in the tantalizing sight before I cross to the bed, longing to push inside her.

But tempting as she is, and as much as I've thought about this for weeks, tonight is not the night, and I must tell her so.

I lower my mouth to whisper in her ear, but before I can utter a single syllable, she snores. It's the sweetest, most delicate sound I've ever heard, and I can't help but smile and laugh silently as I drop my chin to my chest.

So much for making her lose control. I can't even keep her conscious.

She's passed out on top of the covers, so I find a blanket in the linen cabinet and gently spread it over her, tugging it up to her shoulders. Her face is turned away from me, her full lips parted and stained red from the wine. Though I want to taste them, I graze the softest kiss over her brow instead. She doesn't stir, but she *does* snore again.

I admire her, thinking about all we've been through. All we've shared. How desperate I feel to keep her safe. How desperate I feel to claim her as mine. Not just when we make love—the claiming that comes with passion —but the kind of claim announced to the world, as though I might lose her if I don't. Because I care for her, deeper than should be possible.

A pang strikes my chest with all the impact of a fist. Assuredness fills me, followed by a release of pressure, as though some scar tissue that formed over my heart a very long time ago disintegrates. It's been disappearing little by little since I met Raina, but right now, as I ghost a touch across her cheek and tuck a wayward lock of hair behind her ear, my throat constricts around the swelling emotion inside me, and the web strangling my heart vanishes completely.

Perhaps it's impossible to give your heart to someone when it's tethered to your soul by centuries of misery and pain. But regardless of what I face with Admiral Rook and Vexx tonight, there's a freedom inside me, freedom that I haven't felt in...

I can't remember when I felt this way. When everything of meaning or importance narrowed down to one thing. To one person who holds my heart whether she knows it or not.

The truth rises inside me like a growing tide. A truth I can no longer deny to myself, and a truth I can't keep from her much longer.

"Raina Bloodgood," I whisper, leaning in to kiss her brow one last time before I leave. "I think I'm falling in love with you."

❧ IV ❧
ENDINGS

33

RAINA

I wake with a start.

Disoriented and feeling a slight wine headache, I sit up and glance around the dark loft. Night has fully fallen, and I'm alone. The door knocker clangs again. Loudly. Over and over.

I throw on a tunic and leggings and grab the oil lamp that's barely still burning and hurry to the lighthouse's main level. When I throw open the door, it's Hel. She stands beneath the lantern whose flame Dru and Drae haven't yet extinguished, wearing a frown and a determined expression that I know well.

I wipe my sleepy eyes, set my lamp on a table inside the doorway, and form my own expression. One that says, *What's wrong?*

"I saw a man leave Starworth Tor," she says. "In a horse-drawn cart. I'd *just* headed upstairs when Alexus escorted him out."

"Dedrick Terrowin," I sign. *"The smuggler."*

"I heard," she says. "But Alexus didn't turn around and head back to the lighthouse when the man left. He came upstairs and went into Rhonin's room."

"There is nothing unusual about that," I sign. *"And... were you snooping?"*

"Of course I was. Because there *is* something unusual about it. Alexus was supposed to be with *you* tonight. I knew it had to take quite the event to drag him away from this lighthouse."

I shake my head and shiver against a cool breeze, confused. *"So where is he now?"*

Both of her brows rise. "He left. On foot. I saw it from my window, so I thought I'd come find you. Then I passed Rhonin's room." She lowers her eyes for a moment and pinches the tips of her fingers together. "His door was cracked, and I *might've* peeked. He was maybe a little naked, and very nice clothes and a new double dagger harness lay on his bed next to his weapons. He was clearly distracted enough that he didn't notice me. I feel like something's up."

Trying to think more optimistically, I reach for Alexus through the rune, sending a gentle inquiry along the bond, but...

His end of the bond is closed to me. Again.

An uneasy feeling climbs up my spine like phantom fingers. I hurry upstairs and grab my scrying dish, the decanter of water I keep in the room, and my needle. If Rhonin and the Witch Collector are placing themselves in harm's way for the second time today, I will know.

Alexus might close me out of the bond.

But he cannot stop a Seer.

⚜

UNFORTUNATELY, THE WATERS TURN UP LITTLE MORE THAN ALEXUS walking into the city like a handsome devil, shrouded in the night's shadows, an unsettling air about him. Hel and I settle for a different route to gather information.

We catch Rhonin just in time, at the top of the stairs, and shove him back into his room. It takes both of us and all our might to make him budge.

"It's *nothing*," he says, holding his hands up in a defensive manner. "Nothing special. Just business."

I lean against the desk and give him a narrowed look, wanting answers. *"You just so happened to decide to go out at this hour for no reason? Armed in fine clothes and daggers?"*

Rhonin is still learning my language, so Hel translates, blocking the door. "Maybe he has plans with *Mari*."

The air tightens when Rhonin turns that cerulean gaze on her. "Can I ask why you're so worried about Mari? I've known her for a matter of days."

Hel draws her shoulders back, wearing a mask of indifference, trying so hard to hide her jealousy. She gestures at me. "A lot can happen in a matter of days, Rhonin. Where've you been?"

He faces her, smoothing his hand over his finely embroidered vest. "*Me?* Where've *you* been? Finn was here for all of a few hours, and Mari looked at him like he was a god that fell from the sky. He's all she talked about tonight when I helped her in the kitchen. She's been taking him food and clothes and gods' know what else they've done. She's really nice, but trust me, even if she *did* have eyes for me, these clothes would not be for her." He shifts his jacket from massive hand to massive hand and moves closer to Hel, a giant of a man, even compared to her tall form. To both our surprise, he tips her chin up with his finger. "Do you like it? That's all I care about."

Hel's throat moves with a hard swallow as she holds his stare. "Very much. You look quite... regal."

"Regal is good." A tiny smirk curl's Rhonin's lips. "Does it earn me that kiss you talked about?"

I expect Hel to grab his vest and yank him near for a hard, deep tongue lashing. That's just something Hel would do. Instead...

"Tell us where you're going, and you just might get your wish, Spy."

Rhonin shakes his head, and a soft glint of disappointment shines in his eyes. "One day I'm going to kiss you, Helena Majesta Owyn. Obviously not today. But I will, and when I do, you'll kiss me back. Because you want to, not because of a bargain." He folds a single arm around her waist, picks her up, and moves her, clearing the path to the door, which he opens. Paused at the threshold, he points at both of us and says, "Don't get any ideas about following me. Either of you. I mean it. You're better off here. Remember that."

The moment he's gone, Hel and I share a glance. "We can't go through the cove," she says. "Nephele, Zahira, and Yaz are down there having wine. Can you get us through the wards?"

I think of Callan's lesson when we entered Starworth Tor's gate. *"I can try."*

We head to the room she shares with my sister. *"Should we tell her?"* I sign. It feels strange leaving Nephele out.

Hel lifts a single brow. "Not unless you want her to stop us, because she will." When I shake my head, Hel stalks toward the wardrobe filled with the clothes we bought yesterday. "That's what I thought," she says and opens the doors wide. "We need to hurry. You wear the gray dress. I'll wear the black one."

⁂

THANKFULLY, CALLAN ISN'T WATCHING THE GATE.

Though it takes a few tries, I manage to dismantle the spell from the inside by unlocking the runes for protective passage. It's like a puzzle, the proper placement of pieces, and the practice I've had with the prince's barrier helps. Unfortunately, once we're outside the gate, Hel tracks *two* sets of wagon marks in the gravel and sand, one set that belonged to Dedrick Terrowin. The other had to be Rhonin.

We start toward the city anyway, hoping to see other people dressed in finery, headed to the same place so we can follow. Our weapons are concealed beneath our taffeta dresses, our glamours up. My dagger and sheath feel unusually rough against my thigh, the leather chafing. The healing properties of the thermal pool and long baths softened my skin and healed the sore places where my weapon stayed for most of the last several weeks. But I walk on, hoping to acclimate to the feel again.

We don't make it far, though.

Finn jogs around a bend, up the cobbled street toward Starworth Tor's gate, right where it curves away from the city wall and toward the many houses between here and Village Hill. He slows when he sees us, the confused expression on his sweat-dampened face clear under the moonlight as he approaches.

He looks us up and down as he catches his breath. "Where are you two headed? Without escorts, at that? Where's the Collector? Rhonin?"

I can smell the ale on him.

Hel and I glance at one another. "They're *out*," she says. "And so are we."

She starts to move past him, but he presses a hand to her chest and pushes her back. "This is no time for games or lies, Helena. It's very important that I speak with the Collector."

"He is not here, Finn," I sign, hoping he'll believe me. *"We are going to look for him."*

Finn groans and scrubs his hand through his thick, wavy hair. "Leave it to that bastard to leave you unattended. Anything could fucking happen."

I jerk my head back, not shocked that he would say something so ridiculous but pissed off, nonetheless. *"I do not need to be* tended," I sign, widening my eyes and exaggerating the movement of that last word. *"I do as I please. Clearly."*

"How about you tell us what you want with the Collector," Hel says, crossing her arms beneath her breasts. "Then we can go from there."

Finn glares at his sister. I know he loves her. Know he would do anything for her. But... He just isn't the Finn he used to be.

"I met a man at the Bitter Barrel last night," he says. "After a few mugs of ale, he started talking about the war, because he used to be in the Watch. He let it slip that he knows things about the Prince of the East's current plans. I prodded him as best I could. He knew about the Eastlander army coming through Malgros. He knew who the guards were that guided them through the backstreets of the city. He even knows that General Vexx is in Malgros, and he knows his whereabouts."

My blood goes very cold and very still. *"Where is this man?"* I sign.

"In my room, hopefully still waiting. I told him I had someone I needed him to talk to."

Hel presses a hand to her forehead. "Gods. We need that information, Finn. Why would you leave him? Why not bring him here?"

Finn's face contorts into a mask of frustration. "Because I was trying to protect the knowledge that you all are staying at Starworth Tor, Helena. I made certain he didn't follow. That no one did. I wanted to interrogate him, but I didn't know what to ask, not like the Collector would. I asked the innkeeper not to let him leave, so if either of you would like to stand in for Thibault, then perhaps that's what should happen tonight rather than you two running around a foreign city in fancy dresses. This isn't playtime."

Hel's dark eyes flare, and I half think she might punch her brother in the face. Instead, she looks at me. "What the fuck do we do now?"

A sigh escapes me. We have to be careful, but if Finn's man knows where Vexx is...

Gods. A feeling crashes into me, a realization. I've been so busy traveling and worrying and surviving and thinking and *fucking* that I've buried my rage beneath hope and a longing for peace. But right now, at the thought of learning where Vexx is hiding, I exchange immaterial desires for something tangible. Something within my control.

Vengeance rises inside me on a vicious, violent tide. Suddenly, my dagger feels different around my thigh. It feels fucking good and right. It feels like power. Like I'm remembering who I am.

I turn to Hel, recalling her words when we were in the cave in the ravine, and I give her an answer. "What the fuck do we do?" I sign with a bitter smile, closing down my end of the bond too. "We go hunting."

34

ALEXUS

"R unning rooftops." Rhonin presses his hands to his knees to catch his breath. "A skill I've never been particularly good at. Is this entirely necessary?"

"Unless you want me to murder dozens tonight instead of a few, yes."

The Northland Watch had patrols on the streets, so we took to the rooftops, three stories up. I glance at the city wall in the distance to my left, making certain we're still within the shadows of the taller buildings built on the city's slope. Then I stare ahead, into the moonlit night, where Brear Hall looms.

"Come on," I tell him, readying myself to sprint across the rooftop and leap. "We're only three jumps away from our destination."

And a little revenge.

On the last leap across a narrow alley, Rhonin misses by a matter of inches and slams into the building's side.

Clinging to the clay tiles, he looks up at me when I peer over the edge, panic twisting his face into a grimace. "A little help would be nice. Before I end up splattered in the alley."

I bend down, rolling my eyes, and grab him under the shoulders. "You might break, but you won't splatter. You are a literal beast." I groan and heave, but it's like tugging on an oak tree. "Push off the wall with your toes."

"I'm *trying*," he says, voice and body straining.

I don't know if what I'm about to do will work or if it's even wise— probably not—but I summon the night's energy, soak it in, and blast it toward the ground in a thin, concentrated stream. The moment it shatters the cobblestones in the alley, I take a deep breath and draw the energy toward me once more in a mighty swell.

The propulsion of that force can be so powerful, the mightiest wind, one I used to know how to ride through the sky. This burst is small, but it still sends Rhonin upward, flying over me, until he lands two yards away with a loud grunt, face down on the roof's tiled ridge cap.

He pushes up and snaps his head around to look at me. "What the fuck was that?"

I brush dust from the impact off my jacket as I peek into the alley to see if anyone heard us. It's still empty, likely thanks to the activity near Brear Hall.

"Energy," I reply.

He huffs. "That's your answer for everything when it comes to your magick, isn't it? *Energy*."

I stalk toward him, careful of my footing, and help him stand. "Now isn't really the time for a magick lesson. Let's get in there and get this over with."

Quietly, we move to the stairs snaking up the side of the building and hurry down to street level where we slip inside the servant's entry at the back of Brear Hall, glamours up. I've been here before, though never in the kitchens.

The gazes of several servants hang on us as we move through their work areas, but no one says a word, not even when we enter the secured parts of the building. Brear Hall consists of Northland Watch offices, meeting halls, a grand dining room, a ballroom, and an entire floor of apartments dedicated to Rooke's living quarters and rooms for guests, like Colden and me.

Like Vexx.

We step into the busy main hall, shielded behind an old statue of Neri —half man/half wolf. The statue's white marble matches the floors and walls, gleaming under candlelight. Guests are still arriving in their sleek clothes, checking their invitations at the door, and guards stand stationed beneath Tiressian flags hanging from every pillar surrounding the circular entry. They look disinterested and unworried, barely noticing the people who pass before them, which is far more than the twenty Emory mentioned.

"Well, this is bad," Rhonin says beneath his breath.

I try to silence my annoyed groan. Either Emory lied, which I can't imagine, or he was given false information, which is always possible. Regardless, the fact that there are this many people here tonight obliterates my plan to corner the admiral and Vexx at dinner.

I've a second option, though.

I glance at the vaulted entry and the wide, marble stairs. Rhonin follows me as we merge with a group of guests and start the climb toward stringed music filtering down from above. Thanks to our attire and shorter hair, we blend in well enough with the partygoers.

We don't break with everyone else when they enter the third-level ballroom. Instead, we keep moving to the last floor—the apartments. Six surround the stairwell, every door closed and all quiet.

"Any ideas?" Rhonin keeps his voice trained low as I guide him to the other side of the floor.

"I know where Rooke lives. That's all I need to know. He'll willingly divulge all else by the time I'm finished with him."

Rhonin draws his daggers as I pause before Rooke's door and press my ear to the wood. Voices. Laughter. No guards.

Something isn't right.

I turn the knob and push the door open, remaining at the threshold. Two men—one with short, blond hair and sun-tanned skin, the other with gray braids and a ruddy, weathered complexion, a raven sitting on his shoulder—sit in finely carved armchairs near the hearth, glasses of dark liquor in hand. They aren't facing the fire. They're facing me.

Admiral Rook and General Vexx.

Rooke nervously rolls his shoulders inside his dove-gray uniform, covered in an admiral's insignia. He looks at me with a strange expression, one that says he's scared but has placed his faith in the man to his right. A mistake.

"Ah, Un Drallag, we've been waiting for you." Vexx wears a bronze-colored suit, the color of his army's garb, and that familiar, cruel smile is at play on his lips. He glances at Rhonin, and the raven's eyes move too. "I see you brought my traitorous soldier along for the fun. You really made my job too easy."

Rhonin says nothing in response, though he shifts on his feet, no doubt wanting to tear into Vexx. But he has a family to think of. The spy must play the traitor, for now.

Behind us, I hear movement. Footsteps coming up the stairs.

"Guards," Rhonin grits out.

Fuck. We've walked right into a trap.

I step inside the apartment, Rhonin with me, and shut the door.

Vexx laughs. "*That's* not going to keep them out. All I need to do is say the word, and they'll march in here and drag you to my ship. In a matter of days, you'll return to the Eastland coast, whether you want to or not."

"You *know* what I'm capable of," I tell him, narrowing my eyes. My pulse is pumping, my voice so deep and low it sounds foreign to my ears. "You saw, in Frostwater Wood. I can destroy every single one of those men in the blink of an eye. And I can destroy you." I aim my next words at Rooke. "Did the Watch find two guards dead in an alley near the ship-yard earlier today? Chests blown open?" Admiral Rooke's face falls, and Vexx's eyes glisten. "That was me," I inform them. "And I'll do it a thou-sand times more before I let anyone lay hands on me or mine. Know that."

"Oh, they were found, and I *do* know what you can do," Vexx says. "But my plans were made so much easier because I also know your weakness, Un Drallag. The one thing you would sacrifice all of Tiressia for, strange as it is. You paint me and the prince as evil when, in truth, you are no better. At least we fight for more than one person. You would burn everything and everyone for Raina Bloodgood, wouldn't you?"

Vexx's cruel smile morphs into a grin that sparks fear inside me. A grin that says he's been hard at work preparing for this very night—with Raina on his mind.

Heart hammering, I take a step toward him, the room beginning to crackle with my power. "If you so much as lay a finger on her, I will torture you from here to eternity, so brutally that you will beg me to carve out your heart with my hands because that would be a kinder end. Don't think I won't commit to the task. I know how to persist."

"Oh, I know you do," he says, taking a casual sip of his liquor. "But I'm not going to touch her at all. I know who is, though. I hope you said your goodbyes properly."

I lift my hand and draw bolts of blue power into my fingers. "You get one chance to correct the very poor decision to goad me."

Vexx stands and meets my eyes, far braver than he has any right to be. "If you kill me, you lose your only chance of learning what happened to your beloved witch." He reaches up and pets the raven's wing, the black bird staring at me with cold, beady, watchful eyes. "Because thanks to my little friend, Crux, I'm the only one in this building who knows where she is right now, and I've a plan for where she's going. *If* she lives through the night." He lifts his glass. "Go on. Call to her. See if you can. Try to communicate with that mark you burned into her so selfishly. The prince notified me about that, by the way. You shared your power with that little wench, which could be quite handy if—" he holds up his finger "—she's learned how to use it, and you're accessible to her, which you are not tonight. Meaning she's vulnerable, especially in the hands of a sorcerer assassin."

I do try to reach her, internally admonishing myself for closing the bond, my breaths coming faster. I send a heartfelt plea through the rune, along our connection, asking her to please talk to me. *Please.*

There's no answer.

Tears sting the backs of my eyes, and rage burns inside me, hot as the lightning I can command. I want to destroy Vexx. I want to feel his bones crush beneath the squeeze of my power. I've never hungered for the warmth of a man's blood on my hands more than now. Never craved the feel of cold death as it consumes another's life more than in this moment. But Vexx's threat awakens me, makes me imagine a hundred ways I could kill him and still not be satisfied.

"Alexus," Rhonin says, drawing my name out like a question, wanting to know what to do.

I raise my arm and whirl my hand in a wide arc, gathering all the power in the room into a blue eddy, before I fling it at the door, plastering the entry with a web of electricity I would like to see Rooke's men try to come through.

With that same momentum, I sling ropes of power toward Rooke and Vexx, manacling their hands and ankles, and drag them from their chairs across the room.

The raven—Crux—squawks and flies straight for me, wings flapping wildly, but I pull a Raina Bloodgood and grab that bastard mid-air. I slam it against the wall where it thuds to the floor.

I stalk to Vexx and straddle him, bending down to fist a clump of his gray hair. "I don't have to kill you. But I can make you wish you were dead. So if I were you, I'd start talking. Tell me where Raina is. Now."

He laughs again. This time, it grows into a cackle, to a howling guffaw. Then it just dies, his eyes wild, his face cold. "She's in trouble, that's where she is. And this time, you can't save her."

RAINA

"I'm back, Gavril."

Finn motions for Hel and me to enter his room at the Bitter Barrel. The man—Gavril—sits hunched in a chair, his feet boldly close to the fire as if to warm them as he chews a piece of bread.

Hel and I cross the threshold and stand in the center of the cramped, run-down space in our fine gowns. Muffled laughter and music from the tavern reverberate through the floor as I look over the room. Mari has certainly been here. I recognize items from Starworth Tor. A blue and white vase of flowers sitting on a small table near the balcony door, a stack of old books on the desk, a nice woven blanket folded on the bed, and a basket of grooming supplies. At least she's taking care of him.

Gavril lifts his head and studies me with sparkling blue eyes before he shifts a glance at Hel. He doesn't look as old as I expected, maybe only a few years older than Alexus—in frozen years. Early to mid-thirties.

I take quick inventory. He's covered in a stained brown cloak and tattered, drab clothes, making him appear slovenly. But his black hair, though tousled, looks like it's been trimmed recently, and his beard is shaved back to a short clip. When I skim a glance over his hands, they don't match what I imagined either. They're clean and strong, his fingernails neat.

There's an incongruence that makes me wary, the picture of this man not quite coming together, though I seem to be the only one who notices. I take the small chair across from him, willing to hear what he has to say. Finn pulls up a stool beside me, and Hel sits at the foot of her brother's bed, close to Gavril.

"This is who you wanted me to speak to?" The man's words are shortened and sharpened by an accent that doesn't sound like anyone from the Northlands.

"Not actually," Finn says. "He wasn't available. But these two are more knowledgeable than me about the matters that need to be discussed."

Gavril stares at me, his gaze boring into mine before he flicks a glance and a finger at my thigh. "You wear a blade. Take it off." He turns to Hel. "You too."

"Go fuck yourself," Hel says at the same time I instinctively sign, *Not a fucking chance.*

He arches a brow at me. "You don't speak?"

"I speak just fine," I sign again. "You just cannot read me."

Hel translates with a little fire in her voice, and Gavril smiles, but his attention remains on me. "I read you better than you think. You want to know where General Vexx is."

I narrow my eyes. *How do you know that?*

Again, Hel translates, and Gavril shrugs. "He's been here for nearly two weeks. You've been here a few days. Things are overheard. Gossip spreads. The girl with no voice bested the Prince of the East, and now she's in Malgros with the Witch Collector, wanting to hunt down Vexx before sailing to the Summerlands and journeying to the City of Ruin."

My stomach sinks, and gavrI can feel the blood drain from my face as Hel sighs a quiet *Fuck.* If this is common knowledge, we're in more danger than we realized.

Worried, I open my end of the bond and reach for Alexus, to warn him. At first there's nothing, though his end of the rune is as clear as the sun. I close my eyes and call for him.

Find me. Leave. Find me. Not safe.

When I open my eyes, my rune warms to a burn, so hot I gasp and slip my hand under the part of my dress that covers the mark.

Where are you? That's the question that races along the bond from Alexus. *Where are you? Where are you? Where are you? Please talk to me.*

I double over from the power of his plea. All I can manage to communicate is *Finn. Tavern. Finn.*

"Raina." Hel rushes to my side. "Are you all right?"

I shake my head. Alexus is panicking.

"Perhaps you should get her some water or ale," Gavril says. "A cool cloth." Finn agrees, and before I can argue, Hel hurries downstairs to the tavern.

The moment the door closes, my entire world changes.

Gavril flashes a blade through the air so fast I barely have time to look up and flinch. Blood sprays my face, and when I turn, stunned, Finn is gasping, his throat slit from side to side, blood spilling from the wound and then from his mouth.

With those big brown eyes, he stares at me in shock and horror, trying to say my name, and I clasp his throat, blood seeping between my fingers. Already I smell his death approaching—the aroma of a forge fire and leather, of the air just before a rainstorm.

My mind stutters as I search for the glimmering threads of his life and think the Elikesh words to save him. *Loria, Loria, anim alsh tu bretha, vanya tu limm volz...*

But a hot, sharp pain stabs into my ribs.

I gasp and jerk, and Finn slips from my hold—there's so much blood. He collapses on the floor as I look up and meet Gavril's eyes. The man hovers over me, caging me in my chair, his dagger buried in my side. I can hear Finn struggling, coughing, choking, suffocating on his own blood.

And it makes me cold with fury.

Fulmanesh, iyuma.

A ball of fire shoots from the hearth and flies toward Gavril. Something stops it mid-air, the fiery orb spinning in place until it disintegrates into sparks dancing on the floor.

Gavril smiles and grips my throat.

He's a witch. Or sorcerer. A man with magick.

I try again and again, launching fire balls at my newest enemy as he pushes my head against the back of my chair. He catches the raging orbs with his mind and quickly extinguishes the flames.

But one—*one*—blessedly strikes his face, drawing a scream from his chest, a howl of a sound that rattles the room as the fire blisters his cheek and singes his hair.

Shaking with pain, his grip loosens, but he never lets go of me, his weight pinning me. The fire in his hair and on his skin fades quickly though, and he stares down, eyes wild and head half-scorched. "Stupid, foolish woman. You will pay."

Desperate, I call for my magickal blade. *Lunthada, comida, bladen tu dresniah, krovek volz gentrilah!*

The amethyst light sputters into existence but instantly vanishes, as though sucked away.

Gavril's eyes sparkle and glow, that same shade of amethyst, as though he absorbed my magick. He tilts his head back, lips parted, relishing it. I can see the pleasure on his face—like that small bit of magick is renewing him.

In those few moments of distraction, I imagine Finn laughing and smiling. Quickly, I work at weaving his life threads as I gather the side of my dress in my hand and slip my blood-slicked hand over my thigh, feeling for leather and steel.

"I was supposed to let you live," Gavril says. "Get you to Vexx and the prince. But you had to go and summon Un Drallag, didn't you? I could feel it. Feel *him*. He should know that this war is no place for such a delicate thing as you." He leans close, reeking of burned flesh and hair. "When I first saw you, I hated to be the one to snuff out your light. But now I don't care. Some lights burn too brightly, so tonight is your last night to shine, pretty one."

I shove my dagger into his gut and rip it back out. I'm not fucking dead yet.

He stumbles back a few steps, his blade still buried in my side, but now I'm free. I leave his weapon inside me so that I don't bleed out and force myself to stand, kicking my chair out of the way, gathering the energy to fight him. We're both wounded. We both have magick. But I'm armed. He isn't.

Before I can attack, Gavril lunges across the room, knocking me to the floor, sending my dagger flying into the fire. His blade burrows deeper into my side with the fall, and piercing, punishing, pain blazes through my body.

He clasps his hands around my throat and squeezes as blood soaks through his tunic.

I try, but I can't reach the hilt of his knife—my only defense. When I try a second time, Gavril lifts his knee and pins my right arm beneath his weight, then he fights me to pin the other.

The thinnest shred of hope forms as I hear Hel stomp toward the room, but Gavril hears her too. He throws up a hand, aiming it at the door, and though the knob jostles, Hel can't enter.

My best friend pounds her fist on the door. "Finn? Raina?" When there's no answer, she pounds harder. "Let me in." And again, more pounding. "Fucking let me in!"

I buck against Gavril, kicking, each movement agony, and he uses magick to trap my legs, like two strong hands holding me down. He shakes his head, and with a cruel smile, grabs the hilt of his blade and pulls it from my body, the only thing keeping me from bleeding to death on this floor.

My pinned right hand lies in a pool of Finn's warm blood. I can feel his skin against mine, the weak brush of his finger as tears pour from my eyes. I keep trying to focus, trying to save him, but I can feel him slipping.

Memories of him flood my mind. He shouldn't have been here. He should've never come. I wish I would've made him stay in the valley.

Sobbing, I tell myself that this is the worst of it. Gavril will get up and wait until we stop breathing. I pray to the Ancient Ones that Hel gets away. That she hurries downstairs, and the people there help her.

But this *isn't* the worst of it.

Gavril grabs the sweeping collar of my dress and rips the fabric, revealing my rune. "You seem hard to kill in this game we're playing," he says as Hel begins screaming and kicking the door. "And I'm certain Un Drallag is on his way. So if I can't get you to the prince alive, I can at least grant him his second request. I can stop you from entering the Summerlands. All it requires is a little change in your trajectory."

He reaches toward the fire, and when his hand appears over me, he's holding *my* dagger. The last few inches of the tip are glowing with orange light from the heat of the flame.

The air in the room changes, and Gavril begins an eerie chant. I can't process the words as magick swells around me with so much pressure it feels like the room might burst.

I can't do anything but try and reach for Alexus, even as I curl my finger around Finn's, needing someone to hold onto. I close my eyes and send another word along the bond. *Help.*

There in the darkness, my abyss is waiting, beckoning, pleading as hard as Alexus had pleaded, roiling and empty, cold and vast as death. I sense safety in that void, and I almost let my mind fall into it. I come so close.

But Gavril presses the flat side of the incandescent blade to my rune, and my soul screams.

dling on the sand with your father, you just haven't recovered it yet. But surely you feel some familiarity here?"

She does. She said as much as we stared over the water earlier.

Someone touches my shoulder, and I jump, having completely forgotten that we weren't alone in this room. Zahira stands behind Nephele and me like a protective mother, as though she knows we've already had our fill of this little outing.

"I think these two are tired, Ingrid," she says. "Do you have any further suggestions for what Raina and Nephele might do to unearth these memories more fully?"

The woman leans forward, forearms on the table. "If you're going to be here for any length of time, I suggest taking a stroll by the barracks where you and your parents would've lived and spend some hours on the beach. Other than that, perhaps you should have Captain Osane check the years of your parents' time here. That information can be found in the Watch's enlistment logs in the archives."

ALEXUS

White-hot agony washes through the rune with bright familiarity.

It rips through my flesh, my blood, my bones. My *mind*. Gasping around the relentless pain, I stumble and slip on the tiled roof. Rhonin wraps a hand around my arm, catching me before I fall. "I've got you."

"They're taking her from me, Rhonin. They're hurting her."

"I know, my friend." He jerks me to my knees. "But we have to keep moving. The guards are coming."

I can't breathe. The misery of this moment—I remember it well. Someone's reversing the rune.

Tears flood my eyes, and my chest strains so tightly I think my sternum might shatter. But worse, my heart is being torn in two, shredded by an invisible beast I swear I will hunt and kill for this.

"Come on," Rhonin insists. "Think of Raina. We have to find her."

Through the red haze clouding my mind, I struggle to my feet and find my mettle. Rhonin and I run, leaping over one narrow alleyway after another, stair-stepping down rooftops until I know we're close to the tavern. I had to leave Vexx and Rooke behind, too uncertain about killing them in case Vexx was telling the truth. The moment Raina's torment scorched through the rune, I knew he was.

We drop to a one-story rooftop, my knees weak, then on to ground level. The Watch is coming. They might even meet us there.

With my hand pressed to my rune, I burst through the front door of the noisy Bitter Barrel and fight my way up the crowded stairs that lead to the inn. Halfway to the second floor, I falter as a hot, merciless throb pounds through the rune, reverberating in my chest and ribs, threatening to take me to my knees again.

Rhonin is still there, grabbing me from behind, helping me stand. "Clear the way!" he yells in a booming voice.

These people are gathered for a reason.

A spectacle.

When they don't part, Rhonin steps in front of me and shoves forward, moving patrons aside like rag dolls, using his size to forge a clear path.

Standing in the hall, I know which room is Finn's. The door is open, and the innkeeper waits outside the threshold, hands fisted at his sides as he shakes his head. I hurry toward the room. The innkeeper tries to stop me, but I shove him aside.

Then I freeze, grasping the door frame, the wood singed and burned, like someone recently tried to use fire magick to get inside.

Helena sits in the middle of the room, in a puddle of blood, holding Raina and Finn. As she weeps, one bloodied hand rubs her brother's chest, just over his heart, as though she might rub life back into it, while her other arm is wrapped around Raina's shoulders, cradling her best friend's slumped body against her breast. All three faces are pale.

Helena looks up at me and Rhonin standing in the doorway, her eyes wide and distant and filled with tears. "Help them," is all she says.

Rhonin hurries to Helena's side, and I go to Raina, taking her from Helena and holding her in my arms. Using my mind, I slam the door and slide the bed in front of it.

I graze my fingertips over Raina's throat where life still flutters, thank Loria. She's just unconscious, for now. But Finn... I've seen that sickening smile across throats too many times. It's partially healed, likely thanks to Raina, but if his end hasn't already come, it's very near.

"Raina was stabbed," Helena says, trembling as she tries to gather herself. "In her side. She healed the wound enough to stop the bleeding before she passed out. Gavril got away. And her rune is... it's almost gone."

I process three words from that. *Healed. Gavril. Almost.* Carefully, I push the torn pieces of Raina's dress aside. A portion of the mark remains, but it's only a fraction. The skin surrounding it is angry and red, bubbled and seeping.

Burned.

My arms tighten around Raina. I can barely contain what the knowledge of her pain does to me, the rage inside me that makes me want to roar. My power breaks over the room, crackling like lightning along the walls.

Rhonin draws Helena against his chest, and I see the panic and urgency in his eyes. "We have to get them out. Are you listening? There are too many people here, Alexus. Badly as I know you want revenge on Vexx and Rooke, taking it out on their guards will come at the expense of innocent lives."

Taking a ragged breath to cool the fire inside me, I focus. I know he's right. I must think through my hatred, blinding as it is.

"You have a horse and cart nearby?" I ask, my voice shaky.

"Yes, near Emory's. But it only carries two. Three at most. I stole it from the stables."

There's a ruckus downstairs. Shouts and thudding footfalls. The Watch is here.

"If you can see to Helena and Finn," I tell Rhonin, "I can distract the Watch and get Raina home."

His brow furrows, and Helena looks up at me. At the same time, they ask, "How?"

"I don't have time to explain. I just need you to trust me. Both of you." I jerk my head toward the balcony door. "Be sure to take the back streets and ditch the cart. Do your best to enter the tor through the cove. The patrols will be thick. Now go."

Without another word, Rhonin hauls Finn's lifeless body over his shoulder, and Helena leads him to the balcony. They look back at me, concern darkening their eyes.

"Protect her, Alexus," Helena says, dragging her skirt up to retrieve her dagger, even as another tear tracks down her cheek.

I nod once before she vanishes into the night. "With my life."

*

I PULL FORTH ALL THE ENERGY I CAN SUMMON AND LET IT HOVER IN THE darkness outside. I capture just enough to send a ribbon of power through Raina, hoping to wake her. I'm not sure I can do what I need to do with her unconscious. I'll try, if I must.

Thankfully, her eyes blink open. For a moment, I think, perhaps nothing has changed. That perhaps this Gavril person didn't know runic magick so well. But Raina's gaze widens as she takes in my face, and she twists out of my arms, landing in a crouch.

The first pound on the door strikes, and I use some of my gathered power to electrify the entry. Raina's attention flicks toward the sound, but then she looks back at me, on edge. Feral. Ready to kill.

I hold out a placating hand and pour my heart through the rune, praying to the Ancient One, that she can still feel me. *Raina,* I whisper from rot...

Zaaira.

Please, Lorία. Let her remember me. Let her know me.

But her... tell me is gone. All that remains are tattered threads in...

She darts for a dagger discarded by the fireplace, coated in dried blood, and holds it in my direction with violence in her stare. A warning. And a sign.

Her dark blue eyes are cold. I see recognition there, but also confusion and contempt. I'm no longer Alexus to her. I don't know who she sees when she looks at me, but she doesn't trust him.

Another pound, like a shoulder slamming into the door, followed by a cry.

I can't use up my strength. I'm already weakened, and there's only one way out of here now, and it requires my all.

The Witch is here, I sign, hoping to build some sort of unity between us. *We need to leave. Quickly.*

She blinks and scans the bloody room, her eyes filling with tears, as if the realization of the night just struck her.

"Helena and Finn are with Rhonin," I tell her. "It's just you and me. I can take you to them."

She glances at the balcony a split second before shoving to her feet and skirting around me, dagger raised. She sways, staggering toward the exit, holding her blood-soaked side.

Slowly, I stand and face her. I remember this Raina. The one who stood against the world. The one who turns into a deadly warrior when she feels she must protect herself or what's hers. She isn't going to come with me willingly, and yet we cannot just walk out of here unscathed, not without me leaving a massacre behind and a bloody trail that leads straight to Starworth Tor.

I must give her no other choice.

Another pound. And another.

Raina stands at the doorway of the balcony. She steps outside and glances toward the ground. Even if I couldn't sense more guards outside, I'd know of their presence by the look on her face when she turns back. Panic gleams in her eyes.

I let my magick fall away from the door, a little at a time, and in a matter of seconds, guards from the Watch begin pushing against the bed.

While Raina's distracted, I rush her, flip the dagger out of her grasp, and wrap my arm around her waist in one smooth movement. With her hands pressed to my chest and her nostrils flaring, she stares up at me with a glare I recall from our first days together.

"I think I've loved you for my entire life," I whisper. "And when we're both gone, I will love you still." My words are true, but they feel like shards of glass in my throat. As the Watch's guards fight against my magick to enter Finn's room, and the others start up the exterior stairs, cornering us from both sides, I gather my magick close and Raina closer, whether she likes it or not. "Do you trust me?" I ask her.

She shakes her head, adamantly, and pounds her fists against my chest, but I hold fast. I always will.

"Well, you'd better try," I tell her.

A flash of worry crosses her face a moment before I cover her head and send the most powerful blast of magick I can manage toward the ground.

Everything happens so fast. The explosion destroys the balcony, the concussion rumbling through the city. My power shatters windows and sends wood and fragments of cobblestone, gravel, and dirt flying into the air as we fall toward the street, only to be caught in the resulting swell of magick as I draw it nigh, the propulsion so extraordinary it rockets us upward, launching us into the darkness, away from danger. Just the two of us. Safe.

Into the sky.

admiring his handiwork. "This might be the best idea I've ever had," he says with a sexy smirk.

Seductively, he leans down and kisses my rune, tracing his tongue across the mark. I can't fight the shiver it causes.

Before I grasp what's happening, Alexus lies down on his back and uses the leverage of his feet planted on the mattress to push himself toward the head frame, resting his head between my legs, his broad shoulders butting against my thighs.

Heat licks up my throat and spreads across my face as I look down at his muscled body, his cock raging hard against the carved plane of his abdomen. He touches it. Stroking it. Thumbing the already glistening crown.

A ragged breath tremors out of me. This is torture.

"I'm going to feast on you." He presses a kiss to my inner thigh. "No release though. Not until you fill this room with *starlights*, as you call them. And I want your glamour up. Let's see if you can hold two magicks at once."

I send a bolt of bewilderment through the rune, chased by a question. I have no idea how to harness his magick, much less while I'm holding the construct of a glamour in place. We could be at this all night.

Not that I mind. But I do.

Sort of.

Gods above and below.

Alexus laughs and skims his rough hands up my thighs and over my hips, cupping my ass. "My power is accessible through the bond. All you must do is command it. Will it to behave as you wish. Focus."

I make a mental note to call him the worst magickal instructor ever born when this is over. But my mind gets sidetracked quite quickly because he's kissing the inside of my thigh again, and not a gentle press of the lips either. A wet kiss, his tongue making sinuous circles on my skin.

When he stops, he smacks my ass, just hard enough to arouse the slightest, most wonderful sting. "Glamour. Up."

A quiver rocks through my thighs, and my muscles clench, but I hold myself steady and try to think straight enough to erect a glamour. It's difficult, because I can feel his breath, warm on my damp flesh, making me ache even more. But the glamour rises. The magick of it chases across my skin, and my witch's marks vanish.

"Mmm, good girl." He spreads me apart with his fingers, opening me. "Now sit."

Every bit of my self-awareness tightens into a knot in my chest. When I don't move—because I'm so incredibly aroused yet somehow also simultaneously mortified—his arms tighten, and he draws me down to his mouth. I'm angled in such a way that my back is arched, my softness pressed to his mouth just right, just where I need him. But gods' stars. As he pushes his tongue into me, I feel like I'm suffocating him.

I inch up off his face, and a deep chuckle resonates from his chest. "Don't be embarrassed." He lifts his head and drags a long lick up my center, making me tense. "You are perfect and utterly delicious. This is bliss for me." Again, he folds his hand around his cock. As he pumps his fist, his other hand grips my hip. "I can make you climax like this."

No doubt.

He kisses my thigh. "Just call forth my magick," he continues. "And I'll fuck you with my tongue until you can't stand it anymore." He takes my hips in both hands again. "Now, come here."

There's no fight in me this time. No resistance. No bashfulness. I let him feast, let my pleasure build with the tempo he sets, leading me toward the crescendo of a song whose ending I know well.

If I give him what he wants—

I work very hard to compartmentalize everything within my mind: the bond, the glamour, the distraction of Alexus's talented tongue devouring me. Even though he avoids my clit, only licking over it a few times, there's a pressure building inside me, making me writhe against his mouth.

Focus, Raina, I think as I close my eyes.

There, in the darkness, with the world shut away, I see magick across the landscape of my mind. If I look to one side, I see Alexus's life threads, still wound with mine and Colden's. If I look to another corner, I see the pulsing magick of my glamour. In another floats the threads of Alexus's desire, his *passion,* threads I could tangle with my own if the time were right.

Alexus's end of the bond and the glowing threads of his power linger just beyond my abyss, pulsing like a flaring light. A *beacon.* Like a lighthouse across the dark shore of the chasm before me. On a leap of trust, I let my mind cross that pit of nothingness.

There's something there. A presence. A *force*. It's almost like the vestige of another bond, a soft shadow hovering behind Alexus's power. Limned in white light, the shadow is frayed at one end, like a shredded piece of gossamer caught in the wind. I don't know what it is, but it calls to me, as though it needs me to reach out and touch it.

Magick means connection. It always has. Tonight, this magick is about mine and Alexus's connection to each other, so I submit.

When I let my mind graze that shadow, Alexus groans into my flesh, and suddenly, his hands are everywhere. Squeezing my ass. Gripping my breasts. Reaching up to fold those long fingers gently around my throat. His touch is a heady thing, and I rock against his mouth, feeling more desperate for this release than any other before it.

In the next breath, I hear his voice, speaking to me the way he did when we were in the wood, harvesting fire threads. *Fulmanesh, iyuma tu lima, opressa volz nomio, retam tu shabl.*

Fire of my heart, come that I may see you, warm my weary bones, be my place of rest.

I can't explain why, but something compels me to think those words. I repeat them until bold, fiery threads emerge from Alexus's power within my mind's eye.

Bend them to your will. Force them to become light.

Is Alexus speaking to me? Is he communicating through the bond? His voice is so clear, as if he's whispering in my ear.

He presses his tongue harder to my clit, flicking that tender bud, sucking it, reminding me of the reward that lies ahead. With an image of my will in mind—those glowing orbs of light filling this room—I repeat the Elikesh lyrics in my thoughts, until those blazing threads cool into soft, white light.

The sweetest caress of power cascades over my body, my skin heating with desire and need. Alexus keeps feasting, and his hands keep roaming, rougher and harder, as though learning me anew.

Suddenly, Alexus smacks my ass again, making me gasp and arch my back.

More, I plead through the bond.

In answer, he sends a trickle of magick between his tongue and my clit, the pulsing current growing ever more powerful before fading away.

Needy, I close my hands around the silken sashes binding me to the bed and grind against Alexus's mouth. If I'd possessed a demure quality before, it is gone from me now.

The throb between my legs pounds harder and harder, but so does Alexus's magick, trapped within me, beating under my skin, wanting out. My rune heats, and my skin goes taut, drawn upon by a force so strong it's as though my very soul is being pulled from my core.

Alexus's magick pours from me, and the room brightens even from behind my closed eyes. When I open them, I'm met with a loft filled with tiny orbs of light. Hundreds—no, *thousands*—like sparkling stardust.

My excitement floods the bond, and I swear I feel Alexus smile.

He doesn't make me wait for my prize. He lets his magick thunder into me, vibrating through his tongue into my body, and in seconds, I'm in a state of utter rapture, swept up in the wave of a relentless orgasm that spasms through me over and over and *over*.

When I come to my senses, Alexus is soothing my swollen flesh with long, languid caresses of his tongue. But he's also stroking his cock. Hard and fast. I cannot stop watching, especially as a pearl of cum slips free.

I'm still floating in the haze of pleasure, still hungry. My hands need to feel him. I need to taste him. Need to drink him down.

I think of the sashes around my wrists—*the knots*. And with Alexus's magick still hot in my veins, I envision those knots untangling. At my command, the sashes untie and fall away, and I collapse forward, catching myself on the bed in sheer surprise.

Alexus catches me too, by the hips, before a laugh escapes him. "Fuck. Raina. You did it. My talented, wicked little witch."

He has no idea.

Without a second of indecision, I grip his cock, and for the first time, take him into my mouth.

"*Shit*." His voice is rough and ragged around his gasp, his entire body jolting from the contact.

My legs are trembling, but I manage to turn myself around, until I'm on my knees between his legs, my breasts pressed to his spread thighs.

He tortured me. Now I mean to repay the favor.

arms and swim against the weight of the ocean to the surface. The moment the night air hits my face, a low-rising swell pushes us toward the nearby shore.

Starworth Tor was so far before, an impossible distance to swim. Now we're close enough to the cove that the torchlights where Zahira usually sits at night are clearly visible.

My feet quickly meet sand, and by the blessings of the Ancient Ones, I carry Raina from the mighty Malorian and collapse to my knees on the shore.

As creeping waves roll up behind us, their foamy crests dying on the beach, I lay Raina down and call forth all the starlights I can muster, which is only a few. Careful, I turn her onto her uninjured side and rub her back as she coughs and splutters into the sand.

Straddling her, I press my forehead to her shoulder, trying to breathe. At least she's here. At least she's alive. Thamaos and the prince and perhaps even Vexx want her, for punishment, I'm certain. But by the gods, they will not have her.

I hear voices. Soft laughter.

"Zahira!" My voice is a ragged, weathered thing in the night, burned by salt and water. I lift my head. "Yazmin!"

After a moment, they appear from the shadowed curve of the cove, one of them carrying a torch. Their silhouettes move with uncertainty at first, walking with hesitance, being careful.

But then they're running.

There are three. Zahira, Yaz, and... Nephele.

"What in Loria's name?" Zahira cries as they collapse beside me. Nephele drops to her knees next to her sister and stabs her torch in the sand.

"Raina!" She smooths Raina's wet hair back from her face and snaps a look at me. "What happened?"

Yaz falls to her knees too, immediately scanning Raina and I for injuries. She presses her hand to my cheek. "Alexus? Are you both all right?"

I can't answer. I just swallow the tight knot in my throat and shake my head as Raina turns a look on me, piercing my heart with a hateful glare.

Holding her side, she shoves at my chest and scuttles out from beneath me toward the cove, panting, clawing at the sand and struggling to her feet, as if my very presence is a poison.

Every wide eye is on her back as Nephele rushes to her side, folding an arm around her waist for support. "Raina, what is it? What's wrong?"

There's little light—only the moon, my few starlights, and the flickering torch. But it's enough to see what Raina signs. *"Get me away from him. I never want to see his face again. I need to find Finn!"*

"Just go, Nephele," I shout, digging my hands into the wet sand. "Just do what she wants. You'll understand soon enough."

My friend is hesitant. I see her worry. But at my insistence, they slip into the cove's shadows and disappear toward the main house. I swear it feels as though Raina Bloodgood rips out my beating heart and carries it with her.

Zahira clasps my shoulder, her eyes glinting with sadness, the corners of her mouth downturned. "Alexus. I'm going to need you to talk to me."

I shove to my feet and tear off my sodden jacket, throwing it to the ground, and redirect my mind because I have no other choice. "I will," I promise her, swiping the dripping water and tears from my face. "But first, we have to find Helena and Rhonin."

No sooner do I speak their names, Zahira looks past me, and her face falls even more. When I turn, Rhonin and Helena are walking around the rocks that jut from the eastern side of the cove, Finn's lifeless body slung over Rhonin's shoulder.

"My gods," Zahira says, covering her mouth.

And I go to meet my friends.

⚜

A NEW DAY RISES, AND I'M THERE TO GREET IT.

Callan strolls onto the beach and sits beside me on the sand under the early morning light. They hand me a steaming cup of Yaz's tea. "Rhonin finally let Keth and Jaega take over his watch at the main gate. You should let me take over for *you* now. The guards at the wall changed out shifts seamlessly. If Rooke and Vexx knew where you went last night, they would've already sent a legion here. But they don't. They are not all-seeing. You need rest."

city wall's archway a... ep... , taken aback by the sigh...

fountains, and a maze of ... en... ...eights connected by city stree... at... or navigating the labyrinth that is ll... in. ...sit high in the distance, t... view spik... th... ...rets pointing toward the sun.

...lush, green vegetation seem to have sprung up ... er... ...a foothold in the otherwise baked earth, and whe... nd... ...an smell the perfume of dozens of flower gardens ming... ith... ...rich spice.

...Summerlands are truly a world apart, and I've only seen on... ...na catches up and motions for us to follow her into the l... ty.

...t thing I notice are the different types of guards. There ... ot... ...s standing in archways, along streets, and ne... fountains, b... re... ...so mounted guards patrolling the city from at... ble-colored horses ...tisoned in fine red velvet, their harnesses and ... trimmed in silver. ...guards wear bla..., even covering their heads ... faces, their bodies ...with all manner of blades. A polished, silv... ield with a snake ...d into the center f the metal hangs from th... rse's side, as does ...sort of animal h...

...e Dread Vipers ... llan says... ...m the gate to my righ... ing his ho... ...to a wall... eight strides away ... ries papr... ...ver the heads o... othe p...

...tor says as ... es along... ...he presses ... od to the sma... ... of ... leading ... ... be ays at my ea...

...re like two fi... ...and presses ... hand to my b... She sti... ou...

...d ... earlier. A... ... Fia Ocumer... ...t the Collecto... ... is only a few hatred with the images of you two that now exist in her mind. Your time in the wood. The conversations over these last weeks. The intimacy."

"I know what she's feeling." I hold out my wrist, showing them the old scar there, Fleurie's face flashing across my mind. "I've been through this before, only that bond was severed entirely, from both sides. We became strangers, but strangers would be better than being considered an enemy. It's like these last two months have been completely undone."

Callan sighs. "I'm truly so sorry. But perhaps the memories will help and not hinder. A reminder of how far you two had come."

"They haven't so far." I clasp my hands and swallow the constriction in my throat. "I can still feel her. What little of her rune remains is enough that I sense a trickle of her emotions. She wants me, but not as much as she hates me." A swell of sickness washes over me, my chest aching like it's been hollowed out with a spoon. "I don't know how to deal with that. I want to tear down the world for this. It feels like she's gone. Like she died. Only her ghost is still here to haunt me."

Callan swirls the tea in their cup, staring at the leaves settled in the bottom. "You know, when my partner passed a handful of years ago, I thought that was the end of everything. We'd been together for so long that I was sure there was no other for me. But there was, and now he's at Winterhold with our son, and I'm *here*, trying to make this world a better place for them. There isn't anything I wouldn't do for those three."

"I understand."

I don't tell Callan that I lost my wife and child a very long time ago. Or that my heart has been an empty landscape ever since. Until recently, anyway.

They nudge me again, and I look up, meeting their hazel eyes. "That kind of love, the kind that makes you want to tear down mountains with your bare hands, is the most powerful force in the universe. So though it may feel like all is lost right now, remember that Raina isn't gone, and she's no ghost. She's still very much here. It's all right to fight for her. To tell her how you feel. To remind her how much you care. I would expect no less. And I'd bet that if you'd asked her before last night's events, she would've told you that she expected no less as well."

"I never said I was going to give her up." I turn a glance at my friend. "Again, I'm not that good of a man. I tried to be, at Winterhold, when she learned Finn was alive. I was ready to let her go if that was what she wanted. But I don't know that I could've stayed away." I narrow my eyes. "You speak like you know I'm going to have *time* to fight for her."

"She's still undecided about the Summerlands, for several reasons," Callan replies honestly. "She's had many conflicting thoughts to sort through in a short period of time. But a woman like Raina doesn't walk away from a fight that needs her hands. She'll be on Ferrowin's ship. *If* we can still get to it."

I raise a brow. "That is the worry."

"In the bath next hour."

I go to the nexthour. I clean up and change clothes, trying and failing to ignore Raina's absence at the lighthouse. Some of her things are still here. Her robe lies cast aside on the bed. Her pack still sits on the floor. The book she was reading is on the desk, closed, my letters used to mark her place. Another necklace—the gold chain and single pearl—left behind. I gather her robe in my hands and crush it to my face, inhaling the scent of lavender and jasmine. *Fight for her.* As if my heart will give me any other choice.

When I return to the main house, Callan has gathered everyone for a meeting in the dining hall. Zahira and Yaz prepare a simple breakfast of warm breads and fruit, and though others make their plates, I can't stomach the thought of food.

Rhonin and Helena are here, eyes shadowed with exhaustion, and Keth and Jaega soon enter the room. Joran sits to my left as Nephele takes the seat to my right. I haven't seen her since last night when she came to check on me for a few minutes before returning to Raina. She looks tired too. Worried. The skin beneath her eyes looks bruised, the strain of maintaining the shield, thinking of Colden, of me, and now all of this is visibly taking its toll.

Joran fills a small plate with food and pours a glass of juice, then slides it across the table to Nephele, his silver eyes trained on her. "Eat. You need your strength."

Surprisingly, for the first time since this trip began, she doesn't argue with him. Instead, she accepts the offering with a tilted nod, one that feels like a truce, before she turns to me.

"Mari is with Raina and Finn." She squeezes my hand and leans over to kiss my cheek, her eyes bloodshot. When she speaks, her voice tremors. "I want Rooke's head for this, that traitor."

"And I want Vexx's and Gavril's." Helena stabs her fork into an apple. "If that's even his name."

"I want the same," I tell them, thumbing an angry tear from Nephele's cheek. "But we can't risk Zahira and Yaz's safety and the safety of innocent Northlanders for our revenge, which means we can't remain in Malgros much longer." Everyone falls still and attentive. "It was clear last night that Vexx is running the show here, and he will follow standard Eastlander protocol.

"Which is?" Callan says, looking between me and Rhonin. I gesture at Rhonin.

"Eastlander military practice is to observe first," he says. "Then decide how to best engage. Attacks they're certain will be to their advantage are the method of choice. The element of surprise. If the situation and geography allow, this is their primary form."

"Thus the dinner last night," Hel says. "They didn't know where Alexus was hiding, but they knew exactly how to lure him to Brear Hall. He was expecting one thing and found another."

"It's probably why word of the dinner became town gossip, and why Terrowin, a man not normally in such social circles, was invited at all," Zahira interjects, looking up at me. "In hopes that you would hear about it when you came asking questions."

A trap I didn't expect. Because revenge was all I could see.

"So what will they do now?" Callan asks. "Sweep the city?"

"No," Rhonin replies. "That would be a bold announcement of their plans and would require a concentration of too much manpower and time. They will work to maintain control of the situation. Since we—the enemy —are trying to leave, and they've already manned the city gates, they'll intervene in any transportation plans we might've made. The Watch's fleet will seize Terrowin's ship before it reaches land. Any other ships scheduled to sail will be frozen in the harbor, until we're found."

"And it's very likely they'll use their resources here as well," I add. "This is a land of Witch Walkers. They will likely raise a veil along the coast at some point, and if there are any talented witches who can help them seek us out, they will be recruited for duty."

"Fuck." Keth sets his fork aside and pushes away his plate. "So because of last night's disaster, it's us against the entire Northland Watch, their fleet, and a city of witches. If we mean to leave this break."

I feel the punch of guilt he has every right to throw at me.

"Why didn't you just kill those bastards?" he asks.

"Would *you* have killed them?" Jaega asks, her voice smooth as glass. Keth faces her. "If they were the only ones who knew where I was," she says, "and that I was in danger, would you have killed them?"

Silence falls over the room.

"For what it's worth," Rhonin says, his voice low, "Alexus tried to drag Vexx with us, but we had to leave, but... what Alexus was going through was..." He looks up at me, eyes filled with empathy. "There was no other way. We had to run."

"So now what?" Nephele says softly. "What do we do? We can't get to the Summerlands like this."

I take a deep breath, my mind working. "No, we can't get to the Summerlands like this. But Keth, Nephele, you, Zahira, and Callan can get everyone out of Mudros tonight at Starforth Tor's gate. It might require another shielding construct if there are more guards to men this end of the wall. But I have different plans."

Zahira sets her glass of wine aside, disbelief on her face.

I arch a brow. "I love you, but I don't..."

She opens her mouth, then closes it. "Give me until nightfall."

We all look at...

Nephele seems...

help this situation?...

possibly do that...

With a resigned sigh...

between his thumb and forefinger, holding her stare a moment before turning to me. "I'm a water witch. With access to the Malorian Sea. Let me play." He leans forward, arms crossed on the table. "Nightfall and a little trust. That's all I need. But understand that even if you say no, I'm going to do it anyway. I mean to be in Iturinan in a matter of days, not a Malgros or Queziran prison cell. Besides, I've no king, and I've no lord, certainly not you. My asking for the benefit of the doubt is the extent of my courtesy."

Nephele stiffens. "Joran, if they catch you..."

He slides his eyes in her direction. "They won't."

"This seems... unwise," Rhönin interrupts, nervously tapping the table. "No offense, Joran, but I can't see you sailing a ship through the harbor to Starworth Tor's front door alone. Even if you could, we'd still have to get past the Northland fleet to enter Summerland waters. And if you manage that, without Terrowin and crew, we have no idea what to do once we cross those lines. That's asking for a storm of trouble. One we cannot withstand."

Joran looks down the table at my young friend. "I *am* the storm. If anyone need fear anything, it's the Watch." He turns back to me, not looking for permission, obviously, but agreement. "All I ask in return is that you owe me a single favor after this. *If* I succeed."

"What's the favor?" I ask, suspicious.

He shrugs. "I'm not sure yet. Nothing too grand. Maybe better living quarters when we return to Winterhold. My home for the last long while has been... a little cramped."

"Better living quarters. Deal." I agree to this only because my instinct tells me I need to trust him for once. "*If* you succeed," I add. "If you get caught—"

"I'll die before I let them know where you are." He doesn't say these words to me. He says them to Nephele. A promise. And I can't help but believe he means them.

I also don't know what our other options are. Much as I want to rampage into the Watch's headquarters, I have to remember that the Prince of the East wants me, and he wants Raina. I can't risk letting him have either of us.

"Nightfall, then," I say, even as everyone looks at me like I'm making another grand mistake, especially Callan, Nephele, and Helena. Because this will force Raina to decide about continuing this journey or staying behind with Finn. Today. I can't imagine she'll leave him, and I can't imagine leaving *her*. The thought makes me sick.

Joran pushes up from the table. "Be packed and ready. In three days' time, we'll be in the Summerlands."

ALEXUS

Raina and I sleep until we hear the clang of swords echoing from the beach the next morning.

I get up and go to the catwalk door, peeking through the sheers, only to find Rhonin and Hel sparring in the sand, the white-crested waves lapping at their feet.

They move like two lovers dancing, so aware of one another. So comfortable. This synergy has happened over the course of weeks, now their friendship and alliance. But sometimes I wonder when it will become something more.

Regardless, as a man who once taught the sword, I'm impressed by their skill. Watching Rhonin with all his Eastland army knowledge is one thing. But Helena is a warrior to her marrow, something I've known since I saw her bravery in the ravine. She's Rhonin's match in every way, pivoting, thrusting, and blocking as though she's wielded a sword her entire life.

More surprisingly, though, is the sight of Nephele and Joran—also sparring. And not as gracefully.

They're both skilled—I taught Nephele the blade myself. But where Rhonin and Helena move like lovers, Nephele and Joran move like enemies. Their faces are red in the early morning sun, their bodies covered in sweat and on edge.

❧ 39 ❧

RAINA

I think I've loved you for my entire life. And when we're both gone, I will love you still.

Those words won't stop repeating in my head, even as I lie beside Finn, holding his hand. Everything about him feels comfortable and right, except when I think about the Witch Collector. Then everything in my head jumbles into an unrecognizable tangle.

I stare at the red scar screaming across Finn's throat, glistening with Yaz's salve, then I glance at his still-pale lips, wishing he would open his eyes. I'm trying to focus my thoughts on *him*.

But those words...

It's been this way all morning, *I think I've loved you for my entire life* waking me as I try to rest, distracting me when I try to think. One moment, the memory of the Collector staring down at me and saying he loved me makes me want to cry. It makes me want to find him and kiss him and hold him, as inconceivable as that seems. The next moment, any notions of tenderness are smothered by utmost rage, and I feel like I did on Collecting Day, wishing I could plunge my dagger into his heart.

Despite the consuming coldness I feel toward him, I also remember such wild and relentless passion. Though Nephele and Hel assured me that my unimaginable memories of the Collector really happened, it feels like they were only dreams. Being with him in Frostwater Wood. His rough hands on my naked body at Winterhold. All those nights in his tent, his eyes locked with mine as he moved between my legs, fucking me until I couldn't breathe. All our many moments here, at Starworth Tor.

Dreams. All of it. *Unreal.*

My hatred, however, feels strong and true, something to cling to.

I touch the new scar above my left breast, flinching at the phantom ache that lives there. What torture is this? To desire and loathe someone so wholly at the same time? What cruelty?

I crawl out of bed and cringe, my ribs still sore from the blade that barely missed my lung. Gavril's half-scorched face flashes across my mind as I throw on a cozy robe and slide my feet into slippers. I've a feeling I haven't seen the last of that sorcerer, but I shake it off. I won't let his attack create more fear inside me.

Mari looks up from her chair on Finn's side of the bed, tucking a strand of chestnut hair behind her ear. "Where are you going, Miss Bloodgood?"

She's been sitting with us—reading a book on infirmary care—for the last hour, constantly glancing at me as I lay next to Finn. After Nephele told me about the meeting that was held this morning, she went to the lighthouse to retrieve the rest of my things and assigned Mari to care for me and Finn in her absence. She should be back by now, but she isn't, and I need a little time out from under Mari's watchful eyes.

I motion toward downstairs as I move to the door. I then point to the window and take a deep, exaggerated breath, fluttering my hands toward my face.

"Everyone's packing their belongings and prepping the horses," she says, her brow scrunched in confusion. "Just in case they're needed for a quick exit."

That's not at all what I was getting at. Frowning, I grab a shoulder bag of Zahira's and stuff my scrying dish, dagger, the books on curses I've been reading, and a beach blanket inside. I need to check the waters, but I want some fresh air too, and to be *alone*. Thankfully, Mari doesn't argue when I slip out the door.

I bump into Hel at the top of the stairs. "I was coming to see you."

"I need *air, to be on the beach,*" I sign. "*Mari is with Finn. Nephele...*" I make a face and shrug.

CHARISSA WEAKS

One side of Hel's mouth curls. "She's passed out on Alexus's bed in the lighthouse. We all need to sleep, I think." She jerks her head toward the stairs. "Go. I'll lie with Finn, Zahira and Yaz went to the archives and to check on the Watch's movements. If I hear anything at all, I'll come find you."

Out of nowhere, her brown eyes glaze with a sheen of held-back tears. "I love you, Raina. So very much."

She's said that to me several times since last night. She feels guilty for leaving me and Finn, but chances are, she would've been hurt too if she'd stayed. Gavril had only been making his task easier when he sent her away. She couldn't have known. I've tried to tell her this, but guilt has a way of turning truth into lies, a fact I know all too well.

I make the sign for *I love you too* and fold my arm around her neck, kissing her forehead. She wraps her arms around my waist and presses her head against my chest, squeezing tight.

When she pulls back, she wipes a tear from her eye. "All right, now you can *really* go," she says with a soft laugh, making me smile, and in minutes, I'm walking across the veranda and down the flagstone stairs to the cove, intent on a nap by the sea.

One glance at the sky, and I'm remembering how the Collector flew us over the city last night, and that when I finally surrendered to my abyss, it saved us from drowning. I don't know how. I wasn't alert for much of it. I haven't mentioned the strange occurrence to Nephele yet, and I don't think the Collector has either, if he even realized what happened. My sister would've said something by now if he had. Whatever it was—whatever it *is*—I don't fear it so much anymore.

A cool wind blows my hair across my face and plasters my gown and robe to my body as I step onto the beach in the noon-day sun. I stop and take off my slippers, carrying them in my hand. The sand holds meager warmth, but it feels good beneath my feet and distantly familiar, enough that somewhere in the back of my mind, a memory rises, as if loosened from beneath years of forgotten time, like something buried beneath a billion grains of sand. It's a tiny girl building a sandcastle on the shore with a handsome blue-eyed man.

Me and my father.

Shaken by the vivid image, I pause and drop my bag and shoes. I scrape my windblown hair back from my face and glance eastward, searching for that memory, like I might see a father and daughter playing on the beach.

Instead, I see the Collector sitting a few yards away, elbows at rest on his bent knees, watching me with those emerald-bright eyes. I thought I was safe from seeing him. Thought he'd be at the lighthouse with my sister.

He gets up and brushes the sand from his linen trousers. The wind whips his light-colored pants and tunic against his muscled form. I can't recall seeing him dressed like this before. In truth, I keep seeing images of him on Mannus's back, cloaked in black, that heavy hood shrouding his head as he rode into our valley like some dark knight. Worse, I see images of him from his past. Un Drallag. Alexi of Ghent. A killer for King Gher-ahn. Images that only exist because of the bond and our shared dreams and nightmares.

With every cold flash of dreamlike memory, I wonder more and more how I could've let myself care for such a man so deeply, as though my mind is trying to remind me who he really is at his core, and that I should hate him. He's destroyed so many lives in his three hundred and twenty some-thing years. More than he has saved.

But then he walks toward me. He's barefoot, his hands buried in his pockets, his jet-black hair windswept, his jawline darkly shadowed with a new beard. And I'm reminded that I know what he looks like beneath those clothes. What he feels like. What he *tastes* like. And I know there is goodness in him, even if I don't want to see it.

My heart pounds, and my blood heats, mixing with so many other emotions that I don't know what to do but stand there, frozen, staring at anything but him.

Swallowing hard, I fold my arms beneath my breasts as he stops at my side. He's facing the main house, almost arm to shoulder with me. Thanks to the wind off the sea, his scent is everywhere, man and musk and some-thing like oud. I can't stop my chest from rising and falling at his nearness, like I just sprinted to the shore.

"I would ask if you're all right," he says, his voice washing over me like a touch, "but I know you aren't. I feel how torn you are."

I grit my teeth and ball my hands into fists. He can still feel me because I can't close the bond anymore. It feels strange when I even think about it, like our connection was only ever a delusion. But then I close my eyes and see it, and I know it was real, though there's hardly anything on my end remaining. I might as well be trying to shield an open window from a hurricane with a piece of tattered silk.

"Odd that I cannot feel you," I sign stiffly, drawing my shoulders back. I remember feeling him. Hearing him. Knowing his thoughts. Sharing his magick.

"I'm not allowing it. I thought to spare you." A question glimmers in his eyes. "Why? Do you *want* to feel me?"

I turn my gaze straight ahead and stare at the softly rolling sea. *"No. I just want you to go."*

He nods, but he doesn't move. "I'll leave you alone. But I need you to know something before I do."

I take a deep breath and turn toward the house, not even gathering my bag and slippers. His voice is still rough from last night, and it's shadowed with hurt. I don't want to hear it.

"I meant what I said," he calls, his words lifting over the wind roaring in my ears. "I *do* love you. More than you can fathom."

My feet pause in the sand, my chest caving around my heart. *Walk on, Raina.* But I can't.

I begin to force a step, but the Collector's heat suddenly burns at my back, and his hand slips around my waist. I grab his wrist as if to stop him.

His fingers scrape the silk beneath my navel, gripping the fabric of my robe in his fist. Goosebumps race across my skin at the contact, and I dig my fingers into his flesh, my hand so small compared to his.

I don't fight him. I want to hate his touch, rough and firm, and a part of me does. But another part craves that touch and wants it everywhere. The part that notices the elegant and strong shape of his hands and the feel of his sun-warmed skin. The part that makes my nipples harden, and my thigh muscles clench.

"A month ago, I was prepared to let you go if I had to." His deep voice is at my ear, caressing the skin of my neck. "That's the hero in me you like to talk about," he says, flexing and relaxing his fingers against my abdomen. "The part of me that time gentled."

He tugs me around. Hard. The hand gripping my robe slides to the small of my back, dipping dangerously low, while the other grazes my jaw and tips my chin.

I jerk from his touch, but he draws me closer, my heaving breasts pressed to his broad chest as he takes my face in his hand, forcing me to look at him, to feel him.

"But when it comes to saving you, *to saving us*, I can no longer be that man." He glances at my mouth with all the hunger of a starved lion. "If Joran succeeds tonight, and you decide to continue to the Summerlands, I want you to understand what awaits. I've felt him rousing for weeks now, but these last hours have finished awakening the side of me I've kept buried for a very long time, and he's a greedy, determined bastard. Now, all I think when I imagine losing you or giving you up is that *you are fucking mine*, and nothing and no one is going to take you from me. Not the prince. Not a destroyed bond. Not Finn. Not even your stubbornness. If you want to walk away from me and all that has grown between us, I won't let it happen easily."

He lets go of my face, and I push free from his hold. *"And if I do not go with you?"* I sign, my movements sharp, my blood rushing like a hot torrent in my veins. *"If I stay with Finn? If I refuse you?"*

If I go to the City of Ruin, I must leave Finn in Zahira and Yaz's care, not knowing if he'll even be alive when this is over. If I stay with him, I relinquish any power I have in helping to right Tiressia's future, and I send my sister and friends on a difficult journey without a Seer.

Either way, I'm walking away from those who need me. And like it or not, no matter how much desire I might feel for the infuriating man standing before me, it's an illusory thing, where Finn is tangible, a part of my life that has always been.

The Collector slips his hands back into his pockets, and like he said, determination shines in his hardened stare. "If you stay, then I'll find you when this is over, no matter where you are, and I'll do what I must to remind you of what we've shared. Because that boy—" he stabs a finger toward the main house "—could try with all his might for all his life to love you like you deserve, and he still wouldn't set your soul on fire the way I just did with a single touch." He dips his head, holding my gaze. "I know I make you happy, Raina. I've *felt* your joy. Your passion. Your *love*. Even if you never spoke the word to me, I felt it blooming. And I will feel it again."

"You sound so sure," I sign, twisting my face into a scowl. *"As though it will be so simple to woo me. I doubt you can make me forget how much I hate you."*

"I've done it before." He arches a dark, mischievous brow as a smirk crawls across his mouth. "I can do it again."

I scoff, annoyed to my marrow that his words are true. At least half of them. He *has* done it before. And I offered very little fight.

He narrows his eyes, and I note a glint there as he cocks his head. "Wait. Was that a *challenge?*" He smiles with one side of his perfect mouth, the effort carving a dimple deep into his cheek. "Because I'm taking it as a challenge," he says before his smile spreads, and he walks away. On the wind, I hear him say, "One I bet I win."

40

RAINA

The waters are uneventful today. I see Colden and Fleurie chatting, and then Colden and the prince's red cloud together, possibly chatting, but when I think to look for Vexx or Gavril, I simply can't make myself do it yet.

I also can't sit and mourn, though I feel like maybe I need to grieve. It's strange to lose something your mind tells you was precious when another part of your mind screams that it wasn't.

Instead, I decide to lie on the beach and read from the second book I found in Zahira's library on curses again. Reading is an escape, a way to keep worry and negative thoughts at bay, a comfort the Collector provided until now. I promise myself that when all of this has passed, I will curate my own little library and read to my heart's content.

In my few short sittings with *Curses of a Lorian Age*, I've already made it to the halfway mark. I shield the sunlight as I focus on the words, having finally found a tidbit that connects with something buried in my mind.

After being turned, Soul Eaters consumed souls for nourishment. Food from field and meat from forest, river, and sea were acceptable means of sustaining life if more preferred provisions were not available. Curiously, there seems to be consistent record of these cursed creatures tasting the souls which they

consumed, suggesting that souls possess flavor analogous to their life and
living conditions. Many Soul Eaters were said to have developed particular
tastes over their long years. Their kills were often selected using this one
determining factor.

I cringe and try to scrub the thoughts from my mind that these words conjure: the prince eating souls in the wood. "*At least your soul will restore me,*" he had said to me. "*I bet it tastes like smoke and starlight.*"

I also can't help but re-read those first three words: *After being turned.*

He is still my enemy, and I still want to feel his life slip through my hands for what he did in the valley. He chose the path that led to me.

But he didn't choose the path of a Soul Eater. He was *made.*

He was *cursed.*

It makes me think of my father and the God Knife. He was cursed as its Keeper, and now so am I. *But why?* Who would do such a thing to a reaper from Silver Hollow?

That question seems so innocuous, and yet now it holds deeper meaning. Because my father was something more than a reaper from the vale. He was a Head Sentry for the Northland Watch, though I can't piece together how that could've connected him to the God Knife.

Too tired to think on it anymore, I close the book and slide it aside, folding my hands under my cheek. With the sound of the waves, and the sun on my back, and the cool wind racing over me, I close my eyes and hope for a little sleep.

◈

"*RAINA, WE NEED MORE WATER. COME ON, LITTLE ONE.*"

Father extends his marked hand, and I take it, my tanned skin against his pink skin. At his side, I toddle toward the shore's edge and squat low as he collects the sea into our pail. I smile and wiggle my bottom when the foam tickles my toes, and Father laughs, the sound so bright, his eyes clear as the summer sky.

He swoops me up in his arms and carries me back to the sandcastle we've been building all morning. It's a massive playground. I walk through the path my father built into the middle, a moat we will soon fill.

"Go dig for seashells, little one." Father tugs his straw hat down over his blond

hair to shield his sunburned face. "*We'll use them to make your castle so beautiful.*" *He scrapes his hand—covered in lines like tree branches—through the wet sand to show me the seashells buried there, and I head back toward the waves with a small trowel that's still too big for my grasp.*

"*Not too far, love,*" *Father says, and I listen, pausing just where the water slinks back to the sea.*

Squatting again, I start digging. Shiny shells. That's what I want. Big ones. But shiny. One by one, I rescue them, setting each one carefully in a pile.

But then I see something different. Something darker, yet shinier than any shell.

Sunlight glints off the amber stone as I push the sand back, trying so hard with my too-little hands to dig it out. There's more. Something white and smooth and long. I can barely fold my hand around it, but I tug and yank and pull and dig some more. I don't want to stop. I need to reach it. To make it mine.

I don't have a name for the thing I free from the sand. It's nothing I've ever seen. Nothing my Mother or Father or sister have ever named. The stone is cold, but it feels right in my hand.

Suddenly, my father calls for me. He comes running and falls to his knees, grabbing the thing from my grip. It passes to him easily, though its absence makes me sad.

He holds the thing up to the sunlight, panting, his eyes wide and glassy as he studies it closely, his chin trembling as he swallows hard.

"*No,*" *he whispers, face blanched.* "*You were just a dream,*" *he says to the thing in his hand.* "*A nightmare.*" *But then his voice gets louder.* "*No!*" *And he slings the thing into the sea.*

It returns on a wave, the sea leaving it at my feet.

Again, he flings it away. And again it returns. This happens over and over until finally, when he's spent from throwing it into the sea, he lets the thing rest in a cloud of sea foam by my toes.

I pick it up, and my father doesn't stop me, this big thing I cannot name, made from something sharp and black on one end, and the white stone and amber gem on the other. Amber like the sun at dusk.

With a trembling hand, Father takes the thing away once again and draws me close, and for the first time, I see him cry. "*I will protect you from this,*" *he tells me, pressing his lips against the curls atop my head.* "*I swear on all that I am, Raina. I will protect you.*"

GASPING, I SIT UP WITH A START. I'M ON THE BEACH BLANKET. ON THE sand. In the cove at Starworth Tor. *Not* with my father.

Just another dream, I tell myself, my words mirroring his.

But it wasn't a dream. *That* was a memory. One I've never had before now. It's a revelation that sends panic pounding through my chest, a million questions pouring into my mind.

Because no matter what stories he told, no matter what tales I've believed for my entire life, my father didn't find the God Knife on the Malorian seashore.

I did.

⚜

I GATHER MY THINGS AND RACE BACK TO THE HOUSE, MY SKIN WARM and tight from lying in the sun. I don't make it to the veranda before the Collector meets me, hurrying down the flagstone steps. Concern etches his face.

"What is it, Raina? What's wrong?"

How can he feel so much with so little when it comes to the bond? Did he see my dream? Surely not now that the bond is partially destroyed.

But then I glance at the lighthouse and pause. *"Have you been watching me?"*

"There are people who want you dead, or worse, alive, so yes. Of course, I'm fucking watching you. What's wrong?"

It isn't anything I want to discuss with him. I don't even know what I would say. It makes no sense. My father was the Keeper. The God Knife was cursed to *his* keep, not mine.

Perhaps it was just an accident. Perhaps the blade was trying to find him, and I just found it first. But why did he say he'd protect me from it?

I shove past the Collector—he's at fault for that godsdamn God Knife in the first place—and keep moving toward the house.

"Raina." My name falls from his lips like a command, as though he holds that sort of power over me. Perhaps before, he did. But not now.

I don't get a chance to turn around and level him with a few choice words because Nephele opens the exterior door to the great room, and the expression on her face fills me with even more dread.

With eyes that remind me of Father's now more than ever, she looks from me to the Collector and back to me. "Zahira and Yaz are home. They found something."

※

NEPHELE AND I SIT ACROSS THE DINING ROOM TABLE FROM ZAHIRA AND Yaz. Alexus is here, leaning against the doorframe. Not that I want him to be. Nephele asked him to stay.

Zahira slides one of her pads of bound parchment across the polished table. My sister accepts, dragging it closer. I scan the words, written in charcoal, as she reads them aloud.

Citizen: Ophelia Moren-Sar
Born: Elam, Ske-Trana Province, Year 264 in the reign of Fia Drumera, midsummer
Student: Hall of Holies, City of Ruin, Years 286-288
Displaced at sea, practicum expedition: Year 288, spring, refugee at the Northland Watch barracks
Returned to Itunnan: Year 288, autumn
Returned to Malgros: Year 289, early winter
United with Head Sentry Rowan Bloodgood: Year 289, winter
Child: Nephele Moren-Sar Bloodgood, Year 289, summer
Child, Raina Moren-Sar Bloodgood, Year 295, midwinter
Permission for leave to Northland Valley: family, Year 297, winter

I look at my sister, who's already staring at me. Her eyes are wide, and her rosy cheeks drained of color. She turns to Zahira. "Elam. Ske-Trana. These are Summerland locations."

"Yes," Zahira nods. "Elam is a small province not far from Itunnan."

Nephele blinks and tilts her head, as though not hearing correctly. "But our mother was a Northlander."

Yaz's brows raise. "Yes, she was. *After* she moved here and permanently settled with a member of the Watch. But before, your mother was a Summerlander. By birth. And even more importantly, she was a student at the Hall of Holies, under Fia Drumera and her magi. She obviously found herself displaced here and met your father, and when she later learned she was with child, left her home to be with him."

From the doorway, Alexus stiffens, as though something Yaz said tugged his spine into a rigid line. He exhales a long breath and scrubs a hand over the shadow of his beard. "Which explains her ability. And Raina and Nephele's."

I stare at the parchment. Raina Moren-Sar Bloodgood. Not only did I not know about my magick for most of my life, but I also didn't even know who I really am.

I can't help but wonder if this has anything to do with my abyss. If that's some sort of Summerlander ability I just haven't been aware of until recently.

"Instinct guided the historian in me," Zahira says, interrupting my thoughts. "I had a feeling that something was buried in your lineage. It's important to always look deeper. We are not only products of our parents, but the ancestors who came before us as well. Their souls sing a mighty echo in our veins."

"Why would she hide this knowledge from us?" I sign, and Nephele translates.

"That is the question," Zahira says, clasping her hands atop the table. "Perhaps one Fia Drumera can answer once you reach the City of Ruin."

If we reach it. *If* I go. I don't sign those words, but I know everyone else is thinking them too.

When I look at Nephele again, swollen tears teeter on the rims of her eyelids. She blinks, and they run down her face. "I remember Malgros." She wipes her cheeks. "But I thought all those images in my mind were from my parents' stories. I didn't think they were real. I didn't hold on to them as I should have. But..." She pauses. Takes a shaky breath. "I remember Mother calling Raina *Sunshine*, and I loved that." She smiles, the corners of her mouth quivering. "It seemed such a happy nickname. But she called me—"

"Morning Star," I sign, remembering my mother's sweet voice drifting through the cottage at dawn.

Nephele nods. "Morning Star," she whispers. *"Moren-Sar."*

I slide my arm around her shoulders and try to ignore the fact that when the Witch Collector pushes from the doorway and comes to stand at my sister's side, she takes his hand, and he kisses it sweetly. Regardless of him, and regardless of my heart being torn when it comes to Finn, I know what I must do in the coming hours.

For me.

Because my mother was a Summerlander. A powerful mage schooled at the Hall of Holies, a place I don't even understand. But the God Knife was bound with Summerlander magick. Magick attached to me and my father, even though he longed to be rid of the blade, to protect me from whatever danger he felt it held. I only have more questions, but at least, now, some of the missing pieces of the puzzle have come into play, and I mean to uncover the rest.

I stand and address the table before I head upstairs, aware of the Collector's stare locked on me. *"I need to spend time with Finn and think,"* I sign.

What I don't say, if only to prolong the Collector's worry, is that if the chance arrives tonight, I'll be leaving for the City of Ruin.

✦❧✦

WHEN I RETURN UPSTAIRS, HEL'S VOICE DRIFTS DOWN THE HALL, HER words happy and lilting. I open the door, only to be met by Finn's dark gaze. He's lying propped on pillows, eyes half-lidded, a weak smile lifting one side of his red lips.

Hel kneels by the bed, holding his hand in both of hers. She's grinning so big, tears streaking her golden-brown face. Mari seems happy too, standing over Finn, her cheeks pink with an innocent blush.

"I was just about to come find you," Hel says. She stands and leans over to kiss her brother's forehead before eyeing Mari. "Come. Let's give Finn and Raina some time."

Hel squeezes my hand as they leave, and then I'm standing there, facing Finn Owyn, uncertain what to say.

Arm lying on the bed, he flutters his fingers for me to come to him. His expression is soft and open, kind and gentle. Like the Finn I used to know.

Tears spring to my eyes, and I hurry to the bed, carefully lying down beside him, nestled against his side. He kisses my temple, and I slide my arm around him, squeezing gently, needing him to know how happy I am to see him awake.

We lie like that for a long time. He softly caresses my arm as I weep against his chest and inhale everything about him. I've missed my best friend.

After a while, I sit up and wipe my face, noticing how warmly he looks at me, as though all bitterness has faded with the night.

"Did Hel tell you everything?" I sign, sitting close to him, my knee resting on his hip. I realize that I don't even know if he can speak.

"Not everything," he signs, giving me my answer. His movements are sluggish and heavy. "You *tell me,"* he adds.

When I begin, I start with last night, but he stops me.

"Everything," he signs. *"Beginning with Collecting Day."*

He lays his warm hand on my knee and listens. At first, I still feel unsure. Uneasy. But he rubs his forge-calloused fingers softly against my leg, as though soothing me, gently telling me that it's okay to say what I need to say.

The more I sign, the more the floodgates open, until eventually, I even tell him about last night and my dream on the beach today, and about facing the Witch Collector, about how much I ache for that man and yet hate him too, and how I don't know anything about who I am anymore.

He lifts his hand and brushes the tears from my cheek with his thumb before tugging my robe and gown back for a look at the burn scar that has erased most of the rune.

"You have to go," he signs, a pained look in his eyes. *"To the City of Ruin. I will be fine."*

It shakes me to my core that he doesn't fight the fact that he can't go. That tells me all I need to know about how Finn truly feels physically right now, regardless of his effort to hold his eyes open long enough to listen to my story.

"I love you, Raina," he signs. A single tear tracks down the side of his nose. *"I want you here. But this is something you have to do."*

"I know," I sign back. *"And I love you too."* How deeply I mean those words.

He angles his head on the pillow, those constantly mussed black curls tumbling over his forehead. There's a sad tilt to his eyes. *"But not like you love him,"* he signs.

I can't help but make a face. *"I do not—"*

He cuts me off, a languorous grin on his mouth, his voice a ragged, scraping whisper when he speaks. "You are Tiressia's worst liar, Raina Bloodgood."

A breath rushes from me, and I wave my hands, trying to stop him from using his voice, but he continues regardless.

"I'm all right, let me finish," he insists. "It hurts me," he continues. "But I see it. You need to be with him. For now, at least. Go to the Summerlands if you can. Figure out your story. And then," he takes my hand, "if you still want me, I will be here. If you want *him,* I will bear it. I just want you happy. That's all I have ever wanted."

More tears. I can't stop them. It seems that Finn's kindness and understanding have opened a path for me to funnel all my worry and pain and sadness and regret.

He draws me to him, and again, I lie in his arms and cry, thankful that he's holding me.

I admit something to him that I'm not sure I would admit to anyone else right now.

"I am scared," I sign.

He presses his lips to my temple. "I know."

41

NEPHELE

I can't stop pacing the uppermost catwalk of the lighthouse.

The shimmering veil of magick the Watch's Witch Walkers have erected along the coast to keep us on the mainland shimmers like mist on a spider's web. I can get us through the barrier with Alexus's help, I know. But I'm nervous that I won't have a reason to try.

Below and to our far left, on the veranda, Hel, Jaega, and Zahira stare at the sea, watching Rhonin, Hel, Harmon, and his boys as they drag row boats and oars to the shore in hopes we'll need them. Raina is upstairs with Finn. She didn't say as much, but I know my sister. She's packing and torturing Alexus. I have no doubt.

"I'm glad you got some rest today," Alexus says. He stands with his arms braced on the iron railing, his eyes trained to the east. His jaw hasn't stopped feathering since we left the dining room earlier. His concern about Raina choosing to stay behind and what he'll do if she does is evident.

"Me too. Thanks for lending me the lighthouse."

He shrugs a shoulder. "I could see your exhaustion. And your agitation." Bluntly, he adds, "I'm surprised you're so worried about Joran."

"I'm *not* worried about him." And I'm not. Even though Raina tried to see him in the waters earlier and couldn't. From exhaustion, perhaps. "I'm worried about my friends and my sister," I continue. "About Yaz and Zahira and Finn and Mari. Harmon and the boys. About not getting out of Star-worth Tor alive or being buried at sea thanks to the Northland fleet or not getting through that veil or the fact that I'm half Summerlander. I'm truly not worried about Joran. Never him."

"Never," Alexus mocks, his brows curling inward as he gives me a look I know too well. That knowing smirk.

"Stop it," I warn him as I jab his shoulder with my pointer finger, "or I'll toss you over."

"Ow," he laughs, rubbing his arm. That smile is a small thing, but something I haven't seen him do at all today. I miss the days when his laughter wasn't such a rarity.

"Joran seems... changed," Alexus says. "At least a little more tender toward you. Makes me want to kill him less."

I keep pacing and shake my head, cutting Alexus a sharp glare. "Your definition of *tender* is very different from mine if Joran is your example."

Though he *is* a little different. Something I've certainly noticed. He's still an animal, just with a different bite.

I glance toward the water. The waves are calmer tonight. Twilight shadows the clouds and bruises the sky, darkening the sea to a dusky blue. But a strange fog looms to the west, promising a storm.

Or... *something*.

"Do you see that?" I point toward the white haze, pearly and dense.

Alexus turns, and his long spine stiffens. "That's not normal. But it can't be Joran."

Over the next hour, as we both pace the catwalk from side to side, that fog rolls in, along with a chill wind. The previously calm water begins to churn, the waves rolling higher and crashing harder.

Alexus uses a spyglass to magnify things in the distance. Its view only extends a couple hundred yards past the curve of the cove, which is already blotted out by nightfall and something resembling a contained snowstorm hovering over the sea. It's stretching across Malgros's shore and across the city, for as far as the eye can see. Everywhere except right here at Star-worth Tor.

"Ten fucking devils." Alexus lowers the spyglass before lifting it to his eye once more. When he lowers it a second time, disbelief masks his face as he stares at the fog.

"What is it?" I snatch the instrument and aim it in the direction Alexus was looking. It takes a few moments and a few tries, twisting the world into focus, but what he saw *does* become clear. A tall mast and a single square-rigged sail break through the mist. Leaning against the rail are two men, one with brown hair, the other with long silver locks I would know anywhere. I scan the dark words painted on the side of... "Oh my gods. Is that—"

"Terrowin's motherfucking ship," Alexus says with a smile in his voice. "The Lady Belladonna has arrived."

⚜

ALEXUS AND I RUN TO THE BEACH, PASSING HEL ON THE WAY AS SHE hurries to tell Raina that the Lady Belladonna is here. And here it is. For a cog ship, it's big and imposing and possibly visible from the city wall behind the tor.

A thousand thoughts race through my mind. Did Joran find a crew? If not, how will we man this beast? Did he think of food? This ship was set to return this morning, it can't possibly be ready to sail again by now. What about Terrowin? How do we get past the Summerlander armada?

Gods, this journey is going to kill me.

I stand on the beach, facing the veil. I can't bring the whole thing down, but there's no need, I remind myself. We only need a path.

Alexus stands with me, and together we focus on the shimmering web. It's a mind game. A temporary mental rearranging of magickal lines that form the construct, a way to create a hole in the structure without being noticed. It's like poking a hole through a spider's web, carefully enough that the resulting vibration across those sensitive threads cannot be felt, lest we lead every Witch Walker in Malgros straight to Starworth Tor.

But Alexus is a talent. I've never seen him at work with his mind. I've only ever been instructed by him. But with such focus that I can feel it against my skin—a tightness to the air—he alone opens the veil. *In a matter of seconds.* Not a single thread in the web moves. Not even the subtlest, tiniest flutter.

"You'll need to teach me that trick one day," I tell him.

He just gives me a wry grin. "I can't divulge *all* my secrets." He winks. "Now see to your shield, woman."

I face the next battle. My shielding construct, a web of white light to my eyes. Quickly, I weave that web higher and thicker, imagining what I want anyone who might look in this direction to see: the white haze over a shipless sea. That's all.

Where it took Alexus seconds, my work requires several minutes. But Harmon and the boys have already packed the boats with our belongings, so when I finish, all there is to do is say our goodbyes and row out to climb aboard. There are three boats. They each seat four.

"Heading out!" someone calls.

I'm a little dizzy from the rushed effort on the construct, so I turn carefully, my neck tight. Drae, Keth, Jaega, and Callan are already rowing into the sea. Alexus casts his starlights across the beach and over the water to guide the way.

"I'm next!" another voice calls.

Alexus and I look toward the main house. Zahira.

She jogs across the sand and drops her pack in the front of Rhonin and Hel's boat, Alexus watching her every move with a scrutinizing and quite challenging stare.

"What do you think you're doing?" he asks, hands planted firmly on his hips.

The captain grabs an oar and meets his wide eyes. "What does it look like I'm doing?"

He glances back at Yaz, standing on the steps leading to the beach next to a torch, her arms crossed over her middle. "I'm not letting you leave her," he says, gesturing to Yaz.

Zahira throws his words back at him from our meeting. "I love you, but I don't really need your permission, my friend. I need *hers*," she nods toward Yaz. "And I have it."

"Zahira." His nostrils flare. "This is dangerous."

She cocks her head, her big, dark eyes intent. "As though I have not faced danger during my life on the seas? In the Watch? In war? And you need a captain, which I am. So stand aside and let me help."

Alexus shakes his head, working his jaw, but then he looks up, and his gaze hangs on something. I already know from that morphing expression on his face what that something—or *someone*—is.

When I turn, I'm not surprised to see Hel running toward us, her lips skewed into a smile. I'm also not surprised to see the woman stalking behind her.

My sister.

She's dressed like Death, garbed in black leather, carrying her pack in one hand, her swords in the other. Her hair is pulled back from her face in a long, thick braid, loose tendrils blowing in the wind, the silver-handled daggers strapped to her thighs glinting beneath the starlights.

Sand scatters as she walks to the side of Alexus's boat where she dumps her pack and swords. She looks up, staring at the man I know she loves, the very one she now calls Collector, and motions to the sea with a flinty expression.

Alexus doesn't speak. But he does nod at her and smile, if wickedly.

As Dru, Rhonin, Hel, and Zahira row to the ship, the three of us and Harmon drag the last vessel into the water. In perfect time, we row through the night, the sea lit with magick, quickly moving toward the Lady Belladonna.

And a water witch to whom I owe a godsdamn kiss.

V

A WORLD APART

42

NEPHELE

The Malorian Sea
The Lady Belladonna

The ship's oaken deck is slick with cold mist, glistening beneath the light of the ship's many lanterns.

Raina, Hel, and I lean against the railing holding hands, facing Malgros as the ship rocks and creaks on the waves. The world is awash in white, as though we're sailing through a cloud, the ship and Joran's magick carrying us across the Malorian Sea, unseen as a ghost.

My gut twists that we can't watch the Northland Break fade in the distance, but...

"Perhaps it's better this way," Hel says, as though reading my thoughts. "It hurts less if we don't see it."

Raina steps back, her cold hand leaving mine. She wipes her eyes before turning and heading past Terrowin's crew who walk around a bit dazed. In moments, my sister vanishes to the cargo hold where we will sleep for the night.

"We're going to need to help her through this," Hel says, rubbing her temple. "She wants to be here, but I've never seen her in so much pain."

I think about Raina's years without me, the relationships she built, everything she's lost in the last two months, how it must hurt to say yet *another* goodbye. "She's far more attached to the Northlands than she believes," I say. "A life isn't so easy to walk away from, especially when you love the people you must leave behind."

Hel tilts her head, her deep black hair falling over her shoulder. "Was it like that when you chose not to return to the valley?"

A heavy sigh leaves me, and I look out over the fog. I've been waiting for this. I thought Raina would be the one to mention it, long before now, though I worried she wouldn't believe me.

"I had my reasons for staying at the castle. It was difficult, and yes, the pain was unimaginable." Tears well in my eyes, but I swallow them back. "I forfeited time with my parents and my sister because it was important that I learn how to protect Winterhold. And yet, even with years of work and sacrifice, when the time came, I still failed."

I shake my head, a sinking feeling inside me. Before I left on that Collecting Day eight years past, Father told me to stay with the king. It wasn't anything I wanted to hear, and though we cried many tears, he emphasized that I would be needed one day, that I must remain on the far side of the wood to learn and study. And though I was twenty-two years old, I felt like a little girl seeking her father's wisdom, so when he said *stay*, I did.

Hel squeezes my hand, pulling me from my thoughts. "Don't look now, but your boyfriend is coming."

I make a face and look over my shoulder, spotting Joran stalking our way. A stained and dirty burlap bag hangs from one hand, a crystal glass of whiskey is clasped in the other.

Hel gives me a wide-eyed look, raising her sharp brows as she glances around the deck like she's looking for a place to hide. "I'll... just go find Rhonin."

The moment she turns her back on us, Joran drops the bag at my feet. It lands on the oaken planks with a *thud*. "A gift. For you."

Frowning, I study his silver eyes, his unreadable face, searching for a glimpse of a clue. "A gift," I say, dumbfounded. "For me."

"There's no one else on this ship that I would do as much for, I can assure you."

"But we hate one another."

He laughs. "Do we, now? I wasn't sure."

"The sword to your throat the other morning wasn't a clue?"

He smiles at the memory. "You were also straddling me. My brain received mixed messages."

Curious, I shake my head and look him over, trying to see what I'm missing. Because something is so off about Joran these last weeks. Something I cannot pin down. *Yet.* But I will.

When I look at the bag, a nervous twitch tugs at my mouth. My heart beats a little harder, almost like my intuition knows what I'm about to see before my mind does. I bend down and open it anyway.

I lock eyes with those of a dead man whose blond head happens to be removed from his body. I've never met the Northland Watch's admiral, but I know, without a doubt, it's him.

Stunned, I glance up at Joran and swallow the thick knot in my throat, trying my damnedest not to get sick. I killed Eastland soldiers at Winterhold and on Winter Road too. I've seen far worse than a blank, swollen, blue face and a bloody neck. But for some reason, staring into those terrified eyes gets to me.

"You... *You brought me Rooke's head?*"

Joran leans back against the railing and crosses his booted feet at the ankles. "You said you wanted it."

I just stare at him, blinking, utterly perplexed. "What of Vexx?"

Joran shrugs and takes a sip of his liquor, the liquid shining amber in the lantern light. "You didn't mention him. But in all truth, I looked for the general. I just couldn't find him." He rolls his eyes, inwardly. "For some reason, my senses aren't so good these days."

All I can do is close the bag, get up, and keep my shoulders squared as I walk to the railing beside him, thankful for the cool air on my face. He picks up the bag and tosses it overboard into the sea.

"Does Alexus know?" I ask, and he nods.

"I don't owe him anything," he says. "Not even an explanation. But he saw the bag."

"Ah," I reply. "Well, you might owe him nothing, but I owe *you* a kiss."

When I turn my head to brazenly meet his stare, his argent gaze is bright as liquid metal. Leaning in, he slips his cool hand across my neck, beneath my ear, his fingers in my hair, his thumb grazing my cheek. This close, I can see the azure witch's marks rising from behind his collar, and I can smell the warm, rich liquor on his tongue and the cold on his skin. I like it. That crisp scent of water and winter mingled with the sweetness of whiskey.

He lowers his stare to my mouth and tightens his fingers in my hair. Gods, I'm stupidly ready to press my body against his and kiss his face off when he draws back, his hand slipping away.

"Another time," he says, his voice a rasp before he chugs another drink and swallows hard. "When there aren't so many watchful eyes."

The pressure of anticipation that had built inside me moments before eases as I look around the deck. Our group are all below, prepping the hold and cabins for sleeping. Alexus is with Terrowin, having what I'm certain is a colorful conversation. The crew Joran somehow bribed into staying on board have brought out their tin cups and flagons of ale. Some stand near the helm, but a few sit with Zahira and Callan on empty cargo crates that never had the chance to be offloaded. Every rugged, sun-bronzed face looks irritated or confused, but the good Captain Osane, with a smoking pipe dangling from her mouth, seems to keep tensions suppressed as she withdraws a deck of cards and deals a hand.

There are no watchful eyes. Awkward as that feels given it was an excuse for not kissing me, neither of us leaves.

Joran turns and leans onto the railing, his elbow touching mine. He offers me his drink, and I gladly accept, draining the remains. Smiling at the empty crystal, he pulls a metal flask from inside his gray and gold jacket and fills the glass halfway.

"The fleet," I say, changing the subject. "We have to get past them." That's only part of the battle, I know, but the only one I can think about right now.

He motions to the white night around us and stuffs his flask back into his inside breast pocket. "You don't think we will? We've at least ten hours of night. In this fog, those sailors will never see us. I'll navigate this ship right past them."

What else can I do but pray to the Ancient Ones that he's right?

A thought occurs to me, though. "This isn't water magick." I reach over the railing and run my hand through the thick, white haze. It has the feel of magick, enough to mislead, but I sense something altered within it.

Joran lifts a silver brow. "It isn't? Fog is water, no?"

I turn so that my back is against the rail. "I suppose. If that's even fog. Sailors can navigate through fog. Whatever this is makes the world utterly inscrutable." I narrow my eyes. "If you can do all of this, where was this sort of aid in Frostwater Wood when we were being drowned by rain?"

His grin is a force to be reckoned with, broad and white and taunting. "Maybe I just like seeing Nephele Bloodgood dripping wet."

I roll my eyes, but I'd be a liar if I said that his words didn't affect me.

"Well, now I know what you're capable of." I take a long swig of his liquor and hand the glass back to him. "If you withhold help from us again, I will carve your balls from between your legs and wear them as a necklace."

That grin grows even brighter, though his gaze sharpens. "I like your fierceness. Very, very much."

I give him a dirty look. "Enough to lose your balls?"

He laughs. Actually *laughs*. "Enough to let you try and take them. That would be a fun fight, I think."

Again, I study him, so confused. "You act as if you don't remember the kind of woman I am. I don't play games, Joran."

Wearing a devilish expression, he leans in so close, his whiskey-warmed breath on my lips. "And yet you're playing one right now, witch. And loving it." He inhales the night air and draws his bottom lip between his teeth. "I can smell your arousal. It makes my mouth water."

Pressing a hand to his firm chest, I shove him away, though gods' death if it isn't the *last* thing I want to do.

"Go rot in the Nether Reaches, Joran."

Perhaps I'm more desperately lonely than I realized because there's a part of me that wants him to challenge me. To haul me into his arms. To drag me below deck to an empty cabin, tear away my clothes, and fuck me until I can't think of anything else but him.

But he doesn't do any of that. He just turns and, still grinning, struts away. "Only if you come with me, witch," he says over his shoulder. "Only if you come with me."

43

RAINA

I'm struggling to drift to sleep when footsteps sound on the stairs leading to the cargo hold.

Opening my eyes, I rise on my elbow, only to find the Witch Collector's tall figure sauntering down the darkened stairwell. It bothers me that I can identify him even in the shadows, that I know the way his long legs move, that I've memorized the shape of him, his narrow waist, his broad, strong shoulders, the curve of his hands.

He steps into the dim lantern light, head ducked to manage the low ceiling, carrying something under his arm. It isn't until he passes everyone else and crosses through the path Rhonin, Callan, and I made amid the undelivered barrels and crates that I realize what that something is.

He squats down and unrolls one of the thin cots Dedrick Terrowin gave us to make the next few nights bearable. Right beside me.

Fulmanesh, iyuma.

A small flame flares in the lantern hanging from a peg above my head. The light shadows the Witch Collector's face as he crawls onto his cot and plops down on his back. Across the hold, Hel lifts her head from her place beside Rhonin and Nephele, peeking over the crates, and I swear I hear them snickering.

I glare at the Collector. Dedrick Terrowin offered him a cabin in the crew's quarters. There's only one reason for him to be here right now, and that's to annoy me.

The Collector strips off his tunic, bundles it, and stuffs it beneath his head. I can smell the soft musk of sweat on his naked skin, mingled with all the other scents I now associate with him.

A golden gleam from the lantern light shines in his green eyes as he looks over at me, a crooked grin sitting on his lips, the embodiment of cool arrogance. "Something wrong?" he whispers.

It's been a difficult night. A difficult day. I've been tossing and turning for the last hour on this godsforsaken floor, worried and sad, all while trying to acclimate to the ship's swaying and constant creaking and groaning. The Collector's cocky ass is the last thing I need to deal with.

Just ignore him. And do not look at him.

And yet...

I sit up, my gaze quickly traveling over his muscular chest, the iron key hanging over his heart, his hard nipples, down his rippled stomach to that trail of black hair. Gods, the things I have done to that body.

When I meet his eyes again, he looks so smug.

"This will be a very long trip if you make me miserable," I sign. *"Because I can be just as awful, if not worse."*

He smiles, as though he's gotten exactly what he wanted, damn it.

"We both need something to keep our minds occupied," he says, keeping his voice low. "I would love it if you took your tunic off. I would think about nothing else."

I wish I had something to throw at his face, but I don't, so I lie back down and turn away from him.

He rolls toward me, his long body so close his scent envelops me. "I told you I wouldn't make this easy," he whispers against the back of my neck. "In fact, I'm going to make it very, *very* hard."

A chill skitters down my back, and I flip over, ready to shove the heel of my hand into his perfect nose, but... He's right there, and that mouth...

Gods' stars, why does he affect me this way?

"I'm only aggravating you," he says out of nowhere, a little laugh tripping from his lips. "I just wanted to persuade you to take my cabin, which I have a feeling you won't argue about when I come out of my britches next."

"Did you ever consider asking?" I sign with a sarcastic expression.

"Not at all, because you would've refused." He taps the tip of my nose with tender familiarity, and I jerk back at the touch, screwing up my face as he smiles and lies back again. "Go. First cabin to your right. You'll rest better, and I won't worry so godsdamn much. Or I can pester you all night. Your choice."

Blankly, I stare at him. He gave up his cabin for me. And he's right. I would've absolutely said no.

Suddenly, he slips his hand down to his leather britches and loosens the ties, eyeing me with an arched brow. "I'm giving you three seconds."

I *want* to argue. I don't want to let him win. But seeing him like this, with his hand *there*, makes my mind envision the absolute worst images, so I grab my pack and daggers and get up.

"Bother me again, and I will stab you," I sign.

He just laughs and folds his hands behind his head. "Mmm, you're so romantic. Now goodnight, Raina. Go to bed and let me rest."

My temper flares, mimicked in the flaring lantern light a second before I extinguish the flame, stomp across the hold, and wobble up the stairs as the Lady Belladonna rocks on a wave.

For a moment, I find myself wishing I could send the Collector an acrimonious message along the bond. But I can't. So I slip into his pitch-dark cabin, summon a tiny flame in the lantern hanging near the door, and climb into bed, trying to ignore the musty smell and the strange feel of being aboard a ship racing across open sea.

It had been far worse in the hold. I never would've slept. And I think the Collector knew that.

Later, when I still can't get any rest, I get up and prowl through the Collector's pack, knowing exactly what I need, stupid as it is and much as it irks me. I root around beneath his beloved journals, freezing when my hand touches silk.

Our sashes. They're neatly rolled together and tied around a little golden box—the necklace he bought me.

Don't think about it, don't think about it, don't think about it.

But I do. I think about that night with him, and the way he looked lying there beside me minutes ago, and the way he feels when he holds me, when he kisses me, when he's inside me. It all still seems so imaginary and unbelievable, but every time I'm around him, I end up wondering if my imagination is correct. If being with him was as good as memory serves.

These are not thoughts I need to have. I'm so tired, yet so restless, and so...

Gods be damned. I hate him for this.

I loosen the laces of my leathers, and after several moments of indecision, slip my hand down to the apex of my thighs where a tender ache has formed. Parting my flesh, I find that pulsing ache and let memories of us unfurl.

With every needy swirl of my fingertip, I focus on the filthy words he uttered to me—never the tender ones—and the times when he was brutal, taking me like I was meant to be claimed. But then I picture him the way he was our last time together, hand wrist-deep in my hair, his head thrown back and mouth parted as *he* quivered beneath *my* tongue and *my* hands.

I can still hear him panting my name, still see the muscles of his hard abdomen tensing, still hear him moaning as I finally let him spill.

It takes a matter of seconds to climax with that thought in mind, my orgasm shuddering though my entire body, leaving me leaning on his desk, gripping the edge like I might fall off the world, gasping as I ride out the pleasure.

I stand there for a few minutes, my thighs clenched and shaking, my heart pounding. When I come down from that mindless high and can think again, I take a deep breath and shove the sashes back into his pack. I also withdraw one of his woolen tunics.

There are many things I shouldn't do when it comes to him, yet this is another boundary I'm going to cross tonight. I hold the fabric to my nose and inhale deep before I strip free of my shirt and undergarment, replacing them with his tunic, which hangs over my hips.

I have slept in his arms too many times now because I feel so alone without him near. But I would die before admitting that. This will have to do until I learn to be without him. He'll never have to know.

This time when I bury myself beneath the covers, surrounded by his comforting scent, my muscles languid from pleasure, sleep comes swiftly.

𝇗 44 𝇗

ALEXUS

"Think we're past the Northland fleet?" I ask Dedrick, raising my voice over the wind.

We stand with Joran at the prow of the ship, staring over a sea of opaque, white mist that's tinted with something other than magick, something I can't determine no matter how hard I try.

I listen closely, as though there might be an answer in the night itself. But I only hear the usual song of sailing, the rhythm of howling air whipping canvas, waves crashing against the hull, the groan of wood as the ship sails from crest to crest, and the squawking of hungry gulls in the sky.

It feels as though we're flying across the Malorian. The crew cast their maritime log over the ship's bow last night to measure speed, but the white haze makes it impossible to see for counting the knots.

To maintain his balance on the swiftly moving ship, Dedrick grips the railing with one hand and leans on a wooden cane with the other. Carefully, he reaches beneath the collar of his blue tunic and removes a small hourglass attached to a metal chain around his neck. "Twelve-hour intervals," he says, studying the falling sand. "Only a few hours left before time to turn the glass. So I'd say we're very close."

"We are indeed." Joran leans his elbows on the rail as the wind rips through his silver hair. When he notices the draw of my brow, he adds, "I can sense the fleet. On the water."

Water magick is my weakness, and I've never been in the position of depending on a water witch to guide me over a body of water, so I must take him at his word. But my mind drifts elsewhere. Now that I have the two men together, I broach a topic it seemed neither wanted to discuss last night, one I need an answer to.

"I'd like one of you to explain how this situation came to be." I look at Dedrick. "How were you and your men persuaded to do this? The Watch will know. They might accept an excuse that you were taken by force, but I doubt it. This affects your ability to return home." I turn to Joran. "And you have no money. No means to have bought Mr. Terrowin's aid. Did you somehow kidnap these men?"

I can't say I would've done any less, but I'm curious. Joran took Rooke's head, *the Northland Watch's heavily guarded admiral*, seized a ship and crew, *and* created this wall of white to shield us. Alone. Either he's been withholding his ability for years, or something has changed.

I also wonder if Joran told Dedrick more than I cared for him to know, knowledge that could land us in danger if it's pried from Mr. Terrowin with enough force by the right people.

Like the Summerland Guard.

Joran smirks and glances at Dedrick who tightens his hand on the mist-slicked railing, wide eyes facing the bowsprit, back stiff. "We worked out a gentlemanly agreement," Joran says. "We can leave it at that."

Like fuck, we will. I face Dedrick who's far too quiet, his nerves visible. "What happens when you return to Itunnan's port with the same load you left with and half the crew?" I ask him.

His curly hair is blown flat against his forehead in the wind. "I haven't figured that out just yet," he answers. "Perhaps I'll claim we met with a storm or ship trouble and had to double back." His amber eyes are bold against the surrounding mist. "I'll take care of it, my lord. As I promised, I'll see you all safely to my contact. I'll deal with my plight from there."

"Just like that?" I study him for a reaction. "Just like that, you'll risk being detained by the Summerland Guard, questioned, and possibly accused of treason when they return you and your ship to the Northern fleet's control. And you hold no worry for it?"

He takes a deep breath. Exhales. "I figure if Captain Osane is involved, your mission must be a necessary one. That's all. I did hear rumors at the docks, so when Mr. Dulevia approached me, I wanted to help." Nervously, he glances at Joran, so quickly I could've missed it.

But I didn't. And I'm not a fool.

I turn to the water witch and move closer to him, until I'm leaning down in his face. "I don't know what you're holding over his head, but I'm going to find out."

Smirking, he looks up at me with that silver stare. "I'm not scared of you. In the least. And perhaps you should remember that sometimes it's better to leave well enough alone." He glances at the key around my neck and laughs. "Besides, *you're* the man whose past is built on lies. And yet you worry about *my* dishonesty."

His dig is a weak one. Now that the people who matter most to me know who I was, those barbs don't cut the same.

"Just know that I don't trust you," I tell him. "And that I'm watching you."

No more than I am in that moment, because Nephele steps onto the main deck below us, her pale blonde braid snapping in the wind, and as though she'd tapped on his shoulder, Joran turns around, his gaze finding her instantly.

A wave of protectiveness strikes, but before I can say anything, the Icelander shuffles down the steps to greet her, wearing a wolfish smile.

"GOOD MORNING."

I take a seat on the wooden stool in my proffered cabin, a mug of warm cider in hand. Thanks to Nephele and Zahira's efforts in the galley, a mishmash of a breakfast awaits.

With a glance, I raise a bold flame in the unlit lantern hanging near the door to illuminate the lightless cabin. The fire crackles and spits, and Raina peers at me from beneath a mess of dark hair tumbled over her head.

She scrubs the hair back from her dark blue eyes and tosses the blanket aside. Sitting up with a jerk, she wears a grumpy face that I can't help but grin at. If nothing had changed between us, I'd crawl over her, lay her down, and kiss her until she smiled against my mouth.

"Such a joy you are first thing in the morning," I say with a roguish grin. "Such a beautiful, happy light." As the ship tips over a wave, she grips the edge of the bed and glares at me with sleepy—annoyed—eyes. Once the ship corrects, I offer her the mug of cider. "Apple and cinnamon. It's quite good. Made by your sister."

Raina shakes her head in answer and threads her fingers through her tangled hair over and over to tame it.

My gaze drifts down the lovely column of her throat, and... That's when I notice it. The neck of her rather *large* tunic is untied, her beautifully marked chest on display.

I cock my head, lift a finger, and very matter-of-factly say, "You're wearing my shirt."

Her face. If I could capture this moment in etched glass, I would.

Stiffly, she lifts her chin and signs, *"I was cold."*

I nod, slowly. "Of course. Cold. It had *nothing* to do with the fact that you wanted me last night."

She doesn't bother to hide her disgust. *"You think far too highly of yourself."*

For a second, I consider playing nice. She's tired, and we have quite the night ahead. But I cannot let the moment pass.

I glance around the room, my gaze landing on my open pack before it slides to her crumpled shirt and a pretty white undergarment she must've bought while shopping with Yaz.

"Exactly what did you do in here last night?" I ask and take a sip of her cider.

She reaches for her shirt and underthings, snatching them from the desk, then shrugs and makes a face I know well. *What do you mean?* that face says as she signs, *"I slept."*

"Mmm. I just wondered because I felt something through the bond."

Again. *Her face.* All that sheer mortification hidden beneath a poorly constructed mask of indifference. The pretty apples of her cheeks turn rosy, and a flush races up her neck. How I want to taste the heat of her skin.

I lean forward, elbows on my knees, and glance at the loosened laces of her leathers. They lie on her thighs beneath the tunic's hem which is rumpled around her waist.

"I know what you did last night." It was a thin stream of connection across the singed tatters of our bond, but there's no mistaking that feeling. "Did it feel good?" I ask before taking another sip. "Thinking of me while you fucked yourself? Did you think about sucking my cock? Or when I came in your hand? Or when you came on my fa—"

She jolts up from the bed, tossing her clothes aside. *"Stop,"* she signs, standing over me. *"Last night was not about you, and I do not need you to tell me what happened between us. It changes nothing about what I feel for you."*

Leaning back in my chair, I raise my brow. "Which is?"

"Loathing," she signs.

I give her a challenging stare. "And lust."

"Repulsion."

"Attraction."

"Disgust."

"Desire." I wink. "Shall we do this all morning? Or should we fuck and get that part out of the way?"

The moment I present the question, I see it take up space in her mind —a proposal with possibility. But it's a half-lived notion because she squelches it seconds later.

"Tell me what you want," she demands, her hands moving in that sharp, fast way that means she's close to boiling. *"Why are you here?"*

I stand and set her mug on the desk, every inch of my body aware of her nearness.

"One, this was my cabin." I grab the straps of my open pack and sling them across my chest. "Two, we've sailed past the Northland fleet. In fact, we'll be in Summerland waters by day's end thanks to Joran slipping us across the sea like a godsdamn falcon. So if you want to see the Malorian before we get into the thick of danger, now is the time."

She frowns, and her eyes go wide. *"What? Tonight?"*

"Yes, tonight, so get dressed, go get some food, sit above deck in the sun, check the waters, and get your mind right." I head to the door, looking back at her before I leave. "Because come nightfall, the hard part of this journey begins."

A dozen emotions flutter through the bond. I'm not able to decipher them all anymore, but I can guess.

Raina's chest rises and falls on a deep inhale and exhale, and she levels me with a look. *"Prick,"* she signs. *"You could have said that first."*

"What would've been the fun in that?" I smile as she grabs the mug of cider and rears back, but I'm out the door by the time it smacks the wood with a loud *thud*.

Standing in the narrow corridor between the crew's quarters, I scrape my hand over my face, trying to tamp down the maddening ache that threatens to choke me. I'm so in love with that infuriating woman, and one day—*one day*—she will realize how much she loves me too.

45

RAINA

After breakfast, Nephele, Hel, and I stand together on the main deck. We lean over the port side rail, the salty wind tearing at our braided hair as we watch foamy waves churn away from the starboard side. No matter where we look, there's nothing but blue: the dusky indigo of the sparkling Malorian deep that meets the azure sky at the horizon. It's breathtaking.

For a while, there are no other ships in sight, until white sails appear in the distance, speckling the dark water to the west like birds.

"Fishing boats," Zahira says as she walks up beside me, cider in hand. "And likely small cargo ships from the Western Drifts."

The Western Drifts. An archipelago that links the western waters between the Northland Break and the Summerland coast. They're as foreign to me as the City of Ruin.

"Do they sail into Itunnan too?" Hel asks, running her hands along the wooden rail.

"They do," Zahira replies, "though there are more port cities to the west. They're mostly for the people from the Drifts to trade, but they also intercept ships coming from other lands and determine who gets to enter Summerland waters."

Hel gazes out over the sea, the apples of her brown cheeks bronze in the sunlight. "I'd like to see the Drifts someday."

Zahira smiles. "It's a beautiful place, peaceful. Blue-green waters. White sands. When this is over, perhaps Yaz and I can take you."

I recall that the captain has friends there who plan to visit Malgros soon if the Watch lets anyone into the city. At least Finn will have the distraction of new people to keep him from worrying about me and Hel.

With Finn on my mind, I head back to my borrowed cabin with a canteen strapped over my shoulder. I glance across the main deck, only to spot a dove perched on the rail on the starboard side, watching me.

I stop and stare back. The prince manipulates crows and ravens. A dove seems far too innocent for his employ, but this dove—or *a* dove—has been following me since shortly after we left Winterhold.

Again, just like my first day in Malgros, the little death behind my heart flutters. This time I can't help but smile a little and nod in greeting. Perhaps that little one is my guardian, sent from the Ancient Ones.

In the cabin, I sit at the weathered writing desk and fill my scrying dish. Since being unable to see Joran back in Malgros, I've worried that something was wrong with my magick. It's time to determine if it was a simple one-time occurrence, very possibly due to the horrific night I'd had, or if I'm facing a greater problem.

Finn and Yaz are first, my heart heavy for them both. Much to my relief, they appear in the waters. Finn is sitting with Mari on the bed where I left him, a new bandage on his throat, playing a game of dice on a shiny wooden board positioned between them. Yaz sits curled in the chair in the corner, knitting and watching. They look worried, like they're trying to occupy their minds. But they're safe, and that is everything.

Vexx is my next effort. He's standing somewhere along Malgros's harbor, watching as a crew works to prepare a ship for sailing. At least that's what it looks like to my eyes, though I've never seen a ship or harbor or crew until these past few days. His expression is a dark one. Malevolent and rotten. I'm certain he's taking every advantage of Rooke's loss. The Northland Break is now not only missing its king, but the Watch is also missing its admiral, and we've an Eastland menace on our land.

Where's he going? Back to the East? Or is he planning to follow us?

I realize it's probably an unwise hope because the Summerland Guard would surely stop him. But I pray to the Ancient Ones that Vexx sails at our back soon, or that I at least get one more chance to make him pay.

Come find me, you pig, I think as I stare into the waters.

Before I prick my third finger, I'm unsure who to ask the waters to show me—Colden or the Prince of the East. Neri isn't an option. Since the prince is always shielded behind that godsdamn impenetrable barrier, I decide to look for Colden. He so often provides a bird's-eye view of a resting Fleurie.

Only today she isn't resting. And she and Colden aren't in the dungeon.

My heart pounds as I watch the scene unfold. Fleurie is outside, standing on a stretch of red clay with her pretty face lifted toward a blue morning sky, her radiant red hair aflame in the sunlight. She isn't bound. Even the iron collar I normally see is gone.

A vast crumble of old ruins—nothing more than sun-washed and weather-stained limestone now—mark the background, the skeleton of the ancient city's first iteration left neglected and unburied on a hill for all to see.

I know that view from Alexus's dreams. I recognize the lay of the land. They're still in Quezira, at Min-Thuret's old training yard.

Fleurie is surrounded by a prowling red cloud, as if a cloud can be red. As if it can prowl. I know it's the prince, circling her slowly, but she seems unfazed. Unbothered. Even as he and Colden and another man, a guard perhaps, watch her. More guards lurk around the yard, but their eyes are on the surrounding city.

Colden's attention slides to a pale-skinned older woman with coppery red and silver hair. I don't know her, and yet I do, thanks to those familiar family traits that cannot be missed.

Bronwyn Shawcross.

She stands with her hands clasped, nervously working her grip as Colden's view darts back to Fleurie. I can feel the tension pulsing between each person, even though I'm hundreds and hundreds of miles away.

Fleurie lifts her right arm straight over her head and brings it down like a blade. Colden's anticipation moves across time, through the waters, and into me.

But nothing happens.

Relief strikes Colden next, radiating into me, even as the prince's red cloud roils and swells, and Fleurie nods and tries again.

She's trying to open a portal.

When her arm comes down, I cringe, waiting for *what*, I do not know. The world to open, I suppose. But again, thankfully, nothing happens, save for the prince's red mist swirling and twisting before it rushes toward Colden—*toward me*—and then vanishes from the scene, leaving a red vapor to spill over my scrying dish's edges and disintegrate across the cabin floor.

I let out a long breath. The prince's secret weapon isn't ready yet. It's a small favor from the Ancient Ones, but it buys us much needed time.

Given what we still face, I'll take it.

⚜

"I HOPE EVERYONE CAN SWIM. *WELL*."

Every member of our group, plus Dedrick Terrowin, sits on a circle of crates in the dim cargo hold, staring at the Witch Collector with wary faces.

No one speaks up, so he continues.

"The Summerland's first line of defense in these waters is a checkpoint. All arriving trade ships are funneled into shipping lanes that lead to Itunnan's cove and boarded by officers of the Summerland Guard. They check passage papers and walk the cargo hold before allowing vessels into the harbor for further inspection."

"You can hide in my cabin while they look around," Dedrick says. "They're too thorough in the cargo hold."

That makes my stomach twist. The thought of being right under the noses of the Summerland Guard.

"What about Dedrick's papers?" Zahira asks. "The dates are old, and they're stamped with a return status from a matter of days ago. That will spark suspicion." She turns to Terrowin. "Is your cargo list accurate with the cargo count? Did you offload anything before sailing to Starworth Tor?"

"Only five barrels," he says. "One of my men is working on the papers now. Bit of a forger. We just have to hope it works."

"If worse comes to worst," the Collector says, "spill ale on the pages and apologize profusely. They know your name and face and ship. You are not suspect. Yet."

Which means he's obviously good at what he does to have never been caught and to have never aroused caution. That makes me feel a little better about the night.

"And then?" Hel asks. "Once we're safely anchored in the harbor?"

The Collector sits on the edge of a crate. "Then we sneak off the ship and swim to Goma Pier on the eastern side of the cove. Dedrick can get us as close as possible, and Joran can help with the current if necessary. We just can't disturb the other ships in the harbor. According to Terrowin, Goma Pier is always empty at night."

"My contact, Orlena Madar, lives in the warehouse near Goma," Dedrick says. "Her safe house is the only secure route for foreigners into Itunnan. The other docks are more heavily patrolled since the arriving ships come from the west." He lifts a finger that boasts a fancy emerald ring. "You must still be wise and careful because Orlena isn't expecting you, so I cannot guarantee that the guard won't be walking the piers there, or anyone else for that matter. As for the sea wall, it's always manned, but at night, with Goma's darkness, their eyes are avoidable."

"Wise, careful, and silent as the dead," the Collector adds. "If we're seen, we'll be seized and locked in a prison cell for trespassing for gods know how long before we can persuade the Guard to send word of our presence to Fia Drumera. If they would even listen."

"As if they could hold you," Keth says. "Or Raina. Or Nephele. You three could storm us right through the guard if you wanted. I haven't seen what you can do, but I heard Rhonin talking about it. Just blow these bastards to pieces and light anyone on fire who gets in our way, and this trip will happen much faster."

Of all people to reply, Joran is the last one I expect, but he lifts his silver head from his perch on a crate and says, "This land is far different territory than the North. The North is a gentle place compared to the Summerlands. These people have fought for their very existence for centuries. They've perfected and studied ancient magick to the point that it is a methodical part of their learning. They don't play with magick here. They live it. Magick even thrives in the shifting sands, in the cold dark of the desert. It hides in plain sight in the provinces, and you can't fathom the things that live in the Summerland mountains and forests. Don't think these people aren't more than prepared for a little magick like some of you can dole out. Meet with a swarm of Dread Vipers, and this group will be no more than a bloodstain on the Summerland's desert floor."

"Dread Vipers?" I sign.

"Fia's elite guard of military assassins," the Collector replies. "That I can't just kill," he says to Keth. "They are Fia's men. They hunt down trespassers. They are loyal to their queen, and she to them. It probably wouldn't go over well if I slaughter them. But they aren't a concern for us because we're going to keep our heads low and our magick concealed and get through Itunnan and the provinces undetected so we can reach the City of Ruin. Right?"

He looks at every face, then watches Joran closely, his sharp-as-glass eyes saying all I need to know. He's wondering the same as me. How does Joran Dulevia from the northernmost village of Reede know so much about the Summerlands?

Within the hour, we cross the main deck and climb the steps leading to Dedrick's cabin. The air is so warm this far south, the night and sea dark as pitch. Our blue world has been exchanged for one that could've been carved from an obsidian mountain in the Mondulak Range.

The ten of us take turns sitting, pacing, and standing in nervous silence as the ship slows.

"Empty your packs of anything you cherish," the Collector says, pointing to an empty crate in a corner. "Leave it all there. Perhaps we'll have the chance to retrieve everything one day."

I watch as he opens his own pack and removes the golden box that contains my necklace, along with his journals.

His journals.

He holds them for a few minutes, running his thumb over the wool he keeps them wrapped in, before carrying them—and the gift box—to the crate, carefully placing them inside. When he turns and meets my eyes, a deep sadness sweeps through me. To treasure something for three hundred years only to have to walk away from it... I can't imagine what that must feel like, not to mention that earlier today, I had to inform him that his old friend is indeed practicing her skills with opening a portal.

Talk about a past coming back to haunt.

I'm not sure what gets into me, but I walk over and remove the golden box. I can't salvage his beloved journals, and I can't change that his friend unwittingly made a deal with his enemy, but he didn't want to chance losing this little pearl, and something about that softens my bitterness.

I remove the necklace and fasten it around my neck before tucking it beneath my jacket collar. *"Not letting you give away my jewelry,"* I sign.

He smiles with one side of his mouth—the dimpled side—and I can't handle what it does to me, so I walk across the cabin to the single porthole and peer outside. Anything for a distraction.

A smaller vessel rows up broadside, and in seconds, our crew begins shouting and laughing with the guards. I hold my breath, ready for this to be over, and soon enough it is.

Dedrick opens the cabin door and pokes his curly head inside. "Never underestimate a good forger and an even better liar." He curls his lips into a satisfied smirk. "They welcomed us to anchor in the harbor. Time to see what you Northlanders are made of."

46

NEPHELE

The Summerland Coast
Itunnan Harbor

T he night is thick on the eastern side of Itunnan's massive harbor.
I can't see anything in front of me, and my body is screaming. Behind me, dozens of ships and boats and cogs and skiffs
float on the water, their lantern lights bobbing against the backdrop of the
port city's rocky shoreline.

There are sandstone buildings and mud-brick homes stacked tall
against the rugged coast, looming above the ancient torchlit sea wall that
surrounds the docks, their square windows lit with golden candlelight.

Terrowin anchored us away from the other vessels in the harbor, as
close to Goma Pier as possible without seeming odd, the Lady Belladonna
angled to shield us from view. The swim isn't a terrible one, but my pack is
strapped tightly to my back, the weight making the effort more difficult
than it has any right to be. Then again, it isn't as though I've had a warm
sea to tread through every day for the last eight years. The last time I
swam was in the valley, with Raina.

No matter, I keep pushing through the water, telling myself that *I am not alone*. Everyone is out here with me. Somewhere.

Suddenly Joran is at my side, gliding through the harbor like a shark. If not for his silver hair and the smooth slip of his muscled arms just above water every few seconds, I wouldn't know a human was beside me at all.

The water around me cools, which is strange, but there's a propulsion beneath the surface, a stirring undercurrent, a *push* nudging me toward the darkened pier shadowed by a four-story dimly lit warehouse in the near distance.

Regardless of Joran's aid—because I know that's what it is—I still struggle to keep swimming. For all the vast magick I can create, the one thing I cannot do is transport myself elsewhere. What I wouldn't give for the gift of Loria's children right now, or to be like Fleurie, able to slice open the world and move across cities and continents and bodies of water as I please.

Joran sharply angles his trajectory to the left, and I realize I'm veering right—away from Goma Pier. I correct and follow the Icelander, thankful that he stayed behind to guide me.

That he did not leave me.

Just get to the pier, I tell myself. *Just keep going. Push, push, push. You do not quit, Nephele Bloodgood.*

In minutes, we're dragging ourselves through the water beneath the pier and climbing over the rocks nestled there, glamours up to prevent illumination. Joran's strong hands are on me, helping me, but the moment we're clear of the sea, Raina and Hel grab onto my jacket and lead me to sit on a boulder near them.

I pat my body, making certain my weapons are still intact, even as I sense Joran beside me, finding me in the dark with such ease.

We wait there, dripping wet and catching our breath, save for Alexus and Zahira who disappear into the darkness, moving along the rocky bank, checking for any sign of life.

Jaega hisses, and though it's impossible to see anything clearly down here, Joran's deep voice says, "Someone's bleeding."

"It's me," Jaega confesses. "I caught my shin on a jagged rock. Or maybe it was wood. A nail. I don't know. I just know I'm bleeding. I think a lot."

"Raina?" Keth's voice is quiet and shaking, tender as I've ever heard it. "Help her?"

My sister crawls over the rocks toward Jaega, her silhouette a gray scrape against the night as my eyes adjust to the darkness. I know she's healing the young woman, even if I can't see the magick being done.

"It's not a terrible wound," Joran tells me quietly, as though sensing my worry. "A trickle of blood, but she's not bleeding profusely like you're imagining."

His words ease the tension already tightening knots along my shoulders as I squeeze water from my braid. The last thing we need tonight is for one of us to get badly injured.

"I didn't know water witches have such a delicate sense of smell," I whisper.

"The better to track with. I won't lose *you*, that much is certain."

I crumple my brow and tug off a boot to drain the water. "Why do you say that?"

A pause, and then, "Because I've scented your desire, Nephele." His voice is somehow seductive and reticent at the same time. "I won't forget it. I *can't*. I might as well be a dog on the hunt now."

My cheeks heat, and I'm thankful for the shield of darkness. But then it dawns on me that it excites me to know I've affected him in such a way, and he probably smelled that excitement before I even realized what I was feeling.

"That doesn't explain why you're as talented as any hound," I reply, trying to draw attention away from me, hoping the scent of the sea on my skin masks whatever it is he smells.

He laughs. "Just something I was born with, I suppose."

This conversation feels easy, unguarded for us both, so I do something I would never have dreamed I'd do a few weeks ago. "Thank you," I say. "For staying with me. I owe you again."

"I'll make you a deal," he says. "When this is over, I'll claim that kiss. As for the other debt you feel you owe, I won't call it due until I feel like you're ready."

I smile, sensing the innuendo in his words and wondering what in the world is wrong with me that I like it so much.

"Deal," I say, feeling more brazen than I probably should. "I just have one question for you. Regarding the whole scent thing."

Another laugh, and I feel him lean his hands back on the rock. "Ask."

"Did you *scent* me the night of the wedding at Winterhold?" I whisper, bravely broaching the topic of our single night of passion last year.

There's a pause, a moment of debate, perhaps, but then I feel him lean into me, his cool breath on my damp cheek, the side of my neck, against my ear. "Should I have?" he says, sending a shiver down my arms. "Did you want me then too?"

I start to turn my face toward his, to make him feel me as closely in the dark as I feel him. But his words make me freeze.

Surely he didn't forget that night. He hadn't been *that* tipsy. Sadly, I would've settled for just about anyone after that wedding, and he was there, and it just... happened. With this newfound tension between us, I think sex with Joran would be leagues better now, but he should have as clear a recollection as me.

Before I can press him for an explanation, someone moves behind us. Boots whisper from rock to rock and wet leather creaks. Alexus and Zahira.

"All right, the pier and docks are empty," Alexus says, his voice hushed and deep. "Time to go." His arms are stretched wide, hands gripping two of the pier's pillars as he leans in to speak to us. The contour of his shape is barely outlined by the moonlight trapped behind a sky full of clouds, but I can see him.

"The warehouse is being prepared," Zahira says, stepping up onto two rocks like a shadow. "We have a place to rest for the night, and a means to gather supplies tomorrow. We'll work out the other details inside."

"We just need to stay to the shadows," Alexus adds. "There are only a few guards manning this side of the sea wall. Follow me."

Everyone crawls from beneath the pier like spiders from under a rock. Across the rocky embankment we skitter, before hauling our tired bodies onto the wooden dock, moving on quiet feet.

As we slip through the darkness to an extremely narrow passageway leading behind the warehouse, I end up last, only Joran behind me.

"I said something wrong, didn't I, witch?" His voice has a different edge to it. A different depth. It makes something inside me writhe, something squirming and wriggling and demanding to be felt.

I say nothing in reply as the ancient intuition of my ancestors, flowing hot and alive in my blood, sends me a warning.

Wrongness, it screams. *Wrongness.*

My heart pounds. I try to listen.

47

RAINA

Orlena Madar's warehouse is a clean, cavernous space filled with neatly stacked crates of cargo, produce, and wares.

I stare at the rounded rafters that seem so very far above. The upper floors are dark, save for one area to the left on the sea side of the building. Warm candlelight shines through its single door. Perhaps it's Orlena's living quarters. Dedrick said she lived here.

The rest of the floors are only visible in shadow, revealed by whatever dim illumination reaches from that one nook and the lanterns hanging from the stone walls on the first level. I can make out the lines of a few large windows, and a single mezzanine, though there are wood-planked catwalks around every floor.

"Let's get you all downstairs so you can clean up, dry out, and get some rest," Orlena says.

"We can always leave tonight," Joran suggests. "I don't think any of us are exceptionally exhausted, and we need to be moving. Quickly."

"The gates don't open until sunrise," Orlena replies. "The wall is imbued with our queen's magick."

"After all this time," Joran says, eyes narrowed as he shakes his head in annoyed disbelief, "no one has found an alternate route through that damn wall?"

Orlena eyes the Icelander, and in a soft, steady voice says, "Who are you?"

No reply.

I look over at him. With a smirk on his face, he leans against a stone column, his gray skin and wet, silver hair a strange shade beneath the golden lantern light. He stares at Orlena as though he can see right through her, though it somehow feels like the opposite is true.

"I'm a Northlander. To my core. That's all you really need to know."

Alexus and Nephele share an off glance as Orlena studies the water witch with a thorough once-over. Whatever is hanging between them gets left behind, however, for more important matters.

Orlena struts her tall frame toward a large crate that's taller than she is, and motions, without a word, for Rhonin to follow.

A little shocked, he startles and says, "Me?" But then he quickly steps to task.

He looks like a timid little boy as he joins her, likely because Orlena is so beautiful. She wears black leggings and tall boots, topped off with an umber-red silken tunic embroidered with gold thread. Her hair is a mass of shiny caramel corkscrew curls, her eyes a deep, rich black, her skin an earthy, warm brown and utterly luminescent.

Thankfully, save for a reddened face, Rhonin doesn't embarrass himself. He simply helps Orlena push the empty crate aside, revealing a secret passage cut into the floor. Duty served, he steps back to his place next to Hel.

I didn't think he could blush any harder, and yet, when Hel spears him with a look, his face blazes like a summer sun.

Orlena squats and slides her finger into a metal ring on the wooden planks and lifts the door. As though she's done this dozens of times, and I'm sure she has, she snatches a lantern and nods at us, a bright smile on her face.

"Come on. I think you'll like it down here."

It doesn't dawn on me until I'm descending the steep steps to an underground hideout that Orlena helps Dedrick smuggle Northlanders into her homeland regularly. Who's to say she won't help Eastlanders? Why would she do it at all? Is this not why we labeled Rooke a traitor?

I must not be the only one with that thought, because as we follow the rickety stairs into the lower rooms, and Orlena Madar begins lighting lanterns hanging around the space, Callan says, "Why would you help us enter your lands?"

They walk around studying tables and shelves loaded with clothes and shoes, weapons, foodstuffs, and even baskets of documents, most likely already forged, complete with a new name.

Orlena closes the glass on a lantern and meets Callan's heavy stare. "You're here because *he*—" she points at the Collector "—is old friends with my queen. And because the Prince of the East is causing trouble." Though she's speaking to Callan, she glances at Joran, and with a pointed edge to her words, says, "That's really all I need to know."

Callan picks up a dagger and holds it to the light. "You *don't* know us, though. We could be Eastlanders with lies in our mouths."

Orlena clasps her hands behind her back and meets Callan's challenging stare. "What's your name?" Slowly, the Summerland woman walks toward my friend.

Unlike Joran, Callan answers.

"Callan Terzerak."

"Where are you from, Callan Terzerak?"

"The Mondulak Range. And Winterhold."

"How many blades are on your person?"

"Five."

"Who do you most love in this world?"

"My adopted son."

"Who would you most like to kill?"

"I don't want to kill anyone."

"Who in this group do you hate?"

"No one."

Orlena pauses before Callan, almost toe to toe with the rune witch. "And you were honest, about every question." She looks at Joran. "His answer was honest too. I know because that is *my* gift. I do not help anyone who lies to me, or who means my land or my people harm. It's as simple as that."

"She already did this with me and Zahira." The Collector drops his pack in a chair and rests his broad back against one of the four square, stacked-stone piers that seem to be holding up the entire building. "But

I'm glad you all were able to hear," he goes on. "Zahira would never have placed us in danger with Dedrick. I wasn't sure about him or this situation either at first, but I am now."

From across the small room where she flutters her fingertips over a wine-colored tunic, Zahira offers him a soft smile and slight bow of her head. A thank you.

Orlena winks at Callan, then gestures behind herself, to a dark curtain. "There's a sleeping room that way. Only bunked cots, but there should be enough beds for all of you. As for everything you see here—" she motions to the filled tables and shelves "—take what you need. That's why it's here."

Keth heads straight for the weapons table, while Jaega searches through the clothes, probably for new britches now that hers have a rip from knee to ankle. Callan and Zahira begin examining Orlena's collected documents, their faces masks of focused curiosity.

With her confident walk, Orlena closes the short distance between her and the Collector. I don't miss the appreciative look she skims from his head to his feet, nor do I miss the way it makes my chest tighten.

Admittedly, he's a sight to see. Tall and rugged and still dripping, he wears black leathers, his thumbs hooked in the weapons loops at his waist. A white tunic clings to his strong torso, the neck untied and open, revealing a deep slice of rune-marked, golden chest and his iron key, something he didn't part with on the ship. His wet hair hangs in tousled, black waves, glistening around his angular face.

And his beard. It's coming back in with a vengeance. The dark stubble adds a seductive edge to his look, making his already bold eyes appear that much bolder. It's criminal.

"Thank you for this," he says to Orlena. "We have so much ground to cover. We need to reach Fia as quickly as possible, and I can't do that without you."

"You're welcome, Alexus," she says, her voice husky, yet soft. "How about we go upstairs for a drink?" As though I'm non-existent, she moves closer to him and slips a piece of his wet hair from over his eye to behind his ear. "I'd like to hear more about your plans. More about you."

Their eyes are locked, the tension in the air thick. I hate myself when I turn my back on them and cross my arms over my chest like a petulant child. I hate myself even more when I cringe as he says, "I would love that. Go ahead. I'll be right there."

Everything inside me seems to wither like a water-starved flower under a scalding sun. I stare at a wall filled with landscape paintings and framed maps—Itunnan—and focus on one, what looks like a storehouse, trying to appear distracted. I don't know why I don't move. Everyone else is drifting into the sleeping room, and yet I stand there frozen, awkwardly irritated, maybe a little jealous and... deeply, utterly, devastated.

"I'll see you in the morning," the Collector says over my shoulder. "Get some rest. Come sunrise, we're getting on the road out of Itunnan."

And just like that, he's walking away.

I close my eyes and squeeze my fists as he climbs the stairs. His every step on the rickety wood feels like a dagger stabbing my heart. I tell myself they're *just having a drink*. That's all. They don't even know one another.

And yet, later, I startle from a deep sleep, only to peek down at the last empty bed, the one beneath mine, and find he still isn't here.

⚜

THE NEXT MORNING, THE BUNK BENEATH MINE IS STILL EMPTY, THE covers untouched.

It's early, and the last thing I want to do is go upstairs and stumble upon a scene I won't be able to forget. So I get dressed, make my bed, and sit on the bottom bunk alone, hating every single thing about this situation and wondering how I will ever be free of a man who somehow stole enough of my hatred that I'm sulking over him in the dark of the morning.

It's only been a matter of days since the rune was reversed, and I'm already tired of feeling so torn. I suppose I have to figure out how to feel less passionate about him on all levels, yet that seems impossible, because the more I'm around him, the worse it gets—the more I hate him and the more I want him—and we're going to be together for a while. I'm either going to kill him, or I'm going to kiss him. A dilemma I remember feeling not long after we met.

When the curtain moves at the door, I glance up. The Collector enters the room, rubbing the back of his neck, and comes to sit beside me, his knee gently grazing mine. He doesn't smell like himself. He smells like sweet wine, some sort of sharp, earthy spice, and the brine of the sea.

I don't look at him. I can't. And yet, just like last night, I can't move away either.

He leans his elbows onto his knees. "I didn't sleep with her," he says quietly. "We didn't do anything but talk. I know that's what you're worrying about. I can feel it."

It was and it wasn't. I had convinced myself they might've only shared a kiss, even though I'd felt the magnetism between them. Still, I keep my hands on the edge of the cot, my eyes trained forward.

"I fell asleep in a chair after too much wine." He rubs his neck again. "And my body is going to make me pay for it today."

I swallow hard, sensing the truth. He owes me no explanation, though it brings me far too much satisfaction to know that after my night of worry, he's the one in pain.

He slips his hand over mine, threading our fingers. The feel of three hundred years of sword-formed callouses is pleasantly rough against my skin. It reminds me of all the ways he has touched me. Though I allow the contact for a few moments, relishing it even, I still pull away.

He sighs and scrubs his hand over his beard. "How are we ever going to make it through this, Raina, if you want me so badly I can feel it through a severed bond, and yet you won't even let me touch you?" Frustration saturates his voice, but it lies beneath a wealth of pain.

The bite of threatening tears stings my eyes. I get up, grab my pack, and leave him sitting there as I push past the curtain and head for the stairs, hoping to find a perch by a four-story window so I can watch the sun rise and think.

Because I don't know how we're going to make it through this misery.

I just don't know.

⚜

THE ITUNNAN HARBOR IS A STUNNING SIGHT TO BEHOLD.

We stand in a long line that trails against the side of the soaring stone sea wall, glamours up and tightly weaved, waiting for entry. Orlena is several people ahead of us, wisely keeping her distance. The rest of us hold papers in hand that describe fraudulent accounts of our recent journeys and every port stop. My new name is Stassa Farthorne, a woman who sometimes joins Terrowin's crew from Malgros as a boatswain.

I glance over the harbor, wondering what it might be like to roam the world. The docks are swarming with activity, the blue-green water shimmering painfully bright under a warm sun. Already, fisherman have exited the city and set up for the day along Goma Pier, and in the harbor, there are at least a dozen more ships and boats floating in the anchorage than last night. Those that need to offload are anchored at the docks, crew members scurrying to clear their holds while harbor officers walk around with ledgers and papers, inspecting every crate and barrel that touches Itunnan's dockside. It's so different from Malgros, different from everything I've ever imagined.

For the most part, other than the few pieces some members of our group gathered from Orlena's supplies, we're dressed in our own clothes, save for our weapons. For now. And we still don't stand out amid the masses.

There are sailors and trades people here from Malgros, and some from the Drifts, and more from other parts of the Summerland coast, and even more from lands outside of Tiressia, like Persei, Mapor, and Omalli.

I hear languages foreign to my ears and see attire I've never seen, but all the color and life and noise culminates into such a perfect amalgam I wish we could stay here and absorb it all, even if for just the day.

But soon we're passing through the gate. Our bodies and packs are checked for blades, and our false papers are studied with great attention by the guards.

While we stand there being scrutinized, I half wonder if Fia Drumera's magick might somehow sense us. The Collector especially. But familiarity, good forgery, and a beautiful woman seem to be what saves us, because once the guard to my left meets Orlena's onyx eyes and she smiles, he pulls her aside to chat, and we're ignored and waved into the city without further questioning.

The guard takes the copies of our papers and hands them to a man sitting at a small table behind him. The man begins looking through them, and at us, but we are free to go.

We walk through the shade of the ancient city wall's archway and step back into the sun. Immediately, we all pause, taken aback by the sight.

There are people everywhere.

The city is a collection of temples, fountains, and a maze of wooden buildings of varying, staggering heights connected by city streets that elevate with wide, stone steps for navigating the labyrinth that is Itunnan. White-marbled buildings sit high in the distance, the view spiked with hundreds of ivory minarets pointing toward the sun.

Palm trees and lush, green vegetation seem to have sprung up wherever they could gain a foothold in the otherwise baked earth, and when a wind blows, I can smell the perfume of dozens of flower gardens mingling with waves of rich spice.

The Summerlands are truly a world apart, and I've only seen one tip.

Orlena catches up and motions for us to follow her into the busy city. The first thing I notice are the different types of guards. There are foot soldiers standing in archways, along streets, and near fountains, but there are also mounted guards patrolling the city from atop sable-colored horses caparisoned in fine red velvet, their harnesses and bits trimmed in silver. The guards wear black, even covering their heads and faces, their bodies laden with all manner of blades. A polished, silver shield with a snake forged into the center of the metal hangs from their horse's side, as does some sort of animal horn.

The Dread Vipers.

One of them rides up from the gate to my right, slowing his horse from a trot to a walk, probably six to eight strides away. He carries papers in his hands, staring from them to me over the heads of a dozen other people.

"Don't look at him," the Collector says as he comes alongside me, making himself into a human shield. He presses his hand to the small of my back as we walk past a fountain and set of steps leading to another street level. "They can't see through glamours," he says at my ear, "but they're excellent at detecting magick, and you and I are like two fucking comets in a starless sky. I'm trying to shield us, but he's curious."

Oh gods. This is bad. I wish he would've mentioned this *earlier*. And I wish I would've inquired further when Joran first mentioned Fia Drumera's elite guard. He said that enough of them could take down the Collector. How? What are their abilities? I worry about Nephele who is only a few steps behind me, walking with Joran. She's more powerful than me. For that matter, Joran is even more powerful than me. I have to hope that the Collector is protecting all of us.

Three mounted guards come around the corner in the distance. Their faces are unconcerned at first, but as they look past our group, their expressions seem to change.

Orlena pauses and turns to me, laughing over nothing, and slips her arm in mine as though we've been best of friends for an age.

"Let's visit the bazar, yes?" She glances back at everyone with a smile, nodding her head, laughing again as though I said something funny.

The Collector laughs too, widening his eyes at me just enough that I realize that not only is this my worst nightmare, they want me to put on a show as well.

I attempt a smile as Orlena turns us from the main street into a massive gateway that opens to what seems like another city stuffed within the constraints of walls. The lofty ceilings are arched and ornamented with brightly colored tiles, and along the sides of this place are galleries and stalls and shops, overflowing with wares and goods. Every scent imaginable is contained here, from fish to cinnamon to citrus fruits to sandalwood and ambergris to raw leather to cedar. I could pick apart a hundred scents if I tried.

Merchants and trades people loiter in the early morning coolness, chatting as they set up their places of business for the day. Patrons pour into the streets from every direction, carrying baskets to be filled. And here we are, ten foreigners and a smuggler, avoiding murderous guards by hiding within a giant market.

The Collector glances over his shoulder, then looks straight ahead. "They're following us."

The moment he says those words, my abyss awakens, a yawning darkness.

"Let's split up, then," Orlena says. "If you go two avenues down and take a left, then another left and two rights, we can meet at the armory bazar."

"The armory?" Doubt saturates the Collector's voice, but the armory sounds like a grand plan to me.

"If they come after you," Orlena says, "you're going to need easy access to weapons and horses and a lot of magick to get out of here. I can get you to the first two, the last one is on you. Trust me. Do as I say."

Smiling and laughing again, she slips behind us and wraps her arm in Rhonin's. The next thing I know, Hel, Nephele, and Zahira are joining me and the Collector. They lock arms with us and flash fake smiles as we head toward the second avenue ahead. Again, I sense my abyss.

"Don't look back," the Collector says, turning us onto a new avenue just as the urge to check on our friends strikes me. It isn't easy, but I obey.

In minutes, we take another left, walking past a gallery of rugs and tapestries and another of pottery, dishware, and cutlery before—just as luck would have it—we cross paths with a gallery laden with every sort of mirror one could imagine.

After we pass, I snick open the little silver-framed vanity mirror I swiped from a basket of similar affairs.

When I use it to discreetly look over my shoulder, the Collector squeezes my arm and lets out a small laugh. "I can't take you anywhere."

He certainly won't be able to if we don't ditch the Dread Viper riding through this bazar on a horse, heavy on our heels.

I hand the Collector the mirror, my abyss at full attention now, and pick up our pace as we make our first right into another bazar.

The book bazar.

Though we're all now fully aware that we're being thoroughly followed, the four of us women gasp at the same time. There are more books here than if Winterhold and Zahira's libraries were combined and multiplied ten times over.

The Collector looks into the mirror, then shoves it into his pocket. "Ladies, I know this is a mighty temptation, but now is not the time for book shopping."

He leads us onward, and we take that last right into the armory bazar, an avenue bedecked in steel, iron, and rust.

"My gods, this is glorious," Hel says under her breath, restraining a squee of delight in the face of possible danger.

Orlena and Rhonin and the others haven't arrived yet, which makes my blood vibrate with worry. But at the same time, relief pours through me, because we're surrounded with weaponry—new and ancient alike.

I gawk at the jewel encrusted swords as Nephele stares at a deadly dagger. Some of the blades are straight like they mean to spear, while others are curved, as though designed to arc toward a waiting heart.

There are shields too, made of steel and wood and shell, and then there are knives and maces, bows, arrows, and quivers, and armor and helmets. I would've never imagined seeing so many forms of armament in one place. Some are polished to a gleam. Others rusted. But they all look like they can kill, and that's all that matters.

We don't get a chance to peruse what we might need before the Dread Viper who'd been following us turns the corner to my left, halting his tall horse at the entry to the bazar.

Alexus stands beside me, finger tracing the ivory hilt of a short sword with a serrated edge, like a lover tickling a wrist. His gaze shifts, and he stiffens with indecision. I can see it on his face. Feel it in the power rolling off him into me. Do we stay here, surrounded by weapons, and see what the Dread Viper wants? Or do we keep moving and look for our friends?

There isn't time to decide, because suddenly, we're trapped, both exits blocked by Dread Vipers on horseback.

48

RAINA

"**D**on't anybody move," the Collector says, voice low. "Let me handle this." He smiles up at the merchants sitting amid hundreds of weapons who are now eyeing the guards walking their horses in our direction. The other patrons scatter from the bazar, leaving only us.

Cooly, the Collector turns toward the guard who had been following us, and begins an easy stroll to meet him, as though he's greeting a friend and not an assassin.

"Good morning, good sir," he says. "Is something the matter?"

The Dread Viper, only a few strides away now, looks at me. In a deep, smooth voice, he says, "I only want to speak to Stassa Farthorne."

Fuck.

My abyss roils, inviting me into the shelter of its nothingness. I ignore that dark bastard and do my best to prevent absolute panic from over-whelming my face as I turn toward the guard and the Collector.

The Collector's eyes are wide, his stare penetrating, as though he's trying to send me a message I can't receive. A thumping vein stands out in relief along his temple.

I walk toward them because I don't know what other choice I have.

Until matters devolve into a full-on battle in the middle of this armory, I need to maintain calm.

Smiling, I approach, putting on a much better act than earlier. The Dread Viper lowers the fabric wrapped around his nose and tucks it under his chin.

His face is tanned to a deep, dark brown from the sun, his eyes a stark blue that radiate a fierce and uncompromising demeanor. He's a bit older. Lines fan from his eyes and across his forehead, and gray hair runs through his beard, half-covering a rugged face with pretty lips.

"Stassa?" he says again, his brow furrowing. He knows her, but obviously not too well. Enough that he encouraged his fellow guardsmen to help prevent him from losing sight of her, though. I can't sort out how this is possible with me—clearly *not* Stassa Farthorne—standing right in front of him.

I touch my throat and look to the Collector to come up with an excuse as for why I can't speak. I would sign a suggestion, but that seems unwise.

He blinks out of his daze—he's been staring at me and the guard—and says, "She's been ill. Her voice is gone."

Nicely done.

The Dread Viper swings down from his horse.

And smiles.

In the next breath, he's gathering me in his arms and kissing me like a sailor come home from years at sea. I can't really think with his tongue in my throat, but I cannot imagine how he knows this woman to this sort of comfort, and yet doesn't know her face.

When he pulls back, I'm clinging to his vest and gasping for air, waiting for the hammer of realization to fall on this man. But it never happens. His eyes are bright as crystals, and there's an edge to him, the way he curves his body over mine and runs his hungry hands down to my hips. It's a confidence that says he is certain that with the right words, he can have me if so desires.

"Our night together on the Lady Belladonna did not do you justice," he says. "I could tell by the feel of your body that you were a beautiful woman. But it was so dark, and I'd had one too many sips of your beer." He takes my chin. Tips my head up. "You are more beautiful than I ever dreamed."

Oh gods. My abyss shrieks.

Suddenly, the Collector's hand folds around my arm, and he pulls me away from the guard, drawing me next to him. He slides his hand around my waist, resting his palm low on my belly. His body is as rigid as the steel blades at my back, his chest out, his back flared.

"She's with me now," he says, that voice shadowed with the promise of a threat. "Best to keep your tongue and hands to yourself if you want them to remain intact with the rest of your body, soldier."

Nephele exhales a long sigh. This is probably not going to end well, though I'm not certain it ever could have.

The guard stares at Alexus like he could eat him. His eyes go round at the disrespect, and his upper lip curls into a snarl. He rests his hand on the hilt of the short sword at his hip, and the amount of danger we're in shifts.

Clearly pissed, the guard looks at Nephele, Hel, and Zahira, then back to me. "You aren't the kind of woman to bed only one man, Stassa. Commitment isn't really the stuff of sailors. If he's holding you against your will—" another look at my sisters "—*any* of you, and if you want to leave here with *me*, just say so. I will take you and leave his head on the sand."

Nephele walks over to the Collector's other side and slips her hand in his before resting her head innocently on his shoulder. "We're just fine, sir. Though nothing says some of us can't meet with you later tonight. We're in town for a while."

Zahira struts over, behind me, and drapes her arm around the Collector's neck, resting her hand on his chest while Hel joins her, nestled close.

"Just tell us where to find you," Hel says to the guard, her voice dripping with seduction. "We need to get settled today, but come nightfall, we can be yours."

The guard winks at Hel and reaches for Nephele. She takes his hand, and he pulls her close, looking her over with an appreciative stare. She's dressed like the rest of us, and like him, in all black. The starkness contrasts with her paleness, making her sky-blue eyes stand out like the topaz stones in one of the daggers I saw minutes before.

The guard slides his hand up her arm and into her blonde curls, tightening his fingers into a fist. She smiles, a far better pretender than I could ever dream to be.

I peek up at the Collector. I don't think I've ever seen his eyes so frenzied or felt his body so impossibly stiff. I half think he might run the guard through with a blade regardless that three more Dread Vipers still loiter at the edge of the bazar. But he isn't where my worry should lie.

None of us see the battle axe sailing through the air from the opposite exit until it lodges in the back of the guard's skull. It's a stunning moment, one I can't even fully grasp until the guard falls against Nephele, making her stumble before she slides out from under his crumpling weight, and his body topples to the ground.

We all look around, following the weapon's path. Joran stands two galleries down at a weapons stall, seething with cold fury. The rest of our group are frozen behind him, stunned, but the Dread Vipers on horseback, waiting at the exit, are not. They rip free the horns that hang from their horse's sides and blow.

The resulting deep bellow resounds through the bazar. A signal. A battle cry. In the distance, more horns split the morning air with an unearthly moan, and more and more, even as the sound of hooves striking the earth pounds through the avenues.

And just like that, chaos descends.

◌⚜◌

No one has to say anything as six Dread Vipers race into the bazar from the west side, dismounting their horses and freeing their daggers in the smoothest of movements. We all just act.

Dropping our glamours to preserve energy, we rip weapons off walls—swords, daggers, maces—then we turn toward the Dread Vipers swarming into the avenue.

"Run!" the Collector shouts. "Get to the horse market! Get out of the city!"

Orlena Madar sprints toward the eastern exit, the way we came, and everyone follows. As Joran passes, he reaches down and jerks the battle axe from the first guard's head, a wicked look on his face.

"I should drop you right now for this," the Collector tells him.

Joran meets his gaze, everything about him so steady. "Nobody touches Nephele that way. Don't tell me you didn't want to do the same for *her*." He jerks his chin at me, and then takes off behind my sister and the others.

The Collector grabs my hand and we run too. I'm sure we'll be caught. The bazars are in a maze of a building, and that's a problem.

It doesn't even matter though, because before he and I reach the eastern exit, three more Dread Vipers storm their horses into the bazar.

The Collector spins us around. We run, but we end up sliding to a halt, boots scraping against packed sand. We're cornered.

My abyss is an open sea, beckoning me into the swell of its tide. It's trying to help me. To give me a way out like it did that night in the Malorian. It *moved* us. From place to place. From danger to safety.

"Fuck all." The Collector grips a short, curved sword. "Fia is going to be very pissed about this bloodbath."

But I worry about *whose* bloodbath. Until dozens of weapons rise into the air, aimed at the Vipers at the Collector's mental command.

"Stay at my back," he tells me. An order.

I listen. Because when it comes to this, we're better together.

But we're standing against a formidable foe. The Dread Vipers are not human. I don't know what they are, but they are not mere men.

A wave of strange power ripples through the air, and as though they've dismantled his magick, the Collector's weapons fall to the ground, sending plumes of dust into the air.

One of the guards charges us and—with all the momentum of a squall —races his feet along the bazar's sidewall, up the sloping ceiling, until he's ready to drop on us like a spider from a web, daggers raised and ready to stab.

But I won't let that happen.

Just as he falls, I grab the Collector's hand. I don't know this city or this land, not enough to will us anywhere. I just know that I want out of this moment.

I think of the paintings in Orlena's hidden room, of the one I focused on. The storehouse.

Then I let my mind plummet into the abyss.

49

ALEXUS

I hit the ground so hard the air leaves my lungs.

Pain stabs through my shoulder, hot as a lance, as I gasp to breathe again. Raina lies a few feet away, unmoving, on her back. My sword is gone, and so is everything else, including my protective shields.

We're no longer in the bazar. We're outside, in broad daylight. I don't know where exactly. I only know that the city sounds distant—it's quieter here—and that Raina moved us around like dust in the wind, like she did the other night, in the sea.

I roll to face her and roar in agony. My short sword is run through my shoulder, the hilt buried at my back. But worse, a Dread Viper sits on his knees near Raina, gripping her head by the hair, exposing her throat, even though she's unconscious. His dagger is pressed to the soft place beneath her lovely chin, sunlight glinting off the blade. I can see her pulse throbbing.

I reach for my magick, but he's already subdued it. Dread Vipers have the power to paralyze other magicks, if they sense the need, and I am a need.

"Who are you?" His voice is deep and sharp, velvet over a knife's edge.

"A friend of your queen," I answer honestly, wincing. "We mean no harm. We just need to get to Fia Drumera. To the City of Ruin."

"You and far too many others," he says. "I kill people for such trespasses. You need to understand that this can only end one way."

I meet his dark stare. "Then why are you talking?"

He narrows his gaze and points his dagger at me. "Because one of you sifted us here. I couldn't tell which. That is not a power you should have. I want to know which one of you did it. Then we'll get into even better questions."

Sifting. A gift that evolved from the Summerland magi ages ago. It was eventually learned by necromancers in the East who envied the magi their ability, and coveted Loria's children's realm walking between Tiressia and Eridan. The necromancers never could break *that* ethereal plain, though. Only the one between here and the Shadow World—until Urdin sealed it to keep them out. I know because I did it myself.

It's much like when the prince moved between the real world and the Shadow World, an ability that's only possible because he is a thing made from the husks of souls, a man not truly living, only sustained in human form by the spirits of others.

But sifting... That isn't what Raina has done. I don't know *what* this is.

I lie there in misery. With my magick tamped down, I understand what the Dread Viper can do to me to get the answers he seeks. What he *will* do. Not that I have anything to hide. But I'd die before I let him interrogate Raina. Her silence will bring much cruelty, all from misunderstanding.

"It was me," I tell him, though my attention is on Raina as her eyes flutter open for the quiver of a moment. "I'm your man."

The Dread Viper looks at Raina's witch's marks, bright and beautiful, denoting her Northland heritage and skill across a handful of disciplines. But I suppose he's already tasted my power. Already suspected it might be me. Because he drops Raina like a discarded doll, stalks over to me, and jerks me up by my jacket. With a flat glaze to his eyes, he shoves me back to the ground, pounding the hilt at my back for a little extra pain.

Just before he grabs a rock and bashes it against the side of my head.

50

RAINA

"Raina. Come on, Sunshine. Open those eyes for me."
     I blink, looking for my sister, guided by her voice and the cool feel of a damp cloth on my face. The blur over my vision clears, and she appears, leaning over me in a room I don't recognize.

She runs her fingertips over my forehead and turns to speak to someone else. Hel. "Let everyone know she's awake," Nephele says, watching as my friend leaves the room. When she meets my eyes again, I can tell she's been crying. I scrunch my brows together, but she *shooshes* me. "I'm fine. I've just been worried about you."

Groggy, I push to sit up, and she helps me. My head hurts across the back of my skull like someone tried to open it with a blunt spoon.

I press my fingertips to my temples and examine the room. It's small and plain, with one window and two single-person beds. There's a chair and table, large enough for a drink and plate of food to rest, but that's all.

"Where are we?" I sign.

"An inn on the outskirts of Itunnan. A kind person found you and brought you here since a physician lives nearby. Luckily, the guard nor the Dread Vipers were contacted, in case someone claimed you. We only found you because of Joran's *instinct.*" She says the word as though she doesn't believe in it, and with a softer form of disbelief in her voice adds, "How did you get all the way out here?"

An image flashes through my mind like a dream. Everything was awash in white light, and then I was blinded by the sun and falling.

Wait.

I rub the back of my aching head. I *did* fall. With the Collector and the Dread Viper from the bazar.

My breaths come faster, and Nephele reads the question on my face.

"I don't know where Alexus is." She tosses the cloth into the small pail beside the bed. "Orlena, Joran, and Zahira have been out looking for him all afternoon."

Gods. Did the Dread Viper take him? How is that even possible? The Collector could turn him to bloody bits in seconds if he wanted. But again, I recall what Joran said. They have abilities all their own. I just don't know what they are.

"We have to find him," I sign. *"I can check the waters."*

She grips my arms. "We will. But first, I need to know how you went from being in the armory bazar to being ten miles away in an inn. The innkeeper said plainly that you were brought here early this morning. Not hours later. Not in the time it would've taken you to walk here. Not even in the time it would've take you to run."

Much as I don't understand it myself, I decide it's time to explain my abyss to my sister.

"That's almost like portaling," she says when I finish. "Like Fleurie. Or sifting, like the prince."

I don't know what it is, but the thought of being anything like the prince makes me recoil.

"Do you think the Dread Viper somehow *took* Alexus?" she says.

Before I can ask for a dish, water, and knife so I can see if he did or not, Orlena replies from the doorway. "I'm certain he did."

The woman enters the room, Joran and Zahira close behind. They've been listening. Zahira sets the sword Alexus had been carrying against the wall, blood dried on the blade, while the Icelander shuts the door and remains there. He leans one shoulder against the wood, his hand on his hip, and studies me with a curious stare.

"We went to speak with the woman who found you," Zahira says to me as she sits opposite me and Nephele on the other bed. "She took us back to the scene. You and Alexus arrived near an old granary that belongs to Orlena's family."

"I have a painting of it in the safehouse," Orlena says. "You might've seen it along with maps. I created that wall for passers through to become oriented with the city."

Gods. I remember.

"We found a discarded sword and blood soaked into the ground," Zahira says. "A lot of it. And it didn't come from you."

Trying to recollect anything, I scrub my hands through my hair and think. *"The sword,"* I finally sign, and my sister translates. *"I think he was stabbed. Perhaps when we fell."* I take a deep breath. *"If I can see him in the waters, I can get to him and get him out quickly."*

"That wouldn't be safe," Joran says after Nephele translates. "That guard would've incapacitated the Collector's magick and has likely taken him back to their headquarters. If Raina managed to sift there, or whatever you would like to call whatever magick she's doing, they could incapacitate her too."

"Incapacitate?" I sign to Nephele. *That's* what their power is?

Of course it is. That's why all those weapons in the armory fell to the ground like the air had let them go.

Nephele grips my knee, and I see the worry in her eyes as she turns toward Joran. "You said headquarters. Which is where?"

He shrugs. "Supposedly, no one knows."

"The rumor is that the Dread Vipers live in the Aki-Ra Quarter," Orlena says. "Over the years, they've been seen slipping into the area in the middle of the night. But no one dares go knocking on doors."

"You have preternatural instincts and quite the sense of smell," Nephele says to Joran. "You sniffed Raina out of thousands of people like a dog. Surely you can locate Alexus."

One corner of the Icelander's mouth lifts at her gibe, but then falls. "I've tried for hours now. This city is a confusing zephyr of aromas waiting to happen. Would you have me continue an impossible hunt? In search of a den of vipers, no less?"

He speaks to her as though he is under her command. As though all she must do is say the words, and he will respond as she pleases. And I think she knows it.

"Yes, that's exactly what I'd have you do." She stands and grabs two daggers from the other bed, the same ones from the bazar. Somehow, she procured two thigh sheaths as well. She hands me one, along with a blade, then lifts her eyes to Joran again. "And we're coming with you."

❧

FULL DARK FALLS AS ME, NEPHELE, JORAN, HEL, AND RHONIN HEAD toward the Aki-Ra Quarter.

With Orlena's hand-drawn map in hand, we travel along the city outskirts, trying to remain unnoticed, dodging the thinner presence of foot soldiers and Dread Vipers on the lookout.

But it isn't easy. Nephele can't form a shielding construct because it might draw attention since the Vipers have such heightened senses for detecting magick. And Rhonin isn't exactly the type of man an eye can miss.

Then there's me. My head still hurts, which only pisses me off more. Rage hastens my steps, burning hot in my veins. I've felt this rage before, when my mother was killed. The reminder makes the struggle to cope with all the emotions bubbling to my surface tonight that much harder. I only know that, from what I saw in the waters before we left the inn, the Collector is being held in what seems like an underground room, hands chained to a rock wall. He's being beaten, badly, and if I must scour this entire city, somebody is going to pay.

We turn down a shadowed, dusty street that leads toward a cemetery and village consisting of crude little houses, their slanted rooftops covered in red tiles, their white facades dimly lit by lantern light. That's all that's here, though, tucked away in a grove of cedar trees near the western sea wall, all quiet for the night.

Hel nudges me as we pass a couple of roaming, hungry dogs. "He's going to be all right."

"He is," Rhonin adds. "That man has been through worse than this."

I'm glad Hel and Rhonin are here—Rhonin wouldn't let me and Nephele out of his sight—but I'm not so sure my friends are right. The Collector looked wicked and daring as death, grinning with bold defiance as they struck him time and time again, his face bloody, his eye swelling. But everyone suffers from pain when there's enough doled out. And if they decide to kill him? To take his head? Even a curse of immortality cannot save him from that.

The thought makes my entire body burn, and my heart—*my heart*—it feels like a hot coal inside my chest, as though I could become a living flame from all my rage.

"I can't gather what they mean to get out of him," Hel says. "If anything, they should listen and help if they care at all about their homeland."

"Unless they have other word that the prince is in motion for an attack," Rhonin says, "there's little reason to believe the Collector. Certainly not enough to allow him into their sacred citadel to meet the queen. They're probably pounding him in hopes he'll reveal the truth about why he's in Itunnan and how you two moved one of their men from the bazar to the granary in the blink of an eye. We killed one of their men too, so there's likely revenge at play."

We didn't kill one of their men. Joran did.

He must sense my pointed glare on the back of his silver head because he glances over his shoulder, at me, with that cold stare. "Let's get off the road."

We follow him into the Aki-Ra cemetery, dotted with crowded, crooked tombstones, the curve of land crowned in the center by a weathered mausoleum.

"If we find him," Joran says, pausing near the tomb, "you all need to understand that we might not get out. We're walking into Viper territory, where the enemy can lock down any power we may have, not to mention that we're probably going to be surrounded, quickly, by hundreds more of them."

"They must have a weakness," Rhonin says. "Everybody does."

"Orlena said that when they immobilize magick, it takes a great amount of energy," Nephele says. "The stronger the magick, the more energy required, which is quite typical. They must concentrate much effort on the magick caster."

"That's why there are so many of them," Joran says. "Safety lies in their number. If one immobilizes a gifted witch or sorcerer, he may feel the drain of that power, but his brethren can always help afterward."

"So what do we do?" Hel asks.

"Perhaps you send in the magickless human," Rhonin replies.

We all turn toward him. He stands beneath the moonlight, his red hair cast a darker shade in the night.

Hel tenses her hands. "And me." She glances at the rest of us. "I'm not magickal. Not really. I can whip up a little fire here and there if I try hard, but I'm not going into a fight using magick as my main defense." She touches the dagger hilt at her hip. "I'm going in ready to cut someone down with a blade."

"These are highly trained killers," I sign, staring between her and Rhonin. *"And you do not have swords to swing. Only daggers."*

"I'm aware," Hel replies. "Rhonin and I aren't too terrible in a fight, though."

"I will not let you face that alone," I sign.

"Then come with us," Rhonin says.

When everyone looks at him again, this time it's with disbelief.

He shrugs. "We'll create a distraction. Hel and I can get Raina in. Nephele stays out here. If Vipers must focus on the magick caster to paralyze their magick, then we just don't let them see her. It's that simple and that hard. We walk in wrapped in one of her shielding constructs, we free Alexus, and then Raina breezes the three of us out of there. We just have to cling to the hope she doesn't drop us in the middle of the desert."

I give him a look from the corner of my eye, and he smiles.

"That's actually a good plan, Rhonin," my sister says. "If I build the construct correctly, it will let me sense her, like when she was in Frostwater Wood. I'll know when she's gone."

"And then you and I can leave," Joran says, elbowing my sister. "See? You didn't need me after all, now did you?"

She glares at him. "I do need you. We all do. We still don't know where he is. We need you to locate him before sending these three in for a rescue attempt. There are hundreds of homes here."

Joran rubs his hands together. Though he glances toward the sea of rooftops in the near distance, we all know his next words are aimed at

Nephele. "I suppose that means you aren't too worried if I make it out alive."

Nephele keeps her face neutral, her chin high, staring out at the houses too. "If you want to find out, don't die."

Joran offers a small laugh and one last glance at her, then he takes off, running across the cemetery, into the enemy's den.

51

RAINA

Joran doesn't die.

He returns with a location. Seventh street toward the sea, thirteen house on the right.

He also offers a few tips.

"Stay to the shadows. There are more than Vipers living here. There are common people. If you want a distraction, set fire to house number eight. It's abandoned. But be aware that these homes are very close together. The fire *will* spread."

Fire. I feel the blood drain from my face. *"There has to be some other distraction,"* I sign, and Nephele translates.

Everyone's faces grow somber because there really isn't another option unless Joran floods their streets. A fire can be put out. I tell myself that. But I don't know if I can inflict the horror of a burning village on innocent people. In fact, I know I can't.

Perhaps that's why the Vipers have bedded down in the middle of a sprawl of innocent people. Or maybe this is just where they live. Where their families live. Maybe *I'm* the villain in this tale as the Collector says. We're the ones on *their* soil, searching for *their* queen. They're only doing their jobs, and yet I can't stop thinking about how they've hurt him, hurt *Alexus*.

"Can you douse the fire once Raina has everyone safely out?" Nephele asks Joran, as though sensing exactly what's worrying me. "There's an entire sea *right there.*"

A strange look passes over his face, as though he isn't sure if he can or not. "I'll make certain the fire is out when the time comes," is all he says in reply.

"Swear to Loria," I sign, and my sister translates.

Joran hesitates, but then he presses his hand over his heart and says, "I swear. To Loria."

It doesn't take Nephele long to wrap us in a shielding construct. Once it's complete, Rhonin, Hel, and I head into the night, crossing the cemetery, our heads low. Brittle tufts of sun-scorched vegetation crunch under our steps until the terrain changes to baked earth again, though the pathways here are sandier and grittier beneath my boots.

Quietly, we slip across the main road between the cemetery and the village and become one with the shadows. The moon is bright, but with the homes so close together, the in-between places are dark as pitch. Though we're shielded, the darkness creates the perfect hiding place, and staying to the dark gives me an added sense of safety, though it isn't simple to navigate.

That will all change in minutes, though, because the second we reach house number eight, Rhonin gives the interior a quick sweep to ensure its emptiness, and then I light it up like a bonfire.

My nerves tingling, we hunker down between the eleventh and twelfth houses while the fire grows and devours. Impatience eats at me as Rhonin peers around the back corner of house number twelve into the street.

People don't flood from their homes instantly like I imagined. It takes several minutes and Rhonin throwing a small rock across the way at another house for anyone to step outside and notice what I've done.

But they do come. A handful of panicked faces at first, but as the shouting begins and people being running from house to house pounding on doors, more villagers pour from nearby homes into the now fire-lit street as guilt eats at me.

We creep closer to house number thirteen. Four men hurry out the front door, staring toward the neighboring home, their eyes aglow from the reflected fire. Several villagers gather buckets and head to what I imagine is a well so they might drench the growing fire.

My heart squeezes. I don't want to hurt anyone who didn't ask for my wrath. I just need time to do what I came to do.

Joran had better not fail me or these people. Or I will skin him alive.

House number thirteen has a rear entry. Rhonin goes first, moving swift as a wind across the tiled floor into the dark home with his hand raised to me and Hel. The moment he feels it's safe, he flicks his fingers for us to follow.

Voices shout from the front of the house, warning about the fire, but other than the external noise, all is quiet.

Daggers raised, we stalk across layered rugs into the rear workroom, a place where meals are prepared by the smell of it. There's a faint, golden light emanating from the front room through a narrow doorway ahead, and another dimly lit room toward the western side of the house.

But my attention fixes on a rug haphazardly tossed aside on the eastern end of the workroom, revealing what might've, at one time, been the hatch to an underground cellar. Now it appears it's become an interrogation room.

I touch Hel's shoulder, and she in turn touches Rhonin's. They stop as I point to the door, its latch unlocked. The bolt rests on a small wooden table along with a short, curved sword that looks like it was set aside in haste. A poor decision.

Hel snatches the blade like the Knife Thief Vexx dubbed her and studies the door. It isn't the largest entry. I imagine there are wooden stairs or a ladder beneath. I'm not sure Rhonin can fit his broad shoulders through the opening.

"*Me first,*" I sign, but Hel cocks her head.

"*Me,*" she signs back, holding up her new, deadly friend.

Rhonin frowns hard at us both, his scowling face shadowed in the dim room. But I can tell he realizes he might have a difficult time maneuvering into the cellar, and that isn't a scenario he likes. Neither do I. That means we must get the Collector up those stairs if we're all going to travel out of here together using my abyss.

There isn't anything we can do but try. We need to hurry.

Suddenly, Hel grabs Rhonin's face and kisses him on the mouth. It's a deeply passionate kiss, one that ends mere seconds after it began, and yet it says so much as she pulls away and presses her forehead to his. "You earned that, my magickless human."

Rhonin smiles, though there's a sadness to it, and kisses her back, his hand fisted in her long, black hair. Then he moves around to the hatch and grips the iron ring.

He stares at us, one finger raised. If those hinges creak, whoever is below will be alerted. Hel and I will have a fight on our hands before we make it down the steps. There's also the chance that no one is with the Collector. They could all be outside.

Time to find out.

Rhonin carefully lifts the door, and those godsdamn hinges scream through the quiet house anyway.

Hel bounds down the wooden steps like a force, and I follow, a dagger in one hand and a ball of fire in the other. If they can't immobilize Nephele's magick without seeing her, they won't be able to reach me through her construct. I can leave this place in a pile of ash if I so desire.

Before I even see the first Dread Viper, I hear the clang of Helena's sword meeting metal, and her resounding grunt. As I clear the low ceiling, she ducks beneath the swinging arc of his blade's edge and rams her foot straight into his groin, sending him stumbling back, howling in pain.

I hurry down the stairs, met with a dank, dark room lit by two hanging oil lamps, filled with four smiling Dread Vipers, each one hungry for a fight, brandishing swords clenched in bloody fists.

Behind them, the Collector is suspended from a wall, his shirt removed, his sweat-soaked hair in his eyes, his handsome face and scarred body covered in blood.

He looks up and arches against his restraints. "Raina! No!"

But any mercy I'd felt before has already vanished.

Though one of the Vipers lifts a hand with a haughty look on his face, likely to disarm my fire magick, he fails, and I launch vindictive flames at each man, one at a time, until they're consumed and screaming. The sounds of their misery and the smell of burning flesh is a memory I didn't want to relive, but this rage inside me—this absolute hatred—is beyond anything I know how to control.

Hel storms forward and swings her sword, slitting the first man's throat to end his suffering. Then the next and the next and the next, until they're lying in flames around us, the fire catching on the wooden steps leading up the hatch and crawling up the wooden supports along the walls.

Hel spins toward the stairs. "Rhonin!" Then she grabs me, her eyes wide and wild. "We need to get Alexus off that wall! You don't know if you can sift him with him chained like this!"

I can't explain the fighting calm I feel. The assuredness that we will leave this place together, all four of us. It's a certainty that has settled in my bones as we hurry to Alexus's side.

I touch his face, push his hair back, and look into his eyes.

"I told you," he says, his green gaze holding mine. "Don't you ever put yourself in harm's way for me."

He can scold me later because I had no choice. Much as a part of me still wants to deny it, my heart would not have allowed any other end.

With fire quickly eating the room, Hel and I search for keys to the manacles holding Alexus to the rock wall. Too late, I realize that they're probably still on the burning bodies.

I face the smoke and fire, coughing, my mind working through what to do as a deep groan of wood sounds from the hatch.

A curved blade, like that of an axe, juts through the ceiling, again and again and again, sending splinters and shards of wood flying.

Rhonin.

Like some kind of feral animal, he rips the floorboards away from the hatch, widening the hole. In seconds, he drops like a rock into the middle of the licking flames, shoving through their heat with his arm shielding his face.

I don't have to say anything. When he sees Alexus, I swear he's swallowed by the same rage that devoured me.

He reaches for one of the iron stakes driven deep into the rock wall, folds his massive hand around it, and pulls. But even Rhonin can't dislodge them.

Alexus looks up at us, and the swell of his power sweeps through the room, newly freed. It's weaker than before, but it feels like salvation, nonetheless.

The iron spikes shoot from the wall—both those connected to the chains at his wrists and those at his ankles—and he collapses forward.

Rhonin catches him with a smile. "You get yourself into the worst trouble, old man."

A weak grin tugs Alexus's mouth. "Yeah, well, it's about to get worse if we don't get out of here."

I don't hesitate. Rhonin and Hel already know what to do. Hel drops her sword, and we buckle our daggers into our sheaths. They each wrap an arm around my waist as I step close to Alexus and clasp his face in my hands.

"Oh, fuck. Not again," is all he gets a chance to say before I think of the inn and carry us into the abyss.

52

NEPHELE

Thehe moment they're gone, I feel their absence.

I stop my pacing near the mausoleum and lift my eyes to the flames dancing in the sky to the west. Jolted by the knowing inside me, I spin around.

"Now, Joran! Water magick, now!"

He's sitting on a tombstone, leaned back as though there aren't innocent people less than three hundred strides away fighting a fire with all they have.

He takes a deep breath and lets it out slowly as he gets up and walks toward me, his steps longer, his gait different. More like a prowl.

"You know," he says, his voice so composed, "sometimes all the best plans get demolished by one simple mistake." He stops beside me, a strange look on his face as he watches the flames. "Like a suggestion made but not thought through."

I have no idea what he's rambling on about, and I do not care. "Just *do* the magick, Joran," I spit, slicing my hand through the air toward the Malorian Sea.

"Are you sure?" he says.

"Yes! We've had this conversation. This is your part in the game. Now help them!" When he doesn't move, I step close and get in his face. "I swear to the gods, Joran, if you fail these people out of sheer spite or whatever bastard behavior this is, I will create a construct and cage you inside it, and I might never let you out."

He laughs and stares me in the eyes. "If only a cage held any fear for me, witch."

Suddenly, a rolling fog creeps across the cemetery, and the tepid night air turns cold. Not cool, but *frigid,* icy as midnight in the dead of winter in the North.

Something moves in his silver eyes, a tiny fleck of swirling gold in the center of his black irises. But before I can think too much of it, he points over my shoulder. "Watch."

I turn around, expecting a storm, perhaps. A hard, pounding rain conjured from the sea.

But no. It's...

It's snowing.

Snowing. In the Summerlands.

As though propelled by panic, I hurry forward, but I stop, panting in disbelief once I can truly see what's ahead of me.

It *is* snow. Thick as the greatest blizzard, a deluge of so many snowflakes, the sky over the fire is a curtain of white against the night sky.

"Snow?" I shout, balling my hands into fists. It will work—only because he's sending down so much of it—but... "Is this some sort of mockery directed at me?" I ask, spinning again to face him.

My blood ices, and I draw my dagger, because Joran isn't standing behind me anymore. He's on the ground, splayed face first over a grave like he fell from the sky.

Looming over him is a creature I've only ever seen *once*, from a distance. A tall, naked being with crystalline skin and white hair down to his narrow waist.

I skim a measuring glance over him, from his amber eyes to his pointed ears, to his claw-tipped fingers, to his sinewy torso, and the muscled hind legs of a beast.

Neri.

THE NORTHERN GOD MOVES OPPOSITE ME, THE PAIR OF US CREATING A circled path in the cemetery's sand and scrub. A zephyr blows around the mausoleum, gently lifting the long, silken strands of his pearlescent, snow-white hair.

Neri's eyes are the color of molten honey, with an odd ring of brightest gold at the edges. I've never felt so captured by a stare, yet right now, he might as well be the sun, trapping me in his orbit.

"Is this a dance?" he asks.

His voice chills the air even further, making my skin prickle.

"Not for me, it isn't, you son of a bitch."

He *tsks* and wags a claw-tipped finger. "Come now, Nephele. There's no need to disrespect Loria."

I point my dagger at Joran as we keep moving. "Did you hurt him?"

"Do you care?" he shoots back. "His cock was the only thing about him you found even remotely interesting before I came along."

I glare at him, trying to figure out when that was, wishing I could run him through with a sword. "*Did you hurt him?* Answer the question."

"Of course not. I might need him later—if you agree to play nice."

I scoff. "Fuck you, Neri."

He smiles, his fangs showing. "Please?"

Stupidity comes over me. I throw my dagger at his wolfish face.

He catches the hilt midair, and I gasp. I can't understand how he's corporeal at all. He handled Colden in Frostwater Wood, and I haven't even considered that until now.

But Neri is *dead*. A god spirit. One who is ensuring that snow still falls hard as rain in the distance, extinguishing the fire. But he is still Neri. A soul. This shouldn't be happening.

"Why?" I say. "Why inhabit him? You want something, clearly."

"I do," he says, tossing my weapon behind him. "I want many things. First and foremost, my life back."

I shake my head, wondering how I'm going to get my dagger. "No one is going to give you your life back. You can count on that much."

He smiles again, though there's a smugness to it this time. An air of confidence that makes me very uncomfortable.

"Un Drallag agreed to a favor at Starworth Tor," he says. "Same as a deal. And you agreed to a deal too, under the pier last night. So either way, I'm going to get what I want, or there will be consequences."

A flash of anger burns through me. I ball my fists, thinking about magick, about what I can do to this piece of shit irksome asshole. "You tricked me!" I stab my finger at him. "And Alexus! Because you're a liar. A *bastard* liar."

He arches a white, frost-kissed brow, enjoying my fury. "You see it as trickery. I see it as cleverness."

My nostrils flare, watching him step over Joran like he's nothing. "*That's* why you wouldn't kiss me," I say. "To get me twisted up in a deal."

"Oh no, I wanted to kiss you regardless. I still do, and I mean to make it happen, know that. But I'll go back to the Nether Reaches before I feel you through the lips of a pathetic, useless *man*. I couldn't even consider fucking you with his cock."

New rage blooms inside me like a poisonous flower. It's so bright and hot my skin flushes with enough heat I no longer feel his cold. "As though you would've had the chance."

"I would've had it," he replies, still circling and grinning. "I think I already did. And I managed it wearing the face of a man you loathe who didn't even fuck you well. Imagine when I'm whole again. When it's *my* eyes you gaze into. *My* voice that makes your breath still. *My* hands on your perfect little body. You have not known pleasure, Nephele Bloodgood, until you've had me."

I want to scream like a shrieking wraith, right in his face. But instead, I build a construct, weaving the song and threads in my mind, drawing forth the golden sand of the Summerlands and mingling it with the incandescent heat of my bitterness, creating a perfect, gilded cage to hold him.

He stops. Stands still. Watches as my construct quickly rises around him, trapping him. He said he holds no fear of cages. We shall see.

One side of his mouth curls, revealing a glinting fang as he shakes his head. "I'm going to make you the same deal I made your sister. I will not watch Thamaos live again while I'm hunted by his wraiths and sent back to the Shadow World. If you help bring *me* back before the Prince of the East succeeds in digging up Thamaos's wretched bones, I'll help you with whatever you ask of me. You want a god on your side when the prince comes calling to Mount Ulra with his portal witch, determined to unearth Thamaos's bones? I'll be there to stop him. I'll even fight in your war when it comes, and I'll bring beasts of land and air that this Prince with No Name has never seen or even dreamed. But I cannot do any of this if a naughty little witch locks me up in her pretty little cage."

Now it's my turn to laugh.

I step to the bars of golden sand and look up into his amber eyes. "You truly think that I would take *you*, Neri, into the presence of the queen whom you cursed?" I shake my head and look him over as though he's pathetic. "Being locked up inside Alexus made you delusional."

His snow stops falling over the village behind him, but the fire is nothing more than steam in the air now.

"Then go," he says. "Leave me here as a spectacle for the Dread Vipers to torture. You will eventually have to let this construct fall. You can't hold it forever. And when it comes down, I will go to the City of Ruin myself. There will be someone, at some point, perhaps Fia Drumera herself, who deals with me. Only my deal then may not be so kind, and you'll be left to fight your battles without a god on your side." He grips the bars. "Do you understand that I have aided you since Hampstead Loch?" he says. "I held storms at bay as we rode to the Gravenna Mountains. Asked the Great Horns of my land for a sacrifice to feed *your* belly. I killed your enemy and brought you his *head*. Stole an entire ship and most of its crew to grant you safe passage from Malgros. Used my power to sail us to Itunnan as quickly as possible. Aided you as we swam to shore. Killed the Dread Viper who laid his filthy hands on you. Located your irresponsible, itinerant sister. And most importantly, tonight, I helped you save the man who trapped me inside his wretched body for three hundred years, when all I've really wanted to do these last weeks is kill him. And yet, no matter, you still want so badly to see me as the enemy, because the truth is much more difficult to face."

I fold my arms across my chest, knowing better than to say the words that teeter on the tip of my tongue, and yet I speak them anyway.

"And what truth is that?"

He leans close, the cold rolling off him like a chilled breath.

"That you are intrigued," he says. "That you would very much like that kiss now. That you are thankful that I was there all the times I was. That it fires your blood with lust to know I killed for you and would do it again."

I narrow my eyes and shake my head yet again, disgusted and overcome with disbelief. His words aren't true. They *aren't*.

Not even a little bit.

"What about Asha?" I say, and he flinches at her name. "You only desire witches now that there are no goddesses to play with?"

"I desire *you*," he says, that last word finite.

"Well, that was a poor choice," I tell him, "because I am far from the kind of woman you think I am."

He laughs. Loudly. When he finally stops, he says, "I've watched you from within Un Drallag for the last eight years of your life. And I heard you in the wood with your sister and Helena. Pale hair, a brazen attitude, and a big cock are your weakness with men." He tilts his head, his eyes glowing with delight. "Imagine being with a god."

Though the air holds a chill, a sweat breaks across the back of my neck. "I'm leaving you here. I don't care how highly you think of yourself."

I turn and head toward Joran who still hasn't roused.

"What if I offer you your king?"

I stop walking and close my eyes. Godsdamn him.

"Colden Moeshka," he says. "Sitting in a dungeon in Quezira. I can't get to the prince. I'm certain he remains surrounded. But the only thing trapping Colden there are iron bars, not magick. I can get in and get him out. Quickly. Possibly even the portalist if she's willing."

Don't listen to him, Nephele, I mentally berate myself. *Do. Not. Listen.*

But my self-control is clearly lacking because I turn around.

"Raina can do that now. We don't need you."

He smiles with one side of his mouth. "Then she will risk getting caught by the Brotherhood, and the prince will have the opportunity to punish her for ruining his plans in Frostwater Wood. You, nor Un Drallag, would allow her to step into that sort of danger, but you should hope she doesn't consider that possibility, because she's daring enough to try, with or without her sister or her lover's approval."

I take a deep breath to steady my nerves, hating that he's right. "Well, even if I wanted to make this deal with you, I don't know *how* to resurrect you."

"It isn't so complex," he says. "You need a remnant or a sacrifice."

I frown. I've heard about the need for a remnant, of course, because of the God Knife. But a sacrifice?

"What sort of *sacrifice?*" I ask.

He arches a white brow. "A life. That is not the method of choice."

I cross my arms over my middle. "And I don't have a remnant of you, so you are out of luck."

"My remnant is on that fool's body." He points at Joran. "Your sister refused to help me locate it, so when I crossed paths with that drunken bastard at Hampstead Loch, I saw opportunity, and I took it. I warned her that I would find a way."

I narrow my stare. "What sort of remnant?"

"Go look. It's in his jacket pocket. Inside. Left breast."

There's no limit to how hard I scold myself as I turn and go to Joran and haul him over to his back. At first, when I rummage around inside his jacket, I don't feel anything. But then, there's something small and hard.

I withdraw a necklace and pendant with the brightest red stone set into gold. There's an odd light to it, a sort of pulsing I can feel against my palm.

"A magickal ruby?" I say. "Thamaos gave his bone for the God Knife's blade, and you gave... *a ruby?* I'm confused."

"It is no ruby." His voice is deep and slightly annoyed. "It's a piece of my heart."

I bite back a laugh. "That would require you to actually possess a heart, Neri."

He gives me an icy look. "I carved it out of my chest myself. My liegemen kept it for centuries. They were tasked with ensuring my resurrection if anything happened to me, and they failed. It's been in Malgros all this time, in a temple near Village Hill, buried in a trunk beneath the sanctuary. I had Joran's face and his body, and so I walked him into the temple one night while you all slept and took what I needed. It was far easier than I ever imagined. Humans are so simple."

I study him, then the pulsating pendant. He's serious. I'm holding a piece of Neri's heart.

"If I make any sort of deal with you," I say, "*I* am the one who sets the requirements. And there will be many."

This is stupid. I'm stupid. Unless I play this very smart and use it to our advantage. Neri could be a weapon if I forced him to become one. Deals with gods are binding on both sides. I can bind him with servitude if I want.

His mouth crooks up. "Take the time you need to think up your *requirements*. We can discuss them when you choose. If I agree, then your king will be set free and on his way to safety within hours." He holds up a finger. "But, you cannot tell Un Drallag or anyone else for that matter. *That* is a deal breaker."

I think of everything he mentioned earlier. All the ways he's helped us when he could've just as easily been much more of a bastard given that Alexus is in our band. He probably could've killed him if he caught him off guard. But he didn't, and I don't know what to make of that. Gods are vengeful, aren't they? How has he sat and dined with Alexus? Saw to it he ate? That he *lived?*

I snatch my dagger from the ground and flick my hand through my construct. It stretches and disintegrates into sticky threads that fall to the ground and vanish, like pulling down a thick spider's web.

"Get back where you belong," I say to him, pointing at Joran as Neri steps closer.

He smiles when I slip the pendant over my head and tuck it beneath my jacket, and then he's gone. I don't even see the merge happen. Neri is standing before me one second, and the next he isn't. Just like Joran is unconscious one second and the next he's getting to his feet, not at all himself, but a vessel for the god spirit of the Northern lands.

"You first." I sweep my hand in the direction of the street that leads away from Aki-Ra Quarter.

With a bewitching look that's equal parts pompous and alluring, he starts walking back toward the city, back toward the inn. Back toward the people I love.

When he pauses for me to catch up, I flare a web of magick at him, and, though he laughs at me, he continues up the sandy road, leaving Aki-Ra in his wake.

I stay behind him as we sneak through the city, until we reach the inn. Even until we reach the top of the stairs and check on Raina, Alexus, Rhonin, and Hel. Even until we part and go to our own rooms.

And I watch my door, my hand around that godsdamn pendant, until I can't hold my eyes open any longer.

Because I might make deals with gods, but I know better than to turn my back on a wolf.

53

RAINA

Rhonin steps into the hall, closing the door to Alexus's room at the inn.

"He's all yours," he says, before taking Hel by the hand and walking her down the narrow corridor to his room.

I can't help but smile at them, but then my nerves return. I feel differently than I did before all of this, the threat of losing Alexus too real, though I'm still letting the change settle within me. Taking a deep breath, I push through the door.

Alexus sits in a copper soaking tub arranged by Orlena, the room lit by three oil lamps. Most of the blood is gone from him, but the open wounds, bruises, and swelling remain.

It breaks my heart to see him this way, but I remind myself that I'm just here to heal him. Just here to make sure he's okay.

He looks up from the water, his left eye swollen shut. "Are you all right?"

Me. Am *I* all right.

I nod and stand there awkwardly, unsure what to do. I'd expected him to be out of the bath and at least partially dressed.

"I can get out if that would be easier," he says.

Again, I nod, and when he grips the edges of the tub to stand, I quickly turn around.

He grunts from pain, and I flinch with the instinct to help him. Going against the part of myself that knows better, I turn and go to him, wrapping his good arm around my shoulders. The other arm must be in misery from the blade wound piercing his shoulder.

The water running off him soaks through my shirt as he eases from the tub. Once he's ready, he leans against the plain writing desk in the room as I grab the bath linen and set to drying him.

This might be the most difficult thing I've ever had to do. I know that as I gently squeeze water from his hair and begin patting the rest of his body dry. Not difficult in that I'm so close to his nakedness, but difficult in that seeing each wound brings me physical pain and even more anger than I felt before. It takes everything in me to choke back my rising rage.

"You landed us much better this time," he says. "Less like dropping us from the sky. More like rolling us out of the air."

My anger dismantles a bit, and I give him a small smile. I did do better. And I remained alert, as did everyone else. No smacking our heads on the earth so hard it knocked us unconscious or stole all the breath from our lungs. Maybe I'll only improve.

I hurry with my drying, because though he would never say it, I can tell he's having a hard time standing. In a matter of seconds, I've got him in bed, propped on pillows, tucked beneath a sheet to his waist.

There's healing to be done, so I lay the wet towel aside and take a seat beside him on the bed. He lifts his right arm so I can nestle a little closer. It feels so right when he lays that arm across my thighs, his hand soft at my hip.

I lean over him to examine his wounds. There are so many cuts on his face, a bad knot on the side of his forehead, a field of blooming bruises across his chest and abdomen, and that destruction at his shoulder that runs straight through to his back.

"This is going to take some time," he says. "You're going to be quite tired, I imagine."

It will, and I will, so the sooner I begin the better.

It doesn't take long to weave the threads of the smaller cuts on his face, his lips. The knot and his damaged eye prove more difficult mendings, though.

As I work, imagining what I want the result to be, I realize that I've memorized every single curve and line on this man's face. I know that his left eyebrow has a slightly sharper arch than the right, and that his irises have the prettiest flecks of silver and gold saturated right around the pupil. I know the full curve of his lips better than my own, and the smooth feel of the skin along his cheekbones. I know there's a tiny scar under his chin where his beard doesn't grow, and that when he's confused or angry, two deep lines form between his brows. I know his dimple—nature's little proof that tells me when he's truly happy.

He's so lovely, and I think I might miss him.

I weave the glittering red threads, frayed and multiplied, just as they were in Frostwater Wood. There are still three—his, Colden's, and mine. Even if my end of the bond is severed, these are the lives he's bound to.

For the first time since the rune was reversed, there isn't a single part of me that hates that we were so intimately connected. As I weave and weave in my mind, running my fingertips lightly over his face, I realize that, even with the bond broken, perhaps we still are.

His torso is next, and the bruises are deep. Careful, I trace my hands over his body, mending the contusions, and even a broken rib. I can't help but pay close attention to his runes. As many times as I've seen him naked, this is the first time I notice a particular marking on his chest, right over his heart, where he always kisses me. It's partially covered by the dark smattering of hair across his chest. I look up at him, a question on my face.

He glances down. "I'm not sure. It's been there as long as I can remember. It isn't any rune I know. Probably a battle scar."

Compelled and curious, I touch it, running my finger around its smooth edge. It looks like a brand.

His stomach muscles tense, and his nipples harden. "Back to work," he says with mischief in his voice. "Before you make me want to do things I can't."

I bite back a grin and turn my attention to the sword wound at his shoulder, which offers plenty distraction from the rest of him. It takes the longest of all to heal, along with deep concentration and the tedious weaving of many damaged threads. I work steadily, through shattered bone, slashed muscles and tendons, destroyed veins. He's lucky the sword missed an artery.

By the time the skin begins to restore to its usual smoothness and light gold shade, I feel like I could lie down on the floor and sleep for a week. Instead, I meet Alexus's eyes, his gaze already locked on my face, and graze my fingertips across his healed brow.

Tenderly, he kisses my wrist and rubs his hand softly up and down my forearm. "You saved me. Again. Somehow, I feel like you've been saving me forever, in so many ways."

His little death flutters against my ribs as his gaze roves over my face, making my breath come in uneven pants. I focus on his lips, wondering if he sensed the fear I felt for him today, realizing that he must have, because he hasn't questioned my lack of venom in the least.

"Come here," he whispers, and I lean in, just a little, surrounded by his heat and scent. He smiles, and there's that dimple. "Closer."

As though his words are laced with magickal conviction, I touch my mouth to his, and the rest of the world falls away.

His lips feel so very right, soft and luscious, tempted yet tempered, so supple in their yearning. I let him set the pace, a languorous tasting.

Yes. This kiss is a reminder. A welcome back. A promise made. A declaration. His kiss tastes like devotion. It tastes like sincerity and affection and adoration. It tastes like him, like us.

When his mouth releases mine, everything is so still and quiet. I'm captured, unable to move away, his breath a warm plea against my wet lips.

"Stay with me," he whispers. "Just stay. We don't have to do anything but sleep. I just need to feel you."

There's no hesitation in me as I unbuckle my sheath and let it drop on the floor. No reluctance as he begins unlacing my trousers while I tug off my tunic. In moments, I'm slipping beneath the sheet and curling against his chest, nothing between us save for skin.

Tears come then, the events of the night rushing through me. As ever, those crashing waves.

It's a gentle weeping, and Alexus holds me tight through it all, kissing away my tears, tenderly wiping my cheeks. "I'm here," he says. "I'm always here."

But he almost wasn't, and it seems that near loss has numbed the old bitterness and hatred the reversal of the rune reinvigorated.

When I stop crying, I give in to the drowsiness making every muscle in my body heavy, and as I drift, I swear my consciousness touches the edges of a dream not mine.

It's *his* dream, of us, making love beneath a willow tree in a soft rain, the ruins of an ancient city in the distance.

54

NEPHELE

The next morning as I dress, Hel bursts into my room. "Time to go. The Dread Vipers are coming. Joran went to see if they would retaliate. There are droves of them searching the city, and they're headed this way."

She's gone before I get a chance to ask *how* we're supposed to leave. On foot, I imagine.

When I get downstairs, Raina and Alexus are there. I give him the hug I couldn't share last night, then they guide me to the rear of the inn. We step out into the pink light of early dawn into a dirty alleyway where everyone else and five horses await.

Five.

"It's all I could manage," Orlena says to Alexus, though I spot swords on each animal, which is a blessed feat. "There are bedrolls and meager supplies in your rucksacks," she continues. "The food will see you to the Ske-Trana provinces, but from there, you'll need to replenish and find camels for the ride into the desert. And from there, once you reach the Jade River, you'll face Fia Drumera's shield wall. No one gets through anymore save for her magi and whoever they allow passage."

Alexus takes the reins of a sable horse and smooths his hand down its silken flank. "We'll figure it out once we get there. But thank you, Orlena. I owe you a great debt."

She smiles. "Or perhaps I owe you. Thank you for trying to protect Tiressia and the Summerlands."

Alexus inclines his head in a gracious bow, then glances over everyone as Orlena waves goodbye and slips back inside the inn.

"Mount up," Alexus says. "We've quite the ride in front of us."

Though it makes my heart so happy, I'm a little surprised when Raina swings up onto Alexus's horse without prodding, and him behind her. As everyone else begins pairing off, I start toward a horse near the back of the line, its coat a golden, pale blond.

I freeze in my tracks. Joran—*Neri*—appears from behind Rhonin who holds the reins of his horse while Hel mounts. Calmly, Neri slides his hand along the blond horse's reins, peering at me from the corner of his eyes.

"Looks like it's you and me," he says, a smug smirk on his face as he glances at my neck where he knows his pendant lies.

Annoyance crawls through my chest as I glance around. Everyone has coupled off—Raina and Alexus, Rhonin and Hel, Keth and Jaega, Zahira and Callan, and... me and Neri.

"Ladies first." He motions to the saddle and gives a theatrical bow that makes me want to vomit on his shoes.

For a second, I consider asking someone to switch, but Alexus clicks his tongue and leads his and Raina's horse out of the alley, and everyone else starts to follow.

"Would you rather walk?" Neri says.

"Very much," I spit.

He rolls his eyes, and once Rhonin and Hel start down the alley toward the street, he smiles, and my, my, my, how clearly I see the wolf in him now.

"This will give us plenty of time to discuss your requirements," he says. "Consider it business."

I think about stabbing him and leaving him in the dirt to bleed, but I can't kill a spirit, unfortunately.

Irritated, I stalk toward him, grab the saddle horn, and swing up onto the horse, feeling his eyes on my every move. I know he's next, but I'm not prepared for the full-body cringe that grips me once he's fully seated behind me, Joran's thighs cradling mine.

This is seven kinds of twisted, being pressed against the body of a man I once slept with who also happens to be possessed by a god I loathe. I now have some idea how Raina felt when she learned about Neri and Alexus.

He leans close to my ear. "I'm glad it's my heart you're wearing around your neck instead of my balls." I hear the smile in his voice. "And you don't know how long I've wanted this lovely ass against me, just like this." His thighs tighten around mine. "Are you ready for this, witch?"

I tilt my head forward just a little, then I slam my head back into his nose, hard enough to hurt like fuck, but not hard enough to knock him out, sadly. He grabs Joran's poor face and shouts a curse that roars through the alley, which tells me he feels Joran's pain, which is all I needed to know.

"Now I am." I straighten my spine, making certain to put a lilt in my voice.

With a growl, Neri kicks the horse forward and turns us onto the street. "You are a cold-blooded woman, Nephele Bloodgood."

Though I keep my eyes peeled for those telltale red velvet caparisoned horses and guards in black, I grin, thoroughly satisfied. "You haven't seen anything yet."

۞

BY THE TIME NIGHT FALLS, WE'RE STILL IN THE OUTSKIRTS OF ITUNNAN, and the air is growing colder.

This city is so vast. This *continent* is so vast. It will take us far longer to reach the City of Ruin than it took to travel from Winterhold to Malgros. And now that Fleurie is practicing with portals, we very likely don't have that kind of time.

The Dread Vipers have been nowhere in sight, something I have to wonder if Neri caused. I'm not sure how he could have, but much as I hate to admit it, he's saved us many times before. It isn't impossible that he somehow led them on a false trail before we left the inn.

That night, we stop and sleep in the cold, surrounded by whispering sand and—just like Neri told the group when we were on the ship—the constant feel of magick in the air.

Come sunrise, we ride until midnight, crossing empty stretches of land dotted with small villages. Once the horses tire and our empty bellies can't remain empty any longer, we find the ruins of an old temple to camp inside until morning.

It doesn't take long to build a small fire to ward off the chill in the air. We lay out our bedrolls while Callan draws protective runes in the sand around the old temple. The presence we've all felt remains, even stronger now, and I feel so much guilt, because I know it's been Neri this entire time.

Rhonin and Hel sharpen the ends of two long branches they found beneath a lone eucalyptus tree and go on the hunt for meat. Orlena provided nuts, dates, loaves of bread, and wedges of goat cheese, but after one night, supplies are already low. What we have will only keep us going another day or so.

Neri vanishes into the shadowy alcoves of the ruins. Exploring, I suppose. I find myself wondering how many times he visited the Summerlands to see Asha, or for other reasons, perhaps. I can't stand him, but I can admit that it must be strange to see this land after so many years.

I take a seat beside Raina and Alexus near the fire. My sister sits close to him, a new scrying dish and canteen in hand, preparing to take a look around the world. There's still a strange reserve to her when it comes to Alexus, though, still a thread of conflict in her eyes and the way she moves around him. But like these ruins, her walls are crumbling.

"I'm worried about time," I tell them. "We're many weeks away from the citadel, and that's if we have no issues getting there."

Alexus sits with his elbows draped over his knees as he pinches a bite of bread from a small loaf and eats it. I can see the worry on his face too.

"I've thought about that all day," he says. "I'm not sure how we can get there any faster unless I transport us, one by one."

"It isn't a far-fetched thought," I say.

"But it is *dangerous,"* Raina signs, widening her eyes. *"I have flown with him."*

He scrunches his brow at her. "I take offense to that. For something I haven't done in three centuries, I think it went well."

She cocks a brow and gives him a glare. *"Because there was a sea below. Not a desert."*

I think of Neri's proposal and my requirements, which we discussed off and on today as we rode. But he isn't an option for aid in this scenario. Though I have a feeling he could come up with something, I don't know what he's capable of. I also don't know if he could get us there without everyone knowing that he is, in fact, not Joran.

Besides, I need time to think my way through this deal before I commit. I have him paused in an in-between state right now, waiting for the lines of our deal to be laid out. I refuse to place myself, anyone I love—any Tiressian for that matter—at a disadvantage with a god who can make our lives miserable if I'm not careful. I mean for us to benefit from this deal. Not pay.

"I can get us there," Raina signs. *"If there is a way to show me where we are going."*

Alexus looks at her. "Your *flying* isn't much better than mine."

Her brow crumples. *"Untrue. You might lose momentum and leave us stranded at different places across the desert. I have control. We will end up in the same place."*

Alexus sighs from deep within his chest, a man who knows he's just lost all chance of any argument. Because she's right.

"We'll reach the provinces first," he says. "Do our best to suit up with what we need for the desert, and then, if we can find a way to show Raina where we need to go—" he scrubs his hand over his face as though he isn't sure about this at all "—perhaps we'll try *her* route."

My sister looks up at me with sly eyes, the corner of her mouth curling. I remember that expression so well, on my mother's face when she would best my father in a discussion at the dinner table.

It hasn't really struck me until now that we're on our ancestor's land. That this world was our mother's home for much of her life.

"Perhaps we'll cross through Elam," I say.

Alexus lifts his eyes. "We will. It's the first province between here and the desert."

Raina's eyes sparkle at that. In fact, her whole face lights up, even though we both know there won't be time to linger in our mother's village. There may not be time to do anything more than ride straight through.

With that thought, I nod at the scrying dish in my sister's lap. I hate asking her to check the waters. Hate watching her bleed. But she sets to the task without a shred of hesitance.

Careful not to waste what water we have, she pours just enough from the canteen into the dish she stole from the inn. After slicing the sharp edge of her dagger across the end of her finger, she holds her hand over the water and lets a pearl of blood drip into the bowl.

55

FLEURIE

The Eastern Territories
City of Quezira
Min-Thuret Temple, Rite Hall

I'm not sure how much longer I can fail.

I try so hard to only open the portal a matter of a few miles, up to the ruins, or into the crowded city streets, or down to the market quarter. But the prince is wise to me. I'm certain that's why Bronwyn and Thresh are escorting me through Min-Thuret at midnight, across the courtyard and gardens I remember well.

To Rite Hall.

We walk along the cloisters until we reach the massive doors. They groan through the night as Thresh and Bronwyn open them. I'm unchained, but the iron collar remains intact when I'm not *practicing* portaling the prince. But even if it weren't, the greatest curse I bear is that I am forever trapped. My gift has a limit I never could break, no matter how hard I tried. If the collar were gone, I could portal away from here, but I would shortly be drawn back.

I'm tethered to Quezira, to the Eastern lands my father called home. And I forever will be.

With a deep breath, I step into the ritual room, my stomach twisting to the point of pain. A memory of my last time here swells inside my mind, putting pressure behind my eyes. Anger pulses inside me like a heartbeat, and I taste my old fury, bittersweet.

And the prince. He stands across the hall on the other side of the ritual circle, his red shadows swirling over the etched marble floor, the moon cradling the sun. The symbols stand for the Order of Night's vow to protect the Order of Dawn. More importantly, for me, they represent a man from a very long time ago who was willing to give his everything for a woman who was his only light.

I close my eyes. *So many memories.* My mind is awash with them.

Again, I take a deep breath and blink my eyes open to gaze upon the prince. Just beyond him lies the altar and that godsdamn throne. If he only knew how many times he kneeled there, to his own disgust.

He wears a sleeping tunic and pants, his hands tucked inside the pockets, his bare feet shoulder-width apart. He seems unfazed about being here, and that rattles me to my core.

I open my mouth to try and tell him a string of truths that have done nothing but haunt me since I was taken from Quezira to the cliffs. I just want to tell him his name for gods' sakes, in hopes that might shake him awake. But as ever, it's a foolish attempt. My father's invisible torque tightens around my throat, clamping off my speech, the magick so instantaneous and responsive, it's as though he cursed me yesterday, not three centuries ago.

The doors to Rite Hall close, and a look over my shoulder reveals that I am alone with the prince, standing there in my nightgown and robe.

"I thought you might want to chat now that your voice has returned. And what better place than your father's old ritual room." He waves one hand around the fire-lit hall, and I notice that his palm is bandaged, as though he's performed an offering, the kind only my father ever required.

I narrow my eyes, forlorn and amazed. He truly doesn't remember anything, even now, even in *this* room of all places. If so much as a flicker of recollection exists in him, I cannot see it.

"I was sleeping," I tell him. "This couldn't wait until morning?"

He runs his thumb and forefinger back and forth along his smile lines that aren't as deep as I remember. "But *I* wasn't." A long, dark lock of hair tumbles into his eyes. "All I could do was toss and turn, wondering why we keep failing with portaling, so I came here to discuss it with your father."

Cold, phantom fingers walk up my spine. I cringe, drawing up my shoulders as I look around, a reflexive and permanently engrained reaction.

"He isn't here anymore," the prince says. "It was a brief meeting. But he mentioned a part of your gift I suppose I'd forgotten. You don't just open portals and will the thing where to take you. You use farsight. A magickal mechanism that can pinpoint a locale, sure and true. And yet," he shrugs, "we mysteriously keep portaling to places within Quezira. Funny that."

"You are his puppet," I say, all but spitting the words, surprised that they are somehow allowed to fall from my lips.

"No, I am his servant."

"Or his slave."

He sighs. "A slave requires unwillingness. I am quite willing to abide your father's wishes for resurrection. He will ensure that I reign over Tiressia when the time comes. We will be a force."

"He told you that? And you believed him?" I laugh, but only to hide my sadness. I can hardly believe those words just came from his mouth, a man who would've forsaken a throne at all costs many moons ago.

His face darkens. "I'm going to give you one warning, Fleurie, and only one. You have seven days to portal us into the City of Ruin, to Mount Ulra, but that is all. We made a deal, and your deception breaks it. All I need to do is refuse any further efforts to fulfill the bargain, and you'll end up back in Yura's pits, where I'll leave you to rot for a very miserable eternity. So I suggest you prepare."

Defiance fills me, but my ruse has come to a crossroads. I either give in and help the prince resurrect the vilest creature I have ever known, or I suffer a life of agony, alone in darkness, for an infinity.

I can't see a way out of this. And the truth is, I already know he wins. I know that I will take him to Mount Ulra, and that I will portal Thamaos's bones back to this very room. I know that more will be asked of me too. Soon, I'm sure. I'd just hoped that somehow, the future once revealed to me might've been wrong.

But it wasn't. And now the pain truly begins.

56

RAINA

Fleurie abandons the prince's shadows and steps into the night with Bronwyn Shawcross and a guard at her sides.

Having never met her—only having seen her through Colden's eyes—I wasn't certain I would be able to see her. But she appeared plainly enough.

All I could make of the conversation was the dread and bitterness she felt, the sadness and anger, the worry and loathing. But it was still a conversation at midnight, one she was clearly summoned to and didn't want to attend. I cannot help but wonder what was said.

I leave her and bleed into the waters to see Colden. He's asleep in his new bed in the dungeon, his pretty face cast in the golden torchlight.

"He looks so innocent," I sign, and my sister busts into laughter.

Alexus smiles, and I remember him using that very descriptor when he first told me Colden and Fia's story in the cave. But I don't need their reaction to know better. I've met him, and I've seen him fight.

Though I can't believe I'm thinking it, I sign, *"I wish I had seen him wield his power before Neri stole it."*

My sister, trying to contain her laughter, goes stock-still. "His power," she says, as if she didn't read my hands correctly.

I give her a strange look. *"Yes. His power. Over ice and frost and snow."*

She blinks, as though a revelation just dropped into the depths of her mind, and glances at the shadowy alcoves of the temple ruins, where Joran vanished earlier.

"Gods, Nephele," Alexus says, being facetious, "have you forgotten the man already? Is Joran getting to you that badly?"

She tosses a handful of sand at him, and he jerks to the side to miss it, laughing at her. The way she glares at him, her head tilted, her brow flat, makes me smile. They're like brother and sister sometimes, the way Hel and Finn used to be.

Nephele waves her hand at my scrying dish. "Go on. Ignore me, I'm only... thinking."

Alexus laughs again and gets up to stoke the fire as I bleed to see General Hammerin Vexx.

Not to my surprise, Gavril is with him, that fucking bastard. But I can't even think about that sorcerer as they talk because there's something about Vexx. Something that makes me view him from the outside.

His expression is colder than I've ever seen, his grin even more delightedly cruel than in the ravine. He laughs, tossing his head back with malevolent glee I feel in my soul.

Suddenly, he looks out over the dark sea, toward the bowsprit. His grin spreads into an evil smile, and a cold wave comes over me, chills so brutal they make my skin hurt.

I dip back inside Vexx's viewpoint, expecting to see the sharp spar at the front of the boat pointing toward the open ocean and an eastern, midnight sky.

And I do. I can tell by the stars which direction they're moving. Only there's one thing I could never, in all my days, have imagined my eyes would ever behold.

A head. Pierced through the mouth on the tip of the bowsprit.

I press the heels of my hands to my eyes, trying to unsee the image, but it might be imprinted in my mind until I leave this world.

"What's wrong?" Alexus and Nephele say at the same time.

Without looking at the water again, I reach for the dish and toss the liquid on the ground so I can begin anew.

"*Vexx is sailing east,*" I tell them, rushing the words, suddenly not feeling any desire to eat. "*He... harmed someone. You do not want details.*"

No need to ruin their appetites, and I don't want to make Nephele feel guilty. This was clearly retaliation for Joran killing Rooke. The head probably belonged to a sailor or someone he made an example of for his crew of Northlanders. I feel such disgust for him, such utter loathing. If there are any Ancient Ones listening, I pray they hear my plea that I be the one who ends that man's life.

Shaken, I pour more water and bleed again to see Yazmin and Finn. Yazmin sits alone in the cove with a glass of wine, her love and worry drifting all the way across the sea. But Finn...

Finn is nowhere. No matter how hard I look, no matter how hard I think about him, he doesn't appear.

"What's the matter now?" Nephele says, my face obviously telling all.

"Finn," I sign. *"I cannot see him."*

"Perhaps you're only tired," Alexus says. "Maybe rest will help."

Or perhaps I'm *that* disturbed by Vexx's cruelty that I cannot focus. Still, I try again, and again I fail.

Nephele grabs my hand as I lift the dagger to try another time. "Raina, it's all right. Finn is probably sleeping and healing. You're exhausted from last night and today. Try to eat and rest. You can always consult the waters again tomorrow."

Though I don't want to hear it, I know she's right. I put aside the dish just as Rhonin and Hel appear around a stone corner, laughing with each other despite everything, several hares in tow.

Hel smiles and proudly holds up her kill. "Who's ready to eat?"

❦

THE RIDE TOWARD ELAM AND THE SKE-TRANA PROVINCES IS AN arduous one.

The dirt and gravel road is flat and straight, blending into sandier terrain, but the wind is high, whipping our clothes and hair and pelting us with grit. I can smell hot sand carried from the southwest, from the mountains. It's like traveling in a whirl of constant dust.

Even though Alexus tries to shield me from the heavier gusts, my eyes burn from the intrusion and the occasional fleck of gravel that gets lost under my eyelid. Our faces and necks and hands are coated in grime from sweating, and there's even sand in my teeth, grating my throat. All of that while riding as swiftly as possible, in improper clothing beneath an ever-warming sun, makes the trek miserable. We Northlanders were clearly unprepared for the Summerland geography.

We ride like that for two more days, and we don't reach the first sight of Ske-Trana until that second afternoon. Even then, it lies far in the distance, a sprawl of mud-brick beehive-shaped homes surrounded by flat, golden earth and dunes of sand in the far distance.

Imagining my mother here as a child, probably filthy and happy, playing in those sandy streets, helps me endure.

Early that evening, while the horizon is still lit with pink and orange light, we finally ride into Elam, our horses at a walk. I hold my long braid over my nose as another gust of sand swirls around us. The air is beginning to calm and cool for the night, though, and we need shelter. We need food and clothes and to trade our horses for camels too—if I can't find a way to get us to the City of Ruin much faster. That's my goal, even though Keth and Joran and even Rhonin and Alexus are a little uncertain about the endeavor.

There are no inns here. We stop at a few buildings that look like they might be of importance, but the doors are sealed for the day. There's nothing else but mud-brick houses and what must be a school, and a simple temple built from the same mud-brick, which is where Alexus leads us.

Nephele and I share a glance, a realization that this might be part of our ancestry, but it's not where we'll find any living memory of our mother.

We tie our horses and enter the sacred hall, a band of sand and dirt-covered travelers. I don't expect anyone to be here, and yet a brown-skinned man in a pewter gray robe starts down a center aisle lit by standing oil lamps that divide at least fifty individual places for prayer, replete with a rush mat, colorful pillow for kneeling, and a candle waiting to be lit. He holds up a hand to halt us from entering further.

I glance at Nephele. She rubs her dusty cheeks, her eyes red and irritated, as I consider who the people of the Summerlands pray to—surely not Asha.

And yet, my sister raises her brows and glances toward the front of the temple where the stone image of a woman looks over the altar, a sword hilt in hand, the blade standing on its tip. How strange to see what they imagine Asha to be like, this goddess who has lived in stories for me.

Another look around, and I realize that Joran is still outside, staring straight ahead at Asha's figure with the brightest, most penetrating stare. Nephele watches him so closely, but he remains outside, eventually stepping away and returning to the horses.

When I turn back toward Asha, the attendant motions to Alexus who walks deeper into the sanctuary to meet him. They speak quietly while the rest of us walk around the entry room, studying the wooden paintings and woven tapestries hanging on the walls.

Nephele comes to stand at my side, and then Hel, and then Zahira, and then Callan, and even Jaega. We all lean on one another in some way, our days together having created a bond of our own. One of trust, growing friendships, and a wealth of intuition.

Nephele points at the center painting, a river winding through the desert, greener than Alexus's eyes. But it's a birds-eye view painting, revealing mountains to the west and a stretch of desert to the south.

"Is that the Jade River?" Callan says, but then they look closer, studying the words carved into the wood near the bottom of the painting. "Ah," they say. "It is."

"Are you all thinking what I'm thinking?" Zahira says.

Hel laughs. "I'm thinking we let Raina get us the fuck out of this endless journey and breeze our asses to that river," she whispers. "No matter what the men folk say."

"Snatch them in the night, Raina," Jaega says, keeping her voice low. "They can't stop what they can't see coming."

Quiet laughs and snickers travel between us because she's serious, and I'm very much considering doing exactly that.

When Alexus returns, he scrubs his hand down his dirty face. "He can get us provisions, and we can stay here for the night, in the stables with the camels. No defiling the sacred space."

A feeling passes through me, and the same look crosses every face. A silent, yet collective refusal. We're tired. We're dirty. We're ready to meet Fia Drumera, and I can get us to the river that lies within Mount Ulra's shadow. We are not sleeping with camels.

I know Alexus is worried, because this ability with my abyss is such a new and untested thing, but there's a sureness in me that I can't explain, same as there was in Aki-Ra. It's time to start using that gift. I'm not certain where it came from, but I have it for a reason.

When Alexus, Rhonin, and Keth head outside to lead the horses to the stables, leaving us alone, we all look at one another.

"Tonight," I sign, and they smile. And much to my surprise, they all sign back.

"Tonight."

❦

OH, THE DETERMINATION OF A WOMAN AND HER FRIENDS.

Once the temple's attendant and Alexus arrive at the stables with food and two large pails of clean water, we clean up as best we can, then we set to refilling our rucksacks and canteens while the men prepare a small dinner of flatbread and salted snake meat.

It isn't the worst thing I've ever eaten, but we're eating it in a dung-filled stable that smells like dirty camel and shit. I would give just about anything to be sitting by a fire in the open valley eating Mother's custard pie and roasted venison and stewed vegetables and... Gods. Warm, mulled cider.

The night is colder and bright with moonlight streaming in through the single window in the stables. We're surrounded by sleepy-eyed, unsaddled camels, staring at us from their stalls. I've never seen a camel until tonight. They're rather large and extraordinary creatures, but it doesn't appear that we're going to have the chance to get acquainted.

As Jaega wraps up the leftover bread and meat, Nephele and I fill canteens. She glances at the men, her eyes telling me to look. They're laying out our bedrolls on the ground—even Joran—while Callan, Hel, and Zahira make sure to place our rucksacks and weapons near our respective cots so we can carry them with us. But I hadn't thought about the fact that we will be without bedrolls once we arrive. We'll have to survive.

With our bellies filled, we lie down, our beds close enough and in a circular pattern that we can reach one another to form a chain. Rhonin is in front of me, and Alexus is behind me, and Nephele behind him. It will work.

The night air tightens with tension. I take a deep breath as Alexus slips his hand around my waist and moves closer to me, settling in. I am not averse to the nearness anymore. I can remember my hate of him, and it still has sharp edges sometimes, but there's something far more powerful that shadows that now. Besides, the closeness makes my task tonight much easier.

But then he goes so still, and not the kind of still that comes with sleep, but the kind of still that says something is wrong.

Our rucksack and swords and daggers lay between me and Rhonin who happens to be facing me. Alexus reaches past me and pulls one of the swords free with a quiet hiss.

Rhonin opens his eyes, the whites visible in the moonlit night. Smoothly, he frees a dagger.

I don't hear anything, but then Alexus is on his feet as he shouts, "Vipers! Glamours up! Get your swords!"

As though emerging from shadows, the Dread Vipers who must've been lurking outside waiting for us to sleep flood into the stables as we reach for our weapons and lunge to our feet. How they followed us without us knowing, I cannot grasp.

Power crackles through the air, alive as lightning, spiderwebbing along the mud-brick walls, making the camels grunt and bleat and spit.

Before the Dread Vipers have a chance to immobilize his magick, Alexus yells, "Get down!"

A second later, he pours his power into the guards about to rush him.

I turn and throw my arm over my head, and though I don't see it happen, I feel the pressure in the room change and hear their bodies explode with a horrific squelch. In the ravine, the bits of the destroyed men had hung from trees, the limbs glistening with flesh and shards of bone.

Tonight, we're wearing the remains of Dread Vipers.

Shaking and drenched in blood and guts, I turn, just as more guards rush into the stables, though they pause at seeing the carnage. I wipe splatters of blood and sinew from my cheek, trying not to be sick when I realize an eyeball is in my hand.

"Hold!" Hel shouts, her voice reverberating around the mud walls. "Now, Raina!"

It takes a second for me to grasp the command, but we meet eyes as she reaches for Rhonin's arm on one side and Nephele's on the other. I watch the chain happen around the small room, and I grab Alexus's hand.

He looks down, brow furrowed. And just as the Vipers charge toward us, I think of the Jade River, and pray I can carry ten people through time across the desert.

57

RAINA

Summerlands
The Jade River

"You could've told me," Alexus says, sitting on a boulder surrounded by woody bushes I can't name, stripping off his blood-soaked clothes beneath the moon and a handful of starlights.

We're all scattered along the sandy banks of what I hope is the Jade River. It's cold out, and getting wet is going to be awful, but we can build a fire or two. No matter what, we cannot remain drenched in the remains of dead men. I can still smell their deaths, a cluster of scents burning in my nostrils.

I swallow hard and work diligently to come out of my clothes too. *"You would have said no,"* I sign.

"Yes, because it was risky. And painful." He picks away the last of the briars that have been wedged in his skin since landing in a grove of thorny scrub.

It's wrong of me, but I bite my upper lip to keep from smiling as he grabs his pile of clothes and walks up, wearing nothing but the key around his neck. I peel off my tunic, hoping that's a significant enough distraction.

He lowers his gaze to my breasts, but only for a moment. "Carrying ten people at once into your *abyss* could've gone very badly, Raina. You don't know the limits of this ability yet. You don't even know what it is. And I would rather not lose you. You don't know what your body can handle when it comes to this."

He turns and heads toward the riverbank to rinse out his clothes, the muscles of his long body flexing with every strut. Feeling guilty, I finish and join him, dunking my clothes in the cold, lapping waves.

I consider trying to heat an area like I did at Hampstead Loch, but this river isn't still as a lake, and I wasn't so magickally drained then.

"This is a much different scenario than our first time together by a stream of water," he says, changing the subject as he scrubs his shirt against a rock. "I'm glad you're not hating me still."

I grab his hand, stopping his work, because I know him well enough to realize he changed the subject for me.

"I am sorry," I sign. *"I will try to be wiser."*

His frowning expression softens, just a little, and his eyes glint with something delicate and tender. "I don't know what I would do if something happened to you, Raina. That is my greatest fear. I cannot explain it, just like I can't explain much about my feelings when it comes to you. I only know that I would roll this world off its axis if I lost you."

I touch his face. *"I am not going anywhere,"* I sign, but the idea seems to haunt him still.

We finish our clothes and lay them out on rocks to drip-dry, then we thread our fingers together and wade into the cold water. We can't go far because of the current.

Alexus gasps and cups himself. "Well, this is fucking terrible."

I shake with laughter, because it *is* terrible, but we don't have any other choice.

Quickly, we squat down and scrub away the dried blood and awful bits of sinew, then we dip under to rinse our hair. This probably won't get rid of all the gore, which turns my stomach. I say a prayer to the Ancient Ones that I don't wake up tomorrow with someone's flesh still on me.

When we get out, we work to dress in our wet clothes, which isn't an easy task, but soon we're stalking the shoreline, shivering, trying to find a place for a makeshift camp for the night. Callan and Zahira somehow had the mindfulness during the attack to slip their arm through a pack before reaching for their neighbor's hand, so we have a few supplies. We gather those and keep looking, and I can't help but worry that I could've been wrong about where I sent us, and we just can't tell in the darkness.

"This is *the Jade River, yes?"* I sign, knowing Alexus has been here before.

"Most definitely." He points to the west.

I glance that direction, and though it's a faint distinction, I can just make out the jagged tips of mountains rising like monstrous teeth against the night sky. Mount Ulra is out there somewhere.

I cannot believe we're here.

"The citadel is still such a long way from here," he says, rocks and sand crunching under his boots. "Tomorrow, I'll transport you to the citadel. Once you get a good look, we'll return here, and *then* you can bring us back."

A thrill chases through me. We're so very close.

We find a sandy clearing surrounded by more woody bushes. Under the warm glow of Alexus's starlights, we carefully rip out old growth and thorny branches and find stones to create a place for a fire. It doesn't take long before we have heat and a way to dry ourselves.

"Should we find everyone?" I sign, the cold finally starting to leave my bones. I'm standing by the fire facing the river, glancing from side to side of the riverbank to see if I can detect any movement in the darkness. I swear a small fire burns in the distance. Hel?

Alexus finishes spreading out the only two blankets we have and walks up to me, placing his hands on my hips, his body limned in firelight. "I have a feeling that Callan and Zahira are probably going to come back with some inventive idea for sleeping tonight, and I also have a feeling we shouldn't interrupt Rhonin and Hel. They are together, forced to be naked, and Hel can keep them warm. I doubt we'll hear from them until much later, if at all. As for your sister and Joran? If he's pestering her, we might never see him again, but they're quiet, so that must mean something."

I laugh at that and slip my hands up his chest, over his shoulders.

He pulls me close, clasping his wrist at the small of my back. "The fire will guide them here when they want to come. But until then..." He slips his hand beneath my tunic and pauses with his fingers grazing my waist. "I would kiss your neck, but I'm afraid you still have guts on you."

Again, I laugh, loving that he can do that—bring humor into an otherwise difficult situation.

I take his hand and drag it up under my shirt, urging his warm fingers beneath my undergarment. No gore there.

He groans a little, staring into my eyes, and teases my already hard nipple. "I would very much like to have you in my mouth." He pinches my nipple with the pressure he knows I like. "That might make me forgive you for calling me a prick, threatening to kill me, throwing a mug at me, getting me stabbed, and dropping me in a nest of briars. Am I leaving anything out?"

Smiling, I give him what he wants, what *I* want, tugging my tunic up to allow better access. He sucks my flesh into his mouth like I am all the sustenance he needs, and I bury my hands in his hair, holding him tight against me.

He lowers me to one of the blankets and kisses my mouth, deeply, lying beside me, just touching and teasing, playing, wearing a beautiful smile, joking all the while to make me laugh.

Tomorrow, we reach the City of Ruin and all that entails. But tonight, for a little while at least, it's just us.

VI

CITY OF RUIN

58

RAINA

The City of Ruin
Outside the Wall

T he view from the sky at dawn is magnificent. The river is an
emerald serpent slithering from the mountains through golden
dunes that sprawl toward a distant sea in three directions. The
west is an expanse of rocky, rugged mountain peaks coming to life under a
quickly rising sun.

And right in the middle of it all is the jewel: the walled City of Ruin.

I expect crumbling ruins, like the old Quezira in Alexus's dreams. I
expect a war-torn wall, and a temple in near disrepair after so many years,
and something very similar to the mud-brick homes of Elam. I expect
simple and old, a faded ghost of the city Alexus described in the cave in
Frostwater Wood.

The wall is a stunning piece of architecture circling the city within.
And there are indeed temples—not one, not two, not three, but four,
standing at the cardinal points, each one cast in shining white marble. In

the middle stands what can only be a palace—the Fire Queen's home—made of more white marble, its center-domed structure capped in gold.

The hundreds and hundreds of homes are much like Alexus described, but only more lovely: freestanding mud-brick and sandstone houses with square bodies, surrounded by colorful red and yellow flowers. More homes are built into the southwestern cliffs, windows spilling with blooms, and other houses are nestled under rocky overhangs. Some are even crafted into the side of what must be Mount Ulra, because even from here, I can see what can only be the Grove of the Gods.

It looks like someone painted a swipe of forest across the mountain. The trees are massive, their boughs wide and dome-shaped, their leaves sparkling green. I try to absorb more details, but suddenly, Alexus banks left against a western breeze and we're descending. Quickly, I realize why.

With the morning's hazy heat beginning to rise from the desert, and the fact that I sense magick *everywhere* here, it was almost invisible before. But now that we're closer, I can clearly see the magick surrounding the City of Ruin. I hear it too. What I thought was wind roaring in my ears is a mixture of wind and the *hum* of Fia's veil.

A protection. A shield. A barrier.

The final battle separating us and the queen.

This time, Alexus doesn't lose momentum when he lands, he controls it and sets my feet on soft sands with all the grace of a bird settling on a tree limb.

I smile up at him and sign, *"Impressive."*

That grin of his unfurls, and his dimple cuts into his cheek. "I'm glad you think so. Because we get to do it again."

He kisses me, and gods, I can taste his happiness, and it is a drug.

"How do we get through that?" I sign, pointing at the barrier after I can think clearly again. Beyond, an enormous set of golden and jewel encrusted gates await us, reflecting the sunlight in an array of colors across the sands.

"We knock with magick and hope we're able to do it loudly enough that she lets us in."

I narrow my eyes and purse my lips, studying the veil. *"I wonder if I can get us in."*

He arches a brow. "No. We aren't even trying that. If it were possible,

I'm certain someone would've done it by now. I'm not letting the woman I love throw herself into Fia Drumera's magick."

He doesn't give me a chance to argue or respond. In the next second, he's wrapping his arm around my waist again, and his power echoes across the desert, sending up a golden shower of grains as he shoots us into the sky.

I cling to him as we soar. And smile.

⚝

TRAVELING ACROSS THE ABYSS GETS EASIER AND EASIER TO DO.

My landing is as smooth as Alexus's, delivering everyone to the citadel's outskirts in a matter of seconds. We set to work, even though the sun is rising high, and the day is beginning to scorch, bringing sweat to our brows and backs already.

Callan works their rune magick, carving runes in the sand along the edge of the barrier. Runes for awareness—that Fia might sense us. For peace—that she might understand we mean no harm. For pleading—that she might realize we need her aid. And dozens more, all sending a message Callan means to make certain Fia hears.

Nephele attempts to break through Fia's construct since she understands vast magick. She looks so tired, and as though her mind is weighed by as much worry as there are grains of sand in this desert. I want to help her, but vast magick isn't my gift. Unfortunately, there's no singing magick to be done, and even if there were, there's too few of us here who can actually do it.

Alexus might be the key. He can work with vast magick. But instead of helping my sister, he walks back and forth before the veil for a while, thinking and watching her and Callan, until he finally steps to the shimmering barrier and reaches out his hands.

After a few moments, power moves like a storm across the desert. I can feel it coming, rumbling over the dunes, a tremor along the ground, as though Alexus has summoned an unearthly demon. Everyone turns to look, but there's nothing to see save for shifting sands and blue sky and swirling dust.

But gods, can we feel it. A zephyr blows, and I can even smell it, sweet like Alexus's honeyed magick and earthy like heated sand.

Suddenly, the rumble races under our feet and travels past us. Alexus yells for Callan and Nephele to stand back.

On the edge of the next heartbeat, arcs of blue light explode from the earth around him, like lightning bolts shooting from the sands into the sky. That power latches on to the veil and crawls across it, each bolt spreading and fracturing further, creeping along the barrier like a magickal vine looming over the desert.

We all stand and watch, necks craned, amazed, the immensity of both powers vibrating the air, making the hair on my arms stand on end. If Fia Drumera cannot feel this, we have no chance of ever getting inside.

But Alexus isn't finished.

The bolts of power begin to move in a strange way. I stand back and look left to right, studying the veil for as far as my eyes can see in both directions. And I am in awe of Alexus Thibault. His power has come so very far.

None of this is random. He's writing a runic message on Fia's veil. More than that, he's also writing it a second time in ancient Elikesh. Backwards, so her entire city can read it.

"Callan!" he shouts. "You know what to do!"

They must, because they hurry to the sands near the veil where their previous rune work has been destroyed from Alexus's magick bursting from the ground. They begin re-writing the runes, studying Alexus's message, and copying the markings to...

To create the outer line. Callan is acting as Alexus's ritual guardian, just like they did in the wood when Alexus summoned Thamaos. I don't under-stand the rules, but they clearly do, because Callan works fast, dragging a line through the sand and drawing a rune, then repeating that—over and over and over.

Is he summoning Fia? Can that be done?

Hel stands beside me, cupping her mouth with her hands, watching nervously as though something is about to happen. Keth and Jaega sit on the sands, arm in arm, their gazes glued to the veil. Zahira and Nephele stand together clasping hands, and even Joran stands watching, though his eyes might be a bit more curious than awed. Still, we all feel the importance of this event, but we're also moved by such a display of power.

As Callan works, the light of Alexus's magick only brightens, until sand begins to rise from the earth and meld into each rune and letter. The markings begin to change color, from lightning blue to fire orange.

Callan finally finishes, and as though the sun shot a flaming arrow at the veil, Alexus's messages flare with fire across the sky.

He pulls away, steady as an oak even after such a release of magick and examines his work. Callan goes to stand beside him.

The flames die, though they leave behind their mark: messages burned into Fia Drumera's veil.

Nothing happens for a long time. Hours.

We sit in the heat of the noonday sun, needing more water, our bellies empty, and bodies so very tired.

But then, a spark of light catches my eye.

I glance up only to see the city gate opening, and a troop of guards in knee-length umber tunics with long curved swords come marching out onto the sands. They move in two lines.

Alexus holds his hand up for all of us to stay where we are. We freeze, watching and waiting, nerves rattling with anticipation as he walks close to the veil.

The guards step aside, one at a time, until a small figure is revealed draped in a golden gown.

She walks forward, a wind catching her long, black hair and whipping the skirt of her dress. Gold torques wrap her throat and wrists and ankles, glinting in the sunlight as she moves barefoot across the earth, her dark brown legs slipping from slits in her lovely dress. With every step, the sand sprays from her feet, and I swear I see small licks of fire at her heels. Everything about her radiates beauty and power and danger, like a deadly goddess floating across the sand.

She pauses before the veil, and without any fear or hesitation, traces her finger in an arch along the shimmering barrier, as though drawing an invisible door.

When the magick in that small little space vanishes, we see it happen, such a complex working. I think of the veils our village erected, how the Witch Walkers of Silver Hollow could barely hold it intact for minutes during the harvest supper attack, much less for centuries. And to carve from it? I cannot fathom that kind of control.

The woman appears young. Hel's age, perhaps. But I know who we're staring at, and she is over three hundred years old.

Fia Drumera—the Fire Queen.

ALEXUS

F ia's men lead us across the city on horseback.

Raina rides with me, her head turning this way and that trying to take it all in. The City of Ruin is a vast place, filled with many streets, many homes, and many people, all nestled beneath Mount Ulra. I remember it well, one memory my mind didn't lose, but it still feels new.

We are a spectacle, the rarely allowed visitors, and the queen is in our midst too, riding her white horse barefoot and without a saddle. Summer-landers flood into the street to see us—ten filthy travelers from the North and their beloved queen. From the looks on their faces, we Northlanders aren't much to behold. Only a curiosity. But the queen? They toss flowers at the feet of her horse, their faces lit up with adoration.

The air here smells of sand and earth as always, but also of flowers and food and *life*. Children's laughter drifts through the streets, along with occasional music and clamoring voices as we pass the market quarters. Magick is alive in the air, saturating my senses. There are enough magi inside these walls to fight a mighty war for Tiressia, something Fia has had to ask them to do many times. It isn't what she wants. She only wishes for safety for her people, a common life away from war. Something she has never been afforded.

As we turn down a particular street, the palace comes into view, consuming all thought. Its golden dome shines so bright in the sunlight that I squint.

Raina grips my hand as we ride toward the white marble structure, its facade and tall columns seemingly glowing from within. There are so many gardens surrounding the main buildings. I remember lingering behind to admire the fragrant blooms when Colden and I last came here. The city of Ruin hasn't changed. It's as frozen in time as me, Colden, and Fia.

When we arrive at the palace's main entry and dismount, the face of every person in our group appears taken aback by the beauty and size of Fia's home. Except Joran. He stands at his horse staring at the palace with half a smile. I can't pinpoint what it is about that look on his face. What it is he might be thinking. But it sets my teeth on edge.

I'm quickly distracted as Fia and a few guards approach. "This way," she says with a soft smile, and motions for me and Raina and everyone else to walk with her up the stairs into the public building. It seems she isn't fearful of being under the eye of her people. The respect they show her is a sign of her uniting leadership.

Much like at Min-Thuret and the School of Night and Dawn, the public areas are places of learning and study. Scholars and advanced students are quiet at work within the palace's school while other people move in and out of the main library, some with books in hand, others with parchment tablets and pens made of kohl for writing.

We cross through courtyards and gardens, then to the living areas that eventually lead to ballrooms and even more courtyards.

A gaggle of people hurry toward us. Fia's maidservants, I suppose.

"Please see everyone to a private room," she says. But then she glances back at me and Raina, and then at Hel and Rhonin standing hand in hand. "Or perhaps some would like joint rooms?"

"I would like my own room, please," Nephele says, lifting her hand, not at all afraid to speak up. Fia smiles, and I consider how this must feel for Nephele. She and Colden have a history that never included affairs of the heart, but Fia once meant everything to him.

"Consider it done," Fia says. "My staff will get you settled and make certain you have all you need during your time here." She glances at me, and I realize I'm about to part ways with my crew. "Alexus?" Fia says. "Come with me?"

I kiss Raina. "Go. I'm certain a bath is in your future. And rest. I'll be up shortly."

She doesn't look worried. She looks tired but utterly amazed at the glittering palace surrounding her.

In minutes, Fia and I and two guards are walking down a long, wide corridor to her apartments. We step inside, the guards too, and I find myself worrying she doesn't trust me.

Her rooms are a gilded affair, with ornate woodwork covering the fine furniture, walls, and golden doors. Across the rooms, however, are a large floor to ceiling opening with billowing sheers that leads out onto a covered portico overlooking a large packed-sand courtyard. It's the first in a series of terraced courtyards, each one stepping down to a final, vast level that's more of an amphitheater, big enough to hold such celebrations as the one Colden and I attended so long ago. Beyond that lies Asha's old temple.

Fia grabs a pitcher and two glasses and leads me outside, gesturing to a pillow on the stone porch near a small table, both made for kneeling or sitting and visiting.

I take a seat, cross-legged, facing the queen, and she joins me. I look over the courtyards. Even now, people are working to set up for some grand event, covering the space with tables and chairs and flower arrangements and lanterns.

"A wedding," she says. "Tomorrow night. Two of the scholars from the Hall of Holies."

"I'm certain it will be a beautiful celebration."

"I would love for you and your friends to attend."

I give her the most sheepish look I can muster. "Last time you invited me to a party, things didn't go so well."

She laughs. "I think that was Colden's fault more than yours. How dare he bring his beautiful self to the Summerlands," she says in jest, though I'm glad to hear her mention him. "Something quite terrible had to have happened for you to be here right now," she continues, filling our glasses with fresh water. "I can't imagine the journey you've made."

"A difficult one." I accept the offered glass and gulp the water down, my throat parched.

Fia takes a deep breath and exhales, folding her hands in her lap. "It clearly involves me somehow. I'd like to know."

I nod and set my glass on the table. She refills it, giving me a moment to collect my thoughts.

"The Prince of the East has embedded traitors in Malgros," I finally say. "He stole his army through the ports with traitorous aid and rode north into the valley where he wiped out four villages with the aid of a Summerlander siphon. There were very few survivors. Two are in our band. In fact, we have recently learned their mother was from Elam. She was a student at the Hall of Holies years back before she married and moved north to raise her family. Ophelia Moren-Sar."

Fia's eyes glitter with recollection, and she leans in, her head tilted. "Ophelia's children are here?"

"Raina and Nephele, yes. The woman who was with me, and the woman who requested her own room."

Fia chuckles a little at that. "I knew I liked her spark. She gets that from her mother."

I raise my brows. "You knew Ophelia well then?"

"Very well. She was a promising mage. But it seems love changed her path."

I sit there realizing how glad I am it did. Had Ophelia never followed her heart, I wouldn't have Raina.

"I am so sorry to hear of the north's loss, Alexus," Fia says, her face kind and sincere.

"There's more," I tell her, rubbing my fingertips up and down the smooth sides of my glass. "The Eastlanders entered Winterhold as well. Many died, and the prince took Colden back to Min-Thuret."

After a long moment of her blank stare, Fia inhales again, deeply, and lets the breath out, as though needing to collect herself. "He means to use Colden against me, then."

I shrug a shoulder. "Perhaps. I'm certain that's part of it. But there's so much more. Thamaos is communicating with the prince from the Shadow World, I have no doubt. And worse, the prince found Fleurie. I don't know where she was all these many years, but she's now alive and restored. We've been watching them as closely as possible for many weeks. The prince plans to resurrect Thamaos, and to use Fleurie and her portaling ability to do it."

She blinks rapidly at the wall of information I just threw at her. "Wait, let me think about this. Resurrection? That's impossible. The prince would need a remnant or a sacrifice, not to mention skill with ritual." She pauses. "Do you think he means to sacrifice Colden?"

My blood chills. I haven't thought about that second scenario because it wasn't needed. The prince has what he needs without surrendering anybody's life.

"I hope not," I reply. "Raina's father was the Keeper of the God Knife, Fia. I don't know how or why, but he was. When he died, the knife's curse passed to Raina, but the prince still managed to steal it."

I don't tell her the story about me being Un Drallag. That will have to come at another time. I was a spy, in her homeland. I brought no harm, but I am still a man made from the enemies of her past.

"A Keeper? That's a Summerland distinction."

"I know. There was Summerlander magick all over the blade. I couldn't tell who it belonged to, though."

"Perhaps Ophelia figured out a way to give her husband dominion over the blade. If I had the weapon, I might be able to answer that question. Otherwise we might never know." She lowers her head for a moment and scrubs her hands over her face before looking at me again. "Next question. You mentioned Fleurie. As in Thamaos's daughter who was murdered?"

"She wasn't murdered. She lived. I don't know how, but she did. When the prince recovered her, she was little more than bones."

She shakes her head and crumples her smooth brow. "How do you know this?"

"Raina is a Seer. It's a long and complex story, but she can see Colden and Fleurie. The prince is guarded by his Brotherhood from her gift of Sight. Still, he is visible to her in a red cloud through Colden and Fleurie's eyes."

Fia sits back, hands on her knees, her spine stiff. "Why would Fleurie help the prince, though? Her father was so cruel. Best I recall, she hated him."

"Because to live again, the prince forced her to make a deal. At least that's what I figure. Fleurie wouldn't have done it any other way."

Fia looks out over the courtyards, her dark brown eyes bright with worry. "She could portal him right into the Grove of the Gods. Right into this palace." She turns back to me. "Can she portal an army?"

I shake my head. "No, that was always too difficult. I can't imagine her suddenly being capable of such a thing."

Relief passes over Fia's face, but then her expression changes into one of controlled panic. "This is a nightmare, Alexus. We need to stop them somehow. Now. And retrieve Colden before the prince gets him killed."

"We do. But I don't know how."

"If I could portal there, I would take him back myself," she says. "For that matter, I would take the prince too. That man has my wrath ahead of him one day, and I plan to make him suffer."

"Do you have a portalist in your city with that level of ability?" I ask, worried about even mentioning this, though I have no choice. The moment I say it however, I realize that if she did, she would've already snatched the prince and destroyed him a long time ago.

"We had one, yes," she says, "but he died a few years back. He was no godling, though. Most portalists are bound to their homeland. It's an unfortunate limitation to that sort of magick in mortals."

I think of myself, my ability to take to the sky. Much as I wish it were possible, I don't think I could make it all the way to Quezira.

Then I think of Raina. She isn't a portalist, but her talent could swing this situation in our favor. Quickly. The problem is that I can't stand by and watch her risk everything to walk into Min-Thuret in hopes that she can bring Colden back. Certainly not the prince, though that would stop this effort of resurrection in its tracks.

Still, I know that Fia will find out. If I don't tell her, Raina will. She hasn't thought of this solution just yet—there's been too much else happening. But now we're here, in a place of calm, where she can think. It's only a matter of time before she looks at me, those big, blue eyes lit up with clever intelligence, and suggests that she save us all.

"Raina has a gift," I say, the words thick in my throat.

I have such a fear of losing her. An almost irrational fear. It's deep and terrifying, and I cannot understand it. Fear feasts on those with something to lose—Raina has signed those words to me before—and they are true. But this... This is more than that. This is... a knowing.

"What sort of gift?" Fia asks.

I take a drink of water to loosen my throat, or I might not get the words out. "We don't really know. She calls it her *abyss*. She and I were bonded a couple of months ago. When she had to learn to navigate the bond and began going into her mind to traverse the connection, she found the void. It was a fear for her for a long time. Her mother glamoured Raina's magick all her life, so I've a feeling it's something Ophelia knew about and thought it better to hide. It only came into existence after Ophelia's shields fell. But... Raina can use that abyss to... *move*. She must have seen where she's going, but it's how we ended up here as quickly as we did. I would describe it as something between sifting and portaling. If I could imagine realm walking, it might be like that."

Fia slumps her shoulders and rubs her brow. "I wish I knew what it is, but I don't. To my knowledge, Ophelia had no such ability, so it wasn't handed down from her." She looks up, her eyes intent. "She has seen Min-Thuret through Sight, hasn't she?"

I let out a breath and clasp my glass in my hands. "Yes. She has seen it."

Fia reaches over and folds her small, brown hand around my wrist, her eyes soft. "You love her."

I nod once. "I do. And I am terrified to place her in this position."

"But that is her decision to make, Alexus. Hers and hers alone. She could stop the prince before this gets any worse and more people die."

"She could also fail. She could walk into a trap."

Her black eyebrows raise toward her hairline. "You could go with her. I saw what you did at the wall. I'd heard rumors eons ago that your magick was gone because of some ordeal with Neri. But that magick at the veil was not common magick. It's the kind of magick that tells me you can rewrite the moment if you so choose, and that Raina would be safe with you in her midst."

I almost laugh. She hasn't been safe so far. Granted, I wasn't fully in my power, and I'm still not, but I'm close.

Perhaps I *could* go with her. We cannot know what protections the Brotherhood might have in place, what we might be up against. It could end in our capture, though they would have a difficult time holding me, and I would bury all of Quezira to get Raina out. It still seems dangerous, and the truth hits me then. I would sacrifice just about anything to save Tiressia, even my own life.

Just not Raina's.

"I need time to think." I sit my glass on the small table. "I'll have Raina consult the waters, so we have a better sense of our timeline. Fleurie has been practicing portaling, but there's no way to know when she will actually do it."

Fia nods. "In the meantime, I'll send guards to Mount Ulra to stand watch over the grove and over Thamaos's grave. If I didn't need a remnant for his tree to release him, I would exhume that bastard myself and grind his bones to dust."

I smile at her, though I'm tired and worried, so it's a weak effort. "I'm glad to see you are still filled with your usual fire."

Smiling back, she lifts her hand and near-translucent flames race down to her elbow. "Always." She shakes her fingers, and the flames vanish as she sweeps her hand toward the courtyards. "Will you all attend the wedding? It would be an honor to have you."

I tell myself that all this fear that's eating at me is uncalled for, and yet I feel it even now, as though by attending an event at this palace is an omen for trouble. Lives were destroyed the last time I set foot here. But that's a ridiculous notion. History cannot repeat itself with Asha and Neri in their graves.

"Yes," I tell her. "We will come."

NEPHELE

"**I** agree."

I stare at Neri through the portal of Joran's eyes. "You agree. Just like that?"

He huffs a laugh. "Yes. Just like that."

"Tonight," I repeat. "You will fly your godly ass to Quezira, give Colden his power back, and help him escape. *Tonight.*"

He leans back on the gilded desk in my chambers, smiling. "I will. I'll leave shortly if you'd like, but I'll need to lock Joran's body up somewhere. You can have your sister check the waters when I return. Colden Moeshka will be a free man in exchange for you marching up to the Grove of the Gods after the fact and letting me walk you through the ritual to bring me back to life."

I sit on the edge of my bed, wondering if dealing with a god is the worst thing I've ever done. "But once you're resurrected," I add, "you are mine to command. For as long as I live."

Surely everyone will see the benefit in this. If only he could get through the Brotherhood's barrier to reach the prince. Raina had said that Neri holds no power over the magick of men. Only his own and the magick he bestowed while he was alive. Perhaps he can reach the prince once he's no longer bound to spirit form.

He smiles wider, his face full of satisfied seduction, his hands folded around the desk's edge. "Yes. After you bring me back, I am all yours. I don't see how this ends badly for me."

Gods like permanence. That much I'm learning. They like things that are eternal or immortal or ageless. This deal will probably only last for the span of another forty years if I'm lucky, which is a lifetime for me, and but a breath in his existence. And yet he's happy.

"Why are you so content to be my slave?"

He folds his arms over his chest and laughs aloud. "Are you serious? I want you. You're giving yourself to me. Of course, I'm happy."

I narrow my eyes and stand, fidgeting and nervous that I've already laid something out wrong, and that it might already be too late to change any of it.

"You are the one who will be obligated to me. To my wishes. To my commands. To my needs."

He arches a brow. "Again. I do not see how this ends badly for me."

I scrunch up my face. "Is sex all gods ever think about? That's not what I mean. I do not want you for *that,* not ever."

"Not all gods, but I've been known to fancy a pretty face and fiery temper. And the thing you don't understand is that I have the power to sway your opinions of me. It won't be very hard. It will most likely be much fun. Your *wishes, commands, and needs* will morph in time to exactly the kinds of *wishes, commands, and needs* I want to fulfill. If I must protect the North-lands at your order in the meantime, so be it." He laughs again. "I never wanted to be a king, and I never seated kings or queens in my lands either, but I can see you wearing a crown, stalking around Winterhold during the day, then wearing nothing but that crown at night when you're with me. This might be the best deal I've ever made, and I've made my share."

Made. Meaning it's already done. Gods' death.

"First of all," I tell him, closing the distance between us. "I will never take your wolf ass to bed."

"I thought it was a godly ass. You really haven't even seen it in its true form. I bet you change your mind."

My eyes and nostrils flare. "Secondly, you are not allowed to pester me about this constantly."

Another laugh. "You should have mentioned that in your deal. For now, I can do whatever I want. After I'm a living, breathing god and not wearing the skin of a pathetic man, you can command me to leave you alone. Until then, all is fair."

Someone knocks on my door. I stalk across the room and answer. A maidservant stands in the hall wearing a bright smile and holding a silver platter with a small golden, glass jar and a lovely ecru envelope.

"From the queen," she says.

"Thank you so much," I reply, taking the gifts.

When she's gone, I close the door and hurry to the desk. Shoving Neri off its edge, I set the jar on the desktop and pick up the pretty gold letter opener to unseal the envelope.

"It's an invitation to a wedding tomorrow night." I glance up at him as he takes the jar in his hand and tugs open the cork stopper. A flurry of gold dust swirls between us. I cough. "What is that?"

Holding my gaze, he tips the jar so I can see the contents.

"Gold dust? Is everything here made of gold? What the bleeding devils do we do with it?"

He smiles and dips his finger inside, then he reaches out and drags that finger down the center of my chest where my stupid tunic keeps coming untied.

I jerk away before he gets too far and tie it again.

He lifts the jar to his nose and inhales like he's smelling a rose. "Fever lilac dust. An aphrodisiac that's part of wedding ceremonies here. I've been covered in this so thoroughly that my golden, godly ass fucked a woman for a week."

I toss the invitation aside and grab the jar and cork and stuff that damn thing back inside before rubbing the dust from my chest as best I can. Just from inhaling it, and that little bit of gold on my sternum, I'm tingling in places I should not be tingling, not with Neri around.

"Get out." I sling my finger toward the door. "Get out now."

Neri smiles and laughs, leaning closer. "Is someone hot and bothered?" My tunic ties come undone again, and my shirt falls open. "Need some time alone?"

That bastard. Where is a dagger when I need one?

I reach for the letter opener, hold it to his throat, and start walking him toward the door. "Get out. Get out, get out, get out!"

He pauses, his hand on the ornate knob, his smirk enough to make me murderous. "Have fun," he says, "but be careful." He takes a long inhale, and his eyes flare. "I can tell it doesn't take much of that dust to get you wet and ready."

I rear back, but Neri wisely slips into the hall before I impale Joran's face on the end of a letter opener.

I slam the door and lean my back against it, clutching the letter opener between my breasts, panting like I've run a race, even as my blood hums with a tickle of desire.

There is no question. Dealing with a god is, in fact, the worst thing I've ever done. I hope Colden appreciates this.

61

THE PRINCE WITH NO NAME

The Eastland Territories
City of Quezira
Min-Thuret, Prince's Chambers

"Dinner? Actual food and not someone's soul? This is an odd occurrence. Are you planning on poisoning me?"

Colden sits in the chair across from me, flapping his linen napkin before laying it across his lap. I sent him a change of clothes, so he wears a fine pewter tunic and dinner jacket with silver embroidery at the cuffs and collar. He's bathed again, and he smells like rosewood and musk. I almost hate myself for how much I like it.

"You always insist that I mean to kill you," I say, carefully cutting into my lamb.

"Because that's what you mean to do," he replies, taking up his fork and knife. "Or you did when you first brought me here. You didn't feed me for a week, damn you."

After a bite, I grab the wine and tilt the bottle to fill his glass. "Perhaps I'm reconsidering things."

He spears a stewed carrot on the end of his fork. "How so? You're reconsidering sacrificing me to taunt Fia? I somehow doubt daddy Thamaos will be thrilled to hear that. I'd bet my throne he's the one who told you to use me in the first place."

I don't rile at his words. I have a choice to lay before him. We shall see what he decides.

"I've a proposition."

He stares at me, chewing. "I'm listening."

I set my fork and knife aside and thread my fingers together, elbows on the table. "I've come up with an alternative plan to get what I need from the Summerlands. Something that doesn't require using you as bait."

Colden raises his brows. "Fleurie, obviously."

"She's part of it. If a large part of my men in Malgros don't succeed at finding Alexi and Raina Bloodgood. But there's more."

A glint of worry flashes in his eyes. "And that is?"

"A focus on control. On power. To finally begin uniting this broken empire."

He blinks at me. "You realize that it's only broken in physical form, the division of land from natural forces a very long time ago. Any other brokenness has come at your hand and the hand of Thamaos and his many kings."

I take a deep breath. "Sometimes I envy your wholesomeness."

He almost chokes on his wine. "I've been called *many* things, but never *wholesome*. However, I think you mean goodness, and those are two different things."

I shrug. "I only mean that you see things so simply."

"I imagine you did too at one time. Before you let Thamaos dig his evil claws into your brain." He matches my pose, resting his arms on the table, threading his lovely, slender fingers, leaning in. "I bet you were brilliant and beautiful and everything a man like me would want," he says, his voice low and soft over the crackling fire burning in the hearth. "I feel like I see that man inside your eyes sometimes. I saw him thirty years ago. But he's certainly just a ghost now, isn't he?"

Slowly, I shake my head. "He's no ghost. He's still in there. He's just been buried, but you are slowly bringing him back to life. He wants you,

Colden. He just also wants to unite these lands. Something we could do together."

Colden's eyes are dark and shimmering, as though they contain the night and all the stars. "Is that your proposition? Because understand that we would not go about such a thing the same way," he says. "You want to reign over lands that do not want or need your control. I want everyone to live as they so desire."

I narrow my eyes. "That's why you forced people to enlist in your Northland Watch? To leave their homes and shield your kingdom? Is that not how you just described me? Perhaps we're more similar than you'd like to admit."

He laughs, the sound warm and deep. "I am a terrible king. I will never deny that. It isn't a job I wanted. It was cast upon me, and I have remained steadfast. Our lands have maintained neutrality through centuries of war, especially these last thirty years. There are systems in place that allow us to have some semblance of control and order and protection, but ultimately, until you broke King Regner's treaty, my people have been safe from worrying about you or your army. It might not have been enough for all, but it was the best I knew how to give them."

I study him, a three-hundred-year-old man trapped in perpetual youth. We *are* similar, only I'm much uglier on the inside.

"Think about it," I tell him. "There's a little time. But things are about to change here, and war with Fia Drumera will eventually be something I face unless she chooses to finally stand down. I would very much like to have you at my side. Even Alexi, if he will cooperate."

More laughter bursts from Colden as he tosses back his blond head. "The day that Alexus Thibault sets foot on this soil with any other purpose than to bring your end will be the day the sun falls from the sky. He would never serve you willingly, much less power you through whatever ridiculousness you're planning. And I won't be at your side, either. You might no longer be willing to lose me to Asha's curse in the Summerlands because we both know that Fia would have to let me die, but that doesn't mean you win my heart. You want everything at the cost of nothing, and unfortunately, life does not work that way. To *play* with the side of the right, you must be *on* the side of the right. And world domination, or even Tiressian domination, is not that side." He shucks his napkin at his plate and stands, stepping away from the table. "I want to go back to my prison cell, oh kind prince. I've had enough shite for one night."

I stand and, after a moment of hesitance, cross the short distance between us and look into his eyes. I see anger, but I also see frustration and disappointment.

"It doesn't have to be this way," I say.

He scoffs and shakes his head, his brows lifted. "No. It doesn't."

I move closer, and he doesn't budge, but his eyes rove over my face, and I can sense the urge in him that he's trying so hard to deny. It makes my heart beat harder, faster.

"You're right. I want the impossible." I trace my thumb over his full bottom lip, and I don't miss the breath that leaves him at my touch. "This is all going to end soon. You will probably hate me when it does, but I will return you to Winterhold if that's what you want. You have one final role to play, and I'm not even certain what it is, but I won't let any harm come to you."

"No harm?" he says. "Not certain I believe you. You hated me weeks ago."

"I never hated you." I swallow thickly, my throat constricting around my words, some dark part of me trying to control my honesty. But if he hears nothing else tonight, I need him to hear this. "I wanted you," I tell him. "And I knew I could not have you. I left you alone for thirty years because of that, even when my general insisted that I invade the North and make use of your Witch Walkers. I *hated* that you were the pawn Thamaos required me to collect. That it was *your* land I had to destroy. I had to go into the darkest part of myself and let that man reign just so I could manage it. It killed me that *you* were the man I had to lock in my dungeon, when all I've wanted since that night we kissed was for you to be the man at my side and in my bed. I wanted your heart, and yet I had your disgust. I wanted your affection, yet I had your loathing. I wanted *you*, and yet I had loneliness."

"More's the pity," he says, his face hard, his jaw clenching. "You could've refused Thamaos. Or is his poison truly that deep in your veins? Has he scrambled your mind that thoroughly from the grave?" He pauses and studies me. "Perhaps you should consider why Thamaos made *me* the requirement. Was it truly to bring down Fia if you can so easily discard me as a tool in this game?" He tilts his head. "Or is he fooling you? Is he preparing to test your loyalty?"

"He knows nothing about you and me. I would never reveal that."

His brow wrinkles. "Why not? You were already prepared to end me."

"That was before you were here. Before I had to see your face nearly every day. Hear your voice. Your crude jokes. That laugh that infuriated me until I couldn't sleep for hearing it. It was before I watched you move naked across a room, before I saw you stare at me from a bath, before I saw you smile a genuine smile, before you entranced me all over again, you bastard."

He shakes his head, staring at me as though I am a lost hope. "Desire is only desire, prince. Until you're willing to sacrifice something of yourself for another, it is nothing more than that. Nothing deeper. Nothing *real*."

"Nothing real?" I glance at his mouth, take his face in my hands, and press my lips to his. He doesn't stop me, much to my surprise. Instead, he opens for me, as though this is what he's wanted all night.

It's strange, this. I remember the feel of his mouth on mine. The sweet taste of him, of dark wine and temptation. It's so unexpectedly enchanting that I trace his lips with my tongue, each dip and lush curve still devastatingly familiar after all this time.

He grips my hips, tugging me closer. I kiss him the way I've dreamed about kissing him nearly every night these last weeks, the way I dreamed about kissing him for years before. After longing to forget him, and after wanting to hate him with the passion of an immortal enemy, I'm now reveling in his breathlessness, his eagerness, his hardness. The way his body answers to my kiss.

"This is real," I say against his mouth, dragging my hands into his hair. "You cannot tell me it isn't."

He kisses me once more, as though needing a final taste, his tongue sliding along mine, his full lips so soft and hungry, I might think of nothing else after this.

But then he pulls away and presses his forehead to mine. "That is desire. Only desire. If you want more than that from me, you must prove it, and that means not hurting the people I love. It means not hurting people at all. It means not standing at Thamaos's side because you're standing by *mine*."

He lets go of me and steps back, half stumbling as though he's as drunk from that kiss as I am. I watch him move toward the door where Thresh awaits outside to escort him back to his cell.

Before he goes, he turns to look at me from over his shoulder. "What you want, prince, is love. Something you don't understand in the least, and something I haven't given away in a very long time. I could, though, I think. If you were a different sort of man, the sort of man I think you might've been once upon a time. The sort of man I think you could still be. If you could be him, I could love you."

With that, he opens the door, and I let him go.

⚜

"It hasn't been seven days," Fleurie says as she walks into my chambers later that night.

Her bare feet whisper across the woven rug spread over the stone floor. She looks fully healed, her hair somehow an even brighter shade of red, bold against the white tunic she wears.

I give up trying to eat and stand, turning up the glass of wine in my hand. Nonchalantly, I flick a finger for Thresh to leave.

"No, it hasn't," I reply, "but this isn't about that," I tell her as my captain closes the door. "I had a conversation with your father, and the plans have... changed a little."

In Rite Hall, Fleurie had stood so calmly. Tonight, she begins roaming around my room, touching all manner of things, as though inspecting my life.

I've had enough inspection tonight. Time to tuck in my *feelings* and focus on the matter at hand.

"Changed how?" She drifts her finger over my desk. Casually, she lifts a book, reads the spine, and lays it back down.

"You and I are going to have an adventure." I turn, following her with my gaze, the heat of the hearth warm against my left side. "I need a way to subdue Alexi of Ghent once I get him here. I've thought about it for weeks."

Colden will hate me for this, but I've come too far to turn back now, especially for *love*, because the more I think about it, the more I realize he's right. Love isn't something I know how to feel. Only want and hunger and need, the basest emotions stemming from a long life as a Soul Eater, another part of me I cannot possibly change, a part I'm certain Colden could never live with.

Fleurie pauses her perusal at my antiquities cabinet and faces me. "You cannot subdue Alexi of Ghent for a few minutes, let alone any significant amount of time. Even if I can find a way to bring him here to fulfill my end of your deal, he will destroy you. He will destroy Min-Thuret."

"As I said, things have changed, and I have a plan," I tell her, and I do. A plan that Thamaos presented recently in Rite Hall. "You and I are going to make a trial run of your power. I have somewhere I need you to take me. It would be a dangerous excursion for anyone else because the people there can nullify magick, and we need to bring a few back with us. They're fighters, but they're no danger for a godling, I assume."

She lets out a long breath, her jaw twitching, her fists tightening at her sides as she realizes what I mean to do. "I'm a portalist. Not your warrior. I didn't agree to such terms."

I hold up my finger. "Oh, but you did. You agreed to help me locate a sorcerer and to bring them to my palace for safekeeping, no matter what that might entail. This is part of that. I can't keep Un Drallag here if I don't have the means, just like you said. Once he's here, however, with the plan your father helped me discern, we can subdue him, and then my Brotherhood can conceive a more permanent solution."

Honestly, I expect to stoke her ire, but instead, she just looks... forlorn. And perhaps... defeated. As though she knows there's no reason to fight me.

Her face does flush, however, her usually pale white skin changing to a rosy pink. "You want me to take you to the Summerlands."

I narrow my eyes at her. "I do. How did you know?"

She just shakes her head, her eyes downcast. Again, her entire presence is saturated in deep sadness and more defeat. "A guess," she says. "So tell me what you demand of me. Where exactly am I to take you?"

Reaching into my vest, I withdraw the small map tucked away there and cross the room, where I unroll it on the desk. Fleurie comes closer, and stands at my side, studying the drawing.

I tap the area located in western Itunnan, in the Summerlands, a world I've had no access to for decades. Until now. "I need you to take me to a place called Aki-Ra Quarter."

62

ALEXUS

I
t's early evening when we all meet up at the main courtyard for a
dinner with Fia.
  We've scrubbed all proof of our journey away and have been
groomed by the palace's maidservants until we look like we haven't been
through any difficulty at all these last days.

The outside table—decorated with colorful glass lanterns and tall vases
of red flowers—is set for eleven, with Fia residing at the head. She's
dressed in black tonight, regal and lovely.

On the side of the courtyard sit musicians with stringed instruments
including a harp, each one playing their part in a quiet song. Raina sits
beside me, smelling like a rose and dressed in red again, her neckline
plunging to her bellybutton.

I lean over to whisper in her ear. "That dress might be the death of me.
Who needs food? All I want is to take you back to our room and make love
to you for the rest of the night."

A soft blush touches her cheeks, something that might always make me
swoon.

"We are guests," she signs, keeping her gestures small and between us.
"And so present we must be."

And yet, she drags her hand beneath the table, from the top of my thigh to my knee and back up a little past halfway, sliding inward, teasing just the tip of my cock.

"Evil woman," I whisper, and she just smiles.

I'm so glad to see that smile. These are not the easiest of times, and when she checked the waters earlier today, Vexx had arrived in the East, and she still couldn't see Finn. Worry is eating at her, but I'm hoping that tonight provides a little distraction.

"A toast," Fia says, standing at the head of the table with her glass raised in the air. "To the future," she says. "May we be the shining lights who change the days to come."

We clink our glasses of sparkling wine, and the dinner attendants begin passing platters of food around.

"Where's Joran?" I ask Nephele who sits across from me. I point to the only empty place setting, the one beside her. Everyone else is here.

At my question, she chugs her wine.

"No idea, really. Maybe he wasn't hungry." She fidgets with the ruffle running down the front of her jade green dress, then her hand moves to a small ruby pendant hanging from her neck that I've never seen.

I sense a lie. I know her. Perhaps they had an argument.

"Well, I'm famished," Rhonin says, plucking two bread rolls as the basket passes. Helena smiles, sitting close beside him.

"With all that moaning coming from your room earlier today," Keth says, voice low so that Fia doesn't hear, "I can imagine why."

Zahira smacks at Keth's hand, though she wears a smile, and Rhonin turns so many shades of red that I'm certain one of them matches Raina's dress. Everyone seems happy, save for Nephele who looks nervous and on edge. I'm certain it has something to do with Joran.

After dinner, Raina and I walk the terraced courtyards, still sipping wine, before we head back to our room. Standing at the vanity table, I slip off my shoes and strip off my tunic and iron key, neatly laying everything aside. There's already a low fire burning in the hearth to ward off the desert chill, and the candles around the room have been lit.

When I turn around, I don't expect to see Raina standing a few feet away, already naked, holding a small golden jar and wearing a rather erotic smile and a display of bright witch's marks. But that's what I find, and I couldn't be more pleased.

I shake my head in admiration of her lovely body and move toward her, returning her smile. Standing close, I tap the top of the jar. "What's this?"

She unstops the cork, carefully, and hands me the jar. I should've remembered. Fia is a woman of tradition.

"Fever Lilac dust." I hold the jar to my nose to smell that cloying scent, laced with hints of rose and vanilla.

"A gift," she signs. *"From Fia."*

"Do you remember my story about this?"

She arches a brow. *"What do you think?"*

I wrap my arm around her waist and draw her against me. "We can't use too much. That's the only rule."

Though I'm glad her mind is on us, and that she feels like using it at all.

She makes a face, questioning me, asking *why.*

"Because, if I paint you in this like the couple from the wedding will do tomorrow night, we won't leave this room for a month. We still have a king and a world to save."

She pinches her finger and thumb together, squinting one eye.

I can't help but laugh. "Gods, you are so adorable. Yes. We can still try a little."

It is exceptionally difficult to keep myself from covering her in golden dust from head to foot. Trying to think with reason, I lead Raina to the bed and lay her down. Crawling over her, still wearing my black trousers from dinner, I sprinkle a tiny amount of dust between her breasts, right over her heart where two simple flourishes curve over the swell of her breasts.

The dust spreads quickly, glittering her skin with a soft, golden sheen. Using a small taste of my magick, I draw my hands over her breasts, her shoulders, down her arms, feeling her skin pebble beneath my palms. Then I move lower, straddling her ankles as I rub more dust over the curves of her legs and hips.

It's such a sensual experience, touching her this way, taking my time to feel her curves, to memorize every little dip and valley on her body. Before I left them behind, I sketched images of her in my journals from memory. But I think I would like to draw her like this, posed for me so that I might be forced to notice everything. Every scar. Every freckle. Every witch's mark. The sleek line of her spine. The dimples at her lower back.

Already, she's breathing heavy, massaging her breasts, tweaking her nipples. The sight makes my blood rush and my cock hard as steel.

I move between her legs and use my knees to knock hers wider. She opens for me without any resistance, revealing that slick, pink center I'll never get enough of.

Carefully, I sprinkle a little more dust, right over her pussy. I rub her gently at first, working the dust into her flesh, watching her writhe as she grows wetter and wetter for me. I can feel the dust working on me too, a heady arousal that feels like we're in another world, just the two of us.

Kneeling there, I thrust my fingers inside her, fluttering them with a tickle of my power, and she arches off the bed. Her lips part on the sweetest gasp. After long moments, her eyes meet mine, hazed with desire as I work her deep before finding that magickal little place inside that sends her reeling.

"Do you like it when I fuck your pussy like this?"

She nods, a silent whimper visible on her face. It makes me smile as I bend down and drag my tongue up the length of her slit.

"And you like it when I lick your pussy?"

She shoves her fingers into her hair, nodding again, working against my hand.

"Do you like it when I talk to you like this?"

Another nod, and this time, her hands move into *my* hair.

I lean back down and devour her, fucking her all the while with my fingers, sucking and nibbling her perfect little clit until she's grinding against my mouth, seeking the magick on my tongue.

When I pull back to look at her, to see that golden skin shimmering in the firelight, her eyes are all but on fire. She shoves up and pushes at me, grabbing the jar I sat aside. I obey and crawl off the bed.

My feet no sooner hit the floor than her hand is on my chest, and she's driving me backward until I'm pressed against the wall.

I smile, and she holds my gaze while unlacing my pants. Quickly, they drop to my ankles, and I kick them aside.

Raina pours just enough Fever Lilac dust in her hand, then she sprinkles the gold powder over my chest. Using both hands, she spreads it over my shoulders and arms, down my torso, and then she's on her knees—where I think she wanted to be in the first place—gripping my cock with both hands, staring up at me as she twists her wrists, working me in a way that makes me yearn to be inside her.

She strokes me, and the moment she puts her mouth on me, I feel my control slipping. I slide my hands into her hair, ready to fuck her lovely mouth down to her throat. But I pause.

With a tender touch, I brush my thumb over the curve of her bottom lip as she stares up at me with those hungry, dark blue eyes. The sight of her on her knees before me, naked and ravenous and golden, spurns deepest desire.

But there's something else about seeing her like this. Something that makes my blood heat in a different way.

Anger, the fire of a thousand suns, an emotion that shouldn't be anywhere near this moment. But it is, and I need it gone.

Before she can protest, I reach down, sweep her up in my arms, and carry her to bed where I lie beside her and draw her to me.

"This is better," I tell her.

She pushes up on her elbow, dark hair framing her beautiful face, confusion writing itself into the lines between her brows.

"Did I do something wrong?" she signs, a glint of hurt in her eyes.

"Gods, no." I sit up against the pillows and clasp her face. "Raina, there is nothing I want more than your mouth on my body." I lean in and kiss her. "I have ached to take you that way more times than you can count since that night at Starworth Tor. It's just that..." I swallow the tightness in my throat as I search for words, a reason why I stopped her that doesn't sound like madness. And the answer hits me. "You bow to no one," I tell her, my voice graver than it has any right to be tonight. "Do you hear me? Not ever. Especially not to me."

She crawls up my body and straddles my hips. Not another word is said as she takes me inside her, then leans down, one arm around my neck as she moves slowly, taking her time, taking me deep.

I was too eager moments before, so I haven't yet asked, but I think tonight we both might need tenderness. I can feel it in the way she kisses me, as though that simple connection is enough for her to enter my soul, to memorize who I am, who I've become under her care.

I don't hide anything. I have no fear anymore. Any darkness, she has destroyed with her light. Every shadowy, gloomy place inside me feels remade because of her. I feel *healed*.

She tightens her fingers in my hair and presses her lips to my throat, tasting the skin over my pulse as her other hand traces my rune. I fold my arms around her and hold her tight, moving with her, and a different kind of instinct takes over, something so intimate that we begin to move in a beautiful rhythm, our bodies gliding in perfect time, like when we were in the pool at Starworth Tor. Every movement is fluid, every thrust met with slick grace, our hands and mouths finding that sensual rhythm. It's a dance, one our bodies have learned these last weeks, but tonight it's perfected.

Raina kisses me, her mouth brushing mine, the soft drag of her bottom lip enough to give way to sweet pleasure.

I plunge my hands into her hair to the wrists and inhale her, this kiss is so much more than just a kiss. It's a promise. An oath. I already know that before she presses one word to the skin over my heart.

"Mine."

"Yes," I whisper. "Always. El om ze pera. Lohanran tu gra." She pulls back, and I see the question in her eyes, the recollection. "I was supposed to tell you what that means when we were in Malgros." She nods, eager for me to continue. "It means, *There is no other. You are my only temple.* I love you, Raina." I've said those words before, when things were different, but tonight, I can see that she hears me. That my words are etching themselves across her heart. "I meant it," I tell her. "I swear I have loved you all my life. And when we are gone from this world, I will love you still."

"I love you the same," she signs, and I cannot stop the smile that breaks across my face. My heart feels discovered. Like a lost thing finally found by the one meant to hold it.

Tears fill her eyes, and when they fall, I kiss them away. Again, we begin our dance, making love as though we might never have the chance again, lost in a euphoria that makes it feel as though we're floating among the stars.

Suddenly, a strange feeling comes over me. I grip her hip.

I can feel her.

I can feel her through the bond.

Clasping her face, I stare into her eyes. Now, when I look for her in my mind, she's there. As though she never left.

The threads of our magick begin weaving together, a tight braid chasing along the bond.

I shake my head, confused.

"I healed the bond," she signs, laughing and weeping. *"I did not know if I could."*

It is impossible to express the joy I feel. I'm not certain even Raina would understand it. But this—being with her—feels like my fate has finally arrived. The overwhelming relief of this night is incalculable, because the thing most precious to me in this world is *with* me, in my arms, and she's mine.

Hungered like never before, I turn her over, pressing a kiss to the smooth skin beneath her delicate collarbone that used to bear her rune. That still does, I suppose. Inside.

"I hope you aren't sleepy," I tell her as she completes the tangling of our magick. She smiles and shakes her head, and I bury myself inside her. "Because tonight," I whisper, "we're going to rattle this city."

63

COLDEN

The Eastland Territories
City of Quezira
Min-Thuret, Dungeons

Fleurie is gone.

I passed her in the courtyard earlier tonight. I was leaving the prince, and she was going to him.

Now I lie on my cot, staring at this damn stone ceiling, wondering what the prince is doing with her. Is he portaling to Alexus? She's ready to attempt such a feat, but I'm thankful that she has hidden it for as long as she has.

He said that things were about to change, so I fully expect Alexus to show up any time. Though I still, after all these weeks, cannot fathom how the prince thinks he can keep Alexus here.

I also cannot fathom how he thinks I would change everything about who I am for him. That I would stand at his side as he ruled our world with Thamaos. But I also asked him to be a different person. I could love him if he was someone else. The problem is that neither of us is willing to alter ourselves enough to suit the other. Not in this lifetime.

I've almost drifted to sleep when I hear a sound on the stairs. I look up first and see a long shadow. Then I sit up.

The very last thing I expect comes sauntering down the stairs like the prowling wolf he is. Neri.

I blink and rub my eyes, certain that the prince had to have drugged my wine. But when I look up again, Neri's still there, stepping off the bottom stone of the stairs, frost covering the earthen floor in his wake.

"Colden Moeshka," he says, gripping the bars of my cell. "I'm here to set you free."

I start laughing. I don't know what comes over me. I am very clearly drugged, high as a kite soaring on Malgros's shore.

Neri frowns. "You giddy bastard, what's wrong with you?" He grips the bars and again, and frost coats the iron in a blue-white glaze.

Cold drifts into my cell, rolling off Neri in waves, sending a familiar chill across my skin. He's really here.

I get up and start toward the cell door, but I pause, hesitant and untrusting as fuck.

"Freedom, gifted by you, wouldn't be a kindness," I tell him. "I know better than to think it would. You must get something in return. That's simply how you operate."

"I am very much a dealmaker. What makes you think it isn't a deal that brought me here?"

I narrow my eyes. "A deal with who?"

I don't expect him to tell me. I expect a vague reply meant to leave me guessing. Instead...

"Nephele Bloodgood."

My stomach turns heavy as a lump of iron. "She would never."

He laughs, his lip curling back over a fang. "Seems as though I've heard that said about her before. You underestimate that woman's determination to get what she wants."

My blood chills in a way it hasn't since Winter Road, and I stalk closer to the bars. "What did you do? How is she beholden to you?"

It takes him a moment to reply, and for the flash of a second, I swear I see a bruised ego. "She's a clever witch. Perhaps I'm beholden to her."

Though I want to believe that's the case, I shake my head, clenching my fists. "She had to bargain as well. What are you taking from her?"

He leans in, a snarl on his face. "I'm taking nothing from her. She's giving me life in exchange for me returning your power and setting you free. She also gains my servitude for as long as she lives. She and I will be connected for the rest of her days, and there isn't anything you can do about it."

Stunned, I blink and scrub my hand over my mouth. Clever witch indeed, though the thought of my Nephele enduring this beast's presence for the rest of her life...

"I don't have to accept."

A low growl leaves his chest. "You would deny my aid?"

I consider this in a way I don't think I would have months ago. On Winter Road, feeling defenseless—save for my sword—after so many years of having the power to protect myself and those I love, was the closest thing to death I've experienced. My power felt like such a safe haven, more than I realized, and I was unmoored when Neri took it away.

And yet, after some time without it, I feel more like the young man I used to be. I feel the warmth in a touch a different way, the heat of a kiss, the soothing warmth of a bath. Even firelight is a different sort of pleasure now, rain and sun on my skin. Now, all these simple things are comfort to my weary bones rather than a reminder of the humanity I lost.

I might still have eternal life until someone takes my head, but without that old power, I will live those days more like a man and less like a god.

"You need to think about this?" Neri says. "You are captive in the East-land Territories, soldier. Do you remember nothing of your training under my leadership?"

"Apologies, but it's been an age." I keep my voice light with mockery. "Perhaps I don't recall what you're getting at."

Neri hates me, after all this time, a truth that's evident in his glowing, amber eyes. "If an advantage over the enemy is offered, you take it. If it means living to fight another day, you take it."

"Ah, yes." I bob my head. "No matter the cost. We should always strive for the upper hand."

Neri tilts his head, studying me like *I'm* the abnormal one in the room. "This doesn't have to be permanent. If power disgusts you so much, ask your friend, Nephele, to have me take it away after you've used it to its proper end."

I laugh. "You just want me to say yes so that she has no choice but to bring you back from the grave. If I deny you, then the conditions of your deal fall apart, don't they?"

"If you deny me, you fool, then you're trapped here. And if the prince succeeds in resurrecting Thamaos, the Northlands and the Summerlands will have no godly defense against him. I can be that defense. For certain, your witch will force me to the task whether I want to do it or not."

A smile unfurls across my face. God, I adore that woman.

Hands in my pockets, I stroll closer. "Do your deed, then. Curse me. But I'm not leaving. Not yet."

His eyes flare. "Why?"

I shrug. "Because the prince is up to something tonight, and I want to be here to see what it is. Poor timing on your part, but once I'm ready, I'll leave this place in a manner that the prince will forever remember."

I slip my hands through the bars, resting my wrists on the crosspiece. "Do it. And to satisfy your end of the bargain, open this cell door when you're finished. Your deal doesn't require that I leave, right? Only that you free me. Which you will have done."

Even as I say the words, I cannot believe that I'm helping Neri be resurrected. I didn't even know he could be without a remnant, but I suppose, in Nephele, he found a way.

He takes my wrists in his clawed hands and smirks, revealing that gods-damn fang again. "Take a deep breath, *king*," he says. "Because this is going to hurt."

✦ 64 ✦

NEPHELE

"Wake up."

I startle and flip over in bed. A lone oil lamp still burns, though I don't need the illumination to know that voice.

I sit up to find Neri sitting on my bed, right beside me. His amber eyes drift from my face and tousled hair to my satin nightgown.

To my breasts.

I gather the blanket to my chest and glare at his watchful eyes. "What happened?"

"Your king accepted the curse. He is the Frost King once again. But he wouldn't come with me."

I frown, trying to hear an untruth. "What? Why would he not?"

Neri holds up a claw-tipped finger. "I opened his cell door. He had but to walk out with me, and yet he chose to stay because he expects to learn of the prince's dealings from last night. He said he would leave when he's ready."

If I didn't know Colden so well, I would call Neri a liar. But this feels too much like something my friend would do.

"This fulfills my end of the bargain," Neri says. "Now you must fulfill yours."

He stands, an enormous naked, snow white, wolf-man-god, in Fia

Drumera's palace. She would probably bury me alive in the desert if she knew he was here.

"Tomorrow," I say. "Tomorrow we'll go to the grove."

He stalks closer, and I push back in bed a little. "Tonight."

I'm tired and irritated and unwilling to deal with him at this hour.

"Tomorrow," I insist. "I need time. There are guards there. Strategy is necessary. Now go away. Go rescue Joran from wherever you hid him and get back inside him." When Neri opens his mouth to tell me where he hid him, I hold up my hand. "Stop! I do *not* want to know. Just go, and we will deal with this come morning."

Just then, the palace trembles. We both look around, uncertain what that might've been.

"I'll check it out," he says. "But know that tomorrow, your end of the bargain must be met, or I'll change Colden back to a mere man."

He disappears in a whirl of snow and frost, spinning a cold draft through the room.

I drop back on my pillow, dread filling my tired bones. Because tomorrow, it appears I'm raising a god from the dead.

RAINA

The next morning, I wake to a maidservant cleaning our room.

I drag the covers over my chest and look at Alexus, on his stomach, face pressed into a soft pillow, still sleeping soundly. He's stretched out like a golden god on the bed, a sheet barely covering his backside.

The maidservant sneaks a look at him, and I can't help but laugh inwardly. If I were her, I'd sneak a look too.

When she sees me watching her, she startles and straightens from picking up Alexus's trousers from the floor. "Forgive me, miss," she says, her emotive brows drawn upward in the middle with great concern. "There was a disturbance last night?"

I look over the room, remembering, and my face heats. Books have toppled from the bookshelves to the floor, a chair is overturned, the sheers covering the windows are blown up in a tangle above the cornice, every painting that had been neatly hung on the walls sits oddly crooked, the desk was rattled askew by several feet, and I can't even look at we did to this bed.

I can't answer her, but Alexus wakes at the sound of her voice. I wait for him to reply, but then he turns over, groggy, and as if matters couldn't get worse, his morning erection tents the sheet.

The maid's eyes go round, and she swallows. "I'll just... I'll just go. Should you need me, dear, ring the bell outside the door." She turns and rushes toward the hall, but then turns back around, her wide eyes fixed on me as Alexus stretches, still oblivious to being an utter spectacle. "Oh, forgive me," the maid says, "but the queen requested to see you and your sister today. For a visit to the Hall of Holies."

At that, Alexus finally, truly stirs. He turns toward me and wraps his arm around my waist, dragging his naked leg up my thigh. "You'll enjoy that," he says, his voice deep and sleepy.

I nod at the maid, and she turns and rushes out the door.

I shove at Alexus's shoulder, laughing and so embarrassed. I feel him smile against my arm. "I like sensing you again. Such mortification is a delight."

My mouth drops open. *"You were not embarrassed at all!"*

He chuckles and pulls the sheet back, revealing a still very eager erection. "Should I be?" he asks.

"Not in the least," I sign.

He pulls me on top of him, pushes into me, and once more, we take one another with unbridled hunger, though we avoid *rattling the city* this time. Afterward, I leave him to sleep while I go find Nephele.

"What do you think this is about?" Nephele asks me as we head down to the main entry of the palace where we were told our horses await. My sister's nerves are still as visible as they were last night.

"Mother, I suppose?" I sign, and though that should've been the first thought on Nephele's mind, it clearly wasn't.

Fia and two guards are waiting with the horses in the street near the main entrance. She's holding the reins and rubbing the horse's mane, which seems somewhat at odds with how I would've imagined about a queen. She's dressed less formally today. More like us, in leggings, dust-covered boots, and a tunic. Her hair is braided back, and she still wears the torques at her neck and wrists.

She smiles as we descend the palace's stone steps, the sun already beating down. "Good morning." She bows her head to each of us. "I thought you might like to see some of your mother's past."

We smile gratefully and nod, then we mount our horses and follow Fia and two guards into the city.

The Hall of Holies is a long, rectangular sandstone building to the southeast of the city. When we enter, I have a dozen images in my mind as to what it might be like, but it's far simpler than I expected. To a degree, it reminds me of the School of Night and Dawn from Alexus's dreams. The Queziran school is very similar to Min-Thuret, though smaller.

The Hall of Holies is comparable in that it houses a school, dormitories, a grand library, an observatory, a massive dining hall for students, scholars, and magi, and an archival hall.

Fia shows us the very room where our mother lived during her time here. We step inside the tiny space now filled with someone else's life, but it feels good to be here. To be close to her. To know some of her truth that she felt she couldn't share.

We leave there, and Fia takes us to the library next, where our mother would've spent most of her time. I walk past books and scrolls and maps and documents thinking about how much fun it would've been to have visited this place with her, or to ask her questions about this part of the world and fall into a deep conversation filled with her knowledge. It would've been so good.

Fia motions for us to follow her to a small table where we sit. No one here bothers her, and again, I'm moved by the respect her people show her. They revere her, obviously, but there's a feeling of oneness that assures me that Fia Drumera is a people's queen.

She threads her fingers atop the table and looks at me. "Raina, I wanted to chat with you about something Alexus shared with me."

I nod and gesture for her to continue, of course.

"Your gift," she says. "The one that brought you all here from the Jade River..."

Again, I nod, wanting her to continue, though I see the tiniest bit of discomfort in her otherwise flawless armor.

"I had some time to think on it last night, and I keep coming back to the fact that your ability sounds like realm walking."

I blink at the queen, certain she's wrong.

"That would mean she's one of Loria's descended, no?" Nephele says.

"Yes," Fia replies with a soft lift of her brows. "It could be lineage from your father's side."

Nephele huffs a nervous laugh. "That's impossible. We would've known."

The moment my sister says those words, I see worry and doubt swirling in her eyes. She couldn't believe we were born in Malgros either, yet it's true. Denial is her first response to news she can't understand.

"Your father had no markings?" Fia asks. "Those in Loria's direct blood-line gain certain witch's marks once their powers have developed, a dark birthmark and a series of vines somewhere on their body. If you two are part of that line, your markings can still come, with time, but I would think, if my guess is correct, that your father had them."

Nephele and I look at one another. I remember my father's hands. The way his witch's marks branched over his knuckles like tree roots.

"He was a reaper," Nephele says. "He had reaper's marks."

Fia arches one black brow. "Perhaps. Or perhaps he was something more and couldn't risk anyone knowing. Being known as one of Loria's descended would've drastically changed your lives." She pauses, and then says, "It could also explain your affinity for vast magick, Nephele, which might even be a driving force for Raina's moving across time. Vast magick is, at its simplest form, the ability to project will across space and time. Realm walking was a form of that. Holding a construct from many miles away is a form of that. You two might simply have different portions of ability."

Nephele rests her elbows on the arms of her chair and presses her fingertips to her temples, closing her eyes, as though she simply cannot handle much more.

When she lowers her hands, she looks Fia in the eyes from across the table. "Thank you for letting us know. I suppose all we can do is wait and see if we end up with markings like a descended. I've never seen them, but I've read about them and heard about them through stories of a woman back home. Petra Anrova. Her birthmark was on her face. Colden let her stay at Winterhold for a time to protect her until she could manage a glamour."

Fia's eyes sparkle at the sound of Colden's name. "That sounds like something he would do. Your father, or mother for that matter, could've glamoured any revealing makings too. We cannot forget that."

I say nothing. I feel... numb. If this is yet another lie...

"I cannot say for certain if your father was a descended," Fia says. "But I knew your mother well, and there was nothing in her bloodline that could grant you the ability to slip across time." She reaches across the table and places her hand over mine. "All I'm telling you, Raina, is to be mindful with this gift. Realm walking was meant to be used by Loria's children to help them travel between this world and her world. It might not be that. It could be some new ability no one has ever seen. But that only means something could more easily go wrong. So please. Be careful."

I nod, finding it difficult to smile, even in thanks.

Fia leaves us with one of her guards, needing to head back to prepare for tonight's wedding. Nephele and I explore all the areas within the Hall of Holies once more. But then my sister asks me if we can return to the library, for a third visit. I agree, of course, and she spends the next two hours reading about the history of the Grove of the Gods with inexplicable intensity.

"Did you know that each god's name is written on a golden plaque at the foot of their tree?" she asks. "And that there are over one thousand steps built into the side of the mountain to access the grove?"

I flip through a book, my mind unfortunately elsewhere. I didn't know, but I suppose the labeling of Thamaos's name will only make him easier if the prince arrives on Fleurie's wings.

As Nephele and I follow the guard back to the palace, my sister says, "Don't let all of this bother you. Fia might be right. We could be Loria's descended. But she could be wrong too."

I glance up at Mount Ulra, where Loria's bones supposedly lie with the remains of so many other gods. Wishing I could ask her.

THE PRINCE WITH NO NAME

The Eastland Territories
City of Quezira
Min-Thuret, Prince's Chambers

I sit in my chambers, Bron bandaging one of three stab wounds in my back.

"Did you think Dread Vipers would come with you willingly?"

I slide a glare up at my friend as she walks in front of me to gather more bandages.

I thought it would be faster. I thought Fleurie would pop us into Aki-Ra Quarter, we'd snatch a Viper, be back inside an empty dungeon away from Fleurie and Colden in minutes, and then she and I could quickly portal here to my rooms. I thought that if there were trouble, Fleurie would have the ability to stop it.

That wasn't the case, whether by natural condition or planned occurrence, and I bear the stab wounds to prove it. Luckily, my portalist was uninjured thanks to my back taking the brunt of a Viper's rage.

Before I can reply to Bron with a sharp-tongued retort, someone knocks on my chamber door.

"Come in," Bron calls.

I haven't heard word from Malgros since Thresh sent Crux there with a message. I also haven't seen my general since we parted ways in Frostwater Wood. But this morning, Vexx strides into my rooms looking like a sea pirate come home, his long, gray braids wind-tattered, his scarred, ruddy face even more weathered than before.

He takes in the scene but keeps his stance a few feet before me. Respectfully, he bows his head, a line of worry across his brow. "Your Highness. Are you all right?"

"I have holes in my back," I tell him, "but it's nothing Bron can't manage."

He straightens, and I realize that Crux isn't with him. He isn't dragging Alexi of Ghent or Raina Bloodgood into my presence either.

"Malgros was uneventful, I take it."

Thamaos will not be happy.

Vexx clasps his hands behind his back. "I considered following them to the Summerlands, my prince, but we both know I would've been detained at the harbor, if I made it that far. I didn't have the manpower or the magick power to undergo a full-scale attack on the coast."

Bron finishes, and hands me my shirt. "It's not the end of the fight," I tell Vexx. "It's a long story, but I have Thamaos's godling daughter in my possession now, bound by a deal. She portaled me into the Summerlands late last night, so we have a way in."

Vexx looks stunned but excited. "Fleurie lives? And we have her skill?"

Carefully, I shrug into my tunic. "We do. She can't carry more than a few people at any one time, but it's enough to get us to Mount Ulra. I also have a Dread Viper imprisoned thanks to her. Once Alexi of Ghent is here, we can hopefully nullify his magick so that I can siphon from it, but he can't use it."

Vexx smiles and claps slowly. "Well done, my prince. I hope I have the chance to make Alexi of Ghent pay for Crux's death among other things."

"You know the rules. As long as he lives." I glance at Bron who watches me from the corner of her eye with what I would almost believe is revulsion.

It makes me think of Colden. *If you want more than that from me, you must prove it, and that means not hurting the people I love.*

But I am not made for kindnesses, I suppose. I am not made for the tenderness of love. Because when Vexx meets my eyes and says, "When do we begin?"

My answer is, "Tonight."

67

COLDEN

The Eastland Territories
City of Quezira
Min-Thuret, Dungeons

"Y ou might be able to get us out of here," Fleurie says, passing me a pinch of her yeast roll. "But I'm bound to a deal, Colden."

I remove my hand from the bar between us and watch as the ice I started to form falls to the dirt floor of my cell.

I sigh and turn a little, pressing my shoulder to the bars. We sit on the ground sharing the last bites of our dinner, something we've only done one other time since Fleurie regained her voice.

"It would take me too long to get to the Summerlands without you," I tell her. "I'm better off staying and hoping Thamaos still requires my presence, even if the prince wants me nowhere around."

She leans a shoulder against the bars too, facing me, those amber-brown eyes studying me as she sips from her mug of wine. "Is he... Is he in.. love with you?"

She so often speaks like that. Broken. As though unsure if her voice will let her release the words.

"He would have to understand the concept of love first, and he does not."

She nods, slowly. "It seems like he does," she says. "I see it sometimes when he's here. The way he looks at you."

I take a deep breath and sigh it out. "I'm fairly certain that if he loved me, I would not be on the floor of this cell right now, eating leftover lamb and stale wine. Sort of like if your father loved you, he wouldn't have been cruel. Control and desire are often disguised as love. One just has to be able to tell the difference between the fraud and the truth. Besides. The prince and I don't know one another well enough for all that."

Not a lie, though I don't tell her I've had thirty years filled with a longing to know what might've been.

"You're wise for a king." She tucks her deep red hair behind her ear. "Except for the part about accepting Neri's help. That cannot be good. I cannot believe he's here."

"Neri was a bad decision waiting to happen in this situation," I say. "And what, have you never met a wise king?"

I think about the kings in her day, and when she meets my gaze with a sarcastic face, we both laugh.

"Never," she says. "All fools."

"Well. For what it's worth, I plan to use this wisdom to help my friends, and that means you too. When we get to Mount Ulra, if I can prevent the prince from binding my hands in iron, I'll do my best to make it impossible for him to resurrect anybody. Surely he cannot exhume bones from frozen earth."

She looks pensive, chewing her lip. After a few moments, she touches her throat, and again, it's as though she isn't sure her voice will work. "What if... What if I told you... I-I know much of what's going to happen? And that we can't stop any of it?"

Now she has me curious.

"What do you know is going to happen?"

This time, when she tries to speak, no words come. Only tears that finally build her in eyes. She clutches her slender throat and lets the tears fall.

I cock my head, really looking at her, and wipe away a tear from her cheek. "You can't speak certain things. For a reason."

She doesn't nod, almost as though she can't, but relief shines bright as starlight in her eyes.

"Was it your father? Did he curse you?"

More relief. In the form of a shuddering sigh this time.

"You know things he doesn't want anyone else to know."

Again, no obvious outward reply but my guess is clearly the issue. I don't know how she can know the future of this moment in time, though. But if she does, she's been bearing that alone for so long.

Before we can say anything else, the dungeon door opens. I expect the prince to saunter through the door, but it's Bronwyn. She hurries down the worn stone steps to my cell door.

"What is it, Bron?" I push to my feet and hurry to her. "What's wrong?"

Her pale face is pink with the exertion of her sprint here, her eyes clear and focused. "If you have any manner of escape, my king, I urge you to use it now. The prince and the Brotherhood have been with the Dread Viper all day. He's now being siphoned. Everything is in place. You leave for Mount Ulra within the hour."

68

RAINA

After checking the waters for the hundredth time on this journey to no avail, I walk down the steps that line the terraced court-yards looking for Alexus. Colden and Fleurie had been having dinner, talking easy. Yaz is a saddened mess, missing Zahira, in tears every time I check on her. Vexx is at Min-Thuret now. I saw him walking toward the entry with a tall walking stick in hand, the head from the bowsprit now impaled on that instead, held in place from sliding away by two pieces of metal fitted around the wood. And then I looked for Finn but never saw him, as if he's hiding from me.

Oh, Finn. *Where are you?*

The night smells like a forest of flowers filled with the most delectable food. It's chilly out at first, but Fia has enormous golden braziers burning like bonfires on every courtyard landing and perfectly placed on the court-yards themselves. I also think there's a bit of magick hanging in the air, because the warmth from the flames seems to radiate everywhere, chasing away the cold.

There are so many people. I'm not sure I'll ever get used to crowds such as this after a lifetime in the valley. There are at least a hundred party-goers filling each courtyard, not to mention the main amphitheater below.

Maidservants walk around with sparkling wine-filled glasses and mounds of food on golden trays, offering them to anyone who wishes for a drink or a bite.

I think back to the harvest supper, how different things are. There are no barrels of ale or roasting pigs or drunken elders. Everything is elegant, like Fia.

The moment I spot Alexus speaking with the queen in the middle of the stone stairs leading to the last courtyard, my heart starts beating fast. He must sense me, because he turns, wine in hand, and his eyes fix on me, brightening like diamonds as he smiles.

So easily, his attention becomes solely mine. He looks starstruck. So unabashedly in love.

As ever, he's dressed in sleek black, matching the night sky. Tonight though, his tunic has gold embroidery down the front and along his tall collar. Hair down and perfectly tousled, he starts up the steps toward me, unblinking, as though he might miss something if he looks away. Then he's with me, kissing me softly, the purest happiness gleaming along our bond.

He takes my hand and steps back to look me over. "My gods, you are a vision."

I chose a different color tonight. The dress is a warm ecru with gold, embroidered starlights covering every inch. The neckline plunges, something I know Alexus appreciates, and the sleeves are sheer and full, gathered into long cuffs at my wrists. The skirt is flowing, with two slits that expose my thighs when I walk. I'm wearing the pearl necklace he bought me, and my witch's marks are bright. I've also dusted my skin in a golden powder that isn't Fever Lilac dust, but a simple cosmetic offered by my maidservant to match the dress. From the look on Alexus's face, I chose well.

He kisses my hand and gives me the darkest, most deliciously wicked smile I have ever seen. "I need five minutes," he whispers. "That isn't nearly long enough to do all the filthy things I so desperately want to do to you, but for now, it'll save me from utter misery."

He trails a finger down my chest, lingering at the skin over my heart, sending a frisson of longing straight to my core.

"If you can't spare the time though," he says, still smiling as he leans closer, "I suppose I must endure the rest of this night in agony, looking at you in that dress, wishing more than anything that I was buried inside you."

I smirk. *"You will survive,"* I sign. *"We are in public."*

His eyes flare with a challenge. "If you think I'm too reserved to drag you into the shadows and take you like the beast that I am, then you are sorely mistaken, my love." He glances beyond the amphitheater toward the deserted and darkened entry to Asha's temple, just beyond the ancient pylons. "If you're willing, I'm more than happy to prove just how wrong you are."

I consider taking him up on his offer, but the crowds begin dispersing down the courtyards to the amphitheater. I've never imagined such an event for a wedding.

"Later," Alexus says, "I'm going to ruin you in the best of ways, the way I'm certain you're going to ruin me every single time I look at you tonight."

On the way to our seats, which are more like wide stone walkways that wrap the oval arena, we pass Rhonin and Hel, hand in hand. They look lovely and happy, as though nothing can touch them here.

They join us, and we find Keth, Jaega, Callan, and Zahira, and take the seating area in front of them. I don't see Nephele and Joran, which is concerning. Nephele wasn't in her room all evening, which was odd, but she and Joran have been acting so strange. When I mention him, she cuts me off, but I can see the physical tension between them. It's more intense than what I felt when this journey began. There's fire between them now, whether she can admit it or not.

We take our seats, and I note the way the locals are sitting. Lovers or not, people sit in pairs of two, one nestled between the other's legs. I sit between Alexus's legs, and he bends his knees, caging me in as he leans back on his hands.

"You smell so good," he says. "We might have to leave early."

I drape my arms over his knees, loving the comfort between us as he leans down and kisses my shoulder.

Then, the music begins. Clusters of musicians stroll down the stairs lining the terraced courtyards toward the amphitheater which is bedecked with floral arches, beautiful, layered rugs, and glowing lanterns. A magi stands in the center of it all in a crimson and gold robe.

We turn to watch the procession. Behind the musicians are dozens more people, all dressed in golden finery, throwing red and white flower petals to the sand.

When the grooms appear at the tops of the stairs, everyone *awwws.* Alexus looks at me with a smile and winks.

We watch the couple move down the stairs, slipping glances at one another, their smiles bright in the night. It's such a happy moment. Such a beautiful evening filled with love.

Until my sister races across the top terrace behind the grooms, distracting every eye.

Because Neri, the god of the North, is at her side.

69

NEPHELE

"I told you to calm down, witch," Neri says through gritted fangs.

I spin around, not realizing that he was even here. He must've followed me and... just appeared in proper, wolfish Neri fashion.

Oh, gods.

I face the crowd again, panic hot in my veins, making me a little sick. Every face is a mask of shock.

Alexus and Raina jump up and hurry to the stairs along the sides of the courtyards, followed by the rest of our band, while I absorb what's actually happening. When I see Fia Drumera's face, even from a distance, I can feel the fiery fury inside her.

The god that made her an immortal fire queen is standing in her house. Thanks to me.

Alexus reaches me first, pulling me to his side, his eyes aflame as he pins Neri with a glare. "What in the fuck are you doing here?"

"That really isn't the question you need to be asking right now, Un Drallag," Neri says. "Why don't you try *How do we stop the Prince of the East who just arrived on Mount Ulra with magick-laced blood?*"

Alexus's face blanches, and Raina freezes behind him, her eyes wide.

"How..." Alexus pauses and looks at me. "Talk, Nephele. Fast."

My insides wither to dust under his stare. "I'll have to explain everything later. Just know that Neri isn't lying. He saw them on the mount. The prince is here, with Fleurie, Vexx, and Colden, and Colden has his power back thanks to the northern god. But the prince must be siphoning, because Neri could sense magick on him, thick. Things could get very ugly very quickly."

Before Alexus can say or do anything, a woman's wail of fury howls through the night, and a ball of raging fire comes sailing through the air, aimed right at Neri.

He holds up a single hand, and the fire turns to ice, crumbling to the packed sand of the courtyards, sizzling in the braziers. It's magick from his curse, after all.

"I'm leaving, witch," he says to me. "Get them to Mount Ulra and do it fast. I'll be there."

Snow and ice spin around us in a whirlwind of cold, and then he's gone.

I don't know what to say to my friends who have now gathered on the stairs and courtyards, their faces confused, or to Fia who's stalking toward me.

So I look at my sister and say, "You need to get us to the Grove of the Gods. Now."

70

RAINA

Alexus clasps my face, his eyes shadowed with worry. "I don't want you in this. Take me to Mount Ulra and leave me there. Let me deal with the prince."

It's always him before me in moments like this. But maybe I need to save him.

I take a moment to think. Fleurie is here. She brought Colden and Vexx and the prince. I don't know if she means to portal Alexus back to Quezira as part of her deal, but I can't walk him into harm's way. Still, she can get to him whether he's with me or not, but at least if he and I are together, I can give Fleurie a chase.

Her portals versus my abyss.

We shall see which one will win.

"She needs to take *me*." I turn around to see Fia.

"No," Alexus insists, his voice firm as a hammer. "If Colden is up there, we can't know what happens if the pair of you get into close quarters. Your curse could bring down the whole mountain."

Godsdamn Neri.

Near-translucent fire licks from Fia's hands, as though she's barely containing her rage. "I am the queen here, Alexus."

"And a wiser one than her fury," he reminds her.

I don't give anyone else time to argue. There are three of us with the kind of power meant for magickal battles. If I think we need more, I can return. I hope.

I grab Nephele and Alexus's wrists and think about the Grove of the Gods, the view from the sky, the paintings in our room, the drawings in the books Nephele looked through, and without another second of indecision, we're gone.

෯෯

The Grove of the Gods is a cold, lightless forest.

From the sky, I'd glimpsed its massive boughs, its shimmering green canopy. But that was a shield for what lies beneath.

We didn't land together. It was a rough awakening, my body aching now as I crawl over what must be roots, gnarled and puncturing the earth like woody tentacles. I would hold up a palm of fire, but that seems too dangerous a thing to do here in the cemetery of the gods.

Suddenly, a few starlights come into view, and I follow them, still crawling in my dress, my knees and palms scraping on rough bark.

When I find Alexus, he's creeping over and around a mass of roots, big around as his arm, some the size of my thigh, tangled together across the rocky side of the mountain for as far as the dim light allows me to see.

I reach him, and he kisses my forehead. "Gods, you scared me. I was looking for you. Where's your sister?"

I shrug, and he takes my hand as we keep looking, unsure where we are or where we're going.

Alexus sends his starlights a little ahead of us to light the way, making my heart pound like a drum. I half expect to see Vexx's ugly face around a corner any second, or for Fleurie to rip through the air and vanish with Alexus. The thought has my muscles tense, my nerves vibrating with anticipation.

I don't have a dagger. I wish to the gods I did.

When we come upon Nephele, it isn't her I first see. It's Neri, squatting at her side.

He looks up, his shimmering white skin and hair visible in the darkness. "She's hurt. A broken ankle, I think. Can you help her?"

I swear I hear concern in that bastard's voice.

It's hard to hurry on this terrain, but Alexus helps me reach Nephele quickly.

"I'm so sorry," she says, pain and tears in her voice. "It happened when I landed."

Alexus squats beside me as I work to heal my sister's bones. "Where are they?" he asks Neri.

"Further toward the cliffside," Neri points beyond Alexus. "This is the rear of the grove. Loria is here, and other old gods from around the world. Thamaos, me, Urdin, and Asha are all toward the cliff."

Alexus glances over his shoulder toward absolute darkness. "They will see us coming if I light the way."

"I can guide you," Neri says. "But it won't be an easy trek in the dark."

A wave of tiredness washes over me, already. Healing broken bones is a tedious task. I feel the weight of it so quickly.

Still, I finish, hurrying at Nephele's insistence, and we get back on the move.

Neri leads the way, and though I can't grasp it, my sister holds to his hand as though it's nothing, following him into the dark. I hold Nephele's other hand, and Alexus holds mine. The linked chain we've created keeps us together, but it also makes it harder to balance as we navigate, too slowly, over twisting roots.

The only sound here is the swishing of the tree limbs under the touch of a soft, desert mountain wind. It's like the leaves are whispering and dancing, waiting and watching from above. Their hushed rhythm reminds me of a song, like a requiem for the dead who lay buried here.

The hulking white figure at the front of our line reminds me that the gods are not so dead, not even in spirit form, and I have to wonder if the many whispers I hear in the trees are not from them.

We walk for too long. So long that I'm certain we are too late. Though if one of its dead has been stolen, the forest has yet to announce the thievery.

Finally, Neri halts, but he says nothing, and I instantly know it's because he's seen something.

He gets down, the bright white of his body too noticeable against the darkness. The rest of us keep moving, just a little ways, until we're slipping behind a tree trunk that shields all three of us.

I peer around the side. The next tree over is clearly Thamaos's tree. It amazes me how far away it is. At least sixty strides.

The Prince of the East kneels amid a spread of roots, the God Knife in his hand. The only reason I can see him is because Vexx has bravely lit a single torch.

Vexx. Standing there with a torch in one hand, holding it over his prince, while the other hand is wrapped around that pike, that head—probably maggot infested—gaping from the tip.

I don't see Colden, but then Nephele tugs me around to her side of the tree, and I do. His hands are bound in chains, which confuses me. His power is gone, isn't it?

"No," my sister whimpers.

I cover her mouth, even as the three men in our line of sight look in our direction.

And that's when I first see Fleurie.

FLEURIE

Mount Ulra
Grove of the Gods

I glance toward the darkness of the grove and fix my gaze there.

My pulse beats a steady rhythm, even though I know at some point tonight, Raina Bloodgood's rage is coming.

The deep of night reveals nothing yet, but I know she's here. Alexi, too. How I ache to see his handsome face, to hold him in my arms, to hear his voice.

Colden eyes me as the prince returns to his prayers. It's an eerie experience, listening to him have a whispered conversation, knowing that he's speaking to my father whose bones lie somewhere beneath my feet. I can feel his presence, goosebumps on my skin regardless of the desert cold, like a wraith has been lurking in the night, sniffing the back of my neck.

I study this man with the prince, General Vexx, and his prize head. He finds himself terrifying carrying a symbol of his barbaric brutality around like a trophy. A part of me thrills when he gives me a smug look.

Your time is coming, I think to myself. *Your time is coming.*

Suddenly, the prince presses his hands to the roots before him, as though he nearly collapsed. "No," he groans, his voice a low and miserable sound. "No, my lord. You cannot ask such a thing."

My heart begins its breaking. Perhaps it's been breaking for three hundred years. Perhaps it's broken anew these last weeks, seeing my old friend made into a monster. I remember the beautiful boy he was. His pure heart. His soulful eyes. His tender laughter. How did he become this? How could my father reach up from the grave and still destroy someone so good?

I wipe my tears from my face, my breaths trembling. I wish I could grab him. Shake him. Make him hear the words Thamaos has locked inside me for so long. It would stop this if he could truly hear me. I know it would. And yet I'm trapped as I've ever been.

Blinking back more tears, I study the tree that represents my father's life, the growth of his spirit. It makes me want to vomit that he's been granted such a beautiful memoriam when his soul is as dark as the deepest pits of the earth. If he lives again, I will kill him again. And I'll do it over and over if I must. His poison must be blotted out. It *must* be.

The prince leans back on his heels, his shoulders slumped, his demeanor that of a defeated lover. I know what's been asked of him. The thing he cannot bring himself to do.

I revel in that, at least. That a glimmer of his old self lives, enough to say no to the god who rules him.

Even if only for a moment.

THE PRINCE WITH NO NAME

"*There is a way to replenish my bones faster,*" Thamaos says.

"How, my lord?"

"*A sacrifice. The remnant and the ritual can resurrect me, but with the added blood of vital life, I can be restored in days rather than months.*"

"I have no offering, my lord," I whisper. "Save for myself."

I do not mention Vexx. I do not mention Fleurie. I certainly do not mention Colden. And yet my lord laughs.

"*You do, though,*" he says. "*You have a useless king in your midst. One who accepted help from Neri to harm you. One you had to bind with iron to prevent his icy betrayal. One you chose not to use against Fia Drumera. Time to give him a purpose.*"

This command is too much. I fall forward with the weight of a sinking heart. "No, my lord. You cannot ask such a thing."

"*I just did, little prince. You know the needed Elikesh. You know how to summon me from this pit of an existence. Do it. And bleed that king. His blood will be my blood. He will give me life like rain for a thirsty tree. Do it!*"

I sit back on my heels. My soul feels broken. After a moment, I glance up into Colden's black eyes. He watches me closely, a weak smirk curling the corner of his mouth, as though saying *I told you so.*

I can do many things, I've learned. But I cannot do this.

Even as Thamaos whispers like a demon in my mind, I set to work. This isn't complex, not as complex as it should be. A thousand years of change have rendered such innocence enviable, in truth. That Loria ever believed all the gods would deserve a living monument, and that she provided a way for resurrection if a god were needed. She believed humanity would be good stewards of dead power, and yet here I am, restoring power that we might conquer Tiressia.

Something inside me screams at this. It screams and rages and rattles like a monster in a cage. It feels like when I vaguely remember the man I used to be. As though he's trying to get out. To stop this. To remind me who I am.

And yet I cannot listen.

I drive the God Knife into the ground between two roots, returning Thamaos's bone to the soil that binds him.

Then I drag a ritual blade across my palm and begin the summoning.

🐉 73 🐉

RAINA

Mount Ulra trembles.

I grip onto the tree we hide behind, a chill crawling over my skin, even as Alexus's hand on my back steadies me.

The prince is doing it. I know he is. He's awakening Thamaos.

With the others' attention diverted by the prince, Neri prowls toward us, joining us behind the tree.

"I'm going to end this," he says. "I don't know how, but I am."

Alexus steps up onto a root beside Neri. "I'm coming with you." He turns back to me, faceless in the darkness. "I love you more than life. Please stay here."

My breath catches in my throat as they take off across the expanse of roots before I can stop them.

Nephele grips my hand, as though trying to hold me back. But then she sighs. "I know you're going after him regardless," she whispers.

And she would be right.

I don't know what I expect of Neri and Alexus. I never imagined them fighting on the same side willingly, but here they are. Still, I can't fathom anything they can do to stop the moment, other than kill the prince, and I don't know if a man made of shadows, souls, and sin can be killed any more than a god spirit can. Alexus can obliterate anything, but with Colden and Fleurie so close and in his line of sight?

There's a sudden groan through the earth, a great bellow that swells across the night, stretching over the City of Ruin. If a mountain could cry, this sound would be its pleading wail. It's as though it's being asked to give up something it doesn't want to lose, and I realize it probably doesn't. This land knows what happens if this is allowed. It knows it's re-birthing an enemy.

Nephele and I move quickly, but we're stopped in our tracks when a flash of white light and an unholy lament splits the air. We shield our faces with our arms as dirt and rocks and wood rain down around us.

That wasn't Alexus's power. I would know it anywhere. And it wasn't Neri's. I've felt it before.

This power is new—

No. I've felt it too. Just a shadow-kiss, in the wood when Alexus summoned this bastard.

Thamaos is here.

※

IN THE NEXT BREATH, THE LIGHT DIMS, BUT THERE'S A CONSTANT GLOW spilling from the earth beneath Thamaos's tree.

It's enough to illuminate several hundred feet in all directions, meaning we are no longer concealed. Fleurie has fallen to her knees next to the prince, panting. Colden is on his knees too, a few feet away. Vexx is leaning against a tree for steadiness, chest rising and falling fast, his eyes on me and my sister, as though he'd already found us in the dark moments before. Neri and Alexus stand in bold form, only a matter of strides from the prince.

But most importantly, the bones of a long-dead god lie in a berm of upturned soil, and they're moving in odd little twitches, like his skeleton might rise any moment.

Without hesitation, Alexus lifts his hand to call forth his power in the night. To destroy Thamaos's bones or to destroy the prince, I can't be sure, but...

Nothing happens.

I always feel his magick. I taste it. Smell it. But there isn't even a hint of it in the air.

The prince, still sitting on his heels at Thamaos's marker, laughs. He holds up his hand, turns it, studies it like it's an appendage he's never before had. "Power of the Dread Viper," he says to Alexus. "I suppose this is a siphon I need to keep on hand. If only he could power me a bit more strongly, I could march down to the City of Ruin and take it with ease."

Alexus stands so still, so quiet, so stunned. Only his shoulders move as he breathes.

"You bastard," Neri says. "Prince with no name. I can tell you who you are."

Every eye turns to Neri, every breath held. Especially the prince and Fleurie. She looks utterly captivated.

Neri stalks out of the grove to the small clearing that looks over the City of Ruin. He moves past Colden and Fleurie, then he gives Vexx—whose torch is still burning—a grim look and peers up at the head on his staff.

He smiles. "You're in trouble." Then he turns toward the prince.

The prince doesn't seem scared at all. More intrigued.

"Do you want your name?" Neri says.

The prince spits in Neri's face. "Like I would believe you."

Neri laughs and wipes his hand from his eyes to his chin. "You should. I was there. I didn't know you well, but I knew *of* you."

Thamaos's bones twitch even more, as though he's trying to stop Neri from talking.

"You realize that I might be a god spirit," Neri says, "but I can still bring you much harm. Especially now that you're out here unprotected."

"I'm not unprotected," the prince says. "You see, I think of these things." He snaps his fingers to his right, where Fleurie sits and says her name.

She blinks at him and hesitates, as though unsure what to do.

"Fleurie, you have one second!" he screams in her face.

A familiar slice of fiery light cleaves the air, then they vanish. Her, the prince, Thamaos's bones, and the light.

Things change so quickly then.

Alexus's starlights fill the night, his power returned with the prince gone. I watch as Neri turns for Vexx, and Alexus runs toward Colden. Nephele and I bound out of the grove, and she goes to Colden too.

But I stop. I stop and face Vexx who's being held by the throat in the air by Neri's strong hand, so tightly that Vexx's face is red even in the soft light. His steely stare meets mine, and the chance I wanted so badly finally arrives at my feet.

I stalk toward him and Neri and raise my hand, summoning my fire by the power of *fulmanesh*. If I had my dagger...

I shove past Neri and unbuckle Vexx's sheath. I'm strapping it on my thigh when Alexus and Nephele shout my name.

When I turn around, I expect to see Alexus coming for me, but he and my sister sit with Colden, their horrified faces like moons in the darkness beyond them.

"Neri!" Nephele yells. "Protect her from this! Please! I'll do what you've asked of me when this is over! Just... Please!"

Confused, I turn back around, and Alexus's starlights hovering around me wink out.

I grab Neri's wrist. I don't know what Alexus is hiding from me, but Vexx is mine. After all he's done? *He's mine.*

"This is your kill, Raina Bloodgood," Neri says, "Your revenge. I won't take it."

Icy light blooms from his chest. It isn't much, but it's enough that I finally glimpse what my love and my sister didn't want me to see.

Vexx's walking staff is leaning against the wide trunk of the tree, that head I always had to look away from still miserably intact somehow. But then I sense it.

Magick. Probably Gavril's.

I hold my fire closer, a strange feeling swelling inside me, like a bubble about to burst. And I smell the death. The scent of a forge fire, and leather, and the air after a rainstorm.

I see his hair. Those dark, messy curls, and his sleek nose. I know the line of his jaw, even swollen with death, and I know his lips. Lips that have kissed mine. Lips that have spoken words that angered me. Lips that have spoken words that soothed me. Lips that told me to go when they wanted me to stay. I remember his head on that bowsprit, his eyes cast toward a sea and a land he never wanted to know. He was there because of me.

I've felt a fighting calm before. I've felt cold, murderous rage. And they come together now into something fueled by deepest pain.

Neri drops Vexx and steps aside, and when I hear Alexus calling my name and running for me, Neri stops him.

"Let her have this!" Neri shouts. "She has earned this vengeance!"

I owe that god a debt because this cannot be taken from me.

Breathing so hard I'm gasping, I stalk toward Vexx with flames in one hand, a dagger in the other. I slide the dagger into the sheath. I need both hands for this. I want it to be slow. I want to burn him from the inside out.

I hear voices. Rhonin. Hel. Callan. Zahira. Keth. Jaega.

They're here.

Helena cries out in utter agony.

I feel Alexus, his love burns through the rune, his plea, his comfort, but I am already too consumed to be moved. I sense him break past Neri, an awareness of his nearness, and when he does, I think for a solitary moment about Fia Drumera's warning to me, to be careful of my gift, but that thought passes as quickly as it arrives.

Nothing will stop me. I grab Vexx by the throat and carry him into my abyss, back into the deeper part of the grove where no one can find us, no one can stop me, and no one can save him.

I summon fire. I let it flare high from my hands, hot death awaiting.

"Stop!" Vexx screams, scuttling back over the roots. "Stop right now!"

But I don't.

I grip his ankles, this coward. And I call forth my fire, letting it simmer, letting it burn.

He starts screaming, and my rune starts pounding, Alexus knocking to get in.

But I close him out. I close him out and I keep burning. Burning as Vexx tries to crawl away over the roots. Burning as he tries to fight me. Burning when he has no legs or arms to move him. I burn and burn and burn, until General Hammerin Vexx's screams shake the requiem trees, until fire pours from his mouth and his eyes, and he at last becomes nothing but ash.

But then it's over. And when the haze of my rage begins to fade and I can see again, the Grove of the Gods is on fire.

74

RAINA

I hear my name, even over the screams of the Ancient Ones leaving the trees around me.

There's a fast way out, and I try it, but it fails me.

It fails me.

Again, Fia's warning repeats in my head. *Be careful, be careful, be careful.*

I try again but my abyss is still and calm, as though it's tired.

I get to my feet and move, stumbling over roots as the fire spreads, racing along the trees and branches as quickly as it did the night of the harvest supper, lighting up the world in flaming terror. The night fills with thick, woody smoke, and I can't breathe.

This nightmare must end. I cannot lose anyone else. Alexus said that if he lost me, he would knock the world off its axis. I felt the same, although now I realize that if I lost him, it would be *me* who lost their balance. I would never be the same. I would rage for ages, until my pain was met.

I must protect all of them. Everyone in that clearing on the edge Mount Ulra. Everyone who is here because I didn't stop the prince in the first place. I can't let anyone else suffer. I can't feel this kind of pain ever again. I *can't.*

I must stop Thamaos. If I have to burn his bones to dust, I will.

My name is a ghost in the trees. I listen as fiery branches and limbs start to fall, crashing around me.

My rune throbs. Alexus.

The roots seem to crawl as I move, as I try to run toward his voice. I have to get him out of here. I have to get us to safety.

The roar of fire and the groan of wood is so loud though, it soon drowns him out. I keep trying. I just want to see his face.

Ahead, a bright light cleaves the night, and Fleurie appears. I halt, stumbling over a root, crashing to my knees. When I look up, she's a few steps in front of me, holding out her hand. The only thing separating us is a ring of fire.

I can't go with her. I can't let her take me to the prince.

But maybe I should. Maybe then I could end this. Maybe, with her deal done, she would help me.

"Trust me," she says. Only the words don't fall from her lips. She signs them, in my language.

A language she cannot possibly know.

Flames roil through the wood and over the canopy around us both. Her eyes are so sad, tear-filled golden-brown orbs reflecting the light, and her lip quivers, as though her heart is breaking.

"Raina." She shakes her head, face pleading. "I'm going to get everyone out. Come with me. Just let me try to get you out of here too. I can't leave you."

She extends her hand again, and at the same time, my abyss roils to life.

I close my eyes and reach for them both.

❧ VII ❧
INTO THE DIM

75

RAINA

I'm in a vast, dim space that feels like death. If I could imagine what death might feel like. Fleurie is with me, floating and weightless.

I've stepped into my abyss many times now, but this time, it feels more like it did when I first came to know it. Like I'm hanging off the edge of the world, ready to drop into nothingness.

The release of pressure is a sudden rip between me and Fleurie. Her eyes go wide, and she reaches for me, but then I'm cast in one direction, her in another.

Whether I want to or not, I begin the fall into a new void, stripped away from everyone I love, unsure where I'm going to land.

🙼

I HIT THE SLAB OF CRUMBLED STONE, AND THE BREATH LEAVES MY BODY in a *whoosh*.

My ears ring, and I can't see until everything clears—sight and sound— and my breath returns on a gasp that leaves me coughing, the taste of smoke in my mouth.

Trembling, I stare up at a starry night sky. No smoke. No fire. I'd thought of the clearing when Fleurie reached for me. I wanted to be with everyone I love.

This is not the clearing.

Oddly, the night is not cold. It's balmy, like deep summer, too warm on my burned skin. I roll up and cringe, still coughing. Whatever happened with Fleurie feels like it blew me into pieces. I can't stop shaking, everything aches, my eyes and throat burn, and there are pebbles and stones wedged into the skin of my back. The worst part is that my right hand and arm are badly blistered from reaching through the fire.

With my good hand, I rub my fingers over my back and knock away some of the stones, even as the world around me swims. It isn't easy, but I get up and stagger to what's left of a ruined column and stare out over a torchlit city below.

I'm... I'm in Quezira's ruins. The other city of ruin. I saw this view from Colden's eyes, and in Alexus's dreams. It's very much the same, practically unchanged.

Min-Thuret sits to my right, the center glass dome lit by moonlight, and in the near distance, I swear I see Alexus's old home: the School of Night and Dawn, bearing the same three domes as Min-Thuret, only a smaller replica. I hadn't known it still stood.

Fleurie brought me here? Brought me here and left me?

With my lungs trying to expel the last of the smoke, I rest on a broken wall, careful to stay in the shadows, trying to be quiet, and set to mending my burned arm.

Only I can't. I can see the threads, but I cannot weave them back to rights, no matter how hard I try.

I blink and look at myself, at the exposed skin showing through my badly burned dress, the starry fabric marked with holes and an uneven singed hem. My witch's marks aren't visible, yet I'm not maintaining a glamour.

It'll fix itself, I tell myself mentally, trying to keep my nerves from fraying worse.

I get up and try to move around. I don't know what to do. I'm here, and I might be able to find Thamaos's bones and bring him back to the Summerlands, but I could also walk into a trap. I can't be sure of anything. I just need to go home. I need to find Alexus. He *is* my home.

Thinking of him, I close my eyes and seek the abyss.

It isn't there.

Gods. Panic scratches at my chest, and my eyes shoot open, my body shaking. *Try again, Raina. You just landed too hard.*

I *do* try again, but still. Nothing.

I need to sit down. Again, I prop my hip on the broken wall. This is a bad omen. It's just a result of my poor landing, I'm sure. It rung my head to hit the earth so hard. Or maybe I'm exhausting the ability, and it needs time to recover between uses.

Turning, I study the city again. Something isn't right, but I can't place it. A long look at the guards flanking the temple entry, and I realize they're dressed differently than the prince's guards usually dress. Longer tunics, a different shade. Mail, but no cuirasses.

Restless, I walk through the ruins to an opening that looks out over a small pond and a copse of willows. Something about that view feels familiar, but again, I'm too rattled to make any sort of connection.

Footsteps sound at my back, but before I can move, an arm slings around my neck, and the tip of a knife digs into my chin.

"Mistake," a male voice says, only it's edged with more of an accent than I've ever heard from an Eastlander.

I unsheathe Vexx's dagger and send it up behind me in an arc, ramming the tip into the man's face. He screams and stumbles back, his head still caught on my weapon.

Don't think about Finn, Raina. Don't.

I spin and yank the blade free, bringing his eye and other matter with it. It's a fatal twist. The man drops to his knees, then falls face first against me.

I scuttle out of the way, let him hit the ground, then scrape my blade on a stone. In the next instant, two more guards enter the ruins.

Then two more.

For a moment, I hold my dagger at the ready in one hand, even though I'm still trembling, and I summon a struggling ball of fire in the other. But suddenly, the fire in my hand dissolves, like one of the men standing before me sucked it away.

I turn and run toward the willows, only I quickly realize I got turned around, and I'm running toward the temple.

The guards chase me, but I'm not as fast as usual, my body too weary, my lungs filled with smoke.

My heart pounds with every stride, a sweat breaking across my brow. I try my fire again but... nothing.

Panic swallows me, and when my attacker's body slams into mine, we fall, hard, skidding across the grass, sending my dagger flying from my hand.

Pointlessly, I reach for it, but the man's weight is too much.

I turn my head to get a glimpse of him, but all I see is the silver butt of a hilt a second before he knocks it against my skull.

76

RAINA

U p the stairs we go and through a maze of torchlit corridors I could never retrace. The guards lead me outside, into a courtyard brimming with blooms and boughs. The grass is soft between my toes, and the night air is sultry, the sky filled with winking stars.

Then we're inside again, walking through cloisters. I swallow hard. I'm here. I think. But not like I'd hoped.

More stairs. At least three flights. I'm hauled past door after door until finally we stop and the guard to my left knocks.

When there's no answer, he knocks again, harder. "Your Highness, we found an intruder."

Silence. And then—

"For the love of the Ancient Ones, come in."

They swing the door open and shove me inside toward a man standing barefoot at a large, stone hearth in a silken robe. There's no fire tonight, but the hearth is filled with candles.

"Elias, send them away," another male voice says.

I glance around the room to find the owner of that voice sprawled across a fine bed, a sheet draped across his middle.

Clothes are discarded across the floor, and a crimson sash hangs haphazardly around the neck of a bust nearby. Not a sash like the one from a robe, but the kind royalty sometimes wears around their neck. I can just make out the golden embroidery shimmering in the low light glowing across the room. A raven.

I would think this the chambers of the prince, but the man with his back to me at the hearth has dark hair down to his shoulders, very much unlike the Prince of the East. I just saw him. This is not him. And his waiting lover called him Elias, and the prince has no name.

The guards at my sides clamp their hands on my shoulders and press me to my knees. Though I wish it were otherwise, I don't fight. I don't have the strength to do much of anything in the way of magick, it seems.

"Found her snooping in the ruins, Your Highness. She killed Lucius."

Elias pulls the top off a crystal decanter and pours himself a glass of liquor. A moment later, he's back before the massive hearth, swirling the liquid in his goblet as it reflects amber from the soft candlelight.

Even though I can't see his face, I feel the weight of his heavy gaze. Silent as death, he watches me from the shadows.

As he walks toward me, I find I can't look at him. I don't know who it can be, but it's best to keep my head down. Eye contact creates a connection. I don't need that.

The man's feet stop before me. He squats in his robe, the smell of musk and liquor in my face. He touches the burned sleeve of my dress, rolling his fingertip over one of the stars.

Finally, he speaks.

"My, my. Aren't you a lovely little thing. Even though you smell like smoke and starlight and have a bloody face." He touches the stream of blood running from my temple and wipes it away.

A chill chases across my skin, and a bolt of fear shoots up my spine. This is impossible. *I bet you taste like smoke and starlight* the prince had said to me in the Shadow World.

Slowly, I lift my eyes and meet the gaze of the Prince of the East. He looks different. So much different. But I would know that face anywhere.

"Lovely though she might be," he says to his men as though he doesn't recognize me, as though we weren't just in the grove, "I don't want to deal with a trespassing murderer tonight. Tomorrow maybe. For now—" he laughs "—take her to the library."

⊙⋘⊙

THE LIBRARY?

The guards heave me to my feet, drag me across the room, and shove me out the door before I can so much as attempt a glance over my shoulder.

They seem sick of me, not even careful of my burned arm, all but dragging me downstairs and back outside, back through the cloisters and courtyard, back to another part of the temple I don't know if I recall seeing on the way in.

I look up at the night sky, shining through a dome of glass, but it's smaller than I ever imagined the dome at Min-Thuret to be.

Suddenly, we're facing two massive wooden doors, and I'm being hauled inside an actual library. Something inside me twists.

I know this place.

We pass at least a dozen rows of shelves on either side of the main aisle, but my attention locks on the back of the library where a winding staircase leading to another level looms over rows of worktables littered with all manner of books and scrolls and ink pots and quills. Unlit candles and rush lights are strewn here and there, waiting for the lick of a flame to illuminate this entire hall.

This is... This is straight out of Alexus's dreams of the School of Night and Dawn, a smaller version of Min-Thuret. It's so similar to the image in my mind's eye, as though time stands still here.

The guards drag me past the worktables and under the stairs. There's another door, and at the sight of it, everything in me tenses. I don't know this door, though I feel like I should. Like maybe I dreamed about it once, but it was a dream forgotten.

The guard to my right pounds on the oaken slab. "My lord. We have a trespasser. Prince Gherahn said to bring her to you."

That *was* the prince. It wasn't my imagination. He has a name.

Elias. Prince Elias Gherahn.

King Gherahn's... son? How?

A quiver tightens the muscles along my spine. Something isn't right.

The door opens of its own volition, and I'm met with a familiar scent that is so strong it almost brings me to my knees. Rich spices, dark wood, and the honey-sweet aroma of ancient magick.

The guards shove me into this room as well, and though my mind races to try and place the fine woods and the bed and the rugs and the many, many shelves of books, I can't think clearly.

Candlelight flickers around the chambers, making me feel like I'm in a dream, because everything is all wrong. Especially when a naked man pushes up from a silver soaking tub, steps out, and strides dripping wet to a small table where a bath linen awaits.

Because I know that body. I know every single line touched by the shadow of candlelight. Except it bears no runes. Not a single scar on his smooth, golden skin.

And then he speaks.

"Kneel." The guards send me to my knees again, and that voice... "What did she do?"

Tears well in my eyes. I want to wake up. I don't like this dream. It feels so wrong. That voice has whispered against my skin. It has scolded me and begged me and loved me. It has never sounded so empty. It has never sounded so foreign.

"She was in the ruins, my lord. She had fire magick. Killed one of our men with a dagger to the face. She doesn't look like much, but she's trained. Clearly."

My heart pounds and pounds as he wraps the linen around his waist to hide the nakedness he so openly revealed earlier and starts toward me. Something in the way he moves—like a predator stalking prey—makes me want to cry. And I do.

Tears fall down my cheeks as a strange sort of knowing tightens my chest to the point of pain. When he stops a few feet away, and I look up into those sparkling green eyes, I know it isn't him. There's not a single rune mark on his chest, not even the one he made for me. There's also no recollection in his gaze. No love. No happiness at seeing my face.

And yet, faster than I can think about it, my feet are taking me to him. He's whole and well and... free, it seems. And the joy inside me overwhelms.

But I no sooner throw my arms around his neck than he shoves me off him, gripping my wrists painfully in his strong hands.

Using his weight, he drives me back against the wall, pinning me in place, his fingers cutting into my flesh enough to bruise, enough to make my burn flare with pain. "You kneel to me. Do you understand?"

More tears. They fall so fast and so hard I can hardly see. My Alexus would never do this. Never. He would never look at me with such fire, such animosity. He would never allow me to kneel to anyone, and he would never hurt me.

But this man... This man is *not* Alexus Thibault.

Suddenly, he's leaning in, his smooth face so close, his scent enveloping me.

"Who sent you here?" His words squeeze between gritted teeth.

Loria, please let this be a dream. Let me wake up.

When I say nothing, he slams my wrists against the wall again, sending a shudder of fear through me.

"A spy? Who sent you? I *will* find out." He tilts his dark head. "It won't be pleasant when I yank that truth from you, know that."

I shake my head, unable to explain that I can't speak. Unable to explain anything. Even to myself.

Before I realize what's happening, he bends down, heaves me onto his shoulder, and shoves past the guards. He heads into the library, stalking down the center aisle with me draped over his body like a sack of grain.

I can't tell where we are or where we're going, I only know that in a matter of minutes, we're moving down a flight of stone stairs, then another, then another, until he pushes through a door that clangs against its stone frame.

It isn't until he dumps me on the dirt floor of a torchlit dungeon cell and says, "Welcome to the School of Night and Dawn," that I know, for certain, where I am.

It's still confusing, because I've seen Colden and Fleurie in a dungeon just like this so many times. Except... it's not as old. In fact, it doesn't look old at all. The iron bars are still black. The stone steps are not worn in the middle. The torchlight chains are not rusted. And these cells are even smaller.

How is this happening?

I let my gaze travel over the man's unmarked and beautiful torso as he looms over me, and at last, I think I know what has happened. I can't explain it. But I know. The *how* will have to be a discovery, and that terrifies me. And yet, even though assuredness fills me, I still pray to Loria that I'm somehow wrong.

He squats before me, and I think about the first time our gazes ever met: the night of the attack. I think of the way those green eyes felt like they could see into my soul, like he was prying through my mind.

But it was more than that, wasn't it? It was a look borne of recognition. Even if he couldn't remember why, his soul knew mine, even if mine didn't yet know his. I saw that same look in Fleurie's eyes. She knew me. Even if Alexus had forgotten me, she had not.

Gods don't forget.

"Have you any notion how much trouble you're in?" he says to me.

I can only shake my head with disbelief. Because I *do* know. With every passing second, realization deepens like a boulder sinking in the middle of an endless sea.

As he walks from my cell, shuts the door, and locks it with the iron key hanging around his neck, I feel a hammer drop across time, making me tremble so hard my teeth chatter, and I struggle to breathe.

Because this man is not *my* Alexus Thibault. He's the villain the man I love warned me about.

He's Alexi of Ghent.

Un Drallag, the Gatherer.

I crawl backward and press my spine to the stone wall, trying to breathe as he vanishes through the door, leaving me alone down here.

My gods. *My gods.* Fia warned me. And I didn't listen.

I didn't travel *across* space and time to Quezira. What happened with Fleurie... it sent me *back* in time to Quezira.

Three. Hundred. Years.

⚜

Thank you for reading! Did you enjoy? Please add your review because nothing helps an author more and encourages readers to take a chance on a book than a review.

And don't miss more of the Witch Walker series with a special novella,

THE WOLF AND THE WITCH, available now. Turn the page for a sneak peek!

To stay up to date on Charissa's future releases or to join her reader group or Patreon, visit her link page at direct.me/charissaweaksauthor

You can also sign up for the City Owl Press newsletter to receive notice of all book releases!

SNEAK PEEK OF THE WOLF AND THE WITCH

Mount Ulra
The Grove of the Gods

The grove is wailing.

Mournful cries drift through the scorched remains of the cemetery, anguished howls baying from deep within the earth. Beneath my feet, the charred ground is covered with snow, a result of Neri's magick suffocating the fires the same way he did in Aki-Ra Quarter. Above, the ancient, heavy boughs are no more. Now there's nothing but a dense, gray cloud blotting out the night sky.

The only light is from Alexus's starlights. They illuminate the wood so we can see, our little clan desperately searching for my sister as ash falls heavy as Neri's snow.

Shivering against the cold air, I move adjacent to Alexus as he calls Raina's name. His deep voice has gone so rough and ragged that it's almost unrecognizable amid the lament of the grieving grove. He coughs from the effort, the lingering smoke almost too much for any of us to endure.

Save for Neri. Unaffected by our surroundings, the white wolf stalks close behind, returned to his corporeal form. He hasn't let me out of his sight, but my king follows too, freed from his chains by the wolf himself.

"I've been over this grove thrice," Neri says to Alexus. An irritated edge roughens his smooth, accented voice. "She isn't here."

Earlier, he looked Alexus in the eyes and said, "It isn't what you want to hear, Un Drallag, but your woman either died in her own fire, left this wood using her abyss, or she's in Quezira with the prince and Thamaos."

Surprisingly, his words had not been laced with bitterness, not meant to cut or wound. They sounded sincere, spoken to prevent us from doing what we're doing now: wandering through the gods' blistered graves, grief threatening, hoping against all hope to see my sister's lovely face around the next bend. We all felt the ripple of strange power during the fire. A breath-stealing force *whooshed* through the grove like a mighty storm, but almost as soon as we felt it, it was gone.

A pang punches my chest as more tears flood my stinging eyes. Vision blurry, my foot catches on a root, and I stumble on my still-aching ankle.

Neri is at my side in an instant. He folds one massive claw-tipped hand around my bare arm, the other around my waist, keeping me from falling. "Careful, now."

I steady myself against his muscled chest. The smooth skin and human features of his brawny torso are a strange juxtaposition to his animalistic lower half, covered in sleek, white fur.

Regardless of his chimera form, the contact sends a flood of heat pouring into me as his strong fingers brush back and forth over the goose-bumps covering my arm. It's his power. A gift of warmth, momentarily easing my chills.

"Better?" He stares down at me with that honey gaze, and I can't help but notice how, even in the gloom, his skin shimmers like snow under moonlight.

"I'm fine. I think Raina's healing was just too brief to fully mend the bone."

He frowns. "I should carry you, then."

"Try it," I warn, pure venom coating my voice, and a small laugh falls from the wolf's lips.

He skims a glance over me. At first, it's as though he means to take inventory, so I tuck my injured foot beneath the hem of my dress. One glimpse of my swollen ankle, the skin reddened from a mixture of cold and inflammation, and I can envision him sweeping me off my feet whether I like it or not.

His attention drifts from my soot-stained wine-colored dress, the one I chose for the wedding at Fia Drumera's court before everything went wrong to the remnant of his heart hanging around my neck, then to my teary eyes. His gaze softens, but it's still too penetrating. Too knowing. And Colden's night-dark stare, spearing me from a short distance, is too aware. Too watchful.

Questions are brewing, and I don't want to answer any of them.

I shake free of the wolf's heated grip and take a single step away. On a deep breath, I press one hand to my aching heart while the other keeps me upright against a blackened tree. "Raina wouldn't have left us."

I say those words because I believe them. They're the only truth getting me through any of this.

As the crying wood's song abates, Colden starts toward me. He strips off his silver velvet dinner jacket to reveal a tailored pewter tunic marked with streaks from cinders. His pale skin is pearly gray with ash, his usually silky blond locks twisted into heathered tangles. The way he moves is almost as predatory as Neri, but he's far less like a beast and more like a skilled soldier hurrying to protect a man down. Colden is also tall, but he must lift his chin and blink away ash and snowflakes to look Neri in the eyes. He glowers at the northern god—the maker of his curse—baring his teeth before placing his fine dinner jacket around my shoulders and cradling my face as gently as fragile glass in his hands.

Colden kisses my forehead and wipes my tears with his thumbs. "We will find her. I swear it, love. We will find her."

Neri's lip curls back, exposing an elongated fang, and a deep, contained growl rumbles inside him. He postures for a moment, but reluctantly turns and moves on those long and muscled hind legs toward the charred remains of a giant tree, frost falling off him like mist.

His hands clench into fists, a spoiled god seething because he can't have what he thinks he wants. If he were wise, he would understand that I am no trophy. I am no prize.

I am a shrew.

Or at least I will be if our paths truly entwine as planned.

With the weight of the wolf's territorial gaze off me for once, I melt into Colden's waiting embrace. I need the familiar comfort of his arms far more than I can express. "If Raina used her power," I say against his chest, my attention still fixated on Neri, "she would've returned to the cliff's edge after destroying General Vexx. Back to Alexus's side. No matter what."

The other options are unthinkable.

Unbearable.

"I agree," Neri says from over his shoulder. "Which means we should leave this mountainside behind and find out if she's in Quezira. Because if she isn't—"

"She must be." Alexus's voice is as grave as the death around us. He stands in the falling ash, still as a statue. Black and gray soot covers his hulking form, making him look like some sort of creature of the night. He turns his glassy, green gaze on Neri, and a lone tear spills down his face, washing away a trail of ash. "The connection along the bond is faint, but I feel her." He lifts his hand to his collarbone, where the rune he shares with Raina marks the skin beneath his tunic. His eyes shift to me, offering the only reassurance he can. "I would know if she met her end, Nephele. *I. Would. Know.*"

Helena and Rhonin, Keth and Jaega, and Callan and Zahira appear from the back side of the grove. Their faces are grim and gray and stained with tears.

"No luck," Rhonin says, holding tightly to Hel's hand.

The expression on her face is so coldly fierce and quiet it's nerve-rattling. Her mother and sisters first, now her brother and best friend. I probably shouldn't, but I fear for the person who will one day meet with Helena Owyn's pent-up wrath and pain.

When Hel and Rhonin reach Alexus, Rhonin clasps his shoulder. The sorrowful tears in his eyes shimmer like broken glass under sunlight. "I'm so sorry, my friend."

Alexus looks around the grove, meeting each of our gazes, our fearless leader so obviously broken and lost without the woman who stole his heart.

The woman who became his heart.

He shakes his head and swallows thickly as more tears race down his cheeks. "If she's in Quezira, I have to go get her."

I lift my head from Colden's chest as the slightest *hum* vibrates the air.

Alexus walks backward toward a small clearing where the boughs are thin. Still shaking his head, a new kind of fury lights eyes that lock with mine.

"No!" My voice trembles as panic and understanding swallow me. "Don't!"

I push free of Colden, my hand outstretched toward Alexus, but there isn't anything I can do to stop him. He throws his hands out at his sides, and ancient power floods from his hands, blasting ash, snow, and dirt, the force enough to send him rocketing into the sky with an echoing roar that disintegrates the charred limbs within his trajectory.

Gasping and spluttering from debris, we all stand stunned in the suddenly quiet grove. The wailing has faded to silence, as though the dirge is finally, truly over, though a new sort of mourning has just begun.

"Can someone please explain to me when he learned how to do *that*?" Colden peers upward. "And how in the bloody fuck are we going to help him now?"

In those next few moments, I find myself turning toward the *one* being I have no business beseeching for aid, certainly not pertaining to Alexus. But I close the distance between Neri and me anyway, a limp in my step. Again, he stares down at me with those molten eyes, a pointed ear peeking from the shiny strands of his long, white hair.

"You already owe me my life," he says.

With that revelation, the Northlanders behind me make an array of noises—sighs, gasps, curses. Each one is filled with dreadful understanding.

"In exchange for your servitude until my dying day," I remind him, wanting them to overhear.

Satisfaction lights the wolf's lupine features as he casually broadens his stance and clasps his hands behind his back. "Exactly. Once you've resurrected me, I am yours to command. Not before then."

"Please." I step closer as I fight to keep the tears brimming on the edges of my eyelids from falling. "I will do whatever you wish. Just find Alexus and get him back here. Then go to Quezira, find Raina and Fleurie, and bring them home. You're the only one who can."

A tear falls, and he catches it with his finger so quickly that I never even see his hand move.

Though the gesture is kind and might offer a different woman a morsel of hope, I only feel anger and resentment as I wait for him to say no. He denied my plea to protect Raina from seeing what Vexx did to Finn. Had he granted my request, none of this would've happened. He gave her vengeance instead, and what end did it serve?

Neri leans down, still touching my face with a claw-tipped finger as if my skin is his to caress. He's so close I feel the warmth of his breath on my lips. "Tempting as you are, witch, a deal is a deal. Raise me from the dead, and I will do all you ask before the sun reaches the middle of the noon-day sky."

Tempting? The only temptation *I* feel is the urge to smack his smug face, but I force my bitterness down. He will be beholden to me once I give him what he wants. Then I will make him pay for his role in this disaster. But first...

"How?" I ask. "How will you do all of that in a matter of hours? Thamaos left here in a pile of bones. His reawakening wasn't instant. What makes you think it will be any different for you?"

"Good question." He cocks his head. "Your sister left a sacrifice to the grove when she killed that general. Best I recall, all that is needed is a life in exchange for a life. She took that life *after* Thamaos was already gone, so I'm clinging to the hope that my resurrection will be an accelerated process. Where Thamaos's transformation will likely require weeks, if not months, to return him to a truly living state, mine should be fairly instant given Vexx's sacrifice."

My gods. I still hate what Raina went through, and if I had it to do over, I would've pulled myself together and wrapped that pike in so many vines she couldn't have possibly seen what remained of Finn. But in my panic and shock, I didn't, and her rage and pain will be something I forever feel in the guilty shadows of my soul.

Her destruction of the grove wasn't for nothing, though. I found the North a weapon, and by killing Vexx, it seems she might've given me the means to wield that weapon more effectively.

I pull away from the wolf's too-easy touch and gesture toward the cliffside where his bones are buried beneath scorched earth and snow. "Fine. Lead the way. If you want to live again, *under my thumb*, so be it. But don't you dare complain when my rule is not so pleasant."

His mouth quirks as though I'm humorous. "What's unpleasant for one might be pleasant for another." He turns and stalks toward the gloom hovering between the trees. "I rather like your bark, witch," he calls. "Though I'm more interested in seeing if you have any bite."

I stare at his back until he drops to all fours and lopes away like the beast he is, disappearing into the smoke bleeding from the trees. Colden strolls up beside me, wearing a pinched and concerned expression I know far too well.

"Don't scold me," I snap. "I've missed you with my whole heart, but please don't scold me."

He arches a brow and drapes his arm over my shoulders before touching his forehead to mine. "Wouldn't think of it."

"Yes, you would." I grip his wrist, so thankful he's here.

He kisses the tip of my nose. "But I won't."

"I did what I did for Tiressia, Colden. For the North and the Summerlands. Neri will be mine, and I mean to use him."

He slips a finger beneath my chin and tips my head up. "I understand. I understood the moment that bastard explained the situation at my cell in Min-Thuret. I just need you to be careful. I know you're quite capable, but Neri is a *god*. Dangerous and beyond clever." His eyes soften at the corners, as though drawn by sadness. "I want to protect you from this, but you've entered into a deal with a devil, and I can't do a godsdamn thing about it."

A sickening knot of worry tightens my chest as I lean into his embrace, my gaze fixed on the wolf's path toward the cliff, the path that leads to a future with Neri ever at my side.

"I know," I whisper. "Believe me, I know."

❧

Don't stop now. Keep reading with your copy of THE WOLF AND THE WITCH, available now! And find more from Charissa Weaks at www.charissaweaks.com

Don't miss a special novella of the the Witch Walker series, THE WOLF AND THE WITCH, available now! And find more from Charissa Weaks at www.charissaweaks.com

⁂

As Nephele, Alexus, and their faithful companions grapple with the devastating loss on Mount Ulra, the threat of Thamaos's reign rises in the East. To prepare, the crew must strengthen the Northland and Summerland armies, even if it means depending on the one being they never thought would live again: Neri, God of the White Wolf.

Nephele made a deal she can't escape, a deal that not only ensures the Wolf's resurrection, but one that forces her to remain at his side, even when he returns North to bolster defenses and destroy any traitors and enemies remaining on his land. The last thing Nephele wants is to spend her days and nights alone with a seductive, arrogant god, but Tiressia's future depends on Neri being their primary weapon, one only she holds the power to wield.

As Thamaos aims his first wave of destruction at Neri, Nephele finds that not only is the Wolf more difficult to control than she believed, but that he's far more human than she gave him credit for. With every passing hour, the undeniable passion between them burns brighter, until their fire becomes impossible to resist, and impossible for Thamaos to ignore.

Because the only thing he loathes more than the Wolf roaming Tiressia again, is that there's a witch at his side, and her name is Bloodgood.

⁂

Please sign up for the City Owl Press newsletter for chances to win special subscriber-only contests and giveaways as well as receiving information on upcoming releases and special excerpts.

All reviews are **welcome** and **appreciated**. Please consider leaving one on your favorite social media and book buying sites.

Escape Your World. Get Lost in Ours! City Owl Press at www.cityowlpress.com.

ACKNOWLEDGMENTS

They say the sophomore novel is always the hardest. That's no lie! This entire year of Real Author Life has been such an adventure, but I cranked out this beast of a book regardless. The RETURN key on my newish laptop is dying as I type this. That's how much keyboard pounding has been done this year.

First and foremost, I want to send out an enormous THANK YOU and I LOVE YOU to my family. You live without me for days and sometimes weeks at a time, depending on how deep into a book I am. You keep me fed and watered and make sure I get some sunshine ;) You also listen to all the writerly talk, even when it makes absolutely no sense. I love you for helping me make this dream a reality.

Secondly, I want to give a shout out to my Rebel Readers and all the amazing influencers who helped get this book in front of reader eyes. This one is for you! You guys have been the most amazing support system. I can't begin to express how much of an impact you've made on me and my life. Because of you, I can keep doing this. Because of you, I *want* to keep doing this. Every single day, I'm uplifted and motivated to keep going. Thank you for loving Raina and Alexus enough that their world became what it is, and that their romance went from being a novella-length tale to a series full of twists and turns. I can't wait to give you the next book. (Just don't hate me at the end of this one!!)

Tee Tate! You are a rockstar. You have my eternal gratitude. Your notes and comments on this book kept me pushing when I was buried in rewrites and unsure how to piece this story together again. Your 3am stream of conscious notes are the best. Also... I'm certain you're a vampire.

And to my CP's, Alexia and Beth, who never complain about my sporadic emails, and to all the sensitivity readers who gave me invaluable feedback on this book, I appreciate your time and hard work. I'm so grateful for your help through this process, and your sweet encouragement. You helped this book come to life. And to Stacy Choi, Katherine Quinn, and Jess Wisecup for always having a listening ear. Big hugs.

ABOUT THE AUTHOR

CHARISSA WEAKS is an award-winning author of historical fantasy and speculative fiction. She crafts stories with fantasy, magic, time travel, romance, and history, and the occasional apocalyptic quest. Charissa resides just south of Nashville with her family, two wrinkly English Bulldogs, and the sweetest German Shepherd in existence. To keep up with her writing endeavors, and to gain access to writing freebies  and book giveaways, join her newsletter, <u>The Monthly Courant</u> or her <u>Rebel Readers group</u> on Facebook.

www.charissaweaks.com

instagram.com/CharissaWeaksAuthor
facebook.com/CharissaWeaksAuthor
patreon.com/authorcharissaweaks
tiktok.com/@charissaweaksauthor

ABOUT THE PUBLISHER

City Owl Press is a cutting edge indie publishing company, bringing the world of romance and speculative fiction to discerning readers.

Escape Your World. Get Lost in Ours!

www.cityowlpress.com

 facebook.com/YourCityOwlPress

 twitter.com/cityowlpress

 instagram.com/cityowlbooks

 pinterest.com/cityowlpress